Unforgettable Nights

Also By Nikki A Lamers

The Unforgettable Series
The Unforgettable Summer (#1)
Unforgettable Dreams (#3)
Unforgettable Memories (#4)
The Unforgettable One (#5)
Unforgettable Mistakes (#6)

The Home Duet
Dreams Lost and Found (#1)
Finding Home (#2)

For Clean Contemporary Romance read books by
Nicole Mullaney and Ethan Dulane
Ethan Dulane is a character created by
Nicole Mullaney and Candy Cain for Joy & Hope

Ivy & Mistletoe
The Maltese Holiday
Deck the Heart
Magic in Mount Holly

Joy & Hope by Ethan Dulane

Unforgettable Nights

The Unforgettable Series #2

By Nikki A Lamers

Second Edition

Cover design by Jessica Scott, Uniquely Tailored

Frey Dreams an Imprint of Nikki A Lamers

ISBN 978-1-951185-17-6 (paperback)
ISBN 978-1-951185-16-9 (eBook)

Table of Contents

Prologue

10 Years Ago…

Blake

It's springtime in Maine and still bitterly cold outside. The sun warmed up just enough today, so the snow and ice are beginning to thaw. The dark black paved road winds for miles in front of us, wet from the melted snow and filled with large cracks and potholes of all shapes and sizes from the long winter. The sun is starting to set behind the trees and without city lights, darkness and cold in Maine sometimes feels like Alaska to me, not that I've ever been, but I imagine the quiet isolation to feel the same. But I wouldn't have it any other way because this is where my family and friends are; this is home.

I look over at my little sister laughing like she's on a carnival ride as we go over yet another hill. My sister Aubrey is three years younger than me. Her hair is lighter than mine, but she has the same brown eyes as me. I think she's actually cool as sisters go and we usually get along pretty well.

I look up to the front of the car towards my mom and dad and ask, "How much longer before we get there?"

"It's another half hour or so, Blake," my mom answers, her voice tired. "Why don't you play a game on your Game Boy?" she suggests.

I heave a sigh in resignation. We're driving to my aunt and uncle's house for my cousin's birthday. I always have fun playing with all my cousins when we're there, but even a two-hour ride seems like forever in Maine. With all the curvy and hilly country roads, along with looking at what sometimes feels like the same pine trees, fields and farms over and over again, this trip feels endless to me, but I'd probably feel that way no matter what landscape I'm gazing at out my window.

My sister leans over to grab one of her princess coloring books along with a bag full of crayons and begins coloring. I pick my game up from the seat next to me, but continue to mindlessly stare out the window, watching the trees fly by in a blur of green with farmhouses and barns alongside pastures of cows, horses, sheep, or even lama sprinkled between. Aubrey groans in frustration, so I look over at her and prod, "What's wrong Aub?"

"I dropped my purple crayon and I need it for my picture." She tries to reach for it, but her little hands are only about halfway to the floor. She huffs and glances up towards the front seat without moving her head.

"Just use another crayon for now and save the purple part for later," I suggest. She glares at me through narrowed eyes, so I look back to my game and start playing.

A soft click echoes in my ears causing me to look up to see where the sound came from. My eyes widen seeing Aubrey out of her seat grabbing her purple crayon off the floor and attempting to quickly climb back in her car seat.

Suddenly, my mom yells, "Aubrey, get back in your seat! You can't unbuckle..." her voice trails off as Aubrey reaches for her seatbelt. Everything begins to happen in what seems to be slow motion, but I can't do anything to stop it.

I'm blinded by bright lights through the windows as my dad tries to swerve out of the way, but the car doesn't cooperate. Our car slides along the road more like a sled over a field of solid ice. My dad moves his arms frantically, trying to maintain control and keep the car on the road. I feel the back of the car fly out as it fishtails across the highway, slowing slightly as we bounce roughly over a few potholes on the broken road.

The other car bumps into us giving us a slight jolt, sending us in the opposite direction, but everything happens so fast I'm not really sure of reality. Helplessly, I watch Aubrey in upmost horror as she's tossed around the backseat like a ragdoll. The extreme fear in her eyes knowing she's not protected by her seat belt is overwhelmingly terrifying, making it difficult to breathe. I reach for her desperately trying to help her and protect her, but my seat belt has locked tightly, making it so I can barely move.

All at once, the horrendous shriek of metal crunching, pieces clattering and the ear-splitting sound of glass shattering before a deafening silence descends upon us as our car halts instantly and my seatbelt knocks the wind entirely out of me. With wide eyes, I desperately claw at my chest and my seatbelt, trying to catch my breath.

After a moment, I'm finally able to gulp in a few eager breaths, filling my lungs with oxygen, when suddenly I remember the last few seconds. The instant nightmare of my sister bouncing around the car terrified has my eyes frantically searching her out, still trying to catch my breath.

First, I see an enormous tree trunk pushing Aubrey's side of the car in at the back of her seat where she's supposed to be sitting. My heart stops completely when my eyes are finally able to focus on Aubrey's tiny, limp body. There's so much blood dripping down her sweet, innocent, little face and covering her clothes. I'm staring at her in shock, feeling helpless and lost when my mother's blood-curdling, tortured scream vibrates through me breaking the eerie silence.

I close my eyes as tears seep continuously out of them with unrealistic hopes that what just happened is anything but real. I cry feeling scared and completely powerless while we wait for help to arrive.

Chapter 1

Present Day...

Blake

Biting my tongue, I attempt to hold in my sigh of exasperation, wondering if I'll ever be used to this. I'm on my way to a concert with my friends and I'm being tortured; at least it feels that way to me. I'm watching my best friend, the girl I'm in love with, hold hands, smile at and kiss another guy. The guy that she chose over me and the guy she would choose over me every fucking time. I may be her best friend, but he's the one she's in love with while my insides twist into knots.

I will keep suffering through this shit though because after everything she's been through, there's no way in hell I'll ever let her even think I'm abandoning her or our friendship. Although, even I can admit, I know stepping away from her would help me keep my own sanity, if only for a little while.

It has been over six months since I found Bree and helped her for the second time. That night, once I knew she would be okay, I swore for a second time I would never let anything hurt her again, so I'm definitely not going to be the one to do it. It doesn't matter how much bullshit it costs me.

She's worth it.

At first, I was excited about tonight because my best guy friend, Matt Young, drove up from Massachusetts, from the same town Bree, Amy, Matt and I all graduated high school from together. I haven't been able to hang out with him in a while and I miss the camaraderie with him.

Bree's good friend Amy and Matt have a history though, so instead of it being just the five of us, Bree decides to invite her friend Cassie to make it even and make me more comfortable. I know that's bullshit, especially once she revealed that Cassie is interested in me. My stomach clenches with the thought, although it has nothing to do with Cassie. I asked Bree not to set me up.

Honestly, there's enough to be uncomfortable about just amongst the five of us with our complicated history. Sometimes I think the rest of us go along with hanging out together just for Bree. Don't get me wrong, we can handle each other in small doses…mostly. But if I could have it my way, Christian wouldn't be here at all and neither would Cassie.

When I arrived at Bree and Amy's apartment, Bree informed me we needed to wait for Cassie before we could leave. Narrowing my eyes, I gave her an accusing look. She smiled innocently and simply shrugged her shoulders declaring, "We had an extra ticket," knowing I can't say no to her.

Unfortunately, I just don't have it in me to date one of Bree's friends, no matter what she's like. The last thing I need is to be set up by her even though she has the best of intentions. It would always feel like settling to me if I'm dating one of her friends because it's not her. I just can't do that to someone, let alone myself. It fucking hurts just thinking about it, which makes me want to do something drastic to change it.

Thankfully, it doesn't take long before we're parking at the concert. Everyone catches up and jokes around as we stroll inside the venue. Grabbing a few beers on our way to the pit, we weave through the crowd, making our way towards the front, right in front of the stage.

Christian wraps his arms possessively around Bree from behind, while Matt slings his arm over Amy's shoulders, making things even more awkward for me with Cassie at my side. Pasting a smile on my face, I sip my beer, doing my best to be nice to her as she chatters in my ear, but I don't want to encourage her either, which makes tonight even more complicated and that's the last thing I need or want. Heaving a sigh, I run my hand through my hair and drop it at my side.

"I want to go to the bathroom before the concert starts. Do you girls want to go with me?" Bree prompts, glancing at Amy and Cassie.

"Yes!" Amy exclaims, slipping away from Matt.

"Good idea," Cassie adds, stepping away from me.

I can't help but breathe a sigh of relief the moment the girls walk away. With a wave of his hand, Christian follows them, I'm sure still unable to leave Bree's side now that they are back together, let alone with everything he's been through with her. I'm also positive he doesn't want to hang out with me and he's only doing this for her.

I don't blame him, he's not my favorite person either, but that's mostly because he has what I want. He's finally treating Bree the way she deserves to be treated though, so I can't hate him either, especially when he is exactly what she wants, unfortunately. After everything she's endured, she deserves to be happy more than anything. I'll do anything for her. But that doesn't mean I have to like it.

Now, I need to figure out a way to deal with Cassie when she comes back. I scan the growing crowd looking for an out, but I honestly have no idea what the hell I'm looking for. Reaching up, I sigh in frustration, while I rub the back of my neck, trying to release some of the built-up tension.

13

Eventually, I turn back to Matt instead of trying to solve a problem I don't have a clue about unraveling at the moment. I take a deep breath and exhale slowly, attempting to relax. Tonight is supposed to be fun. While the girls are gone, it's probably a good time to catch up with my good friend while I can actually hear him between acts. "So, what's been going on with you?"

"Same bullshit," he grumbles, shrugging. "But it's good to see Amy." He smirks wiggling his eyebrows making me shake my head. "Looks like you're still struggling with Bree," he observes, turning the conversation right back to me.

"Shit," I mumble, my shoulders slumping, hating that it's so obvious.

He chuckles, shrugging. "Relax, Blake. I just know you."

Heaving a sigh, I take another swig of my beer. "It's going to be a long night," I mutter under my breath.

Chapter 2

Elizabeth

"Hurry up Lizzie!" Sara yells at me for the hundredth time. "Soon we will miss the whole thing!"

It's Saturday night and my best friend Sara and I are headed to our first Brett Eldredge concert. Sara and I both turned twenty-one in the last couple weeks; our birthdays are only three days apart. So, we decided we would celebrate our birthdays together this year by going to this concert. We always celebrate together, but it's usually something more like dinner, shopping and lots of cake.

I'm so excited, but I am notoriously late for everything. I've changed my clothes ten times, literally because I have no idea what to wear. I look at my current outfit in the mirror, assessing myself. It's June and summer in Maine is just beginning. Right now, the sun is shining and it's a warm eighty degrees outside, but it will probably be cold by the end of the night, so I keep going back and forth on what I think I should wear. I have on short cut-off jean shorts and a fitted teal tie-dye tank top, matching beaded sandals with a one-inch heel and my straw cowgirl hat. "The shoes aren't too much?" I prod skeptically.

With a roll of her eyes Sara answers, "You don't wear enough heel. That color looks great on you too, perfect with your green eyes."

"Thanks," I purse my lips and squint into the mirror at my reflection. I hate heels; hopefully I won't fall and make a fool of myself. Sighing softly, I lightly scrunch my dark brown hair between my fingers that's coming down in waves from my hat.

"Come on, you promised you would relax and have fun tonight! And all nights this summer for that matter," Sara complains.

"I know, I know," I whine and fidget with my outfit one more time. After this past year, I promised Sara I would try to change the way I did things. I'm one of those girls many people may call book smart. I work hard, I do well in school and I have trouble saying no to people, especially if the one asking for help is a gorgeous guy that makes me either freeze up or have verbal diarrhea. I have been taken advantage of a lot to say the least.

One guy in particular pushed me way over the edge and Sara helped me pick up the pieces. After that, I decided I'm not letting anyone take advantage of me anymore or walk all over me in any way. I'm going to be in control of my life and what happens to me. I don't really know how well that will work with my parents, especially my mom since she likes to control everything about my life, but I can't think about that now. It's time for me to change, for the better.

I take a deep breath and let it out slowly. "Okay, let's go." I jump as Sara squeals so loud I think the windows might break. She grabs my hand, practically dragging me out the door of our little two-bedroom apartment.

We jump in the Uber she requested so we can have a couple beers while we're there. Now that we're legal, Sara insists I loosen up a little bit. She's always saying I deserve to have a little fun. We finally make it through the traffic and the Uber pulls up, dropping us off right at the front of the concert venue.

Slowly, we make our way through security and into the concert. Sara bought our tickets for the front section near the stage, but its standing room only up there. Therefore, it's first come, first served for that section and because of me, I believe we're probably last.

"We have to get to the front. I want to get the shirts I bought us signed," Sara whines. "That's why I splurged and bought us tickets up front. Any ideas?" Sara prompts as she buys two beers from the vendor and hands one to me.

As we make our way over to the side at one of the many entrance ramps overlooking the stage, we stop and take everything in. I bite my lip, thinking. "This is crazy," I mumble as I try to come up with something while I sip my beer gazing down over the crowd.

Suddenly, my eyes freeze and my heart stops, lodging itself in my throat. The most gorgeous man I've ever seen is standing right in front of the stage. He's obviously tall since I can see him through the crowd, but it's tough to judge just how tall from here. He has short sandy brown hair, spiked slightly on top like he's been running his fingers through his hair, his cheeks look flushed from the heat in here and his broad, sexy grin is so big, I wouldn't be surprised to see one of those diamonds sparkle from his mouth like on those toothpaste commercials. I can only imagine what he looks like up close and I think I have to find out.

"Well, since you bought us the tickets and I'm the one who made us so late, getting us to the front is the least I can do," I announce glancing at Sara with false confidence. Her eyes narrow, looking at me curiously as I take a deep breath and lift my beer to my lips. Tipping the cup up slowly, I chug until the whole thing is gone. Then, I take a deep breath and paste a big smile on my face thinking, it's now or never as I shrug, mumbling to Sara, "You did want me to live a little this summer. So, I could use some liquid courage for the new me." I take another deep breath and start walking, shaking at the thought of what I'm about to do.

She laughs excitedly and follows me as I pull her through all the people, weaving in and out of the hot and sticky crowd already smelling of sweat and beer while calling out, "Excuse us," over and over again. I try my best not to step on anyone or get anything spilled on me, but a couple messy casualties and dirty looks along the way seem to be inevitable.

We make it to the front and I stop right next to the beautiful guy I'd been admiring, feeling like I'm going to throw up. I take another deep shaky breath before I reach up to his shoulder trying to turn him slightly towards me.

Pushing up on my toes, I tentatively give him a kiss on the corner of his mouth, feeling a slip in my armor as my body overheats with nerves. "There you are. We have been looking all over for you!" I claim. Gulping hard, I force a smile I hope doesn't look too terrified as I plead with him through my eyes.

He looks back at me in what I can only assume is shock and disbelief, followed by indecision. I see what I presume is one of his friends staring at me over his shoulder with his mouth hanging open and I'm almost positive Sara has the same look on her face behind me. I don't blame her. This guy is even more gorgeous up close with his sun-kissed tan and doing something like this is definitely not me.

Then it hits me, I didn't even look to see if he's here with a girl. I feel my body burst into flames with the thought and I immediately start praying I don't throw up on his shoes. Swiftly, I begin mumbling an apology when I see his heart melting smile slowly return to his beautiful face with a glint in his rich chocolate brown eyes making my voice catch in my throat. My mouth stops moving as I stare into his eyes afraid to speak.

Lightly, he touches my elbow sending tingles up my arm and down my spine as he leans into my ear. I feel his warm breath on my cheek and don't dare move as I inhale a heavenly whiff of mild musky cologne mixed with mint. His deep voice rumbles in my ear, "You have to do better than that if you want me to reward you for how long I've been here holding your spot."

Gasping in surprise, I pull back a little to look at his face noticing his slight smirk, like he's daring me to do something and waiting to see what it will be. So, with trembling hands and my heart about to beat out of my chest, I do the unexpected. I don't know if the beer affected me that fast, which I don't really believe, or if it's my determination and adrenaline, or even his mesmerizing eyes, but I reach one hand up to the back of his neck and pull him down to my lips, kissing him hard.

I feel his smooth, full lips move against mine as his hands drop to my waist resting there gently, his fingers curling in, gripping me. My eyes slowly fall closed with his touch. I nearly melt right there on the spot as goose bumps instantly cover my skin, but I'm anything but cold. I feel the tip of his tongue on my lips urging me for more. I'm ready to open and get lost in his kiss when Sara grabs my arm and pulls me back to reality.

"That was much better convincing," I hear him mumble just loud enough for me to hear. I feel myself flush from head to toe, shocked at my brazen act. Instinctively, I bring my fingers to my lips, still feeling the heat of this gorgeous stranger's mouth on mine.

Sara reaches her hand out to him, grinning. "Elizabeth," she states, stressing my name, "you still didn't introduce me to your man. Hi, I'm Sara. I've heard so much about you," she emphasizes sarcastically with a smirk.

"It's nice to meet you, Sara. I'm Blake. This guy here is Matt," he proclaims. He nods to the guy behind him who finally shakes his head of dark hair, closes his mouth and reaches out to shake our hands. "Matt, this is my Lizzie and her friend, Sara," he states, shortening my name with intentional familiarity, and giving me another chill.

Sara and I shake Matt's hand and murmur a quick, "Hi."

Blake turns to me, his eyes alight with mischief. "The others just ran to the restrooms and to maybe grab some beers," he informs me, smirking at me like I know whom he's talking about. "I'm so glad you made it and you get to meet them."

Sara elbows me and yells in my ear to be heard over the loud music, "I can't believe you actually did that! That alone was worth missing all the other acts! He is so ridiculously hot!"

I nod my head and bite my lip nervously, hoping the concert will start now before I pass out or do something else stupid.

A small group of three beautiful girls and another guy steps up behind them and squeezes in. My heart sinks like it has every right, as two of the girls squeeze on each side of Blake. I watch as one of the girls hands him a beer with a flirty smile. I try to push down the lump of embarrassment already forming in my throat. I just threw myself at a complete stranger. I kissed him and he's here with his girlfriend or at least a date. I groan feeling pathetic and immediately look away in panic, trying to decide what to do.

He turns to me, stepping around the girl closest to me and moving her to his other side so he's next to me again. He wraps his arm around me and grins. "Lizzie, this is my best friend Bree and her boyfriend Christian and my friends Amy and Cassie." All of their eyes widen in surprise, landing on me as Blake's smile grows, appearing smug. "Guys, this is my Lizzie and her friend, Sara," he echoes his earlier introduction.

Bree gives him a strange look and her boyfriend smirks at me, looking like he's trying to hold back his laughter. I can't stop the blush that consumes me, all the way from head to toe as they all eye me with obvious curiosity.

The other girl, Cassie, continues looking from Blake to me and back again like she's trying to make a decision. She finally glares at me and grabs onto Blake's arm, trying to stake her claim on him. Blake drops his arm from around me and before I have a chance to be embarrassed yet again, he pointedly removes her hand and smiles down at her full of empathy, whispering something in her ear. He then takes a step back towards me, draping his arm around me again and making my stomach twist into knots.

He tips his head down to my ear and whispers, "I think this could be mutually beneficial." I notice his friend, Bree looking at him with a more than confused look on her face, while the girl, Cassie continues shooting daggers at me with her eyes. He ignores them all, allowing his huge smile to light up his whole face, taking my breath away. I think I might implode right here.

Before I get the chance to dwell too much on what just happened, the lights dim and everyone starts to scream as the first notes of "Don't Ya" blast out through the speakers. The music vibrates all the way through my body, especially since we're so close to the stage and speakers. I take a deep breath, remembering why we're here as I turn to enjoy the concert with my best friend and the gorgeous stranger with his arm draped over my shoulders.

Happy Birthday to me!

Chapter 3

Blake

As the final notes of "Beat of The Music" play, the crowd goes crazy, cheers erupting from everywhere, the deafening sounds rumbling through my chest. I feel the exhilaration and I can't help but put my arm around Elizabeth again and give her a little squeeze. "Just playing my part," I whisper in her ear, loud enough for her to hear. I laugh as she gives me a quizzical look, thoroughly enjoying myself. "Hey, you started it," I remind her. I smirk, wondering how I got so lucky tonight. I couldn't have planned something better if I tried.

She raises her eyebrows and with a shrug, concedes, "I guess I did," before smiling shyly back at me.

I don't know how the hell this gorgeous girl can pretend like she's shy. She's the one who walked up and kissed a total stranger at a concert, all for a good spot. She continued to let me act like her date the rest of the night, even laughing with my friends.

She is absolutely stunning too. She has wavy dark brown hair and sparkling green eyes with a few adorable freckles across the bridge of her nose. She has a perfectly curved body, which to me is not too much and not too little, and her legs look like they go on forever, but I'm guessing she's probably about five-feet, six-inches to my six feet with the way she had to reach up to kiss me.

She watches nervously as her friend attempts to get Brett Eldredge to sign at least one of the shirts she bought, fidgeting with her hands the whole time. He eventually makes his way over to her and signs both shirts making Sara

22

scream so loud I would almost bet that was louder than the concert we just sat through, but with my ears ringing, I'm sure I'm not the best judge of sound. I shake my head and laugh watching Elizabeth's timid reaction to her friend, before she turns, looking over at me.

"So..." she stammers, "are you headed home right away?" I can't help but smirk again knowing she can't really come out and ask me anything she should supposedly already know about me without ruining the charade. But at this point she's only keeping up the facade for my benefit. She already watched the concert right in front of the stage. I'm not going to be the one to point that out to her though, I'm enjoying this way too much.

I'm really having fun watching her squirm before I finally answer her, "I think we are headed back to Bree and Amy's for a bit. Would you guys like to come?" I offer.

She hesitantly looks at her friend. Sara rolls her eyes and Liz's reaction and focuses on Bree, asking, "Where do you live Bree?"

I continue watching her face in amusement as she listens to Bree give directions to their place here in Portland. I have to cover my mouth to hide a laugh when I see her visibly relax and release a long breath in what I assume is relief.

"That's right around the corner from our apartment. Sure, that sounds good." She looks up and smiles at me making my stomach flip-flop. I love that I'm going to be able to spend more time with this girl. I lean in towards her and watch her eyes go round with surprise as I brush my lips over hers, giving her a quick kiss on her soft lips. I step back and laugh quietly under my breath at her reaction, but I couldn't help myself; I had to get another quick taste.

"So, I'll meet you there?" I prod, raising my eyebrows at her in question and she nods her head in response. "Call me on my cell if you have any trouble," I direct. I smirk again knowing she doesn't have my number and I have no idea how to give it to her right now without ruining this whole charade.

Sara jumps in to assist, questioning, "Didn't your battery die on your phone, Liz?" She glances at her friend, obviously trying to help, but Lizzie just looks adorably confused and this time I don't hide my laugh. "Can I put your number in my cell phone, Blake? That way if there is a problem, we still have your number. Liz is always forgetting to charge that thing," she claims, smiling brightly as she holds her phone out for me.

"Of course," I agree. Grabbing her phone, I swiftly type in my name and number and then text myself, so I at least have a way to get in touch with Sara. "Don't forget to charge your phone next time," I mumble, grinning.

She ignores my comment and gives me a small wave. "Bye, Blake. We'll see you in a little while." She turns and smiles at my friends, "Bye guys, it was nice meeting all of you. I guess we'll see you in a little while."

I watch her walk away, my heart pounding in anticipation of seeing her again. I take a deep breath and give my head a slight shake as I turn back to my friends, knowing what's coming, but I figure I'd rather get it over with now. Matt smirks at me while Bree looks at me like I've been hiding something from her for a while and she's pissed. I don't blame her. We usually tell each other everything and she thinks I've been lying to her.

"She seems nice. Why haven't I ever heard her name before?" she snaps at me accusingly.

"Bree…" Christian warns and reaches for her hand. I involuntarily flex my jaw trying to release the tension as she immediately takes it.

24

"I'm just asking, Christian. That's what friends do; they talk to each other. They tell each other about what's going on in their life. They talk about someone they might be interested in or dating, but I never even heard her name before and I'm supposed to be one of his best friends," she answers. Although, we all know everything she's saying is directed at me.

"Bree, maybe this is something he doesn't want to talk to you about, even though you are his best friend," Christian defends me.

I flinch with his inflection. He knows I used to be in love with his girlfriend for a long time. I say used to be, but everyone including Christian, or especially Christian, knows she's not something you just get over, especially when I still see her all the damn time making me sigh heavily in exasperation.

"Bree," I begin, "I just met Elizabeth recently and I wasn't ready to tell you about her yet," I claim, not wanting to completely lie to her. Even though with how far I'm stretching the truth in this case, it's probably the same thing as lying. She doesn't need to know that recent was tonight. I continue with a blatant lie, "I knew she might be coming tonight, but I wasn't positive, so I didn't tell you. I would've told you about her eventually."

"Yeah, but I wouldn't have brought Cassie..." she whispers.

I quickly interrupt her, not wanting Cassie to hear and feel bad, "I told you not to set me up Bree."

She looks like she's about to say more, but Christian interrupts her, "Bree, leave it alone. I told you to stay out of it. Be happy for him." I give him a grateful look. I wince and turn away as she smiles at him, nodding her agreement before she leans in pressing her lips to his.

"So, Blake," Bree begins as we all climb into Matt's suburban, "tell us more about Elizabeth. How'd you guys meet?"

"Uh, you know, we met while we were out one night," I stammer answering vaguely. She gives me another one of her inquisitive looks, like she knows I'm purposely messing with her.

Christian laughs and wraps his arm around Bree pulling her closer to him after they're buckled and I deliberately drop my head against the window hard trying to shake my constant feelings of jealousy when it comes to this guy. "Bree, leave the poor guy alone. You can get to know her at your apartment in a little while."

"Fine," she concedes melting into his side. I fist my hand against my leg and let out a controlled breath while staring out the window. I have to keep telling myself it will get easier. After everything she's been through, there is no way in hell I can walk away from her. She may be in love with him, but I know she still needs me and I'll do anything for her.

Chapter 4

Elizabeth

Sara practically screeches in excitement as she skips to the curb to wait for a cab, pulling me along behind her. "I cannot believe you did that! And he just went along with it! Who does that? And holy smokes that man is sexy! And so are his friends," she rambles, wiggling her eyebrows.

"Yeah," I mumble in agreement.

"Anyway, you said you were going to start having some fun and not let people walk all over you and Lizzie you did the complete opposite of that. You totally took control of the situation. I'm so proud of you!" she praises as she gives me an awkward side hug in her excitement.

I smile lightly, embarrassed by her compliment. "Thanks," I murmur.

She looks at me with narrowed eyes. "Just accept the compliment. You deserve to have fun, just like everyone else," she insists.

I take a deep breath and try to relax as I settle into the seat next to her in the taxi. She gives the driver the address she put in her phone, so we didn't forget the apartment number. I look at her and nod my head with false confidence. "Okay, Sara. Thank you."

"Oh, don't forget to turn your phone off. You don't want it ringing while we are over there. That wouldn't exactly look too good," she reminds me smirking. I burst out laughing at the thought, releasing some of the nerves and tension pushing at me. "See it will be fine. Let's relax and have fun."

"Maybe we should just go home," I suggest quietly. "I'm really tired," I claim with uncertainty.

"We're going," Sara declares with a roll of her eyes.

"What if he's like a crazy serial killer or something? You never know. We know nothing about this guy or his friends." Sara just shakes her head in amusement and ignores me completely as she stares out the window.

After we finally make it out of the parking lot, it only takes us about ten minutes to get to the apartment building. It's a long skinny building with only two floors and has doors along one side of the building. I'm assuming it's like ours and one door is for downstairs followed by a door for upstairs right above it. We walk to the door with the number they gave us and right when Sara's about to knock I grab her wrist in a panic. She looks at me with her eyebrows raised in question. I whisper, "I don't know if we should be here."

She rolls her eyes at me again and proclaims, "Liz, we should be here. I'm knocking. Relax!" Lifting her hand, she wraps her knuckles on the hardwood, but we don't hear a response, so she knocks again, harder. This time we hear mumbling and shuffled footsteps coming towards the door.

The door swings open and Blake stands behind it with a huge smile on his face. "You came," he states simply, appearing relieved.

"We did," I answer and grin back at him. "I thought this was your friend's place?" I ask, confused.

"Yeah, Bree and Amy live here. She's not expecting anyone else though and I was hoping it was you," he states with a cocky grin. I feel my face blush a deep red and I smile shyly up at him. He grins even bigger at my reaction and gestures for us to come inside.

I hear soft music playing in the background as we walk into a small entry with steps directly in front of us and climb the stairs into the kitchen. The kitchen opens right into the living room where Christian sits with his arm wrapped around Bree on an old brown couch with Amy on the other side of Bree. There's an oversized chair that remains empty while Matt is straddling a pine chair backwards that I assume he pulled from the kitchen and pulled up close to Amy.

"Hi, guys!" Bree states as she jumps up, smiling the moment she sees us. "I'm so glad you came."

Everyone exchanges a quick, "Hello," before Bree offers us something to eat and drink. She pulls out a couple beers and adds more chips to a bowl before bringing it out to the table in the living room. I suddenly realize someone's missing and I can't help but ask, "Where's Cassie?"

"Oh, she was tired. She wanted to head home after the concert," Bree blushes as she answers. Christian chuckles under his breath and she plops back down next to him and elbows him purposefully in the stomach. He lets out an involuntary grunt. "Oops, sorry" she grumbles, smiling sweetly.

"That's okay, you can pay for that later," he jokes as he wraps his arms around her and kisses her on the neck.

"Lizzie, come sit next to me and Sara I can grab another chair for you," Blake offers. Ignoring his friends, he strides to the kitchen and returns with a chair for Sara. He sets the chair down and she smiles at him in appreciation as she sits.

Then he steps over to the oversized chair and sits down, patting a spot next to him. I look at him skeptically and he just raises his eyebrows at me, challenging me with his alluring smile. Taking a deep breath, I walk over and sit with him, my heart suddenly beating out of control. My nerves go a little haywire as I feel the warmth of his body touching mine all the way up the left side of my body. He leans back and puts his arm around the back of the chair behind me.

"So where are you guys from?" Bree asks us.

"We're both from here actually. We grew up together," Sara answers for me.

"Oh, did you guys know Blake from high school?" she prods. I glance at him in confusion.

"Ah, no, we went to Casco Bay High School. You didn't tell me you were from here," I answer honestly and shake my head.

Blake sighs and elaborates, "I grew up here mostly, but I went to Portland High School. During my junior year I moved with my family to Massachusetts and I finished high school there."

"That must have been hard," I mumble. I can't help but notice the tension in his face.

He nods. "Yeah, it was alright. I had a couple good friends that helped," he claims, nodding at Matt and Bree. She smiles back at him with what I think is reassurance. I can't help but feel a pinch of irrational jealousy with the look she gives him. It's a look that says she knows him more than I'd like her to. I sigh to myself. I have no right being jealous. I just met Blake tonight and may never even see him again after tonight. I can't let myself worry so much or he could walk all over me without even trying.

Bree's boyfriend obviously doesn't like it either, though. He pulls her even closer and changes the subject. "So, Bree and I are going up to the lake for the rest of the summer. I'm going to do some work for my dad and Bree got a job helping out at one of the gift shops in town."

I feel Blake tense again and Bree continues, "That way, we can spend time with Christian's family and hopefully my dad will come there when he's home from

London or we'll both go down to Mass. You guys know how important family is to me," she whispers leaning closer to Christian.

"That's great Bree," Blake croaks with a stiff nod.

"I promise we'll come back and visit a couple times too," Bree adds looking directly at Blake. "Plus, I want to see your sister soon," she adds pointedly.

I'm getting more and more uncomfortable with all the tension I feel almost pouring off Blake and I can't help but react jumping up, "Anybody need anything? Bree, Christian, you don't have anything, can I get you a beer or something while I'm up?"

Bree shakes her head and Christian mumbles, "No thanks, I don't really drink anymore."

Amy stands up and glares at Christian. I think I almost forgot her and Matt were even there. "This is why I don't get why you wouldn't be the designated driver tonight. I had to drive Matt's huge ass truck and I had to wait to get home to have a beer," she whines.

He sighs and glances over at Blake, both of them looking pissed off. I know it's time for me to go before I end up in the middle of something I will later regret. I look at Sara before announcing, "Sara, I almost forgot I was supposed to leave a key for my brother tonight so he could crash on the couch. We better get going. He might have even tried to call, but since my phone is dead…" I trail off.

She eyes me inquisitively, knowing I'm lying. She sighs heavily as she stands up resigned. "Okay, thanks everyone. It was great meeting you."

"Bye guys. Thank you. It was nice meeting you and I hope to see you again," I add quickly.

Bree smiles and proclaims, "If you're around Blake, we'll definitely be seeing you. It was so nice to meet you! You guys should come up to the lake sometime with Blake

31

and you can hang out with Christian and me. You could even stay at my house. I'd love to get to know you more."

Not sure how to answer her, I stammer a response, "Ah, maybe, I'm ah, working a lot this summer. I guess we'll have to see."

"Make time if you can, it would be fun!" she insists as Christian gives her a warning look. I just plaster on a smile and wave as I turn towards the stairs.

"Let me walk you out," Blake offers as he steps up behind me. "I'm going to head back to my place anyway. Matt, are you coming?"

"Yeah, I'll be there in a minute. I'll meet you downstairs," he answers.

"Bye guys. Bree, call me this week. I want to see you before you leave for the summer," Blake insists. Then, he leans down to give her a kiss on the cheek before he walks quickly down the stairs and out of the apartment.

He takes a deep breath as soon as we walk outside. "So, do you go by Liz or Lizzie or do you prefer Elizabeth?" he asks with a smirk. I burst out laughing and feel the tension in the air disintegrate almost instantly.

"Whatever you'd like to call me is fine," I answer with a grin when I catch my breath.

He nods his head in acknowledgment as he stares at me. "I have to say, I think tonight was definitely my lucky night," he admits. I feel my face heat, instantly turning red. "Do you think maybe I could see you again and really get to know you? Maybe ask you questions I couldn't ask you tonight? Take my fake date on a real date?" he proposes, arching his eyebrows in question.

I smile up at the expectant look on his face. "Sure, that sounds good," I agree. "Sara can text you my number. Then you can call when you want to make plans," I answer as nonchalantly as possible, while I feel every bit the mess on the inside.

As we stare at each other, I hear his phone beep. He glances down at his phone and smiles. "Thanks, Sara. By the way, you guys need a ride?"

"We are only a couple blocks over, we'll walk," I declare.

Sara groans. "Sorry, Liz, but I'm not walking right now. I'm taking the ride."

I nod my head and walk with Blake over to a black Jeep Cherokee. Matt joins us right as we reach it and gently reaches for my arm, stopping me from climbing in the back. "Why don't you hop in the front with Blake? I'll move after we drop you off," he offers.

I bite my lower lip and climb in the front hesitantly. I start to buckle my seat belt when I remember I saw a beer in his hand earlier tonight. I don't really know him, so I have to ask, "Weren't you drinking tonight?"

He looks me straight in the eye before he answers. "I had one beer at the concert, and I haven't had anything else since. I'll wait until I get home if I want another," he explains quickly.

"Oh, I...I'm sorry," I stutter hesitantly. He immediately interrupts me.

"Don't ever be sorry for asking that question. It's not something to mess with," he insists with obvious strain. Blake pauses and glances back at Matt before looking over at me. "So, which way am I going?" he relaxes, asking with a mischievous grin.

Matt's eyes immediately dart to the front, glancing between the two of us. Then, he slaps Blake on the arm laughing. "Dude, I knew it!"

"Shut the fuck up Matt!" But Matt just laughs harder. Sara giggles, deciding to tell him the story from her point of view as I try to ignore them and give Blake directions to our apartment.

Blake pulls into our parking lot and parks. Sara mumbles, "Thank you. Bye, guys. Hopefully, we'll see you again."

"You too," Matt mumbles, laughing again.

"Thank you," I murmur as we climb out of his Jeep. "It was really great meeting you guys," I add, giving them both a shy smile.

Matt waves as he bursts out laughing again. Blake just shakes his head in response and focuses on me. "I'll call you soon, Liz," Blake yells as Matt climbs into the front seat still laughing.

Sara and I stride into our apartment with a quick wave over our shoulder. As soon as we step through the door, Sara exclaims, "It was so much fun to watch you tonight! You had so much confidence and a huge smile most of the night. I don't know the last time I really saw you like that," she admits.

I take a deep breath and try to accept the compliment. "Thanks." She smiles at me knowing that was hard for me. "It got kinda' weird though at his friend's apartment, right? I had to get out of there."

She nods in agreement. "Yeah, there's definitely some kind of history there."

"What do you mean?" I ask nervous for her answer.

"I don't know. Honestly, it could be anything, but there was some obvious tension. Nothing to worry about, we don't even know them. Don't get yourself all worked up, that's when you jump in too fast or back track before anything even has a chance to get started," she reminds me.

I heave a sigh. "I know. You're right." I pause trying not to think about it too much. "I'm going to bed. I'm exhausted. Thanks for the concert tonight," I murmur, grateful as I give Sara a hug.

"You're welcome. I'm glad I got you out to have some fun!" She reaches into her bag to grab something and tosses it at my head. "Don't forget your shirt!"

I catch it just before it hits me in the face and chuckle. "Thank you."

"You're welcome," she grins. "You definitely earned it tonight!" She laughs and looks at me in awe, "I still can't believe you did that! That was truly epic!"

I smile and shake my head at myself in disbelief. "I honestly don't believe it either. Good night, Sara," I state and spin on my heel, strolling towards my room.

"Goodnight, Liz!" she calls.

I quickly slide off my shoes and change into my grey and purple striped pajama pants and a purple t-shirt. I walk into my bathroom and quickly wash my face and brush my teeth before going right back to my room.

I plug my phone in and turn in on, noticing a text from an unknown number. I quickly open it up and my breath catches in my throat at the message. "Hi, It's Blake Withers. So glad you decided to use me for seats tonight! Dinner tomorrow?"

My stomach suddenly feels like it's filled with lead at his "use" comment. I'm sure he didn't mean anything by it, but after everything I don't want to use someone...anyone for anything. I quickly text him back, "I'm sorry for using you. I would love to go to dinner if you would still like to." I quickly hit send without even thinking about it.

I save his contact information and my phone beeps before I set it down. "Maybe use wasn't the right word, I'm glad you chose me to kiss. Best night! I'm a lucky SOB. I'll pick you up at six tomorrow. Can't wait!"

I smile at his text and breathe a sigh of relief before replying to his message. "Ok, I'll see you then!"

My phone beeps with another text, "BTW, what's your last name?"

I can't help but laugh as I answer, "Stevens." I climb into my bed and close my eyes. I'm exhausted and ready to go to sleep, not able to wipe the small smile off my face and feeling completely relaxed.

Chapter 5

Blake

I grab my keys and my phone just as it goes off again with yet another text from Bree. I hold back a groan wondering if I should even bother looking at this one, knowing it's just another question about Liz that I couldn't even answer if I wanted to. Meeting her halfway, I respond without even reading her text.

We are going to have lunch this week before you leave for the lake. Just you and me. I will answer your questions about Liz then. When are you free?

I can do Monday or Tuesday lunch.

She responds quickly eliciting a smile from me.

Great! I'll pick you up Monday at noon.

I put my phone away not bothering to wait for her response.

I jump in my Jeep and pull out of the back lot at my apartment immediately, turning onto the road to drive over and pick up Liz. My mind keeps drifting to thoughts of her. I still can't believe she just walked up to me and kissed me with her delicious lips not knowing anything about me, not even my name.

I wonder what her story is. I guess I'll see what I can find out tonight. I smile to myself hoping for a good night without worrying about Bree or my family for once. I love them all, but I'm excited for a date for the first time in a long time and they're the last thing I want to think about while I'm out with Liz.

Parking my Jeep, I hop out and slam the door. Running my hand through my hair, I release another sigh trying to let all my shit go as I walk up to Liz's apartment and knock.

Sara answers the door with a huge grin making me smirk at her expression. "Hi, Blake! It's so good to see you. Liz will be right out. Come on in."

"Hey, Sara." I chuckle quietly at her rambling. I take a step inside right as Liz steps out of what I assume is her room. My greeting gets lost on my lips when my eyes land on her. I can't help but let my eyes drift looking her up and down from her brown wavy hair falling over her pale shoulders, her skin looking so incredibly smooth under a light blue sundress that's tight against her full chest and flips out just above her knees, giving me a great view of her long legs. I'm tempted to take a step towards her and run my fingers along her collarbone to see if she feels as soft as she looks.

"You may want to grab a sweater in case it's cold later," Sara suggests, interrupting my perusal.

Pushing my shoulders back, I unwillingly drag my eyes up to hers and readjust my stance to make myself more comfortable. I swallow the lump in my throat and lick my lips as I meet her gaze. "You look beautiful, Liz," I proclaim, my raspy voice revealing my sincerity.

"Thank you," she whispers and quickly turns her head away slightly while she grabs her sweater and her purse, but I still don't miss the blush that fills her cheeks. Her reaction makes me all the more curious about this girl. "I'm ready," she announces.

"Great." I grin and hold my arm out, letting her go first out the door as we both wave over our shoulders to Sara.

"Don't do anything I wouldn't do," Sara yells after us, laughing as she shuts the door. It makes me wonder if that's putting much of a restriction on us at all, but I don't know either of them, not yet anyway. Hopefully tonight I can start changing that.

I help Liz into my Jeep and jog around to the other side to climb in. I can't help but look at her again and smile before I start my car. Then I take a deep breath, calming my nerves and prompt, "So are you ready?"

"For what?" she questions, giving me a funny look.

I laugh at my own question, shrugging sheepishly before elaborating, "I thought we'd go to Andy's if that's okay. Have you ever been?"

She nods her head in confirmation. "That sounds good. Do they still do live music there? I haven't been there in a long time."

"Yeah, I looked to see who's playing tonight, but it's not anyone I've heard. I'm not quite sure what kind of music it will be, but I still thought it would be fun," I enlighten her hoping she'll agree.

"It sounds perfect," she easily concurs.

"What kind of music do you like besides country? Or is it just country for you?" I prod curiously while flipping through the radio in search of a good song.

I see her shrug her shoulders out of the corner of my eye as I keep my eyes on the road in front of me. "Honestly, I like about anything except for the really heavy stuff. I want

39

something I can either sing to or dance to, even though I can't really sing or dance," she admits, huffing a laugh.

I smirk, thinking of the concert. My stomach twists as I recall watching her move, just losing herself in the music without caring about anyone judging her. "I'm pretty sure I can vouch for that," I mumble, teasing, gaging her reaction.

"Hey," she argues laughing hard and I swear I see her whole body begin to relax.

Watching her right now, I know we're going to have a great night. I love when a girl doesn't take everything seriously and is willing to laugh with you. Life has way too much crap to not enjoy the small things.

Unfortunately, I'm all too aware of that.

"You're not much better!" she proclaims as she catches her breath.

"I'm sure I'm much worse," I concede with a broad smile as we pull up to the restaurant. I park and sit back, glancing over. Catching her face light up again as her head falls back in laughter causes my heart to clench.

Damn, I want this to go well.

Chapter 6

Elizabeth

After we sit down and order our food, I feel like we're finally going to have a chance to get to know each other a little bit and try to relax into my chair. "So, you're originally from Portland area, huh?" Blake just nods in confirmation, so I continue, "Why did you move to Massachusetts?"

"Family," Blake answers like it's a closed subject and I feel myself tense again. He sighs, "I'm sorry. I really don't mean to sound rude, but I would like to have fun with you tonight and talking about my family," he pauses and before he looks away, I see pain in his eyes. When he looks back at me it's gone. "Let's just say I have good parents and an amazing sister. They are all in Massachusetts, but I grew up here. What about you?"

I shake my head, trying to understand his reaction, but I guess it's too soon to ask. So instead, I answer him. "I'm from here as well. My mom and dad live on the other side of town with my little brother. He just graduated high school and will be here for school in the fall. I also have a brother that's a year older than me."

"What about Sara?" he inquires. "It seems like you've been friends a long time."

"Yeah, we've been friends since elementary school," I reveal. I smile at the thought of her. "She's a really good friend, one you can always depend on."

"Good, we all need that," he states, smiling lightly. "Matt and Bree who you met at the concert are my best friends. I grew up with my three roommates Thad, Jason and Patrick here and we stayed close, but Matt and Bree are like family to me. It's just different. I guess more of what you and Sara are even though I didn't know them until I was 17," he adds.

He glances down at his phone with an apology, "Sorry, I need to check my messages when they come in. I promise I'm paying one-hundred percent attention to you, but I can't ignore it. I really hope that's okay," he prods. But the way he says it I'm sure it wouldn't change if it weren't okay with me.

"Is it important?" I ask.

"No, not this time," he admits his jaw twitching slightly. "I just have to make sure it isn't though," he explains looking right into my eyes with obvious vulnerability. The look in his eyes makes me want to melt right into those pools of chocolate. I drop the subject as soon as our waitress arrives with our food.

When she leaves, we start eating. He glances at me with a sexy smirk that makes my insides soften to mush and finally questions, "So what would possess a gorgeous girl like you to walk up to a stranger at a concert and kiss him like that?" I feel the blush immediately consume my body. He adds with laughter in his voice, "I'm definitely not complaining, but I'm starting to get the impression you wouldn't normally do something so…daring." I still can't find my voice to respond and he asks with his eyebrow raised in challenge, "Was it really all just for the good spots?"

I take a calming breath and shrug my shoulders. I force myself to lift my head up and look into his eyes before I speak. I admit shyly, "Well, Sara and I were celebrating our birthdays. They're actually only three days apart, so we

42

always try to do something fun together. She was the one that got us the tickets and I was the one that made us so late."

He raises his eyebrows further. "Happy Birthday! How old?" he asks grinning.

"Twenty-one," I reply.

"Same as me," he muses. "I wish I would've known for tonight."

Ignoring his comment, I continue, "I also promised her that I would try to relax and have fun this summer." He cocks his head to the side looking at me curiously as I speak making me start to babble, trying to explain myself even more. "I just have had a lot going on the past couple years and she thought I deserved it and I'm trying to live up to her expectations, so I guess I went a little overboard. And I wanted to make it up to her since we were late and all. She's always doing so much for me, and we were supposed to be celebrating our birthdays and I really didn't want to mess that up for her, but our birthdays were actually a couple weeks ago. This was our big celebration together though and every year…" I stop when I realize his eyes are sparkling with laughter and I haven't stopped talking or bothered to take a breath. I gaze down at my lap, flushed with embarrassment.

"You can keep going. I'm enjoying listening to you. I'm wondering what else I'm going to be able to find out about you." He smiles genuinely and I blush again. We spend the rest of dinner talking about likes and dislikes, as well as different places we used to enjoy going when we were kids around here like the parks, the lighthouse, the museums, the various tours like whale watching or even where he liked to go fishing.

The music soon starts up and our gazes both veer towards the made-up stage. It's a small stage with four guys all in jeans and dark colored t-shirts probably in their early twenties, or even college students. The band consists of a drummer, a guy playing keyboard and two with guitars. Although, I think one may be a bass guitar. They all have microphones to sing, but only one of the guitarists seems to be doing so right now. The music is a cross between alternative and folk. After listening to them for a little while, I express to Blake, "They're pretty good."

Blake shakes his head at me with a gentle smile and points to his ear, letting me know he can't really hear me too well. Halfway through the first song he stands up and extends his hand to me. I look up at him skeptically since no one else is dancing. His smile just grows, and I reluctantly put my hand in his, attempting to ignore everyone around us.

The instant we touch, I feel the heat travel from my hand, up my arm and burst once it reaches my chest, spreading throughout my whole body. He gently tugs me behind him until we're right next to the stage. He stops there and turns to face me, pulling me close to him with a small smile curving his lips. He places one hand on my lower back and I think I stop breathing. His other hand still grips mine tightly and he settles it between us, resting on his chest. My nerves kick up the party in my stomach sending my heart into overdrive, pounding rapidly in my chest. I consciously force myself to breathe slowly, forcing air in and out of my lungs.

I can't help but think I haven't really done this since Kris. "I'm not that girl," I blurt out practically screaming in his ear. He pulls back to look at my face, questioning what I mean with his eyes. I desperately try to explain my outburst. "The other night at the concert when I kissed you, I've never done anything like that before. I'm not that girl," I choke out, needing him to know.

His answering smile lights up his whole face, making it difficult to catch my breath. With his eyes sparkling, he pulls me even closer and whispers in my ear, "Good. I figured after your...speech during dinner that might be what you were saying, but honestly, I'm happy to be your one and only." My entire body heats with embarrassment. "And from this," he whispers in my ear lightly touching his fingers holding my hand to my cheek before tucking it back between us. I stay right where I am, dancing close, swaying back and forth. I hope he can't tell my nerves have gone into overdrive, but then I hear his low chuckle warm my ear and I swear it gets even hotter.

He pulls me even tighter, and I rest my head gently on his chest. I want this again.

I want to feel beautiful, cherished, and safe in a sexy guy's arms.

I want to be able to talk to him and have him talk to me.

I want to be able to put my trust in someone again.

If I'm honest with myself, I want to be able to put my trust in the sexy guy I'm dancing with right now.

That's crazy though, I just met him yesterday. I pull my head back and glance up at him with a shy smile. He looks at me his chocolate eyes turning even darker making my entire body heat with just a look. I bury my head back in his chest and swallow down the lump in my throat.

We dance to a few more songs before we find our way back to our table. "Do you want some dessert?" he asks. I shake my head knowing I might throw up if I add any more food to the dancing butterflies in my stomach. Blake asks for the check and pays the bill while we listen to the music for a little longer before they announce a break.

"Should we head out?" I prompt as my ears ring from the loud atmosphere. Blake nods his head in agreement and stands reaching for my hand again and this time I take it with a smile. He lets me lead the way out and every time we have to pause to get around a crowd of people, I feel his hand graze my hip making me shiver.

45

As soon as we step outside, he drops my hand, but I don't have a chance to feel the loss because he wraps his arm around me guiding me to his Jeep. "I had a lot of fun. Thank you," I murmur timidly and look up at him as we reach the passenger door.

He reaches his other arm around and cages me in looking into my eyes like he's searching for something, but still not saying a word. Never taking his eyes off mine, he leans in until I can feel his breath on my lips and pauses there. My heart begins beating so fast, it becomes the only sound I can hear.

He finally closes the distance between us, his lips soft and sure as he kisses me. I'm afraid it will end if I move more than my lips, so that's all that I dare to do. His hand slides off his jeep to the back of my neck as he flicks his tongue lightly across my lips. I open for him and he leans in further, deepening the kiss. My heart falls into my feet as his tongue pushes to tangle with mine. He tastes of beer and steak and something else I can't get enough of. He groans as he begins to let up and I swear I feel the rumble all the way to my soul. He pulls back, breaking our kiss and I unintentionally whimper with the loss.

He looks at me with the corners of his lips quirking up as he quickly clears his throat. "I had fun too and this time I wanted a kiss from you that wasn't for show." I release the breath I didn't know I was holding, and he chuckles softly, stepping away from me to open my door. I quickly slide in, dizzy from his kisses, knowing I need to sit down somewhere before I fall to the ground like a fool.

On the short ride home Blake asks playfully, "So did you have enough fun that I could convince you to go out with me again?"

I giggle quietly, but answer him with confidence, "I'd like that."

"I'm busy this week with work and some other stuff, but how about next Friday?" he proposes.

"Okay," I agree. I smile and reach for the door handle as he parks in front of my building. "Let me know where and when later this week."

Before I climb out of the car, he stops me with a light touch to my arm. "For the record, I can tell you're not that kind of girl," he pauses and I hold my breath as he holds my gaze. "I like that about you," he states making my insides flutter like a whirlwind. He quickly stops my hand before I reach for the door handle again and gently places his other hand on my cheek leaning in for another slow and gentle kiss. When he pulls back, my lips are swollen and tingling while his eyes are sparkling. He whispers, "Goodnight, Lizzie."

I slowly let out my breath and again fumble for the door handle before replying, "Goodnight. Thank you, Blake." I jump out of his jeep quickly before he can say or do anything else. I feel him watching me as I walk to the door. I turn to give him a quick wave before I step inside and shut the door. I nearly collapse as soon as he's out of my sight and I let the night's events slowly catch up with me.

I walk into the living room feeling like I'm in a fog. Sara is sitting cross-legged with her laptop laying on her knees, but swiftly slams it shut when she notices me, snapping me out of my haze. "Hey, Sara. What are you doing?" I prod narrowing my eyes at her with curiosity.

"Nothing, just going through my email," she claims dismissively. "How was your date?"

I ignore her question, "What were you looking at?" I probe. "Did she put something up again?" I ask impatiently my anxiety already getting the best of me. "I really hate Tori!" I mumble under my breath.

Tori Sheridan is Barbie beautiful, smart, former homecoming queen and captain of the girls' cross-country team, as well as the poms squad from my Casco Bay High graduating class. She writes a blog, although she uses a fake name online, probably for her own protection after everything that happened in high school. We were never friends, but we were never really enemies either until Kris and I became friends.

"No!" Sara denies in her high-pitched voice telling me she's lying.

I slowly step towards her and sit down right next to her so she has nowhere to go. I turn towards her and grumble with fake cheer, "Then you won't mind showing me what you were looking at."

She sighs heavily knowing I won't give in, and I'll go look myself if she doesn't show me anyway. "It doesn't mean anything, you can't let her get to you," she proclaims trying to comfort me before I even see anything. She reluctantly opens her laptop. I read a post with a picture of me at the concert kissing Blake with the caption, "Some things never change..." I push it away not wanting to see any attached comments, already feeling sick to my stomach.

"I check it whenever I can so I can try to stop all her bullshit. I saw this and was just about to respond to her privately. She can't pull this shit again," she yells still trying to defend me just like she did when Tori wrote the high school blog.

Back then, it had everything from fashion advice to what's happening at school and what's happening in the area. In the most popular section, she had people vote on different topics, many times found in old yearbooks like most popular girl/boy, best athlete, best dressed or most likely to succeed. After a while it seemed she liked to focus on negative 'accomplishments' as she called them. She listed the top five votes with a picture of whoever was in the top slot. Starting second semester, after she saw Kris and me together, I won those nearly every time.

She began with just being a little mean, before she turned completely cruel. She listed me first for things like worst clothes, a loser, a fake and a cheater (which actually got my chemistry teacher to question a project I worked on with Kris) to biggest backstabbing bitch, to slut and whore. I didn't want to go to school, but since the internet followed me home and I didn't want my parents to see any of it, I forced myself to go to school. Tori would always find a way of torturing me.

I grimace. "Forget about it, whatever you say won't do anything. Anyone that follows her blog isn't worth it to me anymore anyway."

"Yeah, but..." she starts to protest.

I interrupt her, "Drop it, Sara!" I sigh in frustration and instantly regret snapping at her. "I'm sorry. It's been a long night. I'm just going to go to bed."

"Did you at least have fun with Blake?" she prods, suddenly concerned about my date tonight.

I look over at her and smile reservedly. "Yeah, we had a lot of fun." She squeals in excitement and my smile grows bigger. "We're going out again next weekend."

"That's great, Liz! I'm so happy for you! You have to share some details!" she exclaims. "I knew it!"

"We went to Andy's for dinner, a good band was playing I'd never heard before, we talked, we danced..." I trail off and she raises her eyebrows at me obviously waiting for more.

"That's all you're getting tonight. We'll see how it goes," I claim and shrug my shoulders. I'm just not ready to tell her anything else yet.

She sighs in resignation before nodding in understanding, "Relax, have fun. It will be fine."

I nod just so she won't keep going. "Goodnight, Sara," I rasp and stride quickly to my room.

"Goodnight!" she calls out after me.

Chapter 7

Elizabeth

It's beautiful outside, so I decide to walk the mile and a half to work to wake me up. I really didn't sleep very well. I couldn't get that stupid blog out of my head. Every time Tori posts something new on that thing, I let myself get stuck in the past. I hate that she still gets to me, but I can't help it! I slow down and breathe in the fresh air, letting my mind wander to my ex-boyfriend.

Kris is one of those guys I categorize as having it all, well mostly. He has what I call preppy boy good looks, tall, thin, but strong and very athletic, blonde hair, blue eyes, and a perfect smile. He dresses in clothes like nice jeans and t-shirts or khakis and polo shirts, has good grades, played football, basketball and former captain of our state winning baseball team senior year.

He grew up in a neighborhood that most anyone would be jealous of with his younger sister, mom, and stepdad. His dad died when he was only eleven. I remember all of the kids and teachers alike doing anything for him when it happened, but I didn't know the details of what really happened at the time. I knew a lot of kids whose parents were divorced, but not completely without one of their parents. His stepdad always seemed really nice though and Kris talked about him a lot, but he never wanted to talk about his real dad.

I let myself get lost in my memories of Kris as I walk. He was always nice to me, but for a long time, I basically admired him from afar. Okay, I drooled over him I admit to myself because before everything started, I had a huge crush on him. He dated Tori for two years before he finally broke up with her the summer before our senior year. I tried not to get my hopes up, knowing I wasn't really anyone special, but just looking at him drove me absolutely crazy.

I remember the day Kris started to pay more attention to me. It was the beginning of our senior year and he would ask me for help with homework or projects. I always said yes and was thrilled to spend any kind of time with him, even if it was just to help him. We really had a lot of fun together. He started bringing me treats to school like cookies or brownies his mom made and sitting with me at lunch. He would stay and hang out with me to watch a movie after we were done with our homework. He had a way of making me feel special when we were together.

Just before Christmas, he finally asked me out on a real date and it took me three tries before I could squeak out a yes. We went out for pizza and then we went to a movie. At the end of the night, he leaned in and kissed me making me feel like my dreams had come true.

We continued to spend a lot of time together over the school break; my favorite time spent kissing him. I thought I was in heaven. At least I did until the first time he put his arm around me in the hallway at school. Tori stood there with her mouth hanging open, glaring at me. Even with Kris's arm around me I cowered, terrified of what she was going to do to me because unfortunately for me when she talked, people listened.

I really hate her stupid blog!

The worst parts of her blog were the pictures she put along with her lists. At first, she just found the worst pictures of me she could find or try to take pictures when she knew I wasn't expecting it.

Towards the end of the school year though, she began finding pictures that just made me look bad like Kris and I hugging at a football game, but it looked like he had his hands under my skirt, or a picture of me studying with someone from class, but the angle she took it you can see down my shirt.

The worst one ever though, was a picture from inside Kris's room of the two of us kissing and you could see my naked back. I know exactly when she got that picture. She had stopped by to drop off a book he had left in class and turned on his webcam while in his room. I'm sure she has pictures that are much worse from that day, since it was my first time with him, but she probably doesn't want Kris to hate her or get arrested for that matter, so she didn't use them.

I wipe the tears away from my cheeks as I keep moving towards work. I glance around at the few runners, bikers, or people walking by headed to work, home, or who knows where. I wonder as each person passes by me if they saw any of those horrible pictures of me and choke on a sob I'd been trying to hold back. What if Blake saw one of those pictures? What would he think of me then? I shake my head attempting to rid myself of the panic I'm feeling and wipe the tears from my cheeks again.

I wish the blog had stayed shut down like it was near the end of the school year when a boy from another school made one of those negative lists. He ended up trying to commit suicide due to the cruel backlash from it. Anyone that was believed to be a part of the blog had a three-day in school suspension, including Tori. The whole school also had a mandatory seminar on cyber-bullying. Unfortunately, even that didn't stop the hurtful names people called me like slut and whore. Besides the fact there were pictures of me out there I couldn't eliminate.

Unfortunately, the blog Sara was looking at last night, was the same one Tori eventually started back up after graduation with no connection to the school and without the lists. It appears innocent at first glance, but Tori finds other ways to get to me.

It still hurts remembering the picture she posted of her and Kris dancing as king and queen for senior prom, even though I was his date, but she was all over him for their required dance. Then, she posted a picture of me in a negligée (compliments of Kris's webcam) attached to an article about dressing appropriately in public.

I was completely mortified and too scared to speak up because I didn't want my parents to see the picture. I know it would give them a heart attack, so I did everything I could to hide it from my family and kept telling Sara and Kris not to worry about it. I told them that I was okay even though I was anything but okay. Honestly, keeping that from my family became a total nightmare, but I believe confessing everything to them would've been worse!

I tried to tell Kris she was the one who posted it and it was intentional, but he would always stand up for her and make excuses for why she is the way she is. I just wanted him to stand by me and support me for once. I guess I should have known then, but...I wipe away my tears again and shake my head trying to forget about Kris and Tori before I walk into the café where I work. I'm not about to let them ruin another day for me. They've already done enough.

I take a deep breath before I push open the café door and walk straight to the back with my head down to put my things away. Grabbing my apron, order pad and pen, I head right to the back of house where we meet for a quick meeting to find out any specials of the day as well as our assigned tables before each shift.

I step up next to another waitress and friend just as our manager gets started and pauses, giving me a pointed look. I look down and roll my eyes because I'm never late and my thirty seconds late is nothing compared to some of the others. Katie looks over at me, her eyes filled with concern and whispers, "You, okay?" I guess I must look worse than I thought. I nod my head with a tight smile before trying to take another relaxing breath.

The next couple hours go by quickly with my tables constantly full. I turn to head back towards the back room for a quick break, stopping to ask Katie to cover for me for five minutes when my eyes land on Blake causing me to nearly trip over my own feet. I catch myself from falling and stare openly across his table at Bree smiling warmly up at him. The way she's looking at him makes my heart drop into my stomach with dread. Christian isn't with her and she's having lunch with Blake. I swallow the lump in my throat telling myself that friends can have lunch together and I did hear Blake tell her he wanted to see her before she left in front of her boyfriend.

Why would he do that if this wasn't innocent?

I try to shake off my jealousy and doubt. I'm about to turn towards the back to take my break, but then Blake's look turns serious and he gently covers her hand with his. Panic begins gripping at my chest as I watch them; suddenly desperate to claw my way out. Katie snaps her fingers in front of my face to get my attention. I clamp my mouth shut, quickly running in back again without saying a word to her. At this point I'm pretty sure she thinks I've lost my mind, but I need to pull myself together fast.

I drop down on the bench in the back room, rubbing my hands fiercely over my face. I can't do this again. They look pretty close for being just friends. You don't hold hands like that with someone who's just a friend. She did look pretty serious with her boyfriend when they were together, but I don't really know her. She could be just like Tori. For that matter Blake could be just like Kris and I can't do that again.

I take a deep breath and exhale slowly, attempting to slow down my thoughts. I remind myself that Blake isn't my boyfriend. I went on one date with the guy. I have to stop it now before it goes any further. Why do I already feel like my heart's breaking, like I'm grieving for something I never really had? What's even crazier is I already feel worse than I did when everything happened with Kris. How is that even possible? I let out a frustrated breath when the door slams shut making me jump at the sight of Katie.

"You sure you're okay?" she asks hesitantly.

I heave a sigh and briefly close my eyes pushing back my tears before responding, "I'll be fine. I just had a rough night."

She nods her head in understanding. "Well, I'm sorry to pull you off your break then, but we really need your help. A bunch of people just walked in, and Sally just got sent home sick." I groan and she gives me an empathetic look. "I'm here if you ever need someone to talk to you know."

"Thanks Katie," I mumble gratefully. I reluctantly follow her to the front of the restaurant to get back to work. Maybe if I work hard enough, I'll be able to keep my mind off Blake, Bree, Kris and Tori. I do everything I can to keep my gaze away from the table where I saw Blake and Bree while I work.

Chapter 8

Blake

"Bree, are you sure you're doing okay?" I ask again, practically begging for it to be true.

"Yes, I'm sure! I promise I'm doing really well," she insists with a genuine smile.

"And are you positive you're going to be okay up there at your grandma's with just Christian and his family?" I probe.

She takes a deep breath while I watch as she tries to steady herself before answering, "I like being there. I feel closer to her. It feels like home." She takes another deep breath wiping away a tear that escapes before continuing, "Plus, Christian will keep me busy. We're always going kayaking or something when we're there. It's actually really relaxing and peaceful," she proclaims thoughtfully. "I really like his family too. They treat me like I'm part of their family and..." she trails off.

My heart breaks for her knowing she's thinking about her mom and grandmother. I know how much she misses them. "That's because you are," I offer with a grin, somewhat regretful. She smiles bigger with my comment and the small part of regret I have left vanishes knowing how happy she is with Christian. She deserves it after everything she's been through. I cover her hand with mine and look at her with as much sincerity as I can muster. "I know they love you, Bree. Everyone who knows you loves you." I pause then ask cautiously, "So, is it okay if I come visit you?"

"Yes, please come! We would have so much fun!" she exclaims excitedly. She gently pulls her hand away to finish eating.

"Are you sure it's okay with Christian?" I add quirking my eyebrow.

She ignores my question and asks with a teasing grin, "Are you going to bring Liz with you?"

I can't help but laugh at her response. I lean back and cross my arms over my chest, "So that must be my answer. It's okay to visit you if I bring a girl with me."

She rolls her eyes dramatically, "Not just any girl and you're always welcome at my house!" she defends.

I just nod knowing Christian would never tell me not to come if she wants me there, but I'm sure he's not encouraging it. I sure as hell wouldn't. "So, are you going to make it down to Massachusetts this summer? My sister has been asking for you. She really wants to see you. She misses you," I add feeling slightly guilty for saying that. I don't want to make her feel bad, but it's true and she should know.

Bree smiles at the mention of my sister. "I'll make it down. I promise. I feel bad I haven't seen her in a while," she mumbles and grimaces regretfully. "When you talk to her, tell her I will get there as soon as I can this summer. I want to make sure you're there when I go though, so we can go see her together. Maybe I'll come here, and we can drive down in your Jeep. I could go during the week sometime when Christian is busy working anyway. I'll be working mostly weekends at the gift shop. That's when they're the busiest and since I'm just a seasonal worker, I'll be the one who gets stuck with those hours mostly," she elaborates and scrunches up her nose in displeasure.

"Don't worry, that sounds perfect. Let me know what you want to do after you check your schedule and talk to Christian. You know my work schedule is always flexible."

Bree nods her head in acknowledgement, letting her eyes wander as we wait for our check. "Hey, isn't that Liz over there?" Bree prods pointing behind me. "You didn't tell me she works here!" She smacks my arm playfully.

"Ow!" I rub my arm where she hit me pretending it hurt worse than it did. I glance over in the direction she's looking and spot Liz in her waitress uniform. She's bending a bit to place platters of food in front of her customers and I release my breath slowly. She looks damn good in her uniform, but I'm sure she wouldn't appreciate me walking up to her and wrapping my arms around her right now. We have only been on one date I think to myself. I grin thoughtfully and shake my head before I look back at Bree. "Huh, I didn't know," I admit.

"You didn't know?" Bree reiterates shocked.

I smirk at her reaction. "I told you it was new. When we were out the other night, she told me she had to work today. I knew she was a waitress, but I guess I never asked her where. Now I know." I smile easily.

Bree rolls her eyes dramatically and grumbles, "Men!" Then, she smirks at me. I drop money on the table for both of our lunches. We slide out of the booth and Bree grabs my hand trying to drag me across the cafe. "Come on, let's go say, Hi," she urges and I happily oblige, wanting to be closer to Liz.

Just as Liz finishes placing someone's lunch in front of them and turns to walk away Bree steps in front of her with this ridiculous smile on her face and proclaims, "Hi, Liz!" She startles a little with the greeting and glances at us, then down to our joined hands just as Bree drops my hand she was dragging me with.

It's obvious to me Liz looks a little weary and I can't help but wonder why. She knows Bree and I are just friends. She met her boyfriend the other night, so she knows I'm not on a date. "You didn't tell me this is where you work," I state with a small smile, hoping I'm reading her wrong.

She just shrugs her shoulders in response and stares at me blankly. "Yeah," she mutters, pursing her lips.

I feel more and more uncomfortable as the seconds tic by, like I did something wrong, but I honestly have no idea what I could have done. "Anyway, I can see you're really busy, so I guess I should let you get back to work," I mumble reluctantly. She nods stiffly, not saying a word. "I'll call you later?" I prod hopefully, dreading the uneasy feeling in the pit of my stomach.

She nods robotically again before plastering on a fake smile that makes me cringe. She finally declares stiffly, "Thanks for coming, have a great day!"

I watch her hips sway, taunting me, as she walks away with my mouth hanging open in shock. "What the fuck just happened?" I grumble under my breath. I glance over at Bree finding her glaring at me. "What?" I question, now completely confused.

She turns around and stalks out of the restaurant. I heave a sigh, not able to do anything but follow. As soon as we step outside, she turns on me. Poking her finger into my chest, she demands an answer, "What did you do?"

"What?" I ask again incredulously. "I didn't do anything! We had a lot of fun last night. When I dropped her off, I thought things were great. I have no fucking idea why that was so painfully awkward!" I exclaim.

Bree narrows her eyes at me even more, probably partly due to my language and partly because she believes I'm the one who did something wrong. Still scrutinizing me, she eventually sighs, relenting and shakes her head. "Okay, well you're going to have to call her later and figure it out. You obviously did something."

"Well, I sure as hell don't know what that could be," I grunt in exasperation, but I have a nagging feeling she's right. I just hope this isn't because of my relationship with Bree because that's not something I'm about to change for anyone.

"Maybe you should buy her some flowers. Be prepared to grovel," she suggests. She glances at her phone before returning her gaze to me. "I'm sorry Blake, but I have to go. I'm supposed to meet Christian at his apartment in a little while."

"Okay. Tell him I said, hi," I respond wrapping my arms around her and giving her a kiss on her forehead.

"I will. Thank you for lunch." She gives me a quick squeeze before she steps back and smiles at me.

I nod in acknowledgement. "Of course. Take care of yourself and let me know if you need anything." I grin, adding playfully, "I'd be happy to kick Christian's ass if he steps out of line or anything else you may need."

She laughs and shakes her head in amusement, smacking me in the stomach. "Real funny, Blake," she retorts sarcastically.

"I am, aren't I?" I smirk. "Seriously though…" I add giving her a pointed look.

"I know, I know," she interrupts rolling her eyes again sounding exasperated. "I'll be fine!" she exclaims. "I promise to call you if I need anything Christian can't handle," she jokes even though we both know I'm serious. "I'll see you later and good luck with Liz," she adds giving me one last look of sympathy.

"Thanks, it looks like I may need it." I wave goodbye as she climbs into Christian's white Ford F-150. She looks so small in that thing it makes me chuckle. She turns and waves as she backs out, giving me a warm smile.

I look back towards the café and catch a glimpse of Liz through the window and shake my head in frustration. I slowly walk over to my jeep playing with my keys. I go over the last twenty-four hours in my head trying to figure out what's going through Liz's beautiful head. Maybe she's not interested? If that's the case she sure played me, but I'm not ready to give up yet.

Normally, I don't give a shit, but there's something about this girl.

By the time I get home it's driving me fucking insane! I have to know what's going on. I text her asking if she can meet me after work. Impatiently, I wait for a response and finally get one after an hour.

I'm busy until 7pm.

I'll pick you up.

Quickly, I turn my phone off. There's no way in hell I'm going to give her a chance to say no.

"I'm acting like a fucking pussy," I mumble under my breath.

"It's good that you're finally admitting it," my roommate Thad says as he walks in the room and smacks the back of my head.

Instead of responding I grab a bottle of water and head to my room to change. "I'm going for a run," I call over my shoulder. There's no way I can sit in this apartment until I go see Liz tonight. I need to do something to get rid of my anxiety or I'm going to fucking explode!

"Are you going to the double basement tonight? They're having a party," Thad yells right before I step into my room.

"Aren't they always?" I prod. Then, I shake my head and mumble, "Nah, not tonight, man. I'll catch you guys later."

"Suit yourself, pussy," he jokes, smirking at me.

I just flip him off and hurry to change. I need to get out of my apartment before I lose my mind.

Chapter 9

Elizabeth

At 7:05 I hear the high-pitched sound of the doorbell ringing causing my stomach to immediately churn with nerves. "He wouldn't show up after I told him I was busy, would he?" I ask Sara warily.

She just looks at me with her eyebrows raised and questions, "Are you going to answer that, or do you want me to let him in?"

Instead of responding I huff and trudge to the door mumbling to myself about boys not listening while Sara blatantly laughs at me. I open the door to find Blake on the other side grinning like the Cheshire Cat making my heart beat faster.

He slowly looks me up and down from my head to my toes making me wince as soon as I realize what he's seeing. I'm in my baggy grey sweatpants and University of Southern Maine t-shirt, my hair is in a messy ponytail, and I have absolutely no make-up on. "What are you doing here?" I snap scowling at him. I swear he tries to hide his laugh while I continue to glare at him, only increasing my frustration.

"I told you I would pick you up at seven when I texted you earlier. Are we staying in tonight?" he prods playfully. I narrow my eyes at him even more and this time he doesn't bother hiding his laughter.

"I texted you back saying I was busy," I state in exasperation before trying to shut the door on him. He stops me by placing his body in the doorway and raising his hand to block the door from hitting him.

"You look really busy," he states sarcastically. I glare at him again and he holds up his hands in surrender with a low chuckle. "Okay, okay. I turned my phone off after I texted you because I didn't want to know if you tried to make another excuse why you didn't want to see me," he confesses. My mouth drops open in shock with his admission and I turn away from him.

"You said you were busy all week anyway. What does it matter?" I challenge, not looking at him.

He heaves a sigh and runs a frustrated hand through his hair before responding, "I am, but I thought this was more important right now." My body stills at his declaration, and I wait for him to continue. "Look, at the café today you were acting very different towards me to say the least and I figured I at least deserve to know why. Did something happen? Did I do something?"

I turn back towards him and stare knowing I need to give him an answer. My mouth begins opening and closing like a fish, not really knowing how to respond to him when I'm not ready to tell him everything. "I…" I begin and stop.

"Look Liz, I would normally walk away instead of pushing when it seems like you're no longer interested, but I had so much fun with you the night of the concert and even more so last night when it was just the two of us. I'm really enjoying getting to know you. I like you, Liz," he claims causing my heart to pick up speed again. "I can honestly say I don't remember the last time I could really say that to a girl, but I'm saying it to you. I would really like to get to know you more and see what's between us, but you have to talk to me and tell me if I did something to piss you off. I don't play games." He pauses before asking, "So, are you going to let me in so we can talk? Unless your adorable self is ready to

65

go out?" he challenges as the corners of his mouth turn up slightly making my stomach flip flop.

I cautiously step back from the door and gesture for him to come in, my face heated from his comments. He steps directly in front of me and right into my personal space. My breath catches in my throat as his body heat practically consumes me. He whispers, "Thank you," near my ear before stepping the rest of the way inside.

I close my eyes and take a deep breath to get rid of the chills he's causing and to calm my nerves before following him to my living room. "You remember Sara," I mumble gesturing to her perched on the couch.

She suddenly jumps up and grins. "Hi, Blake. I just remembered I have some things to do in my room. I'll see you later," she proclaims, quickly excusing herself.

Blake makes himself comfortable in the middle of the dark tan couch in my living room and gestures for me to sit with him. I press myself into the farthest corner I can and he sighs again, shaking his head. "What did I do?" he inquires almost desperately. "I hate having to ask, but I have gone over everything that's happened since I met you and I can't come up with anything."

I sigh looking at him seeing that it's obvious how much this is bothering him. I don't know his real reasons, but I decide I have to let him know the truth, at least some of it. "Blake, I don't know if you did anything," I admit quietly. The look on his face becomes even more confused but I don't blame him. I take a deep breath before I continue, "I have a huge issue with trust because of stuff that happened with an ex-boyfriend. I don't know if I'm ready for anything. I saw you alone with Bree, holding her hand, and honestly, I panicked."

I can see a level of understanding in his eyes and I wait for him to speak. "Liz, I don't know what happened with your ex, but I can tell you that Bree is with Christian, not me." I swear I see a bit of regret pass through his eyes when he says this, but that could be my overactive imagination again.

He runs his hand through his hair, sighing heavily before continuing. "Look, Bree and I are very close. In fact, she is my best friend. We've been through a lot of shit together. She's been through so much the last few years especially and I need to be there for her, but there's nothing between us."

I nod my head in acknowledgement and look down at my lap after seeing the sincerity in his eyes. "I'm sorry," I grumble, not even sure if it's loud enough to reach his ears.

He scoots closer to me and reaches for my chin, gently lifting it until I meet his gaze. "So, how about we just go for a walk tonight down by the docks? We can talk some more, and I can spend the evening trying to make you smile," he proposes.

I smile reticently back up at him. "Okay," I concede with a small smile curving my lips. "Just let me go change," I request, glancing down at my clothes, then looking back at him.

His smile broadens. "Don't change on my account. I think you look adorable, like you're ready to cuddle up in my arms." My grin grows and he adds, "Or I could help you change if you want."

I blush and rush towards my room ignoring his question. Glancing back, I call over my shoulder, "I'll just be a couple minutes."

I quickly throw on a pair of jean shorts and a plain faded pink V-neck sweatshirt over my t-shirt. I grab my socks and sneakers before applying powder to my face and a little bit of mascara and lip-gloss. Glancing in the mirror, I leave my hair up in the messy ponytail, so I don't keep him waiting too long.

I step out of my room and Blake looks up from his phone and gives me an appreciative smile. "Wow, you are fast. *And*, you look fabulous."

I feel myself heat easily and mumble uncomfortably, "Thanks." I grab my purse from the kitchen table and yell to my roommate, "Sara, I'm going out with Blake for a little while. We'll be back soon." She steps out of her room nodding at me in acknowledgement as she points to her phone held to her ear. I wave and quietly follow Blake out of my apartment.

I step up to his Jeep and he's right there, opening the door for me with a smile. "Thank you," I mumble again.

I watch him run around the front of the jeep and jump into the driver's seat, immediately starting it up. He glances at me with another smile, giving me chills. He puts the jeep in reverse and throws his arm over the back of the seat while he backs out. I can't help but fidget nervously with my sweatshirt not knowing what to say.

Blake glances at me again before throwing the Jeep into drive and looking out at the road in front of him. "Are you okay?" he prods looking concerned.

"Yeah," I reply trying to get my body to listen and relax. We remain quiet for the short ride down to the harbor. I'm thankful when we get there, anxious to get out of the car.

He steps around to my side of the jeep and immediately starts laughing. I look up at him with a questioning glance and he just asks, "What are you doing?"

I pause at his question when I realize I must look like a complete fool. I'm standing in the parking lot shaking my arms, bouncing back and forth on my feet, while rolling my neck and mumbling to myself to attempt to lessen my nerves like I'm about to start a race. I chastise myself in my head this time and my whole body turns red, consumed with embarrassment. "I...I..." I stammer before realizing at this point the truth can't hurt me. "I'm just trying to get rid of my nerves."

"Damn, you're adorable," he declares taking a step towards me grinning. He pauses right in front of me making my breath hitch as his body heat mingles with mine.

I freeze, staring at his firm chest, waiting to see what he's going to do. He reaches for my hand and entwines his fingers with mine before pulling it to his lips and brushing a light kiss over my knuckles. I can't help but melt a little more at the sweet gesture.

"Are you sure you're the same girl that kissed me at the concert the other night?" he teases. I think he feels me tense because he immediately changes the subject, "Thank you for coming out with me tonight."

"I'm sorry I was being so difficult," I say for lack of a better word.

"It's okay, I get it and you weren't being difficult. Do you want to tell me what happened with your ex?" he prompts as he turns to start walking along the harbor holding my hand tightly.

I try to swallow the lump in my throat as I look around. We stroll side by side and I glance around at the sailboats, speedboats and ferry boats docked for the night. They're all normally flooded with tourists and locals alike during the day for fishing, whale watching, puffin watching, tours and various other things.

I eventually slowly release the breath I'd been unconsciously holding and open my mouth to answer, "I guess you could say he broke my trust and faith over and over again mostly by his support of everyone but me, especially one particular girl."

We take a few more quiet steps. When he realizes that's all I'm going to say for now, he proclaims sympathetically, "I'm sorry he did that do you, but I need you to know that's not me. I do everything I can to support and protect those I'm close to." I nod my head, wanting to believe his words are the truth as I continue walking, staring at the water.

He eventually tugs at my hand to stop me, so I look at him. "Liz, I'm sorry to start this way, but after hearing you say your big issue is trust and after what happened today, I need to be blunt for my sake and yours. I need you to know that Bree isn't just my best friend; she's like family to me. I know I said this before, but she's been through a lot of shit and we've been through a lot of it together, but most of it is not mine to explain to you. I'm telling you this though because I do plan on being there for her. But she's with Christian and he's fucking crazy about her. There's nothing going on between us, but I will do anything for her."

My heart tugs hearing him talk that way about someone else. I want that with someone. He stares into my eyes like he's trying to read me before continuing, "I like you. I'd really like to date you. I haven't said that to someone in a really long time," he emphasizes, "but I need you to be understanding of my relationship with her and I need you to trust me. If you don't think you can do that, I'm fooling myself into thinking this might work."

I bite my lip, wondering if I should just walk away after that declaration. I barely know this guy. We've only been on a few dates and with what he's telling me...I don't know if I can do that, but there's something about him that's keeping my feet glued to the ground. I just can't walk away from him. He sounds like he's being truthful, but so did Kris. He may have thought he meant it, but...I look at Blake and see something so honest in his eyes that I unexpectedly find

70

myself saying, "I like you too and I know you haven't gotten the best impression of me today, but I'd like to try if you'll let me."

He doesn't say anything right away in response and I let my nerves get the better of me. I trip on one of the wood planks in the boardwalk, stumbling forward. Blake acts quickly, swiftly pulling my hand as he reaches around my waist with the other to catch me. "Whoa," he mumbles, placing me back on my feet and letting his hands linger on my waist. "You okay?"

"Yeah," I rasp, nodding woodenly in confirmation.

He gives me a light squeeze, instantly heating my body before letting go. "How about we plan on hanging out on Friday night still?" he suggests. "If you decide it's too much, text me before and we'll just be friends," he grumbles, his face turning bitter with the last word.

I nod in agreement and immediately change the subject. I just can't talk about my trust issues anymore. "So, you mentioned you have to work this week," I reiterate and he nods his head in confirmation. "Where do you work?"

"I work up at the outlets in Freeport, but I'm more of a seasonal worker. I work around holidays, breaks and of course summer. But even then, I need a flexible schedule, so I limit my hours."

"Do you keep a flexible schedule for school?" I ask curiously.

His body tenses slightly as he answers, "No, I need to travel down to Massachusetts quite a bit."

"What for?" I prompt, my curiosity growing.

"My family is there," he states on an exhale.

"That's right. You mentioned that was where you moved during high school. Your family still lives there?"

71

"Yeah, my mom and dad are in a small town outside of Boston. That's where I guess you can say I'm from besides here. And, my sister lives in Boston."

"You and your sister get along well?" I prompt noticing a sparkle in his eyes when he mentions his sister.

"She's the most amazing person I know," he proclaims his jaw tense and voice full of emotion. I pause not really knowing what to say when his words don't seem to completely correlate with his body language. "What about you, you mentioned you have two brothers?"

"I did?" I ask trying to remember this conversation.

"Yeah, the night of the concert at Bree's you said one of them was crashing on your couch and you had to get home to let him in. Then, the other night at dinner you mentioned you have two brothers."

I feel my face turn red for two reasons; one I can't believe he remembers that and two, I was lying to escape Bree's apartment. "Yeah, I uh have one brother who's younger than me and still at home with my parents, but he's starting here in the fall. His name is Scott. Then I have a brother Jax who's a year and a half older than me and lives in Brunswick, but he would rather crash with me when he comes home to visit. Obviously, he doesn't live too far, but it's just easier all around if he stays with me."

"Scott, Elizabeth and Jax?" he repeats.

"Yeah, Jax is actually Darren Jackson. He never liked his name for some reason and after," I pause not wanting to explain my brother's story, "well, eventually he just started going by Jax instead. It fits him."

"I get that," he mumbles. He glances down at me through his long eyelashes, his look giving me the strongest urge to tell him more, to share myself with him.

"As for me, my parents have always expected a lot of me, but they don't really expect much of anything from him.

He sees it as they already think he's a failure and whatever he does is a bonus in their eyes. I'm expected to be the helpful one when it comes to everything, including him. If he stays with me, it's an excuse for both of us to stay away from home. Then, Scott can do no wrong."

I release a sullen breath and try to pull my hand away feeling less and less like this is where I should be since my mouth doesn't seem to connect with my brain. I shouldn't be telling someone I have only been on a couple dates with about my family problems. "I'm sorry," I whisper shaking my head.

"What are you sorry for?" he probes, not letting go of my hand.

I let out an exasperated breath before stopping to explain, "I shouldn't have told you all of that."

"Liz don't ever apologize for talking to me about your life. I want to get to know everything about you. I want you to feel free to talk to me, to tell me anything and everything. To share something like that shows me that you are working on this trust thing," he claims. He smiles encouragingly at me, and I feel myself blush from the attention. He's happy I shared my flaws? I must look confused because he chuckles softly before adding, "I'm glad you're showing me a piece of you that you don't like to share with other people."

I smile bashfully, admitting, "I guess you're just easy to talk to." He beams and I feel my heart pick up speed. I take a deep breath trying to calm my rapidly beating heart before glancing down at my phone. It's almost eleven pm and I can't help but sigh with disappointment, not wanting to stop talking with him. I want to know everything about him too. "I'm sorry Blake, but I should get back to my apartment. I have to work the breakfast shift tomorrow at the café, so I have to be to work at 5:30."

"Wow, that's early! I guess I should get you home," he agrees regretfully. We turn around and begin walking back towards his Jeep letting the conversation turn light to things like work and any of the tourist boats that either of us has been on.

Before I know it, he's walking me to my door and his hand gently cups my cheek as he leans in and lightly brushes his lips over mine. The kiss is over quickly but leaves memorable tingles spreading throughout my body.

"I'll see you Friday," he declares with a small hopeful smile. He steps back before spinning on his heel and striding back to his jeep.

I step inside the apartment just as he slams his car door shut and collapse against my front door. I smile and gently touch my fingers to my mouth trying to remember the exact feel of his soft lips against mine.

A loud laugh snaps me out of my reverie. "Wow, you're already crazy about him!" Sara exclaims with a grin. I start to shake my head in denial, but I look in Sara's eyes and know I don't need to bother. She knows me so well.

I whine, "Sara, I'm so screwed!" I tear myself off the door and follow Sara to our couch so I can catch her up on my night. Maybe she can talk some sense into me.

Chapter 10

Blake

The text from my parents this morning has me on edge.

> *Hi, Honey, we need you to come home as soon as you can. Don't worry, but we have something important to talk to you about.*

I quickly called in to work and told them I had a family emergency and wouldn't be able to work until next week. I'm incredibly fortunate they're so accommodating when it comes to my family and being so flexible. I hung up and texted Liz.

> *I have to go home, but I promise I will be back in time for our date.*

I tap out a quick text to Bree.

> *I have to go home in case you need anything.*

> *Are you okay?*

I don't answer because honestly the whole drive to my parents' house, I worry so much about what in the hell my parents could have to tell me now. I struggle to keep calm and hold my hands steady on the highway.

I pull into my parents' driveway in nearly record time and stare at the house. We have a white colonial with a typical white picket fence out front on a decent size piece of property, just like the rest of the houses in our neighborhood. Our house looks different though. Ours is the one beginning to look rundown due to lack of care and regular maintenance because we haven't done any improvements since we bought it. Ours is the house we never really could call a home, but a place to put our things because it's close to my sister. Maybe that's why I always call it my parents' house and not home. To me this is the house where my parents became more like strangers and friends like Matt and Bree became my family. I know I can depend on them for anything.

I heave a sigh full of dread as I grab my duffel bag and backpack off the seat next to me before throwing my door open and stepping out of my Jeep. I slowly trudge up to the door not really knowing what to expect this time. I cautiously open the front door and I'm greeted by my mom's black cat scampering through my legs and out the door. Pushing the door shut I yell, "Mom? Dad?" and wait for an answer, anxious from the silence.

"Blake is that you?" I hear my mom finally reply and I release the breath I didn't know I was holding. I follow the sound of her voice to the kitchen. "I'm so glad you're home," she expresses and rushes around the counter to hug me.

"Hi, Mom," I greet her, hugging her back. "Where's Dad?"

"He's in his office, working on some of your sister's things," she explains. I nod in understanding, not wanting to ask anymore. "I'm making her favorite for dinner tonight.

Since you came home, I thought we could have a nice family dinner."

I wince with her words but nod my head to appease her. I hate when she's like this. "I'm going to bring my stuff upstairs to my room and I have a phone call to make. I'll be down in a little while," I huff out my excuse quickly, needing a few minutes to myself already and I don't even know why I'm here yet.

"Okay sweetie. I'm so glad you're home," she reiterates sweetly and waves at me.

I quickly stride back down the hallway and grab my bags I left by the front door before sprinting up the stairs two at a time. I step into my room, drop my bags and collapse onto my bed. With my arm resting on my forehead, I stare at the ceiling hoping for answers.

My room feels nothing like me anymore. It's filled with trophies and awards from when my mom insisted I play basketball and baseball, posters of my favorite MLB players and the Boston Red Sox. The only part I feel still represents me is my bulletin board. On there I have pictures of me with my friends. There's a few with Matt, Bree and even Amy. My favorites though are the ones with my sister and me over the years. She's just so incredible.

I sigh in frustration and reach for my phone. I quickly send Liz a text.

Hi Lizzie! I made it to my parents. Wanted you to know I couldn't stop thinking about our date this Friday the whole drive. I'm really looking forward to this weekend.

Hopefully she won't back out. Hell, maybe it would be better if she did. Seriously, what the fuck is wrong with me?

I scroll through my messages and see one from Bree.

Checking in, you ok?

I sigh and instead of answering her, I click the phone icon to call her. "Hello?"

"Hey Bree," I say on an exhale.

"Blake, are you okay?" she prods. I notice the obvious concern dripping from her voice.

"Yeah, I'm fantastic! I haven't seen my dad yet, he's working on some things for my sister and my mom is making Aubrey's favorite dinner so we can have a nice family dinner," I retort full of bitterness.

She gasps, "Blake, I'm so sorry. Do you need me to come down?" she offers making my heart clench.

Before I have a chance to answer I hear, "What the fuck, Bree?" very obviously coming from Christian. I don't blame him, but I can't hide my chuckle when I hear an instant, "Sorry," from him. I can even picture the glare she's definitely giving him and the groveling he'll be doing after we hang up.

"Nah, that's okay. I'll be fine. Besides, I'm going to go visit my sister tomorrow and Matt on Thursday. Then, I'll be back in Maine by Friday."

"Okay but give your sister a hug for me and tell her I'll come see her soon," she insists.

"I will and thanks," I emphasize sincerely.

"We're not leaving until Saturday, so come see me on Friday when you get back. I'll be here packing."

"I'll be there. See you Friday," I promise.

"Bye, Blake," she says before adding, "Call if you need me."

I press end and continue to stare up at my ceiling. I may have helped Bree get through all of her shit, but I'm just as grateful for her. Some nights if it wasn't for her, I wonder if I could have survived my own life.

My phone beeps and I glance at it seeing Liz's name. A smile instantly covers my face.

> *I'm looking forward to the weekend too.*

I laugh, trying to release some of the tension. I do feel a little of the burden lift off my chest when I think about her.

I text her back, teasing.

> *So, you don't want to admit to me that you're excited to see me this weekend?*

I picture her blushing and flustered as I read her next text.

> *I am! Have fun with your family. I'll talk to you later.*

I sigh with the reminder of my family.

> *Ok.*

"Dinner's ready," my mom yells. I slowly push myself up and off my bed with a groan. I trudge downstairs praying for a somewhat normal night.

For the first half of dinner, if anyone was watching us, they might think we look like a typical happy family. We're just eating dinner around our dining room table with one empty place setting I try not to look at. We all do everything we can to talk about things we know are non-issues. The discussions go from my mom asking my dad about work, my parents asking me about the end of the school year to my mom talking about working in her vegetable garden, which is her favorite form of therapy.

Then my mom turns to me and asks, "How's Bree?" proving she never listens to me.

I grind my jaw and take a deep breath before answering her. "She's fine," I finally spit out my simple response. I'm already dreading where she's heading because I know that's not the end of this conversation.

"Why didn't she come with you?" she prods oblivious to my change in attitude.

"She's got a lot going on Mom," I reply bitterly, my body filling with tension. I have no idea how to talk to her when she's like this.

"Yeah, but I'm sure she has some time for her boyfriend," she suggests with a small smile and I can't hold back my visible cringe.

"She does, Mom. She has a lot of time for him. In fact, she's with Christian right now. The guy she's been dating for almost a year and the guy she was with long before that," I grit out gripping my silverware so tight my knuckles are turning white.

"I always liked that girl," my dad mumbles between bites.

"I don't understand why you ever broke up with her. She loves your sister so much," my mom states shaking her head in disappointment.

80

I take a couple more deep breaths attempting to calm myself down before I dare speak. "We were never together," I grumble, enunciating each word. "We went on one date like four years ago. She's my best friend. That's all it is and that's all it ever will be! Get over it!" I snap.

My dad levels me with his stare. "Blake," he grunts in warning.

My mom looks over to my sister's empty chair. The chair that haunts our lives practically screaming at us with what could have been. The chair that has never been filled by her since we lived in this house, except for the rare occasions we bring her home, like holidays. She still sets a spot for her every night I'm home, like she'll walk through the door at any moment. "Are you going to visit your sister tomorrow?" she asks quietly not tearing her eyes away from the chair.

"Yeah, Mom," I acknowledge with a sigh.

"Maybe you can bring her some dinner. It's too bad she couldn't make it tonight, even when I made her favorite, spaghetti and meatballs." She finally looks away from my sister's chair, her eyes full of sadness.

I feel like an asshole for yelling about Bree. I close my eyes and swallow the lump in my throat, realizing tonight is another night of complete denial. I guess it's better than the times she completely flips out or when she goes into such a deep depression, she has trouble finding her way back. "I'd be happy to bring her some food Mom," I concede.

"You know, she misses you. She is always asking about you and why you're not around as much anymore," my mom states calmly. It feels like she's twisting a knife in my gut with her words. I'd do anything for my sister.

"I come home as much as I can. Now that school is over for the summer I'll be back more often. I promise," I murmur. My mom looks at me like she's not sure if I'm telling the truth. I can't stomach any more of her scrutiny. I set my fork down and throw my napkin on the table. "May I be excused?"

"No Blake, please sit and talk with us. We miss you. We hardly ever get to have meals as a family anymore," my mom begs.

Her words push me over the edge, and I lose it, not able to stop my outburst. "We never get to have meals as a family anymore Mom! Aubrey can't just jump in a car and drive home for dinner on the weekends! Pretending she can, won't make it happen no matter how much we all want it to! None of this is normal!" I yell gesturing around the room.

My mom's mouth drops open in shock. My dad slams his fist on the table and glares at me. "Blake!"

"What Dad? It's the truth! Nothing about this is normal! Ever since the fucking accident nothing about this family has been normal! Mom blamed you for so long that you just disappeared from our lives. You just stopped being mom's husband and you stopped being Aubrey's and my dad for years. Then you come back and you act like nothing is wrong."

I pause and shake my head at the ceiling, but I can't stop the hurtful words. I've kept it all in too fucking long. "You can't just jump back into our lives and pretend to be father of the year. You may be my father, but you are not my dad anymore and I'm not going to listen to you tell me what to do! You two act like we're this perfect fucking family, but we're not! That night changed all of us. Stop pretending it didn't!" I rant.

I glimpse at my mom. Tears are streaming down her face and I'm immediately filled with regret yet again. "I'm so sorry, Mom," I stammer. Spinning around, I run quickly out the front door, slamming it behind me.

"Fuck, fuck, fuck!" I scream, stuffing my hands in my pockets. I start striding down the street, not caring where I'm going. I just need to give myself some space from them and from that house.

I keep walking until I end up at the park. It's the same park I used to meet Bree at when we were both trying to escape our lives for such different reasons. I collapse on a swing with my memories from after the accident on replay in my head, reminding me why I'm here. I grab my phone and scroll through my earlier messages from Liz and unconsciously press call before placing the phone to my ear.

"Hello?" I hear her timid voice answer and I almost breathe a sigh of relief.

"Hi Liz, you busy?" I prod hesitantly.

"No, Sara and I were just watching a movie. What are you doing?"

"I'm just sitting at a park, thinking about you," I respond.

"Um, a park?" she asks sounding confused.

"Yeah, there's a park near my house. I like to come down here when I just need to get away," I admit.

"Is…Is everything okay Blake?" she stammers.

I sigh. "Yeah, just family issues. I'm good."

"You know you can talk to me, I'm a great listener," she encourages me sounding a little nervous.

"Thanks Liz, I'd really fucking like that," I confess with a heavy sigh wiping my hand up and down my face. "I think I'd rather have this conversation face to face though. In the meantime, I thought the sound of your voice might help me calm down if that's okay with you," I tell her, not really asking.

I can almost hear her blushing through the phone when she responds all flustered, "Uh, I, um…okay I guess, sure."

I chuckle lightly already feeling better. I turn the rest of the conversation light, asking about work today and the movie they're watching, just to hear her talking. The sound of her voice helps me forget about my parents and our issues. Eventually I murmur, "Thank you Lizzie. I really needed that. I'll see you soon."

"I'll see you later," she answers with a smile in her voice.

I begin walking back to my parents' house, feeling as if I can handle being here after talking to Liz. As I step out of the park, I realize for the first time in a long time, Bree isn't the person I wanted to call when I needed someone. A small smile touches my lips thinking of Liz.

Chapter 11

Blake

The next morning after I get back from a short run, I walk straight back to the kitchen to grab a bowl of cereal and some fruit. I'm hunched over my bowl at the kitchen table when my mom walks in from the back yard with her gardening gloves on. I take a deep breath and push out my apology immediately, "Mom, I'm so sorry about last night. I didn't mean to lose it on you. I know it's no excuse, but I get so pissed about what happened sometimes and I just couldn't," I trail off shaking my head. "I'm just so sorry." She doesn't deserve my anger. My father does for abandoning us and the drunk asshole who pushed us off the road does, but my mom doesn't.

"It's okay Blake. I understand," she murmurs. She gives me one of her sad smiles making me feel like even more of an asshole.

I walk over to her and wrap my arms tightly around her. "I'll be home as much as I can this summer, I promise. I'm only helping out at the outlets part time so I can get home to see you, Dad and Aubrey. Besides my boss is incredibly understanding with our circumstances. He lets me be really flexible with my schedule, so if you need me, I'll be here." I feel her nod in acknowledgement into my chest now that I'm taller than her.

My dad walks into the room and clears his throat. I slowly step back from my mom. "Morning," he grumbles looking at us over his glasses.

I nod towards him before apologizing robotically, "I'm sorry for last night." I know my mom needs to hear me say sorry to him whether I want to or not and I'll do what I need to for her. He nods his head in acceptance and I sit back in front of my cereal to finish eating. I breathe a sigh of relief, knowing I don't have to say anymore to him because my simple apology is all I have in me for him.

The first year after the accident, we all focused every effort on Aubrey and helping her. My mom, my dad and I had cuts and bruises from the accident, which healed relatively quickly. I even have a scar on my right shoulder from the broken glass, but all of us basically returned to a new normal. We were told over and over again how lucky we were I think bitterly.

Unfortunately, Aubrey will never completely heal. Her cuts and bruises healed like ours, but she had permanent brain damage. She needs help all the time. Every day I wish I could have done something else to protect her. Now all I can do is try to do what I can to protect her and her life now and I'm sure as hell going to do it.

I think finally admitting that Aubrey would never be the same is what pushed my mom over the edge. That's when she needed someone close to blame. My dad took it and separated himself from us. Eventually he stopped coming home, but my parents never got divorced or even legally separated. He went to see Aubrey, made sure we all had what we needed to survive, but he stopped being my dad.

"Blake, we need to talk," my dad begins looking hesitant. My stomach fills with dread at the look on his face.

I sigh heavily and push my nerves aside. "Dad, I said I'm sorry. I'm headed over to see Aubrey today. Can we talk later?"

He glances at my mom who nods her head stiffly and I feel my body tense in fear. I attempt to swallow the lump building in my throat and ask, "Is Aubrey, okay?"

"She's fine, Aubrey is good," he quickly reassures me. My shoulders relax only slightly and I exhale slowly with mild relief. "It's about something else, but it's important. It's why we asked you to come home."

I nod, afraid to say anything with the strange tension in the room. I push my bowl away and place my elbows on the table with my hands balled into fists in front of my chest. I nod again, looking him in the eye as if to say I'm ready for whatever he's got to tell me.

"So, when you were younger and I was gone for a while," he begins.

I can't help but interrupt him, "You mean when you left us when we fucking needed you?" I probe bitterly.

He clenches his jaw and continues, ignoring my words, "I was seeing someone. She knew I was married. I told her I'd never leave my wife, but…"

"Is that why you were gone so long? Why'd you come back five years ago then? You abandon her too?" I spit at him accusingly, my voice rising with each question. "Is that why you found a place for Aubrey so quickly so far away from the only home we had ever known and moved us to Massachusetts? Was it even about helping Aub or were you just trying to escape again? Did you even think about how what you did would even affect the rest of us?" I shake my head in disgust.

My father looks as though I just punched him, but after everything he put us through, I don't give a shit. He deserves to hear how much he fucked us all up!

I put my hands on the table and begin to stand up. I don't want to hear any of this, but then I feel my mom's gentle hands on my shoulders, and I let her guide me back to my seat. "Please listen to your father. You need to hear this," she pleads with me in a shaky voice. I press my fists even tighter and listen, feeling dizzy with hate.

"She got pregnant. I mean, we got pregnant," he stammers his face contorts with anguish and my jaw twitches with tension. I must have heard him wrong, but he continues, "I helped her throughout her pregnancy and when the baby was first born before I came back here to all of you. I would never abandon any of my children, Blake, no matter what you believe. I still make sure they're taken care of. Just like I made sure you and Aubrey were taken care of while I was gone." He takes a deep breath before looking me in the eyes again, "Blake, you have another sister and I'd really like you to meet her."

This time when I push up from the table my mom lets me go. I can't even respond to him. What the fuck does he expect me to say right now? I feel all this anger inside me building up and I have no idea what to do with it. My whole body is becoming so tense I feel like I'm about to break and I have to get out of here before I do.

I turn stiffly to my mom and croak out, "I'm going to see Aubrey and I'm going to stay at Matt's tonight. I don't know when I'll be back, but I'll call you later."

I can't even look at my father as I run upstairs hearing my mom call my name. I throw the few things I have on my bed back in my duffel. I grab both of my bags and my keys before rushing out of the house and slamming the door behind me.

I'm able to put on enough of a false front to enjoy my time with Aubrey. She deserves the best of me every day and I hate when I can't give it to her. Luckily, she finds the fact that I smell hilarious. Then again, I did run out of the house so fast earlier that I didn't even shower after my morning run. She always sees the good in everyone and everything. When the nurse tells me she needs rest because she had a rough night my heart practically breaks. I hate the thought of her having a rough night and I never like leaving her, but I will always do what's best for her. So, when I have to leave for the day, Aubrey signs I love you to me and I give her a genuine smile. "I love you too, Aub."

"Next time, bring Bree," she pushes out her words with an innocent smile, sounding child-like.

My smile grows and I feel the overwhelming sense of my love for her. "I'll try. She misses you and wanted me to tell you she'll come visit you very soon." I grab her hand and look into her eyes. I have no idea what makes me say it, but I blurt, "Maybe my friend Liz will be able to come soon too. I think you'll like her."

She beams at me in response. "I love meeting your friends!"

I give her another quick hug before waving goodbye. "I'll see you soon Aub."

I walk out the front door of Aubrey's adult home feeling better after seeing her face, but then I remember what happened with my parents this morning and I feel sick again. I drive to Matt's letting all this shit flow through my head.

I don't like the idea of having another sister. I don't want Aubrey to ever think I'm replacing her because I never could. Let alone her thinking our asshole of a father is replacing her. "Fuck!" I swear slamming the steering wheel and just wanting to forget about everything for a little while.

When I pull up to Matt's, it looks like a party is already underway and forgetting about everything just got a whole lot easier for tonight. I walk up and into the house, not bothering to greet anyone as I go. Tossing my duffle bag in Matt's room first, I immediately make my way to the refrigerator. Yanking it open, I grab a beer, tip my head back and down it as fast as I can. I reach for another bottle and shut the fridge door before scanning the room for Matt.

I push through the crowd of people when another guy we graduated with, Brett, slaps me on the back and hands me a shot of something. "Blake! Good to see you man! Are you around for the summer?"

"Nah, I'm just home visiting my family for a few days. I'll head back up to Maine after hanging with Matt and the rest of you for a bit." I smirk and he laughs in response toasting me with his own shot. I swallow it in one gulp, feeling the burn go down my throat and chase it with a few swallows of beer. "Have you seen Matt around?" I ask still scanning the room.

"I think he's out back by the fire," he replies.

"Cool, thanks." I nod and grab another beer on my way to find him.

I smile stiffly at a few of my old classmates as I walk by them, but there are also a lot of people I don't recognize. I finally find Matt sitting in an Adirondack chair in front of a small bonfire. He has a blonde girl I don't recognize sitting in his lap. "Matt," I interrupt the girl's flirting and she turns to glare at me.

"Blake! I wasn't expecting you until tomorrow night man!" Matt proclaims the same time he picks the girl up and sets her down on her feet so he can stand to talk to me. I toss my empty bottle into a nearby trash bin listening to it clink with the other glass. "I have a cooler here if you want another one," he gestures behind him.

I step around him and grab another beer before turning back. "Thanks."

"So, I guess that means you're crashing here tonight?" I nod stiffly and take another gulp of beer. "All good?" he prods with a quirk of his brow.

I just give him a look that says, "What the fuck do you think?"

He sighs, nodding his head. "All right, Blake. Have it your way for now. Are you up for some drinking games?"

I shake my head and suggest, "How about just straight drinking?"

He laughs, but I'm serious. I'm already starting to feel the burn of alcohol flow through to numb my thoughts and that's exactly what I want tonight. I'm not going anywhere, so no worries. Matt lifts his bottle to mine in a toast, knowing exactly what I need tonight, no questions asked.

Chapter 12

Blake

I startle, waking up to the slam of a door and my head pounding. Grabbing my head, I squint trying to pry my eyes open. A blurry vision begins coming into view, reminding me I'm on Matt's couch as I see his face come into view with a cup of coffee in his hand. He knees me in the side, eliciting an involuntary groan from me. "Ugh!"

He flops down in the recliner near my head. "What the fuck is up with you man?" he questions, demanding an answer.

I don't respond, not wanting to move, fearing more pain will ensue. He eventually continues, "You never drink like that, but last night you were on some kind of fucked up mission. You kept telling everyone except me to leave you the hell alone. I have to say you made it pretty fucking easy on everyone to do exactly that." I still don't say anything and he sighs heavily in frustration. "Look, Blake, I understand trying to forget about things, but last night?" he begins, pausing as he stares at me, arching his eyebrows in challenge. "That wasn't you man for soooo many fucking reasons. I know when you come to me it's usually for kicking back, joking around and not having to talk about whatever is going on, but last night was complete bullshit! Even for me," he emphasizes. My already nauseous stomach turns, his words making me feel even worse. Matt lets so much roll off his back, but not this. It had to be bad. I feel like an asshole. "So, this time I'm not going to wait, I'm going to push you because I think you need it. What the hell is going on?"

I groan and eventually open my dry, pasty mouth to answer. "My family is just more fucked up than I even knew," I whisper, heaving a sigh. I wipe my hands down my face in exasperation, trying to pull myself together. "Sorry if I caused any problems, Matt," I shake my head then groan in agony from the movement. I grunt, "I can't believe I drank like that! I guess after finding out I have another sister, I kinda' stepped out of my own head and jumped in headfirst."

"What?!" he questions in shock.

I just nod stiffly and give him a look letting him know he heard me right, but I can't go there yet. I slowly sit up, placing my feet on the floor and my elbows on my knees. I let my head drop to my hands between my legs, while I try to stop the room from spinning.

Gaining momentary control, I grumble, "Yeah, like I said, fucked up family." I release another sigh and rub the back of my neck. "Did I…did I do anything stupid?" I ask hesitantly.

Because of the accident, it's rare I drink too much, knowing drinking too much many times leads to doing stupid things and I can't have another night like that ever! I don't know if I would survive. But I knew I wouldn't be going anywhere, which honestly makes me fear my own stupidity. I don't think I've ever forgotten what happened after a night of drinking, but right now, my brain feels foggy as shit.

"Well…after you found me out back, you just seemed to be pounding beers glowering at everyone and everything. Anything beyond that?" he prods staring at me. I shrug my shoulders and wait for him to continue since that's all I really remember. "I guess after that you did some shots with Brett as well and kept mumbling about assholes."

93

"Shit," I cringe at the possibilities of what I could have said. I hope Brett didn't have a clue what I was talking about. That's the last thing I need.

Matt continues, "Cheri tried hitting on you, but you wanted nothing to do with her. You kept saying she wasn't Lizzie, so she peeled herself away from you pretty quickly. Anyone that came near you after that, you told to fuck off. After that, you honestly didn't talk to anyone but me. You were the epitome of anti-social," he states. He grins and shakes his head at me in disbelief. "Dude, I wasn't even expecting you 'til today!" he exclaims exasperated. "Anyway, I got you some coffee and I picked up some egg sandwiches and bagels."

"Aw, he does have a heart," I tease. Dropping my head back on the couch, I close my eyes. I grunt as a pillow unexpectedly slams into my head.

Pulling myself back up slowly, I rub my eyes as a bottle of aspirin hits me in my arm. "Take three with the water on the table. Eat and drink your coffee. After that, get in the shower dude, cause you fucking stink!" he instructs.

"Aw, are you taking care of me?" I ask in mock admiration. His gaze narrows as he gives me a look in warning. I sigh, grateful as I pop the aspirin into my mouth followed by water to wash it down. Taking a deep breath, I quickly finish the whole bottle of water, knowing I need it.

"Eat too," he reiterates.

Picking up the cup of coffee, I mutter, "Thanks," toasting him with my morning energy and praying for my head to stop spinning. I quickly wolf down the sandwich and try to figure out what to do with the information my parents gave me. Matt just raises his eyebrows at me knowing my head is going around in circles with something heavy with what I just shared.

"You still hanging out today?" he prompts.

"I think I might head back," I mumble. "Bree is leaving this weekend to spend most of the summer up at her grandma's place with Christian. He's working for his dad or some shit and she got some job at one of the local shops," I enlighten him.

He narrows his eyes, giving me a knowing look and opens his mouth to say something. I quickly interrupt his thoughts, anticipating what he's about to say, "That's not what this is about. It really is about this thing with my parents."

He tilts his head the side, assessing me, but he eventually nods his head in acceptance. "Okay."

I continue, explaining, "I just think I need to talk to her before she leaves. Besides," I begin, grinning for the first time today, "I have a date with Liz tomorrow night, so I really need to get rid of this fucking hangover before then."

"Nice! Maybe getting laid by that hot piece of ass will help," he proclaims, smirking.

"Shut the fuck up, Matt! Don't talk about Liz like that." I cringe, not able to hear him speak so crudely about her. "She's not just another girl."

The corners of his lips curve up in amusement, obviously enjoying my reaction. "Interesting," he mumbles thoughtfully. I look at him with a question in my eyes and he instantly explains, "Same reaction you always had with Bree."

I heave a sigh and shake my head, knowing it's pointless to argue. He knows me almost better than anyone. Ironically, better than anyone except Bree.

Not too long after lunch I'm finally able to peel myself off the couch without spinning. I take a quick shower and brush my teeth, needing to get all the horrible smells off me.

"Thanks, Matt," I mumble, giving him a one-armed hug with a firm pat on the back as he does the same.

"Anytime," he replies before I jump in my jeep to start the long drive back to my apartment in Maine. Staring at the road in front of me, I continue stewing about everything that's occurred in the past twenty-four hours, not even the sound of the upbeat music playing on the radio able to drown out my dark thoughts.

It's past dinnertime by the time I make it home. Trudging into my place with my bag slung over my shoulder, I wave to my roommates, Thad and Patrick, sitting on the couch, both staring at the screens on their phones. Stopping at the refrigerator, I grab a couple bottles of water on the way to my room.

"You look like shit. You okay, Blake?" Thad questions.

"Fine," I mutter. "I just need some sleep," I claim, giving him a partial truth. He nods his head in acknowledgement, glancing back down at his phone.

I make it to my room, collapsing on my bed and staring at the white ceiling. The rest of the night, I spend trying to figure out what the hell I'm going to do, thoughts of my upcoming date with Liz giving me my only momentary reprieve.

Eventually, the sun rises without getting much sleep. I quickly shower before heading out to get some coffee and donuts to bring over to Bree's place. I need to talk to someone, and I want to see her before she leaves, make sure she's okay. Besides, I did say I would help her pack today and I have plans with Liz later. A smile tugs at my lips just thinking about seeing Liz again. I can't wait until tonight.

Chapter 13

Blake

I knock on Bree's door with a cup holder containing three large coffees in one hand and a pink box filled with donuts in the other. When I hear no response to my knocking, I kick the door hard with my foot a few times, a few seconds later I hear shuffling around and Bree's sleepy voice, "I'm coming!"

I can't help but chuckle to myself waiting for her to answer. The door flies open and I plaster a huge smile on my face when I look at her wrapped in her robe and her chestnut brown hair falls messily around her sleepy eyes. "What are you doing here?" she prompts. She reaches for the coffees and stumbles back up the steps without waiting for an answer.

I chuckle softly, following behind to her kitchen, trying to keep my eyes off her ass. "You invited me."

She scrunches up her nose, looking all kinds of confused and asks, "For breakfast?"

I shake my head and reply honestly, "Not exactly. You just said to come over today when I got back. You said you would be here packing." I drop the donuts down on the kitchen table and we each grab a coffee before sitting in one of the chairs.

I watch her pull her feet up and curl them underneath her before taking a sip of her coffee. "Yum!" she grins appreciatively into her coffee cup, "Just the way I like it, thanks."

I give her a small smile and she asks, "You just now got home? Did you drive during the night or something? You do kinda' look like shit," she adds with a smirk.

I chuckle, "Thanks and not exactly. I came home last night and couldn't really sleep." I sip my coffee waiting to see what she'll say.

She reaches for a paper plate out of a pile left on the table. She grabs a jelly donut and takes a bite before looking at me, assessing me. I swear this girl can read me like a book and honestly, it's scary. "What's wrong Blake? What happened with your family?"

I sigh and run a hand through my hair like I've been doing for days. At this point I wouldn't be surprised if I had a Mohawk even after showering. "Yeah, you could say something's wrong with my family," I croak out and her eyes go suddenly wide.

"Is Aubrey, okay?" she inquires, panicked.

I throw my hands up and shake my head to quickly reassure her, "No, no nothing like that. Aubrey's fine. In fact, she asked about you. She misses you. She asked if you would come see her soon."

"Of course, I will. I love your sister. I miss her too. We'll have to make a plan when we can both go down there to see her," she proclaims, smiling gently. I nod in agreement but remain silent collecting my thoughts. "So, what's going on then?" she prods.

I shake my head in disbelief. "My dad," I begin when I hear Bree's door click open. I don't have to look behind me to know that Christian is standing there.

"Morning, Blake. You're here early." He steps over and kisses Bree on the top of the head and gives me a smug grin. "And you brought me coffee?"

"You can fight Amy for it," I offer, holding up my own cup to acknowledge him.

"First come…" he starts and wraps his hand around the coffee cup. He nods appreciatively at me, "Thanks. It sounds like you guys might need some time. I have to head back to my place and finish up packing anyway if we're going to be leaving tomorrow morning," he adds looking at Bree.

He leans down and presses his lips to hers with a possessive kiss. She mumbles, "Thank you, Christian," trying to gently push him away, blushing in embarrassment. The corners of my mouth, surprisingly to me, turn up watching their exchange.

"I love you, Bree. Don't forget to pack." He smirks and gives her another chaste kiss before pulling away. I don't feel my body tense like it usually does, but I'm sure it's just from lack of sleep.

"I love you too, Christian and don't worry, I'll make Blake help. We'll get everything done, promise," she insists.

"Not with any of the good stuff or I'll have to kick his ass," he jokes, giving her another playful kiss. Christian grabs a donut and starts for the stairs. "I'll see you for dinner Bree. Thanks for breakfast Blake."

I barely grunt in acknowledgement. Bree looks back at me studying my face like it will give away what I'm thinking. The front door slams at the bottom of the stairs and she asks, "What happened with your dad this time?"

I sigh and close my eyes, wishing the reality of what happened would just go away. Eventually, I open them back up and lean my elbows on the table staring across at her. "You know how I told you my dad had just come back when we moved by you?" She nods her head with her eyes crinkled like she's trying to figure out where I'm going with this. "Well, you know all the scenarios I used to try to go through to figure out what he was doing during all the time he abandoned us?" She nods again and I announce, "Well, one of them was real."

Bree shakes her head in confusion, prompting, "Blake? What are you talking about? What one was real?" she questions her voice wobbly, emotional for me.

I shake my head, still not ready to believe his confession. I swallow the lump in my throat and push the words out, "He has another child." Her eyes round in shock. I continue needing to get everything out there right away. "He met a woman, got her pregnant, stayed with her throughout the pregnancy and the first year to make sure they were taken care of and then came back to us. He said he still makes sure they are okay and helps take care of them, but we're his family," I say with bitterness.

"Blake," she begins looking at me with sadness and empathy.

I immediately interrupt her, "That's such bullshit, Bree! If we were his family, he wouldn't have left us when we really fucking needed him! We were barely keeping it together between trying to take care of Aubrey, me going to school, my mom in a complete depression and still trying to work. You know how it was when he came back too. He doesn't know what the fucking word family means!" I rant.

I take a few calming breaths and look up when Bree finally speaks, "How was your mom with it?"

"Fucking fantastic!" I retort resentfully. "She seemed anxious, but I think she was just nervous as to how I would react. Then again, I guess she was right to worry. I stormed out of there yesterday after I found out and spent the day with Aubrey. After I left Aub, I went to Matt's and he had a party going on at his place." I shake my head regrettably. "I don't remember much else after besides what Matt told me."

"What do you mean?" she prods with wide eyes. I give her a look and she screeches in response, completely shocked. "You got drunk?!"

I roll my eyes and grumble, "Yeah, yeah, I know, it's not like me. I already heard it from Matt take it easy. I knew I was sleeping there though, so...I had more than my normal few and..." I trail off and she snaps her mouth shut knowing not to go there.

I take a couple deep breaths, grasping my chest before admitting painfully, "He wants me to meet her Bree. He said, 'You have another sister and I want you to meet her.'"

A look of understanding crosses over Bree's face and she scoots her chair closer to mine so she can give me a gentle hug. I melt into her for a minute, needing the comfort. She sits back and looks directly in my eyes, "She's never going to replace Aubrey. No one can."

"You're right. No one can replace Aub in my heart. But I don't want her to replace Aubrey in his heart either. I may hate him, but she loves him and she deserves only the best." She gives me another hug and I groan in frustration and sit back. "I don't know what to do Bree," I admit painfully.

"I can't tell you what to do Blake. I can tell you, no matter what you decide to do, you have to do what's right for you. You're always so worried about everyone else, Aubrey, your mom, me..." she trails off, taking a deep breath. "You have to think about you sometimes. Have you talked to Liz about any of it yet?" she asks.

"No. She doesn't know about my family yet. I thought it was a little early for too much bullshit and I also thought it should be a face-to-face conversation. I called her last night, but I wasn't about to say shit over the phone." I sigh again and apologize, "I'm sorry Bree, I know I shouldn't be bothering you with this shit, but I didn't know where else to go. I'll tell Liz everything eventually if things keep going well. I may even tell her some tonight when we go out since I can't get it out of my fucking head," I groan.

She shakes her head. "You never bother me Blake, you're my best friend, my family," she admits smiling shyly at me.

I sigh again, this time in gratitude. "And you're mine, Bree." I reach for a donut and take a bite so I can avoid looking at her. There's just too much emotion rolling through me right now. "How about we start getting you packed? I can start with your bikinis."

She rolls her eyes and smacks me in the arm. "You're lucky you didn't say something else or I would have had to use my foot and aimed lower."

"Ha-ha!" She looks at me in challenge, so instead I mumble, "If Christian were here…"

"He'd kick your ass for me," she jokes, but I know it's true, at least he'd try.

"Seriously though, I need to hear it from you one more time. This is what you want to do this summer?" She nods her head with the corners of her lips curving upwards. "You'll be okay and call if you need me?" I prompt. She nods her head again. "Okay, then tell me what I can do to help you," I insist.

"I have a couple boxes in the trunk of my car. Would you mind grabbing those for me while I throw some stuff in my suitcase?" she asks. "I have some pictures and some books I want to bring and leave at my grandma's house."

I nod in agreement and we spend the next hour putting her stuff together before collapsing on the couch. Amy comes strolling out of her room as soon as my ass hits the cushions. She gives Bree and I a tired wave before walking towards the kitchen. "Where's my coffee?" Amy squeals when she sees the donuts and empty coffee cups on the kitchen table. I burst out laughing while Bree hides her smile and offers to make some. Amy just mumbles under her breath, "Damn Christian." I'm sure she's damning him for more than the coffee, but she'll never admit it to us.

The three of us spend the rest of the afternoon watching a couple eighties movies, my favorite being The Breakfast Club and joking around. Every once in a while, Bree remembers something else she wants to throw in her suitcase, but mostly they just help me forget for a little while and that works for me.

Bree stands up to stretch when the front door slams making her jump. Christian yells up the stairs, "Bree, you ready?" He immediately stops when he reaches the top and sees me sitting there. "You're still here," he grunts. I just nod in acknowledgement. He shakes his head before walking quickly over to Bree, "Hi Bree." He wraps his arms around her and kisses her like he's claiming her. I'm yet again aware of the lack of jealousy fueled tension in my body, although I do notice Amy's quick exit.

Bree gently pushes him back, blushing again. "Give me a minute and I'll be ready for dinner." She gives him a chaste kiss before stepping out of his arms.

"I have to head out anyway, I want to stop over and see Liz. We're supposed to go out to dinner." Bree smiles at my comment. "Thank you, Bree," I proclaim and step in to give her a quick hug and kiss her on the top of her head. I can't help but notice Christian trying not to glare at me and chuckle softly. "You let me know if you need anything and I'll be there," I declare and smirk trying to goad him.

"I promise," she agrees. "Thank you for helping Blake and call if you need to talk," she adds before heading to her room.

I turn around, grab my keys and start to walk towards the door. I yell over my shoulder, "Thanks for letting me borrow your girl, Christian."

"You can borrow my ass," I hear him grumble making me laugh even harder before I walk out the door.

I leave feeling lighter, but I'm not ready to go to my apartment. I decide to head straight over to Liz's place like I said and hope I catch her home. I did tell her I would be back tonight for our date.

Chapter 14

Blake

In no time at all, I'm standing in front of Liz's apartment waiting for her to answer. She pulls the door open and without even a hello she gets a panicked look and I can't help but smile. "You're early."

"Yeah, mind if I come in?" I ask with my eyebrows raised in question.

"Um…yeah…sure," she mumbles and gestures inside. When we reach the living room, I make myself comfortable by sitting on the couch. She just stands there staring at me looking absolutely beautiful in white cotton shorts and an aqua blue tank top. Her hair is up in a ponytail and her arms are crossed uncertainly. My lips quirk up when I notice she's staring at me expectantly while I take her in. "I uh…I thought…don't we have a date tonight?" she asks apprehensively.

I nod my head and chuckle again. "I love this flustered look on you. You're gorgeous," I murmur and watch as the beautiful blush covers every inch of her visible skin.

She looks even more confused and she finally prompts, "Do we still have a date tonight?"

I smile lightly, my heart picking up speed just looking at her. "If you'll still have me," I answer reaching for her hand and pulling her down on the couch next to me. She blushes beautifully again and I can't help but broaden my smile.

"Umm…Blake?" she prods still hesitant.

I sigh, not wanting to stop teasing her. "Lizzie, I've had a really shitty few days and I don't really want to go anywhere tonight," I finally concede. "I was wondering if I could take you out somewhere tomorrow night instead?"

"Oh, ok," she mumbles, not doing anything to hide her disappointment when she answers me. She looks anywhere in the room except at me, like she's trying to figure out what to do next. She moves to stand up, but I hold tight to her hand. "I can just do something with Sara tonight instead," she offers halfheartedly and my heart speeds up again noticing how adorable she looks right at this moment.

"No," I state. I laugh at her reaction shaking my head.

She turns towards me and a little bit of a smile lights up her face. She looks at me like I'm crazy, which at this point I'm pretty sure I am. "No?" she asks incredulously.

"No," I repeat with a salacious grin. "I was wondering if I could hang out with you here, tonight? Maybe order some Chinese food, watch a movie and maybe some other stuff," I tease playfully.

Her whole body turns a beautiful shade of red and she fumbles with what to say, stammering, "Blake I…I mean…I… What? Um…"

I laugh even harder, feeling better than I have in the last few days. "Don't worry, Lizzie, I'm not about to do anything you don't want me to. I just really need to fucking chill tonight," I emphasize my free hand running through my hair.

Her eyes turn soft, and her calming green eyes look at me, assessing me. "Are you okay?" she asks with concern.

I shake my head not really wanting to think about it. "I don't know," I eventually answer honestly with a sigh.

She nods and gives me another small, but encouraging smile, "Okay, then." Suddenly I feel like

106

everything will work out. I relax into the corner of her couch while she orders some Chinese food for us. Then she returns to the couch and sits next to me but leaves three feet between us.

"You can come closer, I don't bite. Unless you want me to," I tease with a growing smile.

She rolls her eyes and scoots closer, "Does that line actually work on anyone? That was pretty pathetic."

"It just worked on you," I proclaim, smirking. She rolls her eyes again trying to hide her smile by turning her head away from me for a few seconds.

"You want to talk about it?" she asks hesitantly as she turns to face me again.

I groan in frustration, but I have to admit I feel so much calmer looking into her sparkling green eyes. It's like my heart and nerves have steadied just being in the room with her. "Can I ask about your week first?" I prompt hoping to put off the conversation for just a little bit longer.

"Sure, but there's not much to tell, just work, work and more work," she answers, shrugging her shoulders.

"As long as you were thinking of me the whole time, I'm good with that." She smiles at me again and I want to keep showing her my playful side. I need to keep seeing that beautiful smile. Her smile is like my own personal drug. "I have to say, it's surprising how shy you are. You're not at all what I expected after the first night I met you at the concert." Her rosy cheeks again show her embarrassment. I'm quick to comfort her. With a squeeze of her hand and a smile I insist, "It's a good thing, I promise. I think you're absolutely amazing."

She looks up at me from under those long eyelashes and I brush a stray wave of hair away from her face. My hand lingers on her cheek as I stare into her expressive green eyes. I notice with anticipation when she glances down to my mouth while she bites her lower lip making me want my turn to bite. I lean towards her and gently push her teeth away with my mouth. Her tongue quickly collides with mine as my eyes close. She tastes like sugar cookies and I can't seem to get enough of her sweetness. I let go of her hand and use it to slide up the other side of her soft face. I hold her in place, afraid if I let go, I won't be able to stop. She groans into my mouth making me want to devour every part of her.

The doorbell suddenly rings, interrupting us. I slowly pull back with a frustrated groan of my own and drop my forehead to hers. She mumbles breathlessly, "That must be the food."

She attempts to get up, but I place my hands gently on her shoulders to keep her down. "I'll get it. Those beautiful swollen lips are perfect sitting right there, waiting for me." She blushes again and I smile as I stand and walk to the door. I hand the guy some cash before quickly grabbing the bags of food and shutting the door. I make my way back to the couch and park my ass right next to Liz. I begin taking all the containers out and notice Liz just watching me. I glance at her and smile. "You hungry? Or are you just enjoying the show?" She blushes again and I laugh, "You make it so much fun to tease you. You blush so easily. I never would have guessed."

"I'm sorry," she apologizes, looking embarrassed again.

I immediately stop and put everything in my hands down. I lightly grab her chin and tilt up, so she'll look at me. "There is absolutely nothing at all for you to be sorry about. Blushing is gorgeous on you." I brush my lips over hers and add, "As is everything else."

Her eyes go wide and she blushes even deeper mumbling, "Thank you."

"You don't like compliments, do you?" I prod, watching her curiously.

"I like them, it's just…" she pauses trying to find the right words, fidgeting with her hands. "I guess it's hard for me to believe them. I don't really get many compliments meant for me."

"What? What do you mean by that?" I question in surprise. She shrugs her shoulders in response. I take a deep breath to calm my growing anger. Someone has to be responsible for making her think like this. What the fuck? I shake my head in disbelief and speak slowly, "I have no idea what or who would make you think you can't believe compliments when I'm just speaking the truth, but I'm going to do everything I can to change that. You're incredibly beautiful and when you blush, your eyes and skin light up. You get this look on your face and I want to get as close to you as possible every time I see that look."

I can tell she's still uncomfortable. Maybe eating dinner and a change of subject will help. I grab the plates she put on the coffee table earlier and hand her one, "Let's eat. I'm hungry." After we fill our plates with Chicken Chow Mein and shrimp Chop Suey, I ask, "Where's Sara tonight anyway?"

"She went out with some friends for dinner." She sits back and watches me while she eats for a little while, a small smile curving the corners of her lips. I can't help but enjoy the comfortable silence between us now that she's more relaxed. "So, are you ready to talk about your week yet?" she eventually asks hesitantly.

I take a few more bites as I search her eyes. I don't know what I'm looking for exactly, but what I see makes me think it might be time to open up a little bit. I guess it's time to let her know about my family so I can share the rest of what's going on. Something only Bree and Matt truly know what the whole story entails. My roommates know about the accident. Since we all grew up together, it was impossible to miss. I wouldn't be surprised if Liz or her family saw reports about it when it happened, but if you don't know who the people are, most people just think, "That's too bad," or "It's so sad what happened to that poor family," but it's not memorable to them. I think I'm ready to let someone else in.

Not just anyone else, I think I'm ready to let Liz in.

"Well, to understand my week, you need to know about my past," I admit quietly. "My dad and I don't really have the best relationship. We used to, but everything changed after the accident." I take another bite before setting my plate and fork down. I rest my elbows on my knees and fist my hands together. I can feel her looking at me and take a quick glance in her sparkling green eyes and see nothing there but support and comfort; no judgment, giving me courage to continue.

I take another calming breath and start from the beginning. "About ten years ago this past spring, my mom, dad, sister and I were on our way to my aunt and uncle's house for my cousin's birthday. We still lived in Maine at the time. Well, being from Maine you can understand the roads can be pretty icy in the spring, especially at night or early in the morning and it was just getting dark. There was a car driving erratically on the road and my dad swerved to miss him, but we started fishtailing and the other car shoved us right off the road into a small snowdrift and a tree nearly three feet in diameter. The tree actually came into the car right behind my sister Aubrey." My voice cracks and I have to take another soothing breath before I can continue. "I still don't know if it was a bad thing or a good thing, but my sister had just taken her seatbelt off to pick up a crayon she had dropped on the floor. I remember just sitting there watching her, feeling completely helpless because my

110

seatbelt was holding me back and it happened so fucking fast." I shake my head like I can shake away the memory.

"My mom, my dad and I all ended up with just some bad cuts and bruises." I pause realizing a couple tears have fallen onto my fists and I take a couple more breaths trying to steady my emotions. I feel a soft touch to my back, then on my arm and I close my eyes and relax a little into Liz's gentle embrace, needing her comfort.

After a few minutes I open my eyes ready to continue with her support. "My sister not only had broken bones, but she had severe brain damage from the trauma to her head. At first, she had a severe brain bleed and she was in a coma, but I believe the doctors kept her in the coma for a while until the swelling in the brain came down and they were able to assess the damage. I don't know exactly because my parents didn't tell me everything. They were trying to protect me, I guess. I used to try to listen to them though to find out what was going on with Aub."

"It took a few months before they finally brought her out of the coma and with therapy, they tried to bring her back to us. But so much of the damage was permanent. She has trouble speaking clearly and we had to learn sign language to communicate better with her. She uses it a lot when she can't get the words out. The doctors say she won't ever develop emotionally past the age of 8. That's how old she was the night of the accident. There are so many things she had to learn to do again, like eating and basic personal hygiene, it was like starting over."

I pause shaking my head in disbelief thinking about what Aubrey's been through. "She's truly the most amazing and strongest person I know. She's been through so much and yet she's always happy. She always has the biggest smile on her face when I see her. I will do absolutely anything for her!" I give Liz a tight smile, my hands shaking while thinking about my sister.

"She sounds wonderful!" she exclaims with quiet emotion. I'm finally able to look up at her and catch her wiping a couple stray tears from under her eyes. I try to swallow the lump of emotion pushing up my throat from her reaction.

"I told her about you. I'd love for you to meet her sometime, when she's ready," I admit quietly.

"I'd like that," she smiles timidly at me. I know in this moment I want to do everything I can to protect this girl sitting in front of me too. "What happened to the guy that hit you?" she asks hesitantly.

"It was a thirty-seven-year-old rich asshole who hit us. He was drunk off his ass at five at night and he didn't even remember a fucking thing. He was arrested right away and later he hung himself in jail before he was even sentenced. His family helped pay for our medical bills at first, but my parents didn't fight for much. They said they suffered too which I think is bullshit! They are living a good life while our family falls apart and we struggle to help my sister," I vent angrily.

"How do you know that?" she asks in confusion.

I shrug slightly. "Not long after we moved to Massachusetts, I did some research. I needed a reason to get away from everyone and I had to know more about his family. My parents were acting like everything was completely fine, Matt was always with Amy and Bree was on the lake with her grandma and Christian that summer. I just needed to know," I emphasize and look to her for reassurance.

"The guy had a family, a wife and two kids, one our age. His wife got remarried not long after he died. They moved on with their lives almost right after the accident.

112

Besides the fact that they seem to have everything, while my family is still fucked up. I keep thinking they could have done something to stop him. I don't see how that's right, and I don't know if it's fair or not, but I can't help but fucking hate them!"

I settle more into the couch and wrap my arms around her and she leans her head back into my chest. "Is this, okay?" I ask and I feel her nod her head in confirmation. "Thank you, I need to feel you in my arms to keep talking," I admit. She squeezes me tighter, and I swear her squeeze gives me the strength to keep going.

"Anyway, my parents were always fighting. My mom blamed my dad for the accident. I think she just needed someone to blame since Aubrey…" my voice cracks with the memory and I have to pause.

I take a deep breath and try a different direction instead. "About a year and a half after the accident, my dad started disappearing more and more. Eventually he stopped coming home. He sent money, but my mom and I were the ones who were there every day taking care of Aub. She was always at one doctor or another with my sister since she had so many different therapies she had to do. My mom was so depressed, but she insisted I stay in all my sports and activities. I always wondered if it was because she was too much into her depression and just didn't want me around when she was home or if she truly wanted me to do something for me besides take care of my sister. The thing is, I didn't give a shit about sports anymore, but I did it for her. I wasn't about to make anything harder on my mom than it already was."

I pause and take note of the fact that we have maneuvered ourselves into a lying position on the couch and Liz is cuddled into my side with her face on my chest. My arms are wrapped tightly around her and her right hand is lying on my chest lightly drawing comforting circles. I admit to myself that by telling her all this crap, everything is starting to feel a little lighter. I let my right-hand tangle in her soft dark brown hair and inhale the scent of her strawberry shampoo before gently kissing her forehead.

She lifts her head and glances up at me with her mesmerizing green eyes, looking a little glassy from tears, more tears for me. "Are you okay?" she asks. I just nod as my heart gets lodged in my throat, staring at this beautiful girl I'm wrapped up with. "Do you want to tell me more?" I don't answer her. Instead, I kiss her on the forehead, then her nose before I give her a chaste kiss on her full lips. I huff another sigh, dropping my head back to the couch. Eventually, I feel her head fall back to my chest.

I slowly open my mouth to finish the rest of my fucked up story. "About five years ago, my dad decided it was time to come back home and my mom let him. He tried to pretend like nothing had changed while he was gone or maybe he was trying to pretend he never left," I ponder and sigh. "My sister loves him though, and she was so happy when he came back, so I did what I had to do to watch out for my sister and my mom. I wanted them to be happy, so I didn't say anything, but there's no way in hell I would ever trust him. Not long after he came home, he said he found a great place for Aub in Boston. He immediately sold our house in Maine, pulled me from school and we moved to a small town just outside Boston."

"That was when you met Matt and Bree right?" she asks without looking at me.

"Yeah, Matt and I hung out a lot. Then he started dating Amy, so when Bree got back from Maine, we were all together a lot. At the beginning of my senior year, a spot finally opened up at the adult home in Boston my parents wanted to put Aub in. They said it was what was best for her, best for all of us. My parents were fighting all the time and I just couldn't listen to them or let them take it out on me, which they seemed to do all the fucking time. Just because I couldn't pretend we were one big happy family when Aubrey wasn't around..." I sigh, trailing off. "Anyway, I stayed home my first semester of college because I wasn't ready to be so far away from Aubrey, but I made it here in January freshman year, Bree talked me into it."

"She wanted you with her?" she probes and although I hear the jealousy in her voice, I can't even acknowledge it. I can't help but tense thinking about what happened with Bree that January and how I almost didn't leave because of it. In fact, I missed the first two weeks of the semester because of it, but I would have stayed to help her if she let me.

"No," I rasp out. "She stayed home. She came sophomore year. But that's not my shit to talk about," I declare with obvious tension in my voice. "She wanted what was best for me."

She looks up at me with regret. "I'm sorry, I..."

I just shake my head and run my fingers through my hair, needing to ignore her bit of jealousy right now. "So, this week..." I begin letting her know I'm ready to tell her why I had such a shitty week. She nods and places her head back on my chest and waits for me to speak. "Apparently I have another sister from when he left us and my dad wants me to meet her."

I hear her inhale quickly in shock. "How old is she?"

"I...I don't know," I answer with confusion, realizing I didn't even think about it.

"Do you want to meet her?" she prompts cautiously.

"I...I don't know!" I answer with too much severity, and I feel her flinch against me. I instantly regret my reaction and give her a gentle squeeze. I sigh, "I'm sorry, I don't know. Let me explain. I have an incredible sister who was hurt so badly in a car accident that she will never be the same. In fact, she does better when she has constant care, someone that can better help with her needs than her own family. She is the most remarkable person I know, and I will do anything to protect her. Just like I'll do anything to protect anyone I care about," I add holding her a little tighter.

"Now I all of a sudden have this other sister I never knew about because my dad abandoned us after the accident. She's healthy and has the whole world out there ready for her. My sister will never have that," I emphasize feeling the pain stab at my chest. "I don't want Aub to ever think I'm replacing her. I don't want her to ever think my asshole dad left just so he could fucking replace her," I spit the last words out with complete venom. "She loves him too fucking much and he doesn't fucking deserve it."

Liz rolls slightly so she can pull back and look me in the eyes. The concern I see reflected in her green gaze practically overwhelms me. "Blake, I don't know your dad and I would never speak for him. But I can tell you that since the first time you mentioned your sister, I see the love and admiration you have for her and I'm sure she does too. I may not know her, but I don't think she would ever think you would replace her under any circumstances. The love and loyalty you obviously show her is overwhelming in a good way. I know I would give anything to have someone love me like you love her." I try to catch her eyes with at her last comment, wondering her reasons behind it, but she turns towards my chest and won't look back to me.

Eventually she slowly brings her eyes back to mine and continues, "I believe there are no doubts in her mind how much you love her. And you never know, maybe she would be excited to have a little sister," she suggests.

"Maybe," I answer thoughtfully. "She always calls Bree her sister. Maybe she would want a real one." I feel Liz tense at the mention of Bree, but again, I don't say anything. I can't add that conversation to this one. It's too much. I need to try not to mention her as much. She has to learn to trust my relationship with Bree if this is going to work between us though because I will always be there if Bree needs me.

"She is always so shy and nervous about meeting new people," I continue talking about Aubrey. "Unless it's someone I've talked about for a while before introducing her, she doesn't do too well. My mom brought one of her friends with her once and Aubrey completely shut down. It completely freaked my mom out. She only goes alone or with me or my dad now and she's there nearly every day."

"Maybe you can find out a little more information about your new sister. Then maybe it won't seem so scary," she proposes.

"Maybe," I concede and hold her tight while thoughts of Aubrey and I having another sister consume me.

"You okay Blake?" she prods her voice full of concern.

"Yeah, thank you Liz. I guess I needed to talk about all this more than I realized," I admit feeling completely vulnerable and that scares the crap out of me. I haven't put myself in this position since Bree.

"Anytime," she offers and I watch her Adam's apple bob up and down as she swallows hard.

"I haven't shared that with someone in years," I admit. Thank you for listening," I whisper into her hair.

"I'm happy I was here to listen to you Blake," she whispers with the strong emotion evident in her voice.

"You think maybe we could just stay like this for a while?" I request, giving her a little squeeze. She nods her head in agreement. I pull her into me and place a kiss on the top of her head, then her nose, and follow it with a light kiss to her soft lips. I take a deep breath, pushing my nose into her

117

soft dark hair and loving her fruity smell. I close my eyes feeling exhausted and content with her in my arms.

Chapter 15

Elizabeth

I'm getting myself ready for my date with Blake. I'm so nervous I think I'm going to throw up. Sara's advice was to "Go for it." Last night she came home and found us asleep on the couch wrapped in each other's arms. She accidentally woke us while getting ready for bed.

Blake then left to go home with a "Thank you" and a quick kiss, promising to pick me up tomorrow night for our date. So, here I am with my long workweek over getting ready to go on another date with a guy that is way out of my league.

I can't stop thinking about what he told me last night. He seemed so vulnerable and the way he held me felt incredible, like he needed me. He's been through so much with his family and his sister sounds amazing. But his dedication to protecting her and how much he loves her completely astounds me. I want to be cherished and feel safe like that because of someone's love, knowing he'll do anything for me. I have to admit I still feel jealous of Bree even though I do everything I can so I don't, but it's not easy. It seems to me she has his loyalty. I'm trying not to feel that way, but the way he reacted to some things…anyway.

I look through my clothes and realize I have no clue how to dress because I have no idea what we're doing tonight. I grab my phone to text Blake, but then I decide to call him instead. I want to hear his voice and make sure he's okay after last night. On the third ring, a girl answers the phone and I glance at my screen to make sure I dialed the right number, but I did. "Um, Hello? I'm uh…" I stammer in confusion.

"Liz?" she asks.

"Um, yeah, who's this?" I question perplexed.

"It's Bree. Blake left his phone here yesterday when we were hanging out. I just saw it was you and thought I should answer since he said you guys have a date tonight. I didn't want you to think he wasn't coming or something," she explains.

"Okay," I drag the word out feeling even more out of sorts. He hung out with her yesterday?

"I'm dropping his phone off at his place in a few minutes when I leave for Christian's. We're heading up to the lake today. I'll tell Blake you called as soon as I get there, okay?" she offers cheerily.

"Okay, thanks…" I mumble trailing off not really knowing what else to say. I hang up the phone feeling confounded. I thought he had just gotten home when he got here. I thought he came to talk to me. But he spent the day with her first? Why didn't he say anything? Maybe she's the reason he didn't have the energy to go anywhere I think full of frustration.

I throw on a pair of white jean shorts and an olive-green tank top with sparkles. I definitely don't feel like wearing a dress anymore. I grab my black sweater for later and my bag before waiting impatiently. I've already done my make-up and hair as much as I feel like it. I huff in irritation. I can't help but wonder if I'm getting into the same kind of mess as before, like with Kris. I wish I could talk to Sara, but she left this morning to go home for the rest of the weekend. Even though she's right up the road, I don't want to disturb her time with her family. I have to admit, right now I feel completely confused and alone. I have no idea what to do.

I flop down on the couch and stare out the window, deep in thought. Before I know it there's a loud knock at the door, making me jump a mile. I shake myself out of my stupor and trudge over to answer the door. I open it to Blake and his heart-melting smile. My heart begins pounding against my will and I grind my teeth together trying not to let it get to me. He has a small bouquet of Gerbera daisies in his hands and holds them out to me. "For you. You look beautiful."

I look at him skeptically and take the flowers. Instead of a thank you I stupidly snap, "Did you get your phone back?" I turn towards the kitchen to find something to put the flowers in. He shuts the door and follows me into the room with an audible sigh.

"I did, Bree just dropped it off," he confirms. "I thought you said you were okay with my relationship with Bree?" he reiterates. Then he watches as I bang open all the different cabinets looking for a vase.

"I did, I mean I am. I just don't understand why you never told me you were hanging out with her all day before you came here. You made me feel like you came right to me because you couldn't wait. I guess I feel like you lied to me even though you didn't. I know it's not my business, I'm not your girlfriend and you can do what you want with who you want, but..." I pause slamming the last cabinet in frustration.

Blake pushes off the counter and opens the cabinet with all the glasses in it. He grabs the tallest and fattest glass he can find. He fills it with water, takes the flowers out of my hand and places them in the glass, "I didn't want you to strangle the poor things anymore," he jokes. I glare at him in response. He sets the flowers down on the table and walks over to me slowly. He cautiously reaches for my hand, and I let him take it, waiting to hear what he has to say. "Listen Liz, to me it is your business, I'm just not used to telling someone about everything I do. I wasn't trying to keep anything from you I swear and I sure as hell never lied to you, at least not intentionally. I went over to talk to Bree for a while because I promised her, I'd go see her before she left. She is my best friend. And honestly, she knows my family and was worried about me too. Amy was with us most of the afternoon and then Bree left with Christian for dinner and I came here."

I don't say anything as I let him pull me closer while I try to process his words. I try to remember what Sara said and how I can't let Kris and his mistakes ruin everything else for me. He smirks slightly and peers at me like he's trying to read me before adding, "As for the girlfriend part, are you dating other guys that I don't know about?"

I shake my head and huff, "No."

"Thank God I don't have to kick anyone's ass today!" he exclaims with a chuckle. He pulls me between his legs and I go willingly. "Well, I'm not seeing anyone else either and I don't want to. So, I guess that would make you my girlfriend if you're willing? We can even seal it with a kiss," he jokes arching his eyebrows suggestively.

I roll my eyes at him and smile. "You are so corny!"

"I know you really meant to say charming, and you love it." He smirks and gently nips at my bottom lip. He raises his eyebrows at me in question and I do the only thing my body and heart seem to want, melting into him and pressing my lips to his. Before I get a chance to deepen the kiss he pulls back. With one hand on my cheek, he looks into my eyes and it feels like he can see my soul. "You make all the bullshit in my life just fade into the background Liz and with my family there's a lot of bullshit."

I melt further into him with his words. He tilts his head and lets his lips collide with mine. His tongue quickly slips into my mouth and tangles with mine, leaving me breathless. My heart pounds so hard and fast I start to feel dizzy with his kisses when he pulls back again and I whimper lightly with the loss. He chuckles quietly. "Come on, I want to take you out tonight. It's a beautiful night."

"Okay," I whisper reluctantly and nod into his palm. He gives me another chaste kiss and pushes off the counter. He threads his fingers through mine and starts for the door. "Wait," I laugh. "I need my purse." He won't let go of my hand, so I drag him with me laughing back to my room to pick up my purse before I let him lead me out the door.

As he starts up his jeep, I turn to him and inquire, "So where are we going anyway?"

"It's a surprise," he declares smirking at me. I can't help but smile back at him as I settle into my seat. I have to learn to relax and enjoy being with him before I ruin this. I don't think he's anything like Kris, at least I hope not.

In almost no time at all, I look out the window and start laughing at where we're pulling in. "I haven't been here since I was a kid!" I exclaim.

"Well, you said roller skating was one of your favorite things as a kid and I haven't been here since who knows when either, so I thought it would be fun," he claims.

I jump out of his jeep insisting, "It will be!" I throw my arms around him and he lifts me and spins me around laughing before setting me back on my feet and grabbing hold of my hand.

We walk through the first door where he pays the cashier. He holds the second door open for me and I smile looking around the rink, feeling like a little kid again. We rent our skates and throw our things in a locker. Then, we quickly lace up our skates and when I stand up, I feel a little off-balance. I look at Blake and tentatively step out onto the skating rink feeling wobbly as Blake pushes past me

123

proclaiming, "You have to jump right back into it." Then, he raises his eyebrows and yells, "Go for it!"

My body warms with his smile and I grin back at him. He skates around the rink and eventually catches up to me from behind. He reaches for my hand pulling me and I stifle my shriek. I soon feel confident again and am relaxed and laughing with him. He's holding my hand and skating around the rink while Bon Jovi's nineties music blasts over the speakers echoing throughout the whole place.

Eventually, we decide to take a break. We order a couple hot dogs and fries for dinner at the snack bar. "Greasy fast food at its best," he declares. He smirks and plops down across from me in the booth.

"Thank you, Blake. This is a lot of fun! I would have never thought we would be doing something like this. It's perfect." I say smiling broadly at him. He nods happily and I add, "Parks, roller skating, what other things do you have up your sleeve?"

"Yeah, I guess I'm always thinking about all the things Aubrey likes to do. Last time I brought her to a place like this, I was still living at home. She had so much fun! I couldn't get her and Bree off the rink at the end of the night."

I see his smile fade and realize I must have grimaced with the mention of Bree's name. I really have to get over that if I want this to work. I swallow a sip of my soda and plaster a smile on my face. "It sounds like you have a lot of fun with your sister."

He looks at me like he's searching for something before agreeing, "I do! Aub is just so much fun to watch. She enjoys the little things so much it makes you want to do everything you can for her."

"She's lucky to have you as a brother," I murmur sincerely.

He shocks me again when he looks me in the eye and states with such strong emotion and conviction, "I'm the lucky one." There's something in his eyes that makes me wonder what he's thinking, but he looks away and stuffs another fry in his mouth before it registers. "So, what were you like in high school?" he questions, obviously trying to change the subject.

I shrug my shoulders and mumble, "I don't know. I studied hard, did some tutoring and hung out with Sara mostly. We'd go shopping together, but that's more her than me. In fact, she likes to dress me up like I'm her Barbie doll."

Blake laughs, "I can definitely see that!"

"The only sport I ever did was cross-country."

Blake raises his eyebrows in question, "Really?"

"Yes, really, I was a pretty good runner!" I exclaim, teasing him like I'm offended.

"I didn't mean it like that," he explains. "I like running. I did other sports in school, but I enjoy running now. It gives me time to get away and think."

"That's exactly why I always liked it too. I could stay away from home for longer and still not have to interact too much with girls I didn't like, even the ones on the team." He looks at me curiously with my comment and I feel the need to explain myself. "Sara has always been my best friend, but I was really shy around other girls and boys when I was younger."

He smirks, arching his eyebrows. "Really? Yet you kiss strangers at concerts," he jokes. I smack him playfully in the arm from across the table. He laughs hard with an exaggerated, "Ouch! So brutal."

I roll my eyes at him, laughing. "Anyway, until my senior year that was about it for me."

"What happened senior year?" he asks. I blush realizing my mistake.

"Umm, nothing really. I just had a boyfriend and I guess I did more things then," I explain, fumbling with my hands and words.

"Ah, the one who made you lose trust in all men." I smile tightly. "It's okay Liz. You don't have to say anything until you're ready. But I hope sooner or later you'll be able to trust me."

He looks at me with those sincere chocolate eyes and I feel a heated flutter in my chest. "If you can trust me with your family problems, then I should be able to trust you with this."

He smiles. "How about we go skate some more and we can talk about the heavy stuff on another night?" he proposes. I can't help but breathe a sigh of relief. "I've had too many difficult conversations in the last few days. How about we keep the rest of tonight drama free?"

I smile bigger, incredibly thankful for his suggestion, "That sounds wonderful."

"Come on," he pushes out of the booth onto his skates and reaches for my hand to pull me up. He stares intently into my eyes and my heart begins hammering in my chest. He slowly moves closer to me and my eyes close just as he presses his soft lips to mine, sending the butterflies aflutter. He pulls away and I stare into his pools of chocolate almost forgetting we're not alone. When he turns around towards the rink I trip over my feet. I blush when his grip tightens on mine so I can catch my balance and I hear his low sexy chuckle.

We spend the rest of the night skating, laughing and singing horribly to the eighties and nineties music blasting throughout the skating rink. When we go to leave, I smile at him and proclaim, "I understand where your sister and Bree are coming from." He eyes me quizzically and I continue, "This was a lot of fun and even though my legs are so incredibly sore, I'm sad to have to leave." He gives me a genuine smile causing goose bumps to creep over my whole body and warmth to spread throughout my chest.

"Maybe next time we go skating we can go to the one near my sister and bring her," he suggests, reaching for my hand as we walk outside towards his jeep.

"I'd really like that," I reply smiling shyly up at him.

When we get back to my apartment, I invite him in to watch a movie. He lets me pick the movie and we curl up together on the couch. Almost as soon as I press play on the Nicholas Sparks movie I pop in the player, Blake starts kissing my neck and I sigh breathily turning into him. "I can't watch a movie tonight with you in my arms," he admits quietly. Then, he kisses up my neck towards my ear sending chills down my spine. He follows along my jaw before meeting my lips. I roll completely over so we're lying on our sides, chest to chest, not breaking our kiss. His hand glides from my side around to my ass and gently squeezes. I push further into him trying to get as close as I can, kissing him frantically. My hand glides over his chest to his tight stomach and around to his back trying to pull him closer.

He tears his lips away from mine and we both gasp for breath. "Lizzie, maybe I should go," he mumbles. I look in his heated eyes and am about to open my mouth when he runs his hand up my stomach and gently over my breast. I completely forget what I was about to say as my breath picks up speed and I can only think about Blake and where he's touching me, burning my skin. He rubs his finger gently back and forth over my nipple making my eyes roll back in my head. A whimper comes out of my mouth as his lips come crashing back to mine and he completely consumes me.

His hand drifts down to my waistband and although I feel myself throbbing and I really want him to go there, I know this is going too fast for me. I quickly force out his name, "Blake." He instantly stops and pulls back to look me in my eyes. I catch my breath and whisper, "I'm sorry, but I'm not ready for that yet."

Although I see disappointment in his eyes, I also see complete acceptance and resignation. He places his hand back on my side and kisses me again, but this time much slower, like he's trying to calm things down. "First of all, don't ever be sorry for something you're not ready for. I'll wait for you to be ready. Second," he kisses me gently moving against me, "I'm really sorry, but I have to go."

He gives me another chaste kiss and peels himself away from me, sitting up. I sit up next to him and look at him asking shakily, "Why?"

His smile covers his face as he looks at me and places his hand on my cheek. He looks into my eyes gently shaking his head. "Don't get any ridiculous ideas in your beautiful head. You're amazing. I had a wonderful time tonight. I have to go because I don't want to do anything you don't want to do and tonight, I can't seem to hold it together. You drive me too fucking crazy!" he smirks. I blush and try to look down at my lap, but he doesn't let me. "Thank you for tonight," he states and kisses me tenderly. "May I see you tomorrow?" I nod my head in agreement with a shy smile.

He pulls me up, "Come walk me to the door so you can lock it behind me and I can get my goodnight kiss," he states, more than asks. He smirks and I laugh following happily.

Chapter 16

Blake

Throughout July, I take at least one day a week to go to Boston and visit Aubrey, but avoid my parents' house at all costs, making constant excuses. My mom keeps leaving messages for me, but most of the time I return her calls when I know they won't be home. I realize it's slightly juvenile, but I need some time. Once in a while, I call when I know my dad's not home, but as soon as she turns the subject to him or my new sister, I find a reason to rush off the phone. I'm just not ready to go there.

I pick up more shifts at the outlets when Liz is working and I try to spend her days off doing something with her. We spend a lot of time going to dinner, or movies, swimming at the beaches or checking out the museums on those rare hot days in Maine or having a picnic and playing Frisbee in one of the parks on the warm summer days. Some of my favorite time with her is spent walking down by the docks and talking, like we are now, hand in hand.

"So, tomorrow Bree is coming back and we're going to head to Boston to see my sister," I inform her glancing at her face to see her reaction. She claims she's okay with my relationship with Bree, but Bree has been at the lake with Christian for the summer. I have no idea how she'll react with me making plans with her. I notice her shoulders tense slightly and I run my hand through my hair anticipating the worst. "Aubrey has been asking for her and she hasn't been down to see her since the spring semester ended in May," I explain.

She nods her head and swallows before speaking, "Is Christian going too?" she prompts, trying to sound nonchalant.

"Not this time. He has to stay there to work. Plus, Aubrey doesn't know him. Even though Bree talks about him, she hasn't met him yet," I answer watching her carefully for her response.

She lets out a shaky breath and inquires, "When do you think you're leaving?"

"Probably in the morning sometime, depending on when Bree gets here. She said she'll leave first thing in the morning, but we didn't set a time," I add still assessing her.

She nods her head and blinks her eyes a few times, focusing on anything but me. I squeeze her hand and pull her to a stop, waiting for her to look at me. Eventually her eyes settle on me and I ask, "Don't you think it's time to tell me why you have such a hard time trusting my relationship with Bree, trusting me?"

She releases a huge sigh and nods her head in agreement, albeit reluctantly. We walk in silence again until we come to a bench where I figure we can talk. When we sit, she pulls her hand away, placing it in her lap and separates herself, moving away from me slightly making my stomach twist. She begins to fidget with her hands and I want to comfort her, but I'm not sure what she wants from me right now, so I try with words, "You don't have to worry about what you have to tell me. I'm not going to judge you or anything if that's what you're afraid of."

"It's not that," she dismisses glancing up at me. "It's just that thinking about this is hard. I try to bury it you know?" I just nod in understanding, thinking about everything I wish I could bury every day. I watch her and

130

wait for her to tell me her story, hoping I can give her whatever she needs from me right now to support her.

"So, I already told you I worked really hard at home and school. I even did some tutoring and stuff like that," she begins staring at her hands fisting them together nervously in her lap. "Well, senior year Kris and I were assigned to do a project together and then I started helping him with some other schoolwork, although I don't think he really needed it. Then, over Christmas break we spent a lot of time together outside of school and homework and we started dating. He was my first real boyfriend." She glances at me and I smile at her encouragingly.

"Anyway, he had dated this girl Tori all through sophomore and junior year. She already made it known she didn't like me helping him. So, when we went back to school and she found out we were dating, she didn't like it at all," she admits grimacing. "I know normally it wouldn't be a big deal, but in this situation it was. You see, Tori was always very popular, and her family has money so she believed she could do whatever she wanted. So, she did," she chokes out. I reach towards her to wipe away a tear, but she shakes her head and I drop my hand, trying to hide my flinch.

This isn't about me.

She takes a deep breath, gathering her courage and continues. "Tori was also on my cross-country team. She talked about me to all of my teammates and made me feel like a fool, but at least I could run it out." I nod my head in realization. This is what she was referring to when she said she didn't have to get along with her teammates. I can't imagine how hard it must have been for her.

She pauses looking up at me and I try to show her as much compassion as I can through my eyes and body language. She relaxes slightly, although she looks even more nervous with what she's about to say. Her voice catches when she starts, "Tori wrote a blog everyone at school read. She never wrote a word about me for the longest time because to her I was a nobody. Until I started dating Kris and unknowingly, she declared me as her enemy." She shakes her head and grumbles, "I was so naïve!"

She sighs, "She harassed me whenever Kris wasn't around. Then, with her blog she always claimed the readers had submitted the columns or articles, so whenever there was anything about me, she got away with it. She started to make me a focus on her blog and became more and more cruel as the year went on and Kris and I stayed together. He would always stick up for her, saying she was going through a lot or nobody believes it anyway. He even claimed it wasn't her fault."

Anyway, she continued to harass me, but eventually the blog was shut down and anyone associated with it was suspended. Other people who were hurt complained, including parents from another school since their son tried to commit suicide because of something she said about him. The whole school went through a mandatory assembly on cyber-bullying." She continues, "Anyway, at the end of the school year, Kris had a party and we found her in his room at one point. He kicked her out, but what we didn't realize is she turned on his computer and webcam."

She pauses turning a deep shade of red and I begin to fear where this is going. My stomach fills with lead. I attempt to reach for her and she blocks me again with her hand, "He…he…he was my first that night." Her tears are now falling and I want so badly to wipe them away, but I don't think she'll let me. "She started another blog, but we can't really prove it's her. She put pictures up of me from that night, but none that you could really see anything, but Kris and I knew what they were. It didn't matter though, even after that, he still defended her. He claimed it could have been anyone who snuck into his room, even though we caught her in there. He kept saying the pictures weren't that bad anyway."

She sobs making my heart feel like it's fucking breaking. I open my mouth to say something, but she keeps going, "She would make a point to run into me when I was working and tell me she has pictures and videos of me being a whore. She'd tell me she'd use them if I didn't leave him, but Kris didn't believe me. He kept saying she'd never do that to him. Then with all of us at the same college, she turned all the girls in the dorms against me freshman year, so Sara and I moved into an apartment as soon as we could."

"Wait a minute," I interrupt her, "they both go here?" I ask feeling sick.

She nods her head without looking at me and continues, "Anyway, it ended with Kris on a night I don't think I'll ever forget. Tori showed him a couple pictures of me he'd never seen from that first night. She had the pictures doctored and he thought it was me with someone else. He thought I cheated on him. Instead of coming to me, I went to find him since he wasn't answering his phone. I found him in his dorm room with her straddling his lap and her skirt hiked up around her waist, kissing him. He sort of panicked when he saw me, saying nothing happened. Then, he snapped at me saying, unlike me who was a cheating whore." She squeaks out the last two words. I again try to pull her towards me and wrap my arms around her. This time I'm incredibly grateful she lets me.

"Sara went to him to prove the truth and when she did, he came back to me apologizing and begging forgiveness, but he wouldn't even help me when it came to her. He still defended her actions, even after what it did to us, to me..." she sobs into my shirt and I hold her tight rubbing circles on her back. I take deep breaths hoping I can calm her down without letting her know I feel like finding her ex and this Tori girl and beating the shit out of them.

Eventually she quiets down, but still huddles close to me. She whispers, "The worst of it is everyone in my life does that to me except for Sara. My mom, dad, brothers all expect everything from me, always wanting me to give and forgive, but never support me. I feel like a doormat for everyone to walk on and use." I notice she says use like it's a swear word causing my heart to ache with a flashback of when I attempted to joke with her the first night I met her and said the word use. Now it makes sense.

When I think she's done talking I do what I can to appear calm before I hesitantly begin, "I'm not excusing any of your friends or family's behavior, but maybe they think you can handle more than you can. You do take on so much for your friends and family. Have you told them how you feel?" I inquire. She shrugs in response. "I can't even imagine what you went through with that bitch Tori and that asshole ex of yours. Why didn't you ever press charges like Sara suggested?" I prod as calmly as possible, still attempting to tame the anger wanting to erupt inside me.

"I didn't want to deal with it. I thought it would be too hard. I didn't want to ruin her life. I just want her to leave mine alone. At this point she only does anything when Kris seems to pop into my life," she admits.

I stiffen. "You still talk to him?" I painfully growl.

I feel her shake her head and I release my breath slowly trying to let go of my tension while she speaks, "No, but like I said, he goes to school here and he's from here. I know he feels bad about everything and tries to talk to me once in a while."

I attempt to swallow down the sickness rising in my throat. "If he comes around again let me know." She shrugs and I pinch my lips tightly together, struggling not to say anymore. I want her comfortable with me. She doesn't need any more bullshit. I swear if I ever see this asshole, I will kick his ass and if I could punch a girl…holy shit I need to calm down. I've never felt so much hatred toward a girl in my life! I take another deep breath and release it. "Lizzie, I'm not him," I grunt with obvious rigidity in my voice. "You know that, right?"

She smiles timidly and claims, "I'm learning." Then she takes a deep breath, exhaling slowly. "So, have I overwhelmed you so much that you're ready to run scared?" she asks jokingly, but I see a bit of fear in her eyes, almost like she expects me to walk away.

"Never," I croak out. Holding her tightly against me, I stare out at the water. "No one should ever be bullied like that! I hate that someone did that to you. I really wish you would report it." She shakes her head again and I sigh in frustration. How do I protect her if she won't let me help? "There's something you should know about me," I mumble only half joking. "I have an obsession to protect the people I care about, but you have to let me." I can't help but think that's one of the reasons I almost lost Bree, she didn't let me help with everything until it was almost too late. I squeeze Liz tighter with the thought, not wanting to lose her, but needing her to trust me too.

She looks at me and gives me a tight smile, wiping the last of her tears away. "Just believe in me, support me, and don't keep me in the dark with what's going on with you" she requests. Then quickly adds, almost as an afterthought, "And if you have a question, talk to me."

I try to give her a comforting smile as I mumble my agreement, "I can do that."

"Well then, I will keep working on this whole trust thing," she declares. "Go see your sister with Bree tomorrow and come see me when you get back."

"Sounds like a plan. We'll probably get home really late tomorrow night though, 'cause I won't want to leave Aubrey until I have to. So, I'll stop in to see you at work Tuesday and we can hang at your place or mine Tuesday night and watch movies," I suggest.

She nods in agreement, "Perfect."

We walk back to my jeep, and I drive her home in silence with everything she just told me tumbling around in my brain. It fucking kills me thinking about what she went through! I can't believe assholes like that exist, let alone harass my beautiful girl.

Huh…my beautiful girl. Maybe I am finally over Bree. I'm sure as hell crazy about Liz.

We pull into her apartment complex and I park my jeep so I can walk her to her door. "You don't have to walk me to my door. I'll be okay."

She smiles shyly at me and I jump out and walk around my jeep just as she's getting out. "I need to tonight…for me," I claim. I grin broadly at her and her smile brightens. Wrapping my arm around her, I walk her the few feet to her door. She turns and looks at me with her hand on the handle and before she can say a word, I cradle her cheek in my hand and gently press my lips to hers. I feel my heart creep up my throat as I kiss her soft lips, trying to show her how much I care about her. I force myself to pull away, even though I want to press her body up against her door and claim her as mine.

I swallow down my emotion at her pain and whisper, "Thank you for telling me." She nods in acceptance and my thumb goes up to push another tear away from the corner of her eye. I lightly kiss her again and struggle to hold in my groan as I let my hand fall away before whispering, "Good night, Liz." She spins on her heel and steps into her apartment without saying another word.

Chapter 17

Blake

The next day Bree and I make great time down to Boston. We arrive just in time for lunch, excited we're able to take Aubrey out for a picnic, one of her favorite things to do. We play tag with her, letting her win and enjoying her smile and laughter. At dinnertime the nurse asks us to leave to let Aubrey rest when she starts choking on her food in complete exhaustion, giving all of us a scare. Aub hugs Bree so tight when she says goodbye it warms my heart like always. I give my sister a hug of my own and promise to see her soon, wishing I could bring her with me.

Before we even leave Boston, Bree and I go to a Mexican restaurant for dinner. "I'm starving!" I exclaim as we sit down in the booth.

"Me too. I had so much fun today. Aubrey looks fantastic!" Bree proclaims grinning at me.

I nod my head in agreement, "Yeah, she does. Her nurse said she hasn't had any episodes lately besides her choking episode today, so I guess that's good. She seems really strong too. She was trying so hard to run when we were playing tag and she lasted so much longer." I pause making sure to catch her eye before I say, "That could be partially because of you, too. She really missed you."

"I missed her too." She pauses appearing thoughtful before she asks, "Do you think she might be ready to meet Christian?"

I'm somewhat hesitant in answering, even though I knew this was coming. "He wants to meet her?" I prod, curious what he thinks about her.

"Well, I talk about her all the time and Christian knows how important you and Aubrey are to me. You guys are my family," she emphasizes.

"And you're mine Bree," I answer without pause because that's what she is to me, my family.

"I talk to Aubrey about Christian all the time too. She says she wants to meet him." I nod in response. "I mentioned Liz today too and she said you talk about her all the time. In fact, she said you can't shut up about her!" she informs me, smirking.

I burst out laughing. "Did she really say that?" She nods her head, clearly amused and I continue to laugh. "Well, maybe we can figure out when she can meet both of them."

She smiles and looks back at her menu. We order and she settles back into her seat with a smile. "You look happy," I observe. She looks at me quizzically and I elaborate, "You look really happy again for the first time since…" I trail off knowing there's no need for me to finish my sentence. "It's just really fucking good to see you like this, Bree."

She blushes. "Thanks. I am happy. I miss my mom and I especially miss my grandma, but I'm happy."

"So, I guess that means things are good with dickhead?" I smirk. She rolls her eyes at one of the many nicknames I used to call him before the two of them had things figured out and I can't help but chuckle. I love getting a rise out of her.

"Christian is good, ready for his last year of school so he can work on his own business ideas. I think more than anything his family is driving him crazy, but it's good for both of us. His brothers and sister are rarely around right now anyway. They're all away doing their own thing."

138

"So just the parents driving him crazy, I can understand that," I admit.

She cringes slightly. "Yeah, have you talked to your parents?"

"My mom calls all the time and I've answered one or two of her calls on my way out the door," I admit without remorse.

She rolls her eyes at me. "So, no, you haven't talked to them." I sigh and wait for the rest I know is coming. "Blake you're going to have to talk to them about it sooner or later," she insists.

"I know…" I begin.

"Aubrey asked me today if you knew that you guys had a new sister," she interrupts and waits for my reaction.

"What?" I ask shocked.

"When you went to talk to the nurse," she explains. "She said she was excited, but she wanted to know what you thought."

I sit there stunned, not even knowing how to respond. I rub my hands up and down my face and groan into them. "What the fuck? Shouldn't they have let me know they talked to Aubrey about this?" I ask exasperated.

"Maybe they could have if you would answer their calls once in a while." I roll my eyes and groan again. "You, okay?" she prompts full of concern.

"I don't know," I moan. "So, she seemed, okay?" I ask scanning Bree's face for any hesitancy.

Bree nods her head in confirmation. "She was mostly worried about you. I guess for good reason. She's pretty mature for someone they said wouldn't mature emotionally past eight years," she adds with her eyebrows raised.

I nod feeling completely drained. "Yeah, I think they're wrong on so much when it comes to her." I sigh again and rub my hands over my face and through my hair. When I remove them, the waitress is right there setting our food down in front of us. I look up at her to say a quick, "Thank you," before she turns to leave.

"So how about we make a plan?" Bree prods.

I look up at her curiously, afraid to agree before I hear what she has to say. "What kind of plan?"

She rolls her eyes like usual before letting me in on her idea, "I was thinking you could bring Liz up to the lake one weekend in the next couple weeks and we could all hang out. Then, on Sunday night I can go back to Portland with you guys. Then, first thing Monday morning we can come back here to Boston to see Aubrey and you can talk to her about your new sister."

I smile and release a breath I didn't know I was holding. "Well, I can handle that kind of plan. It sounds really good!"

"Good," she affirms, then looks down at her plate. "Then we can stop by my house so I can check on things and you can talk to your parents," she spits out quickly and stuffs her mouth full of enchilada.

"Bree," I grumble threateningly, glaring at her. She mumbles and points to her mouth, indicating she can't talk with food in her mouth. I can't help but laugh and shake my head. I eventually sigh and run my fingers through my hair again feeling defeated because I know it has to be done. I can't procrastinate forever. "Okay, you're right," I concede. I guess that's our plan. I'll talk to Liz and see what weekend she can get off of work."

She smiles huge and drops her fork clapping her hands together like a child on Christmas morning, "Yay!" I can't help but laugh even harder.

By the time we finish dinner and drive back to Maine I'm dropping Bree off at her apartment at ten pm. I give her a hug and mumble, "Thank you," before she goes inside with a wave.

My jeep veers towards Liz's place without even thinking about it. I park in front of her building and grab my phone, sending a swift text, "Just got in, are you up?"

She responds quickly with, "Welcome back! I'm in bed reading."

I smile wide as I hop out of my jeep. "Want some company in bed?"

Her response just has a bunch of question marks and I laugh out loud as I knock on her door. I hear her yell, "Coming," followed by her footsteps rapidly approaching the door before it flies open. I watch in complete amusement as I take in her expression of shock, her mouth opening and closing like a fish before she finally blurts out, "What are you doing here?"

I smirk. "Is that how you greet your boyfriend after he just had to spend hours in the car?" She just stares at me, while I take the time to gaze over her from head to toe. Her dark brown hair is pulled into a low ponytail and she's wearing a fitted black Matt Nathanson t-shirt and gray Capri sweatpants. "You look absolutely adorable," I proclaim stepping into her. I place my hands on her hips and lean down to press my lips against hers with a low rumble in my throat. I pull back with a small smile curling my lips, "You taste good too."

She blushes looking down. "I have to work early, so I was just reading in bed before I went to sleep."

"So, you weren't going to wait for my call," I joke.

"I...I..." she stammers.

"I'm kidding. But we got in a little earlier than I expected, so I thought I'd see if you were awake." I pull her close and lean in giving her another sweet kiss on her luscious pink lips, pushing inside with my tongue, needing to really taste her, before I pull back slightly. I look into her sparkling green eyes and try to keep the laughter out of my voice when I murmur, "Alright, I got what I came for, I'll see you tomorrow."

I step away and all I hear are her sounds of exasperation, "I…Er…Um…What?" making it so I can't hold my laughter in.

"Seriously, completely adorable," I reiterate pulling her towards me again. "So do I get to come in for a few minutes?" I prod looking at her confused expression.

She shakes her head and groans, "Yes, yes, come in."

I pull the front door shut behind me and follow her to her room. She pushes her door shut behind me and plops onto her deep purple floral comforter. She watches me as I look around her room. Her dresser, nightstand and desk all have a whitewash finish. Her dresser is covered with her personal things like a brush, make-up, and a deep green jewelry box. Her desk has a cup of pens, a stack of papers and a few books piled neatly. Above it lays a bulletin board filled with pictures. I walk over to her desk to get a better look. A bunch of the pictures are Liz and Sara together, but there's a couple with her and two guys. I point to them and raise my eyebrows in question.

"Those are my brothers," she informs me as she walks over to me. "That's Jax," she says pointing to the taller guy dressed in ripped jeans and a t-shirt I can't read. "That's Scott, my little brother," she adds pointing to the guy with dark jeans and a plain blue t-shirt. "Well, he's not so little, but younger anyway."

I nod and glance over at her. I don't know what it is, but I just can't stop staring at her tonight. The more I stare, the more nervous she seems to become, before she finally blurts, "What are you doing here anyway? I thought you were coming by the café tomorrow?"

I chuckle softly. "I was planning on it. I still am if that's okay." I sigh and run my fingers through my hair. I sit on the corner of her bed and look into her eyes. "It's just been a really long day. I really needed to see you, even if it was only for a few minutes, even if you didn't even let me through the door," I confess.

"Oh," she murmurs turning a gorgeous shade of red. I pull her between my legs and wrap my arms around her. She cautiously puts her arms around me and I immediately flip her onto her bed, enjoying her startled screech. I chuckle as I give her now barely exposed stomach a kiss, feeling her shiver under me. I move up her body and prop myself on my elbow so I can look into her eyes. "How...uh how did everything go? How's your sister?" she stammers.

I brush her loose hair out of her face answering, "She's good. It went pretty well." Then I lean in and kiss her collarbone, her neck, her chin and finally her soft lips. I hear her gasp and my body floods with heat. Holy crap this girl is gorgeous. I run my tongue along her mouth and push my way in to meet hers. She comes willingly making these tiny whimpering noises that drive me fucking insane. My hand lightly trails up her side, grazing her breast and nipple as I go and I can't help but push myself into her because I want more. I want it all. I want it now. My hand wraps around her and slides down her back and into the back of her capris over her little round ass and I swear I'm about to fucking explode.

"Blake," she pleads my name with both heat and fear, clearly hesitant. The way she says it puts me over the edge and makes me pull back at the same time. She's not ready. It takes all my strength to force myself to back away from her. I remind myself I can't push Liz. I can wait until she's ready. It's my job to protect her. I slowly raise my hand up to her back and roll her over so she's leaning on me. I slow our kisses before pulling away and dropping my head back against her pillows trying to catch my breath. Her head follows and lands right in the crook of my neck. She fits there perfectly. I take a deep breath, attempting to calm down without a cold shower. I push my nose into her hair, smelling her strawberry scented shampoo and all that's her.

I give her another quick squeeze before she questions, "Are you sure you're okay?"

I sigh. "Yeah, just…Aubrey knows we have another sister."

"She does? What did she say?" she prods.

"I don't know," I answer. She lifts her head off my shoulder to look at me in confusion. "She told Bree," I explain. "She wanted to know if I knew. She's worried about me. Isn't that ironic?" I admit sarcastically.

"She's your sister and she loves you. Of course, she's worried about you. That doesn't come with an emotional age," she claims.

"Yeah, but still, I'm supposed to be the one protecting her," I insist.

"Maybe she wants to be the one to protect you once in a while," she suggests.

I shrug. "Bree wants us to go visit her and Christian up at the lake either this weekend or next. Do you think you can get off work?" I prompt, changing the subject.

"Yeah, I'll try to figure it out tomorrow when I go in. See what shifts I need to cover and I'll let you know. Does it matter which one?" she inquires.

"Just whichever weekend you can get to work for your schedule," I tell her casually.

"Okay," she concurs. She nods in agreement and places her head back on my chest, warming me inside and out.

"Then maybe you can come meet my family after," I suggest shocking us both.

144

"I would love to if you want me to," she admits shyly talking into my chest.

I nod my head and ask, "Can I just lay here with you for a while until you fall asleep?" I draw endless circles on her back with my fingers waiting for her answer.

"Sure, I'd like that," she responds and cuddles into me even further. I hold back the groan fighting to come out.

"Thanks," I grunt quietly. "Goodnight Liz," I finally murmur as I try to relax with her in my arms.

A feeling of contentment comes over me for the first time since…well, I'm content now anyway. I hold her tightly in my arms until she falls asleep. Eventually, I know I should get home, so I slowly slide my arms out from under her and tuck her into her bed without waking her.

I try to sneak out of her room quietly. After I close the door, I look up to see Sara looking at me seriously. "Hi, Blake."

I grin and give her a small wave. "Good night, Sara," I mumble before turning to head to the door.

"Blake, wait," she urges as she starts taking a step towards me. I stop and wait to hear what she has to say. "Be careful with her, she's been through a lot."

I nod my head in understanding. "I know."

"Just…please don't hurt her," she quietly begs.

I look her in the eyes before I even open my mouth, "I will do everything I can to protect her. The last thing I want to do is hurt her," I tell her honestly.

We stare at each other for a few minutes before she nods in acknowledgement, and I turn to leave. I step out the front door knowing I'll try to protect her, but I realize she still has a long way to go before she really trusts me. I have to be careful not to let this fuck me up too much either. I can already feel myself slipping far more than I ever did with Bree. Although I'll only admit it to myself right now, my

145

heart can't take much. I need to figure out a way I can protect both of us. I know it won't be easy.

Chapter 18

Elizabeth

Nearly two weeks later, Blake and I are headed up to the lake to visit Bree and Christian in his jeep. It's only a little over an hour drive, but when we're halfway there my nerves begin churning in my stomach. Things have been really good with Blake. We don't seem to hold anything back from each other now; at least I don't think we do. I feel like he really listens to me and understands me. He always seems to be worried about me, watching me and reacting to me.

I really like that. No, that's not true, I love that!

I think he really wants to be with me. He shows me he wants to be with me with his words, his actions and especially his kisses. Oh my God, his kisses make me go weak just thinking of them and I feel myself blush.

Blake smiles when he glances over at me, "You okay?"

I blush even deeper and his smile broadens. He reaches for my hand and squeezes it, leaving it between us on the seat. I swear he can sense what I'm thinking sometimes. It's strange though, every time things start to heat up with us, he pulls back. I'm not complaining. I honestly don't know if I'm ready for sex after everything with Kris, but I'm not sure what his reasons are and that's what scares me. I know I told him I wasn't ready the first time, but I haven't said anything since. I'm not naïve, he is a college guy and what college guy doesn't want sex? I guess that's why I'm so nervous about this weekend.

He says Bree is like family to him. I still wonder what he means by that. Is she like, a sister to him or is she something else, something more? What if she wasn't with Christian? Would he want to be with her then? I can't help but question their relationship and what I'm walking into. Maybe Bree is the reason why he's holding back with me. My questions keep running through my head and my gut clenches in pain with my judgments.

"Are you sure you're okay?" he prods startling me out of my thoughts. I look down and realize I'm fisting my free hand nervously in my lap. I sigh and shake my hand out, trying to jiggle away my nerves.

"Yeah, I'm just nervous, I guess. I don't really know them very well and now we're going to spend the weekend with them," I explain telling a partial truth.

He nods and states, "I understand, but you'll also be spending it with me." He quirks his eyebrow at me waiting for the reaction I assume I give him when he chuckles. "And besides, they're good people. I know you're going to love Bree and everyone will love you! It's really important to me for you and Bree to spend time together and get to know each other better." I notice he says Bree, not Bree and Christian making me sigh in resignation. I guess she is his best friend, not Christian, but...I can't read too much into it. "And there's so much for us to do here. Let alone it's absolutely beautiful," he adds nodding towards my window.

I turn my head and glance out at what appears to be a small overlook as he drives slowly. There's a small field of tall pale green grass completely surrounded by all shapes and sizes of pine trees in various shades of green. The sun is shining brightly, almost sparkling, over the top of those trees with a large sliver of the lake visible from here just beyond the pine trees. It looks so dark blue, almost black from this angle. Beyond that is what appears to be an island covered in pine trees with water slipping around the other side before more land covered in pine. "I wonder if that land is connected over there," I think to myself.

"I don't know," Blake answers and I laugh realizing I had spoken out loud. He just smirks at me with raised eyebrows probably questioning my sanity. "It is beautiful." He squeezes my hand one more time before slipping his hand out of mine to place back on the steering wheel. "Relax Liz. We're going to have fun this weekend. I promise."

He turns onto an unpaved road. I can feel the vibrations of the rough road. I can't help but ask, "Why are we going into the woods?"

He laughs, shaking his head. "This is Bree's driveway."

"Oh." I take a deep breath trying to calm my nerves one more time. "Will her grandma be here?"

Blake visibly swallows and pales slightly. "Um, no. This is Bree's house," he croaks out.

"Oh," I mumble surprised. "You said we were going to her grandma's, I thought..."

"This ah, this was her grandma's house. She died last year, and she left the house to Bree. They were very close." He answers in a tight voice. I want to ask more so I don't say the wrong thing later on in front of Bree, but I'm not sure I should with Blake's tense reaction. "Christian's parents have a house just down the lake from here. I've never been there though," he adds.

He pulls the car up to a small house and I can't help but stare out at the view. There are more pine trees leading down a dirt hill, covered in twigs, leaves and brush, ending at a beautiful lake. The lake now appears to be a lighter blue and sparkling brightly with the sun shining on it from this angle. I step out of the car mumbling, "This is absolutely spectacular."

149

I glance over towards the small cedar house when I hear a high-pitched shriek. The sound is coming from Bree who runs out the door with Christian following directly behind her. She slams right into Blake wrapping her arms around his waist. He envelops her in a hug with a look of love and contentment briefly covering his face, but in an instant it's gone. I almost wonder if that's really what I saw. "I'm so happy you guys are here!" she exclaims as she steps away from him and over to me startling me when she hugs me too. I awkwardly hug her back while Christian shakes Blake's hand and then smiles at me.

"How was the drive?" Christian asks.

"Short," Blake answers then laughs. "Honestly, that's nothing when I'm going to Boston basically every week."

Bree pulls on my arm, urging, "Come on in and I'll show you where you can sleep."

"I have to grab my bag," I begin, but Bree waves me off.

"What are boys for if not to carry our bags?" she jokes. She smirks at Christian and giggles softly.

Christian grabs my bag out of the jeep and charges Bree picking her up and throwing her over his shoulder as she squeals in protest. "Anything else I can carry for you, dear?" he asks sarcastically.

She laughs smacking his back. "Christian, put me down!" He ignores her heading towards the house and throwing open the door. He waves us through first before following with Bree. He drops my bag before slowly placing her back on her feet just inside the door. She laughs and smacks him in the chest again, declaring, "Trouble!"

He smiles wide. "You started it, but hell yes, I am," he answers proudly. Then he leans down and kisses her lips tenderly before pulling back and looking into her eyes with the sweetest smile. I awkwardly look away, feeling like I'm

150

disrupting a moment between the two of them, or maybe if I didn't know better, I'd say he was staking his claim, but...

Bree shakes her head with a wide smile. "Anyway, so this is the kitchen and the living room." She gestures around her and then turns towards the back of the house where there is a small hallway and a few doors. I quietly follow her as she opens the first door on the right. "This is the bathroom, obviously. There are fresh towels in the closet right there." I look back and realize I'm the only one following her. She reminds me, "Blake's been here before and once you've seen it, it's small enough that everything's easy enough to find." She smiles and pats my arm.

The next door she opens is a small bedroom with a full-sized bed. "Here's the guest bedroom. You guys can stay in here." She stops short; blushing slightly and quickly adds smiling shyly, "Unless you're not comfortable with that, Blake would be more than comfy on the couch."

"I'm not sleeping on the couch!" Blake yells down the hall. I blush wondering what this girl is thinking.

She rolls her eyes and yells back, "You'll sleep where I tell you to sleep!"

"We'll see about that!" he calls back.

She laughs looking over at me. "Don't let him get to you. I know he's kidding." She steps back into the hallway and points to the door across the hall, "And that's my room if you need anything, you can always knock."

"Thanks," I mumble smiling genuinely. She really is nice. "What's in there?" I ask pointing at the last closed door and watch as a shadow passes over her face. I think I know before she even answers and already regret my question.

"That was my grandma's room. I've been using it to slowly go through all of her things," she answers quietly her face full of sadness before turning back towards the kitchen.

151

"I'm really sorry about your grandma," I declare sincerely and reach a hand out to her arm hesitantly.

She stops and lightly closes her eyes, appearing to be fighting back tears. She swallows before looking me in the eye and saying, "Thank you," with a sad smile.

She eventually turns and steps back towards the kitchen. She walks immediately to Christian's arms to give him a quick hug. He wraps his arms around her and squeezes, obviously knowing she needs the encouragement. Then, he keeps one arm around her as he lets her go. What bothers me though is the look of sadness on Blake's face as he watches them. I know he cares about her, but I swear there's something more in his look. Maybe I'm just imagining it.

"Why don't we go out to the back porch?" Bree finally suggests. "I just put some snacks together while we were waiting for you guys to get here and I made some fresh lemonade."

I nod in agreement. "That sounds great, thank you."

"I'm going to put our bags in our room quick and then I'll be right out," Blake informs me before grabbing our bags and turning towards the hallway.

Bree grabs a tray filled with food and Christian picks up the pitcher of lemonade and some cups. "Can you grab the door?" Christian asks nodding his head towards the slider behind me.

"Oh, I'm sorry, of course," I stutter. "Can I help with anything else?" I prod as I pull the door open.

Christian smiles and Bree answers, "No, thank you, this is it." They set everything down on a small table and Christian starts pouring the glasses of lemonade and offers me the first one.

"Thank you," I state taking it. Then, I look out over the rail to the lake. "This is absolutely breathtaking," I murmur.

"It sure is, isn't it?" Christian prompts before he laughs. I look over and watch as a look of love passes between him and Bree. I can't help but smile to myself watching them together.

"So, do you like to kayak?" Bree asks.

I shrug my shoulders in response. "I don't know, I've never been," I admit shyly.

"Really? I thought Blake said you were from Maine?" Christian asks shocked, just as Blake steps outside. "We are going to have to take your girl kayaking, she's never been!" he continues not waiting for my answers.

"I didn't know that. We talked about different water sports. I guess we never talked about kayaking. Do you guys have enough for all of us?" Blake asks and I feel my panic start to set in.

"Yeah, we can borrow my sister's and one of my brothers' from my parents' house. Plus, if we want to do any water skiing or knee boarding or jet skiing, all of that is over at my parents' house anyway," Christian adds.

"So, you live right down the lake?" I prompt, swallowing down my fear of trying something new. Maybe we won't end up going or maybe it won't be so bad.

"Well, my parents do. I've been staying here with Bree this summer," he answers, and I swear he sticks out his chest just slightly when he says it. "I'm not about to let my girl stay here alone."

Bree rolls her eyes, blushing slightly. I glance at Blake who reaches for the last lemonade glass gripping it pretty tightly. I'm getting the same feeling I did the night of the concert, but this time I don't really have anywhere to escape, so I have to figure out how to change the subject and talk to Blake about it later. I nervously look around and my eyes latch on to Bree's snacks. I take a step towards them and start babbling nervously, "Wow, this is great Bree! Cheese and crackers, pretzel sticks, hummus, grapes and chocolate covered strawberries; you didn't have to go through so much trouble." I grab a strawberry and proclaim, "And chocolate covered strawberries are my favorite!"

She laughs. "It wasn't any trouble at all." She grabs a strawberry as well. "These are one of my favorites too!" she exclaims and glances shyly over at Christian. The way he looks back at her could melt anyone's heart. I have an overwhelming feeling in my chest wanting that with Blake, but I'm afraid to look at him. I'm afraid of who is head and heart are truly with right now.

Blake and Christian step over to us and grab their own snack off the tray before we all finally collapse into the chairs. Christian slides closer to Bree and reaches for her hand while we all talk. My feeling of jealousy regarding their relationship continues to grow in my gut, especially when Blake doesn't move to take mine.

We all eventually relax while I mostly listen to the three of them talk. They keep making jokes and telling stories, while I just continue to take everything in. I do answer when I'm asked a question, but I realize I'm more quiet than normal and I'm sure I'm not the only one who notices. We finish off the tray of snacks followed by two pizzas that Bree had thrown in the oven before I realize how dark it's become. "I'm starting to get eaten alive," I state slapping the mosquitos away from my legs.

Blake chuckles and stands up putting his hand out for me and I feel my heart jump to my throat, maybe all this is in my head. "Come on then Liz, let's go inside. I don't want you getting eaten by anything but me." Christian chuckles and Bree smacks him on the arm as I feel my whole body turn beat red. My nerves multiply ten-fold in the pit of my stomach. "I'm kidding," he whispers in my ear just loud enough for everyone to hear to ease my embarrassment, but close enough that his breath gives me chills right down my spine and all the way to my toes.

Bree looks like she's about to stand to come with us when Christian pulls her back down. "You guys go in. We'll be there in a minute."

Blake pulls me inside and tugs me onto the couch next to him. He drops my hand and wraps his arm around me. His touch helps to comfort me and I relax into him. "See, it's not so bad. It's going to be a fun weekend," he insists. I nod my head, even though I'm not completely convinced yet. I admit I feel a little better with his arm wrapped around me holding me so close.

When his friends come in, we decide to watch a movie since we are all pretty tired. So instead of worrying about what to say or how to react or other people's actions or reactions, I curl up next to Blake, wrapping my arms around his waist, ready to watch The Breakfast Club. "Bree had never seen this before until the beginning of this summer, now she's completely obsessed with it!" Christian exclaims then laughs. He gives her a light kiss when she rolls her eyes.

I smile at their antics and turn my eyes towards the television. The next thing I know Blake is lifting me into his arms "What are you doing?" I ask him groggily.

He smiles sweetly, enlightening me, "You fell asleep. I don't think you even made it to the opening credits," he states chuckling softly.

"Oh, I guess I was tired," I attempt to squirm out of his arms when he tries to open the door, but he just holds me tighter. He steps into the room and gently places me on the bed, kissing me tenderly before standing back up. An involuntary sigh slips from my lips when he moves away.

He smiles down at me, then grabs something out of his duffle bag. "I'll be right back if you want to get changed without me here."

155

I nod, not having the energy to voice my answer. I hear him chuckle as he steps out of the room. I push myself over to my bag grabbing teal green pajama shorts and a matching tank top. I change as quickly as possible before grabbing my toothbrush. I turn towards the door right as Blake steps into the room and I come face to chest with him. He has on blue pinstriped pajama pants and no shirt. I can't help but gawk at him. I always knew he was thin and he was fit, but I've never really stared at him too much when we were at the beach, afraid of making a fool of myself, I guess. But without his shirt on and him standing right in front of me, I'm struggling to close my mouth. He's thin but toned and my eyes follow the lines of his muscles, completely ogling him until he chuckles and steps around me. My body heats instantly with embarrassment and I rush out the door into the bathroom to brush my teeth.

I pause in the hallway after I'm done with my hand on the doorknob enjoying the silence. I haven't slept in the same room as a boy since Kris and I have to admit to myself how nervous I really am. I take a deep breath mumbling, "It's just sleep," before I finally turn the knob slowly and step back into the room. Blake is sitting on the bed with his back against the headboard, leaning his elbows on his propped-up knees with his hands hanging loosely.

I smile shyly at him not quite sure what to do with myself and he returns my smile and pats the bed next to him. "It's okay Liz. I'll be a perfect gentleman." I slowly creep towards the bed like I'm afraid something is going to jump out at me, before gently sitting next to him. I quickly stuff my legs under the covers. "I like your pj's," he murmurs scooting himself down to look in my eyes. "You look adorable," adding with a quiet growl under his breath, "And so damn sexy."

My whole body instantly blushes and I whisper a choked, "Thank you." I really want to touch him, but I'm too nervous to even think about it.

"So, what do you think of this place?" he asks watching my every move.

"It's beautiful. Tomorrow should be fun," I answer robotically.

"You don't sound too excited about it," he states, studying me intently.

"I guess I'm just nervous around them still. They are nice though." Blake looks at me curiously before nodding his head in acknowledgement.

"You okay with this?" he prods gently laying his hand on my hip and I blush deeply in response. "I mean with us sleeping in this bed together. Like I said, I'll be a perfect gentleman." I don't answer, completely frozen. He leans a little closer until I feel his breath on my face as he mumbles, "Well, mostly." He closes the distance and touches my lips with his so lightly I almost wonder if it was real after he pulls back. "I promise I won't do anything you don't want me to do."

I attempt to swallow the lump in my throat and squeak out, "Yeah, I'm okay with this." I let my eyes close and lean into him wanting more, but terrified of the same thing. My heart is pounding so hard I can't hear anything except the blood rushing through my ears. I press my lips to his and shakily let my hands trace the lines of the muscles on his chest. His tongue slips into my mouth and tangles with mine while his hand grips my side tighter, like he's holding on for dear life. I try to deepen the kiss but he pulls back. I roll onto my back sighing in frustration, while I try to catch my breath.

"I'm sorry Liz, I just...knowing I'm going to be laying here with you in my arms all night..." he sighs and runs his hand through his hair before continuing, "I just don't want it to get out of hand."

"Well, it doesn't have to," I begin.

"It will if you keep kissing me like that," he admits. He raises his eyebrows and waits for my reaction, but I don't know how to react.

Does he really want me?

He reaches up and brushes my hair off my cheek. Leaving his hand there, he looks into my eyes, "You are beautiful, absolutely fucking gorgeous. Everything about you is amazing to me and I'm just trying to do what's right for us. I want you to be confident in where we are, not nervous as hell, wondering if you're doing the right thing. I don't want you to have doubts about us and I can tell you're not there yet."

I nod, understanding what he's saying and surprised he's reading me so well. "Yeah," I whisper gulping down the emotion in my throat. He knows I'm not quite ready. He's doing this for me I think with an overwhelming feeling filling my chest and bubbling into my throat.

"Besides it's not very often I get to hold an amazing girl in my arms all night," he adds smiles genuinely.

The slight bit of relief I just felt knowing he's been holding back for me vanishes. I know I shouldn't respond; it was meant to be sweet, but I feel compelled to ask him after his last statement. I'm pretty sure I'll regret it, but...I bite my lip wondering if I should say anything and when I see Blake's questioning look, I blurt it out, "When was the last time you did that?"

"What?" he asks confused.

"Just slept with a girl all night?" I question wondering if I really want to know the answer.

He removes his hand from my cheek and looks slightly away, obviously taken aback by my question. "I...uh...a long time..." he stutters.

The way he answers makes me nervous again and I stupidly want to know more. "Was she your ex-girlfriend?"

He laughs sounding slightly bitter, "Not exactly. Why are we talking about other girls right now?"

I look down and try to bring back the small bit of confidence I just had, but I don't feel it when I force out, "I guess I'm just trying to know more about you. I don't really know anything about the kind of girls you like."

He looks up at the ceiling before slowly releasing his breath and settling his eyes back on mine, "Let's get one thing straight, you are the kind of girl I like. The only girl for me right now is you. I don't do overnights with girls. This is a first with a girlfriend."

"But you just said..." I begin.

"I know what I just said," he interrupts tightly. "The only other girl I've done an overnight with is Bree, not as a girlfriend, as a friend. No kissing involved!" he huffs.

He sounds seriously pissed at me and I don't know what to say. I mumble, "I'm sorry."

I try to fight the tears I know are trying to surface. I feel worse hearing him say his overnights were with Bree, even if it's just as a friend. There's just something about the way they look at each other that makes it seem more than friendship to me. I don't want to hear him tell me how close they are. I roll away from him, not wanting him to see the tears I can't hold back anymore as jealousy consumes me.

He sighs loudly and I know he's frustrated with me too. I don't blame him. I feel his hand on my arm and his body inching up towards my back. "You have no reason to apologize, Liz, none at all. I'm sorry," he murmurs caressing my cheek gently, and wiping a tear away. "I just don't want to talk about Bree, or any other girls. I don't want to talk about other guys. There's no one else in this relationship except us, so can we please keep it that way? I just want to talk about you and me. That's what's important to me right now. You, right here, in my arms," he emphasizes giving me a gentle squeeze.

He leans into me, kissing me lightly on the corner of my mouth, my cheek, my neck and then he wraps his arms around me, pulling me into his chest. I know he's right; I wish I didn't have so much trouble letting go, but there seems to be something more between the two of them than I'd like to admit. I just can't seem to drop it. I can't be the clueless girlfriend again. I stare into the dark room, making myself sick questioning why him and Bree had overnights at all. Eventually, I fall asleep in his arms, long after I feel his breathing slow for sleep.

Chapter 19

Elizabeth

The next morning my eyes slowly blink awake to find Blake staring down at me. "Good morning, sunshine!" he mumbles brightly, giving me a lazy smile.

My stomach does a summersault and I lick my lips, smiling back at him. "Morning," I murmur shyly.

"Did you sleep okay?" I just nod at him in response, not ready to talk quite yet. He smirks at me and teases, "So, do you talk in the morning or do I have to kiss your words out of you?"

I feel myself blush and begin to stretch. He leans down to kiss me, slowly moving his lips over mine, as if waking them up.

I start to kiss him back before I let a giggle escape. He narrows his eyes at me, but him pretending to be tough with me right now, only makes me laugh harder. He immediately starts tickling my sides causing me to screech. "Blake, no, stop!" My pleas not doing anything but encouraging him more. "Please, stop!" I squeal laughing and trying to catch my breath.

"But it's working and I love your laugh," he chuckles, reaching for me, he tickles me again. After a couple minutes we're both laughing hard causing tears to pour from my eyes.

I practically jump out of my skin when someone suddenly pounds on the door. "No fooling around in there!" Christian yells through the door, followed by his low chuckle.

"Go away, Dickhead!" Blake grumbles.

I hear Bree's muffled voice, urging, "Christian, leave them alone."

"If you're making me get out of bed, so is he. Besides, if we don't get any privacy, neither does he," Christian responds before I hear what I think is a slap, followed by Christian laughing and their feet moving down the hallway towards the kitchen.

Blake looks down at me and asks teasingly, "So are you blushing or is that from my magic hands?" I feel myself turn a deeper shade of red in response. He laughs and claims, "That answers my question."

"Blake," I mumble, shaking my head in amusement.

He leans down brushing his lips lightly over mine causing me to smile with his touch. "About last night, are you okay?" he prods looking at me tenderly.

"Yeah, I'm sorry I'm such a mess. I'll try to concentrate on us, I promise," I proclaim. I'm grateful we're able to get that conversation out of the way first thing today. I don't want that hanging over our heads.

"Good," he smirks then kisses me before his face grows serious again. "Because honestly, Liz…we are what matter," he emphasizes. He leans down and presses his lips to mine, his tongue slipping in to find its mate. Tilting his head, he deepens the kiss and I sigh into him just as there's another loud thump at the door causing us to break apart.

"Fuck! I got it, Christian!" Blake yells, glaring at the door as if Christian can see him.

I hear Christian laughing on the other side of the door making me giggle. "Come on. Let's go see what we're doing for breakfast," I urge. He sighs and kisses me quickly before jumping off the bed and throwing a t-shirt over his head. He glances at me, handing me a sweatshirt. I just look at him like he's crazy and insist, "It's way too hot for that!"

He rolls his eyes and grumbles, "Fine, at least throw on your bra then." I blush and give him a small smile at his request. But I do what he says, grabbing my bra and slipping it on under my shirt with Blake watching me. I have to admit, I feel my confidence growing with the way he's eyeing me.

"Man, that's hot," he grumbles reaching for me. I quickly step around him and stride towards the door throwing it open. Blake shakes his head mumbling under his breath before following me out of the bedroom and I feel my self-assurance cultivate even further.

We step out into the kitchen and Christian lifts his gaze, smirking over at us from the stove next to Bree. "How'd you sleep?" he prods.

"Good," I answer. Bree turns around with a huge smile. "Christian and I are making breakfast. Are you guys hungry?"

"Sure, can I help?" I prompt. Blake steps around me to the cabinets grabbing a couple coffee mugs.

"Sure, you guys can set the table if you want," Bree suggests. "Christian and I already have our coffee though, thanks Blake."

Blake steps over to the half empty coffee pot and pours us both a cup, then adding cream and sugar before grabbing plates and handing them to me. Then, he reaches for the silverware and places everything quickly on the table. "Smells good, Bree."

"Actually, Christian made the eggs and bacon, I did the hard part of helping to shop for the pastries and making everything look pretty," she claims grinning.

"You standing there makes anything look pretty Bree." She chokes on a laugh and rolls her eyes at Christian.

"He's dramatic, but he's a good cook," she adds smiling at him. "I guess he's worth keeping around," she jokes.

163

He leans towards her with a smile, placing a chaste kiss on her mouth before grabbing the serving dishes out of her hands. "Thanks."

There's something about watching the two of them that makes you feel like you're watching a great love story and at the same time, sharing a private moment. I can't seem to get rid of this slight jealousy I have over them, but only because I would love to have that with someone. No, that's not true. I would love to have that with Blake.

"Are you okay?" Blake prompts reaching for my hand and pulling me down in the chair next to him. I nod smiling shyly and swallowing down my emotions. I realize I probably look ridiculous standing there staring at them and blush.

"So, we were thinking we should head over to my parents after breakfast. If we want to go kayaking, we're better off going in the morning before the lake gets busy. Then, we can always use the boat after to ski or tube or whatever you guys are up for," Christian suggests.

I glance over at Blake and nod stiffly as my nerves begin to take over my stomach by storm. He answers quickly, "That sounds great!" He smiles at me so big my insides turn from chaos to liquid heat and I wonder what he's thinking. Hopefully, I don't make a complete fool of myself today.

Chapter 20

Blake

I don't even know if I could explain kayaking with Liz if I wanted to. She kept steering herself into the rocks or she had trouble turning herself around, but at least she didn't tip herself over. I've never seen someone kayak like she does. She is so fucking adorable when she gets flustered! Watching her is now my favorite hobby.

I stuck close to her while we stayed out on the lake, more than happy to help her with every move. We remained close to Christian's house while Bree and Christian ventured farther, which works for me. Don't get me wrong, I love Bree and Christian is growing on me, but I can only take so much of them when they're together. Plus, I love being able to spend time alone with *my* girl.

Eventually, I help guide her back to shore and I support her as she shakily climbs out of the kayak exhaling deeply with what I assume is relief. I try to hide the laugh rising in my throat, but it surfaces anyway. "Are you laughing at me?" she shrieks and tosses her life jacket in the kayak.

I hide my smile behind my hand but then reach for her and pull her close letting her see my smile. "No, I'm laughing with you babe." She blushes and I'm not sure if it's from my comment or me calling her babe, but either way I fucking love it!

"I'm staying on land next time, or someone else has to be with me to steer the stupid boat. I suck at this!" she vents.

"We can always try a two-man kayak next time," I suggest. "That way I can do most of the work and you can look cute without the worry."

"They have those?" she shrieks. I love the shocked look on her face. "Why didn't we use one of those then? I'm horrible at kayaking! I really shouldn't have been out there by myself!"

"You weren't by yourself, you were with me," I proclaim watching her get herself all worked up. "Relax, Liz," I urge, brushing her hair out of her face. "It doesn't matter how well you do, the point is to have fun, together."

"But no one wants to kayak with someone who's so horrible she can't even steer away from rocks and trees," she complains shakily. My heart clenches as I notice tears building at the corners of her eyes. "I'm surprised I didn't end up in the water the whole time."

"I want to kayak with you. I want to do everything with you," I insist pulling her in for a hug. I wrap my arms tightly around her and feel her shaking. "You, okay?" I lean back and ask cautiously, rubbing her arms up and down.

She nods slightly, "I'm not used to the encouragement. I knew you guys all wanted to go kayaking, so I tried for you." She sighs shakily and I feel my heart shattering listening to her confession. What does she mean, not used to encouragement? Is this one of the things she was talking about when she said her parents always expect her to be perfect? "I don't really like to try new things because my parents, especially my mom, kind of expect me to be perfect at everything, so when I'm not..." she trails off.

I admit, I don't know if I can hear anymore. I attempt to swallow down the lump in my throat, along with my anger

166

before speaking. "It's supposed to be about having fun and being together. I want you to remember that with me no matter what we do! I don't care if we never make it away from the dock or go around in circles for hours! The only thing that matters to me is that we're together and you're having fun. I don't ever need you to be perfect at anything. I need you to just be with me," I emphasize. I take another deep breath before adding, "You better start getting used to hearing encouragement from me because you deserve to hear it and so much more," I stress my voice breaking at the end.

"It's not that exactly. They didn't do anything if I wasn't good at something," she sighs. "My dad works a lot so my mom either made me practice all the time, or she'd get me help until I was perfect. Like with the flute, I had a tutor until I made first chair and even after that my tutor still came once in a while because my mom wanted to make sure I stayed at first chair. Or if I didn't do well, like with soccer, she told me to quit and stick to what I know; things I was good at like school. She never really wanted me to try new things, so I stopped."

"Honestly, what I hated most of all was the look of utter disappointment if I wasn't perfect at something or when she would tell my dad about all the things she said were wrong with me. He would come home from his business trips, and she would give him a list of things I did wrong while he was away, never anything I did right. She would ask him to talk to me, said I needed a firm hand or something. The look he gave me when he walked in my room..." she mumbles, shaking her head gently.

The look of overwhelming sadness on her face right now is fucking killing me. I hate that anyone would put so much pressure on her, let alone her own parents. I feel my fists tighten thinking about what it might have been like for her with her mom. I take a deep breath, trying to calm my

167

anger. "Look, I want to be able to try new things with you. It doesn't matter how good or how bad you are at them, as long as we're having fun together. Nobody is perfect. Nobody," I emphasize. She nods still not looking me in the eyes and I need to do everything I can to make her relax, I need to help her feel better.

"So next time we can take a double kayak if you want," I say clearing my throat. "Or we can just stay here and do this," I suggest. I put my fingers under her chin and tilt her head up to mine, leaning towards her full lips, I kiss her with all I have. If I could make her understand how special she is just through our lips, I would do just that. I really can't get enough of her! I move my mouth over hers and feel more than hear her whimper as my tongue enters her mouth and tangles with hers. My hand travels down her back to the curve of her ass and I leave it there, pulling her as close to me as possible. She has to be able to feel just how much I want her.

Just as I start to get lost in Liz, my back is suddenly soaked making me tense. Liz gasps and pulls away with her mouth hanging open. I turn around glaring at a laughing Christian, while Bree looks at me with a knowing smile. I shake my head and mutter loud enough for him to hear, "You're going to pay for that," which just makes him laugh louder.

"Pretty sure I'm finally getting the chance to pay you back," he grins. I shake my head in amusement when Liz joins in the laughter, feeling more relaxed again. Christian quickly pulls his kayak and Bree's with her in it ashore before he helps her out.

I help Christian clean up the dock while the girls go into the house. While we're alone for a few minutes, I ask him for my own peace of mind, "How's she doing Christian? She seems good."

He smiles. "She is good, man. She's really good. She has her days here and there, but honestly, she smiles more now than the summer I met her," he admits and I turn away remembering that summer myself.

"You'd tell me if she wasn't okay, right?" I probe needing an honest answer from him.

He gives me a hard look before responding, "Yeah, Blake, I would. I promise. After everything you've done for her, I at least owe you that." He turns and starts walking towards his house and I follow.

I put a hand on his shoulder to stop him before he steps through the door. I look him straight in the eye, knowing I need to say this no matter how fucking hard it is, "Thank you, Christian."

He looks at me, probably trying to make sure I'm genuine before nodding his acceptance and stepping into the house.

After lunch, we take the boat out and Bree tries water skiing a couple times before Christian and I each take a few turns around the lake. I attempt to get Liz to take a turn, but she insists she learned enough for one day and she's more than content just watching us. I wish she would understand there's no judgment with me and truly relax, but I don't want to push her too hard too fast either. Since we don't want the girls to spend their day just watching us, we end up pulling the ski rope in and dropping the anchor so we can all swim. "You have to get your bathing suit wet at some point," I insist smiling at Liz.

Christian sticks his foot in the water testing for cold spots. Bree sneaks up behind him and tries to push him in while he's off-balance. She succeeds, but he grabs her hand as he's falling and accomplishes taking her with him. Liz and I laugh as they both come up sputtering. The next thing I know, Liz flies right by me in a blur of blue. I dive in quickly after her. "This water feels good!" she exclaims.

I swim right for her. "Glad you're finally enjoying it," I proclaim.

"I was always enjoying it, just differently, I promise," she admits with a grin.

"Good," I reply. I wrap my arm around her bare waist, pulling her to me. I need to get my hands on her and give her a quick kiss. I sure as hell can't keep her nearly naked body so close to me for too long with an audience or I won't be able to climb out of this water. "God, you're beautiful," I mumble against her lips, kiss her hard, then turn and dive under water to cool down. When I surface, I find Liz floating on her back and I turn to swim back towards the boat. I pull myself up and let my feet hang off the back as I watch her swim.

Eventually, Christian and Bree swim back to the boat and climb in. Liz follows close behind. I grab her hand to pull her up without taking my eyes off her. "What?" she prompts. My eyebrows furrow as I look at her quizzically. "You're looking at me like you did earlier. What is that look?" she probes. I raise my eyebrows trying not to laugh because she has to be fucking joking.

Christian doesn't hold back his laughter and answers for me, "It's the look of a man enjoying the view of his girlfriend in a wet bikini!" Bree smacks him in the stomach and Liz blushes from head to toe as I see her eyes immediately search for a towel.

I lean down to whisper in her ear, "Sorry, but he's right." I kiss her cheek just below her ear and pull her towards me as I watch her blush deepen. I know the instant she feels just how true Christian's statement is when her breath hitches and her blush turn into goosebumps covering her flesh.

170

Christian raises the anchor immediately turning towards the dock and his parents' house. Before my eyes have the chance to soak her in anymore, she pushes me away and quickly grabs a towel wrapping it tightly around her. I chuckle and grab her by the waist, pulling her into my lap. I wrap her in my arms and whisper, "The towel did nothing to get the image of you wrapped around me with or without your bikini out of my head." She opens her mouth to say something but immediately snaps it shut. She leans into my chest and stares straight ahead at the dock almost wishing us there. I laugh quietly and slide her body off my lap and next to me for the short run back to the dock. I rub her arm lightly trying to get her to relax.

We quickly reach the dock and tie up the boat. "Why don't you girls go inside so you can change and clean up upstairs while Blake and I finish up with the boat and put everything away," Christian suggests. He gives Bree a chaste kiss and she turns to Liz with a smile. I give Liz one last squeeze, kissing her behind her ear before she jumps up still wrapped in her towel.

"Come on Liz, I'll show you where everything is," Bree prompts. Grabbing her hand, she pulls her along up to the house. Liz turns and gives me a wave with that shy smile of hers that makes my heart skip a beat. I grin and watch her disappear into the house with Bree.

I glance over at Christian wondering what the fuck is going on because it's obvious he wanted me alone to say something. He's busying himself winding the towrope while I watch him, waiting for him to speak. I honestly don't know what else to do but laugh. He glances over at me like I'm crazy. "It's not like we're best friends," I say and shrugging my shoulders by way of explanation. "What the fuck is going on?"

He puts the rope away and looks at me sighing, "So, things seem to be going well with Liz?" he prompts begrudgingly.

This just makes me laugh harder earning myself a glare from him. "So, Bree put you up to this, huh?" I prod with a smirk. He doesn't respond, knowing I already know the answer. "She asks me herself all the time. She either wants a guys' point of view, hoping you'll get something else, or she's trying to force us to bond."

He shrugs his shoulders like her reason doesn't matter. But then again, we all know it doesn't, he'd do anything for her, we both would. "Pretty sure it's both," he finally admits.

I nod my head in agreement. "You can tell her things are good. That's all you're getting out of me."

"No skin off my back." He eyes me warily and I raise my eyebrows waiting for him to say whatever he's thinking. Instead, he shakes his head and continues cleaning up the boat. We finish quickly and walk up to his house to wait for the girls.

"Where are your parents?" I ask.

"They're down visiting my sister, Theresa in Boston. She never comes home anymore, so they drove down to see her," he answers.

"I didn't know your sister was in Boston. Why don't you ever come when Bree goes to visit my sister?" I ask curiously.

He looks at me like he's deciding how to answer before speaking, "I know your sister has a hard time meeting new people and I don't want to make anyone uncomfortable. Bree absolutely adores her. She talks about her all the time and I think she sounds pretty great. She's part of the reason Bree switched her major to occupational therapy and recreation. She wants to work at a place like where your

172

sister lives and help people like her who have been through so much."

"Huh," I mumble feeling proud of Bree and a little jealous she didn't even talk to me about this. "She never told me she switched."

"She would have told you, eventually. She has her reasons, ask her," he encourages. I look at him knowing with everything in me, he really is good for her and I'm honestly completely okay with that.

"She talks to Aubrey about you," I reveal. With his look of confusion, I add, "My sister." He nods his head in understanding. "Bree and I were talking about bringing you to meet her. She really wants to introduce you. I think Aub will be ready soon if she isn't already."

"I'd like that," he admits and it feels almost like a truce between us. Even with our respite, I swear I hear him sigh with relief when we hear the girls' footsteps coming down the stairs.

Chapter 21

Blake

We go back to Bree's and all help with making a simple dinner. Bree throws a salad together and Christian grills some burgers and hot dogs. Liz and I grab the potato salad, coleslaw, drinks and condiments from the fridge along with a couple bags of chips and bring everything to the table with paper plates and plastic forks. After a day on the lake, we're all starving and eat with barely a word spoken between us.

The rest of the night we relax and hang out. We spend a lot of time joking around and just talking. For one of the first times since I've known Christian, whom I called dickhead for so long, I don't feel like punching him. I don't even mind being around him. I can't help but believe at least part of the reason is because of her. I reach for Liz's hand and entwine her fingers with mine, giving her a squeeze. She smiles and my breath catches as her eyes sparkle back at me.

I like hanging out with my friends, but I'm ready to wrap Liz in my arms and keep her all to myself, at least for the night. I open my mouth to say we should call it a night when Christian gives me a serious look, "Blake, there's something I forgot to mention earlier, can I talk to you for a minute?"

I glance towards Bree and she looks absolutely giddy, so there's no way I can say no. I figure this must be what he looked like he wanted to say earlier, but never did. I sigh, standing and reluctantly letting go of Liz's hand. I follow

Christian to the back porch and we step outside. He hands me a beer from the cooler before grabbing one for himself. He immediately pops the top and takes a huge gulp. He leans his elbows on the rails, looking out at the lake while I take a sip of my beer, waiting for him to speak.

"I've been back and forth on whether or not I should say anything to you at all, but to Bree, you're her family and I'm trying to respect that here," he admits. He takes another sip of his beer while I study him, trying to figure out what the hell he has to say to me. Finally, he spits out, "I'm going to ask Bree to marry me," before glancing at me over his shoulder to watch my reaction. "I'm not exactly sure when yet, but it will be sometime between now and Christmas. I already have the ring. I just have to figure out the right time to ask." I stand there speechless and he continues, "I talked to her dad last time he was back from London, but with everything that's happened," he pauses and I watch the pain pass over his expression, knowing exactly what he's thinking about. I watch his jaw tense and he visibly swallow before saying, "If it wasn't for you, she may not be here with me. I thought you should know out of respect. She considers you her family and I know she would want it this way." He looks at me, his eyes full of emotion, "I love her, man and I will do right by her."

I nod in response gripping my beer so tight my knuckles begin turning white. I know I need to say something, but I'm struggling to open my mouth. I tip my beer towards my lips and gulp the rest of it down before dropping it in the recycle can next to the door. Then, I take a deep breath and look Christian in the eye, "Congratulations, you're a lucky man." He nods in agreement still watching me closely. "And if you ever fucking hurt her, I will come for you," I threaten meaning every word. He again nods his acceptance before he dumps the rest of his nearly full beer over the side into the dirt then tosses the empty in the bin. He steps past me and walks back inside.

I need to get my head on straight before doing the same. I grab another beer, popping it open and downing it immediately. I toss the empty and reach for yet another beer collapsing onto one of the Adirondack chairs. I'm staring out at the lake when Bree pokes her head out. "Christian and I are going to sleep, I wanted to say goodnight." I open my mouth to answer her when she arches her eyebrows in surprise and asks, "Are you drinking?"

"Only a couple beers, just enjoying the lake while we still can," I answer not looking at her. I can tell she wants to say more, so I try to cut her off before it starts. "Goodnight, Bree," I mumble, hoping she won't push it right now and just walk away.

She stares at me for another minute before she finally answers, "Goodnight," and shuts the door.

I quickly finish my beer and grab another when the door opens again and Liz steps out, looking at me apprehensively. I just raise my eyebrows and bring the beer to my lips for a drink. "Everything okay?" she prods hesitantly, I feel almost guilty for being pissed, but it doesn't matter. I nod my head and take another drink. "Want some company?"

"Be my guest," I answer automatically gesturing towards the chair next to me.

She sits down cautiously and watches me for a few minutes before speaking again, "Did something happen with you and Christian? I thought you usually didn't drink that much," she asks eyeing the empty bottles in the clear bin next to me. I can't help but laugh bitterly shaking my head. "What were you guys talking about?" she pushes gently.

"You want to know?" I snap a little smugly. She presses her lips together in a thin line nodding uncertainly.

"He wanted to inform me he's going to propose to Bree sometime between now and Christmas. He thought I should know since she considers me family and he's trying to respect that after everything we've all been through," I answer her bitterly.

Liz's eyes begin welling slightly and I know it's because of the way I'm talking to her right now, but I don't know if I can stop. I need to lighten up, but the shit going through my head right now is making it hard to calm the fuck down. "Isn't that a good thing?" she asks shakily.

I look down at her and spit out, "You'd think, wouldn't you?" Then, I toss another empty towards the bin and I see Liz cringe as it bangs into the others. I try to explain to her what I'm thinking, "I just don't think she's ready for this. I think it's too soon."

"Shouldn't that be for them to decide? And how long is too soon to you? How long have they been together?" she challenges, obviously hurt.

But instead of comforting her like I know I should, I answer her question. "I don't know. They met the summer before our senior year of high school. They broke up that fall, then got back together last fall but they broke up briefly again before finally staying together."

"Why did they break up so much?" she questions and I clench my jaw not saying a word. "Then, what do you mean, too soon since what?" she prods biting her cheek so hard I think she might draw blood.

I shake my head in frustration. "I can't tell you that. It's not my story to tell."

"Well obviously it has something to do with you since it gets you so worked up!" She tries to reach for me and I shrug her away. I notice her wince with my rejection. It's not about her, but she doesn't know that. I try getting my

177

head back on straight. I don't want to hurt Liz, just because I'm stressed.

"It's Bree's story to tell. I may have been there and yes, it affected me a whole hell of a lot, but it is NOT something I can talk to you about," I declare with my anger still shining through, even though it's not at her.

I watch a tear escape as she jumps up. I reach for her to explain, knowing I'm doing a shitty job so far. I don't want her to get the wrong idea. "It's just she had a lot happen this year and I don't think I have any right to tell anyone about it. I don't want her making a huge life decision based on other shit." She shakes her head, backing away from me. She steps inside quickly, backing away from my anger and my stupidity. How else am I supposed to explain it to her?

I groan, knowing I fucked up, but sometimes I can't explain the emotions that come with everything that has happened with Bree. The extreme anxiety that clutches at my chest because I'm terrified I'll find her lying on the floor unconscious again if everything goes bad with Christian. The visions I have of seeing her unconscious and not sure if I'll be able to help her haunt me. After everything she's been through, I don't think she could handle losing him now. She's finally at a place where she believes she has it all, so I'm afraid he's jumping in too fast. If they get engaged and then it doesn't work out, she would be wrecked! But how the fuck do I explain that to Liz without betraying Bree? How do I make her understand it has nothing to do with the way I feel about her? I'm doing my best to tell her what I can.

She's just gotta' fucking trust me!

Eventually I sigh and step inside where everything is already dark. A small light above the stove in the kitchen is illuminated so I can find my way. I walk down the hallway slowly and hesitantly step into the guest room with Liz, quietly clicking the door shut behind me.

178

I feel completely helpless when I look at her shaking form, knowing she's crying because of me. I sigh and run my hand through my hair in frustration before I kick off my shoes. I step up to the bed and lower myself gently behind her. "Liz?" I place my hand on her back and begin rubbing in long slow circles to try to calm her down.

It takes about fifteen minutes before her body isn't really shaking anymore. I try nudging her to roll towards me. "Can you look at me? Please? I just want to talk." She doesn't answer. "I promise you, it's not what you're thinking," I plead. She finally slowly rolls over and peers at me, "I'm just worried about her, that's all. I'm worried this is going too fast for her. What if something happens?"

"She's a grown-up," she cries. I look at the ceiling in frustration, knowing I'll never be able to explain this without the whole truth. "Are you in love with her?" she asks tearfully.

I shake my head, but the tortured look in her eyes lets me know my non-verbal no is not enough of an answer. "No!" I answer with the confidence I wouldn't have been able to give even a few weeks ago. Unfortunately, I don't think she really believes me anyway. I have no idea how to get her to understand.

"Why don't we go to sleep and we can talk on the way home tomorrow?" she suggests.

"That's what you want?" I ask wondering if I should really let this go right now or if I should try harder to explain.

She nods her head, "Yeah, that's what I want," she squeaks out. She closes her eyes, making another tear fall and I wipe it away with my thumb. I feel so completely defeated and I have no idea how to change any of it without betraying Bree. I want to wipe away her sadness, but I was the one who caused it this time and I fucking hate myself for it! I lean in giving her a light kiss on her lips. She lets out a small whimper and I barely contain a responding moan.

I sigh with her taste of sadness. "You taste salty," I whisper trying to turn the mood around.

"And you taste like stale beer," she grumbles scrunching up her nose in distaste.

"Sorry," I apologize. "I'll go brush my teeth and come right back," I inform her and quickly do just that. When I return, she's facing away, so I figure she won't mind if I change right here. I don't want to leave her for too long. I kick off my jeans and throw on my pajama pants. I swiftly pull off my t-shirt and toss it on the floor before climbing back in bed next to Liz to curl up behind her. I pull her into my chest, incredibly grateful when she lets me, making me breathe a sigh of relief. I kiss her cheek tenderly, holding her tight, attempting to wish the tension between us away. "Goodnight, Liz," I whisper in her ear, enjoying the goose bumps appearing on her neck, wanting to kiss them all away.

"Goodnight, Blake," she answers barely audible. I grimace with her reaction and hold her even tighter. I watch her chest rise and fall with her breaths until they slow into the steady rhythm of sleep. I lightly brush my lips against her cheek again and breathe her in as I close my eyes hoping everything will turn out just fine. I don't want to lose her now that I finally found her.

Chapter 22

Elizabeth

The drive home remains pretty quiet, besides Blake constantly flipping through the radio from Carrie Underwood to Gavin DeGraw to One Republic back to Sam Hunt. "Leave this on," Bree requests. "You okay Blake?" she prods looking concerned.

Bree is riding back with us because Christian has to stay and work this week and she wanted to take the trip down to Boston with us. I guess she wants to see Blake's sister again and also told him she'd be there for him with his family drama. We're going back to Portland for tonight and we're all supposed to leave tomorrow morning.

Blake says he wants me to come meet his family, but I don't know if it's the right thing to do, especially after last night. He doesn't answer Bree, so she turns to me attempting to start a conversation again. "Do you see your family a lot?" I nod my head. "Do your brothers live close by?" I nod my head again. "What about work? Do you like your job?" she asks trying again.

I shake my head no, shrugging my shoulders before I sigh. "I'm sorry Bree. I guess I'm just tired from the weekend." I don't miss the look she gives Blake though, which only encourages my destructive thoughts. They say they're only friends, but there's obviously something more. I mean, what decent girl has overnights with a guy who is just a friend? And Bree seems decent. And what guy gets so pissed off when he finds out his best friend will be engaged soon, that he starts pounding beers and won't really tell his girlfriend anything? And why do I feel like a third wheel sometimes with these two when Christian isn't with Bree, like right now? Blake and Bree obviously have some kind of connection, but he won't tell me anything, so how the hell am I supposed to trust him? He knows about my past too! He knows I need him to give me something.

"Liz," Bree taps me on my shoulder shaking me out of my internal rant. "I'm really glad you came up with Blake. I had a lot of fun with you," she declares. She smiles genuinely and I can't help but smile back. It's so hard not to like this girl. She's incredibly nice and generous.

"Thanks for having me. I had fun too," I answer timidly.

"I'll see you tomorrow?" she prompts.

"Um, I'm not sure. I may have to cover a shift at the café," I stammer, "I got a text." I can feel Blake staring at me now. I wave quickly at Bree and look down at my hands fidgeting in my lap.

"Oh, ok…Bye," she falters looking confused. Then, Blake steps out of his jeep to give her a hug and wave goodbye. The wave of jealousy burns right through my insides, not able to stop it.

He climbs back in his jeep and I can feel the tension radiating off him before he asks stiffly, "A shift at the café? Someone else can't cover it?"

"I…I don't know," I stutter, but he interrupts me.

"You know what?" he snaps with frustration. "This obviously isn't as important to you as it is to me. I'm going to have a stressful enough few days trying to deal with everything with my dad and if you don't want to be there, I don't want you there either. And my sister definitely doesn't need any tension around her! Maybe it's not the right time for you to meet her. I thought we were past all this bullshit, I thought you could trust me, but I guess I thought wrong," he states glaring at me.

He starts up his jeep and backs out, driving in silence. I don't even try to defend myself as I attempt to hold the tears at bay until he stops in front of my apartment. When we pull up, I make an effort of apologizing to him, but I don't even know how to explain myself right now without sounding like a jealous fool. "Blake, I'm sorry. I just...I'm sorry," I rasp out desperately. He only nods in response, still holding his jaw tight. "I really did have fun this weekend." He gives me a stiff smile. "Thank you," I mumble even quieter.

He sighs. "I really am glad you came Liz." He looks at me then closes his eyes as if in pain before opening them again. "I'll call you as soon as I get back. I'm not sure if it will be Thursday or Friday. I guess it depends how everything goes with my parents. But I know Bree will want to get back up to the lake by the weekend. Call me if you need anything." He looks towards my front door and then back to me. I nod robotically and try to force a smile, but it probably looks deranged with the pain I'm fighting inside my chest.

I finally turn and reach for the door handle, stepping out of his jeep. I quickly grab my duffel and give it a tug as I stumble out of the car and run towards the door. Right before I turn the doorknob, I feel his hand on my shoulder spinning me around making me suck in a sharp breath. He wraps his arms around me, making me feel safe and warm and most of all for a moment I feel happy again. I know I can trust him, what is wrong with me? He pulls away and gives me a kiss on my forehead, making it feel like a goodbye, instead of a see you later. He's about to turn to go, but I have to stop him. I can't let him go like this. "Blake, wait. I'm sorry. I don't know why I'm so nervous about all this," I claim, which isn't exactly true and we both know it.

He nods his head and mumbles, "I know." He heaves a sigh, hugging me again. "I know. And I get why you're so nervous. Maybe that's why I'm still here. But I'm asking again, please just trust me," he whispers into my hair. I can feel the pain radiating off him making me believe I do. "Maybe come with me next time?" he prods. I nod my head, realizing he still isn't ready for me to meet his family, especially his sister after my behavior. I don't blame him. This time he leans down and gently kisses my lips. He pulls away and runs back to his jeep before taking off with a wave.

I slump into my front door and push it open with a groan. "I'm so stupid!" I scream.

"Oh boy," I hear Sara answer. "What happened?" she asks with concern peering over the couch. I drag myself away from the door and toss my bag towards my room. I flop down on the couch next to Sara and groan. She grabs the remote and flips the TV off while staring at me with her eyebrows raised and waits for me to start talking.

I huff, "I keep overreacting about Bree. Her and her boyfriend, Christian are all over each other. It's obvious she's crazy about him."

She narrows her eyes at me. "What do you mean by overreacting? What did you do?" she asks cautiously.

"I...I...I don't know," I stammer. I guess you could say I keep acting like the jealous girlfriend whenever their history comes up or their friendship for that matter."

"I'm not surprised after Kris, but not everyone is him," she reiterates attempting to reassure me.

I put my face in my hands with an exasperated groan, "That's what Blake keeps telling me."

"You told him about Kris and Tori?" she questions shocked. I nod my head, keeping my face in my hands before finally peeking through my fingers to see a small smile curving her lips. "That must mean you really like this guy!"

I drop my hands and roll my eyes. "It's not going to matter if I don't figure it out. You know how I was supposed to go to Boston with him tomorrow?"

"What do you mean supposed to?" she prompts narrowing her eyes at me.

"Well," I squeak out, "I kinda' freaked on the way home." She looks at me funny and I blurt out the whole story as fast as I can, "Christian told Blake he was going to propose to Bree sometime between now and Christmas when the time is right. He wanted to tell Blake since Bree considers him family. Then when we went to sleep, Blake was really pissed about the whole thing. He says it's just because he's worried it's too soon with everything they've been through, but I don't even know what it is they went through or even if he's giving me the real reason. They supposedly broke up a couple times and I don't know, but sometimes I wonder if Blake was the reason they broke up. Christian doesn't seem to love them hanging out either. He just seems to deal with it for her. Then he also told me Bree was the only other girl he ever had sleepovers with." I gasp for air at the end of my explanation.

"You slept with him?" she interrupts with apparent shock.

I immediately shake my head, "No, no, no! Just slept, like actual sleeping with a little kissing and cuddling. He said with Bree it was always only ever as a friend, but still," I whine. "Who has sleepovers with friends that are guys in high school or college and doesn't do anything? And why did they have them anyway? Then she seems to know everything about him, things I don't know. She is even close to his sister who it seems he doesn't bring a lot of people to meet, but she goes to see her all the time. I know we haven't been dating long, but they have history, and it just reminds me of Kris and Tori's history only stronger. Even if he's telling the truth, they are so close it hurts! I think I'm going crazy," I confess. Sighing, I slouch further into the couch.

"You're not going crazy Liz. I get it, especially..." she trails off. "Have you ever asked him what did happen between them?"

I shrug. "He just says most of it's not his story to tell. I know she's been there for him with his family stuff, but...he keeps saying I have to learn to trust him. It's just so hard when all these doubts start crashing around in my head," I complain.

She pats my arm sympathetically. "Well, if you want it to work with him, that's exactly what you're going to have to do," she pauses. "Or you could try talking to Bree." I can't help but look at her like she's crazy. "Ok, ok, sorry I suggested it."

I jump in to explain, not wanting her to get the wrong idea. "She's actually really nice and everything, it's just what would I say?"

"What's up with you and my boyfriend?" she recommends with a smirk.

I shake my head, "I would feel horrible saying that! We've only been dating a couple months and that sounds like I'm accusing her of something."

Sara gives me a look. "Yeah, you've been dating a couple months. You should be comfortable enough with her to talk to her since she's his best friend or comfortable with your relationship with Blake that you trust him and it doesn't matter. You have to let the past be in the past."

I can't think about it anymore right now, so I try changing the subject, "Anyway...what's going on with you?"

Sara looks away from me and starts mumbling, "Um, nothing really."

"What's up Sara?" I ask already able to tell she's hiding something.

She releases a defeated sigh, "I just...it's not really about me. It's something else about you." My stomach twists in knots waiting for her to go on. "Kris left a message on our answering machine. I guess he figured you weren't listening to the ones on your cell phone. He's coming back from his cousins' house early and wants to talk to you. He said he'd be back this weekend."

I groan in frustration, "This is so not what I need!"

"Maybe you need some closure with him. It has been over a year. Maybe it will help with Blake," she suggests.

"It's not just about him anyway! I don't need any closure. It's been over since the night he ruined everything!" I snap at her.

She raises her eyebrows and I immediately realize my reaction did the opposite of helping my case. "Yeah, you're not bitter at all and it's definitely not affecting your relationship with Blake. Not even a little bit. That's why he's leaving for Boston tomorrow with Bree and without you," she states sarcastically. "Why did you tell him you couldn't go anyway?"

I scrunch up my nose in disgust with her comments and with myself, "I said I might have to cover someone at the café."

"Might?" she screeches shaking her head. "Are you fucking kidding me? I'd be pissed too! I think you need to talk to Kris. You need to get over the whole mess with him."

I sigh, feeling overwhelmed. "I'll think about it," I concede.

She smiles, "That's all I'm asking. I just want you to be happy you know."

"I know. I just hope I didn't ruin everything with Blake because of my insecurity. I think I finally met a really good guy," I admit. "So did you talk to the guy from your accounting class?" I ask needing to change the subject off me for now. Her smile practically explodes on her face when I ask. I breathe a sigh of relief, knowing the subject is closed for now.

I have to figure out what to do about Kris, but the thought of seeing him or talking to him about anything makes my stomach turn. I don't know if I can handle it. Every time I see his face in my head, I see Tori straddling his lap and I feel the betrayal all over again. It makes me so afraid Blake would do the same and choose Bree over me. He's always trying to protect her, just like Kris did with Tori.

I send Blake a quick text before I go to sleep, "I'm sorry. Thank you again for a great weekend. Drive safe tomorrow!"

His reply pops up, simple, "Thanks."

My stomach flips with fear at his cold response. I really hope I haven't ruined everything with my stupidity. I have to figure out a way to get my shit together and fix this when he gets back.

Chapter 23

Blake

"So, Liz had to work huh?" Bree asks and I continue to stare out the front windshield without answering. "How are things going with you guys?" she tries again and I clench my jaw still not answering. "Blake," she insists, "tell me what's going on! Don't clam up on me!"

My lips curve slightly watching her squirm and she smacks me on the arm. "Ow, watch it I'm driving." I smirk, "and clam up? I haven't heard that since I was like ten." I know she's rolling her eyes at me, but I have to do something to lighten the mood or I'm going to lose my fucking mind. I take a deep breath and stretch my fingers on the steering wheel, while Bree remains quiet. I know she's waiting for me to speak.

After a few minutes I finally admit, "She's having a hard time with our relationship." I glance over at Bree to see her reaction and she's giving me a questioning look. "I mean my relationship with you Bree, like every other girl I try to date." She nods her head in understanding. "I don't really know how to explain anything to her without…" I trail off.

"I understand. Christian was there for a lot of it and he knows most of what he wasn't there for, but sometimes he still has a hard time with it, even though he loves you." I can't help but give her a look like she's lost her damn mind. She hurries to defend him, "He does love you, Blake. He's extremely grateful for everything you've done for me. He's just…"

"You don't have to explain, I get it," I claim. Sighing, I clench my jaw. "I really like her Bree," I admit quietly.

"Wow, I've never heard you say that about a girl before," she states and then she blushes deeply looking away. Yeah, at least not one that wasn't you I think to myself.

"Anyway, she has some trust issues because of a past boyfriend, so she's having trouble with how close we are. She says she likes you. She says she trusts me, but it's pretty fucking obvious she's still fighting with her memories on this. I have no idea what I'm supposed to do," I admit.

Bree stays quiet for a minute before whispering in a shaky voice, "You can tell her."

I gulp down the lump in my throat. "I don't feel like I can do that, even with your permission. It's not my story to tell, Bree."

She stares out the window for a few more minutes watching the highway fly by before asking, "Is it okay if I talk to her?"

"You would do that?" I prod, mildly shocked.

She nods, "Of course I would. I can tell she really means a lot to you, and I'd do anything for you Blake," she admits gently touching my arm. Her soft gesture feels like a sister's comforting touch causing me to gulp down another breath at that realization. "I do understand where she's coming from too. From everything Christian has said and how you two are around each other."

"What do you mean by that?" I probe with only mild curiosity.

"Oh, nothing," she laughs.

I roll my eyes at her and she laughs harder. I tilt my head to one side and then the other trying to relieve some of the tension that has built up in my shoulders. "Right now, I need to try not to stress about Liz though. I need to concentrate on my dad's shit. I still can't believe I have another sister."

I feel Bree's stare out of the corner of my eye. After a few minutes she finally states, "You know it's okay to be afraid." I just raise my eyebrows, not even daring to look at her. I know she rolls her eyes before she speaks, "Did you ever want a brother to play with when you were little?" She doesn't wait for me to answer before she continues, "I always wanted a little sister. Someone I could boss around. Someone to play with that would like the same things as me. I know you and Aubrey had each other and it's different from being an only child like me, but it seems to me, a lot of girls want a little sister when they're younger. I think Aubrey is excited at the idea of having a little sister, someone she can play with. She just doesn't want to hurt your feelings because she loves you so much. She's worried about what you think and how you feel."

I take a deep breath trying to process her words. Before I know it, we're pulling up next to the house Bree grew up in. I put the jeep in park and before she steps out of the car I reach for her hand and give it a quick squeeze in appreciation. "Thank you, Bree."

She smiles and gives my hand a gentle squeeze back. "Why don't you go talk to your parents and then come back here to pick me up. I should have everything done here by then and we can grab some dinner." I nod in agreement and she slams the door shut behind her. She gives me a quick wave yelling, "Good luck!" before I pull away making my way to my parents' house on the other side of the park.

I pull up into my driveway and mumble, "I need to just get this over with." I step out of my jeep and stride up to the front door. "Mom, Dad," I call, "I'm home."

"Blake, we're in the kitchen," I hear my mom yell back. I walk down the hall to the back of the house and into

191

the kitchen. My mom puts down the spatula with whatever she's making and steps around the counter wrapping her arms around me in a tight hug. "I've missed you so much lately! You can't go that long without coming home."

I feel a huge wave of guilt consume me. I apologize to her immediately, "I'm sorry, Mom. I just...I got really busy with work and I've been spending a lot of time with my girlfriend, Liz," I partially explain. I can't tell her I've been avoiding them because of my dad and my new sister, although I'm sure she knows that's part of the reason.

She drops her arms from around me and interrupts me in shock, "Girlfriend? What do you mean girlfriend? You've never mentioned anyone named Liz," she accuses.

I feel my face flush and my mouth hangs open in surprise. "Mom, I've mentioned her before on the phone. I've been dating her for a couple months now. I was even going to bring her to meet you this weekend, but she had to work at the last minute."

"What about Bree?" my father asks and I turn towards the sound of his voice in disgust.

"Bree is just a friend. She's been with her boyfriend, Christian for a fucking long time!" I yell, trying to keep my anger in check.

"Don't you swear in front of your mother!" he admonishes me, but I ignore him.

"If you had stuck around and actually listened to me once in a while you would know that and you would know about Liz! I know denial is common around here and all but leave me and my life out of your sick game," I retort bitterly with a clear threat in my voice.

My mom clears her throat and my eyes snap back to her. Guilt begins eating away at me again when I look in her watery eyes. "I'm sorry, Mom. I have been able to drive down every week to see Aub though," I try changing the subject to my sister to get rid of some of the tension in the room. "She seems like she's doing really well."

"But you couldn't take five minutes to see your mother?" she questions making me flinch. She notices my reaction and sighs. "She does, doesn't she?" she concedes. She smiles and I grin with relief back at her.

"I've been telling her about her sister," my dad begins. "She seems to be getting excited to meet her, but she doesn't want to do it without you."

I draw in a deep breath and run my hand through my hair. I close my eyes and release my breath before finally looking over at my father. "That's why I'm here. I'm ready to hear more about her and meet her when it works for everyone. I want to be there when she meets Aub." I pause and look directly in my father's eyes emphasizing, "I need you to make sure Aubrey knows no one will ever replace her!"

My dad watches me and nods his head in one quick, definite nod of acceptance. He takes a step closer to me and quietly states, "I'm glad she has you." I nod in affirmation, my jaw clenched not knowing how to respond to him.

"I'm making a blueberry pie for you to bring up to Aubrey and the nurses tomorrow," my mom's voice interrupts our tense conversation.

My dad shakes his head as if pulling himself out of his thoughts. "I can pick her up from her mom's and bring her tomorrow after you talk to Aubrey if that's okay."

"How about I talk to Aub and if she's ready tomorrow I'll call and let you know. In the meantime, maybe you can tell me a little more about her?" I request. A small smile appears on my dad's face, looking more like relief than anything.

I grab a bottle of water from the refrigerator and sit down with my mom and dad at the kitchen table. He pulls a picture out of his wallet and hands it to me. "That's her. Her name is Kari and she's five years old." My heart jumps up to my throat when I take in the picture. She looks just like Aubrey did at that age. Innocent smile, brown eyes, but her hair is black as opposed to Aubrey's light blonde hair. I can't swallow down the lump in my throat as I listen to both of my parents talk about her. Even my mom's face lights up with the mention of this little girl. I didn't realize my mom had been getting to know her too. The guilt of not being here, of not protecting my mom, of not protecting Aubrey is all getting to me as I listen to them tell me about her.

After listening to them talk for a while, I finally get my voice back and ask cautiously, "Aubrey may be ready to meet her, but is she ready to meet Aubrey?"

They know what I'm asking. My parents exchange a hurried look and their eyes quickly focus back on me. "We've all talked to Kari about both of you."

"I don't give a shit about me! I need to know she won't upset Aubrey," I demand.

"Blake, Kari is a very gentle little girl. She would never want to hurt someone's feelings. She's very excited to have a big brother and sister." I laugh in disbelief, but my dad continues before I can say anything. "I've talked to her about Aubrey, and I believe she understands the best she can until she actually meets her. She'll be fine."

"How do you know?" I plead.

"She's going to meet Aubrey whether you're ready for it or not Blake. You can be a part of it, which is what your mom, your sister and I all want, or you can stay out of it, but it's going to happen. I'm done waiting," my dad states with no room for argument.

I'm seething inside. My jaw clenches tightly with my dad's words. All I care about is protecting Aubrey and I don't know if I will be able to under these circumstances. But I

194

will be there for it. There's no way in hell they'll stop me. I try to speak without tension layering my voice, as I grit out, "I will be with Aubrey when she meets Kari. I wouldn't have it any other way. Can I meet her first?" I ask hoping to get the best handle of the situation I can.

"Your mom and I were going to meet her and her mom tonight for dinner. Why don't you come along?" my dad suggests.

"I'm picking up Bree for dinner, maybe we can come meet you for ice cream after." I know I can invite Bree or even cancel, but I need someone to talk to and a little bit of extra time to prepare myself before I meet her.

"That will work," my dad agrees. My mom smiles encouragingly at me and gives my hand a squeeze, telling me I'm doing the right thing.

I stand up, announcing, "I'm going to head over to her house now to pick her up. We'll meet you around seven at The Ice Cream Shoppe."

My mom stands up giving me another hug, squeezing hard. "I've really missed you, Blake."

"I know Mom, I'm sorry," I apologize again hugging her back briefly before letting my arms drop. "It won't happen again. I love you, Mom," I proclaim before turning with barely a nod to my dad and walking out the front door.

I'm at Bree's house in less than five minutes. I honk the horn and stare out my windshield, waiting until she comes out. I guess I zone out a little thinking about everything when I jump to the sound of her opening the door. "Sorry to keep you waiting so long. I was just trying to finish going through the mail for my dad."

I shrug and mumble, "No big deal."

She buckles her seatbelt and I drive into town, parking in front of a place called 'Hole in the Wall Pizza'. We walk inside and I immediately order us pizza and drinks before we sit down. "So," she breaks the silence, "How'd it go?"

I sigh and then blurt everything out at once. "You and I are going to meet up with my parents after dinner to meet my little sister Kari for ice cream. She's five years old. Then, tomorrow we'll go see Aubrey and if it seems okay, my dad will bring Kari in to meet her while we are there."

She stays silent for a few minutes, probably trying to assess my reaction to all of this. "I think this is a good thing, Blake. Maybe you should call Liz and tell her. She was supposed to be here with you. I don't want her to think…"

"Stop," I interrupt, knowing where she's headed. "She backed out of coming. I'll let her know what's going on, but if she doesn't trust me, there's nothing I can do."

"Blake," she hesitates.

"Bree, I can't go there right now. I really have to concentrate on Aubrey at the moment." She nods and for the rest of dinner she changes the conversation to plans her and Christian have with his family for Labor Day weekend in a week and a half.

It feels like no time has passed, but we're already nervously waiting at a large corner booth in The Ice Cream Shoppe. My knees are bouncing continuously and I'm mindlessly drumming my hands on the table. Bree sits quietly across from me, knowing I won't hear anything she's saying to me at this point. The front door opens and I freeze. I stare with wide eyes as a little dark-haired girl looking so much like Aubrey skips inside with a huge smile on her face, followed by a woman I don't know and then my parents. I stand on shaky legs as my dad points over to me and her brown eyes follow his finger and land on me. Her eyes light up even more and I release the breath I didn't know I was holding as my heart melts a little at her bright smile.

"Are you my brother?" Kari asks in an adorable high-pitched voice.

I nod my head, swallowing the lump in my throat. "Yeah, I'm Blake." She wraps her arms around my legs and I look up at the ceiling, trying to blink away the unexpected tears.

"What kind of ice cream are you getting? I like the one with the Oreo cookies in it," she announces joyfully tugging on my sleeve.

I look down at her and know I'm done for. None of this is her fault. This beautiful innocent little girl is my sister. I nod my head and clear my throat barely squeaking out an answer, "That's one of my favorites too." She reaches for my hand and starts pulling me towards the counter.

When we reach the register, she tells the guy what she wants and I do the same. She then looks at me with a huge smile so full of trust and love, yet she just met me. I take another deep breath trying to smile back. At this point I know I'm going to do everything I can to protect her, just like I do Aubrey. "Would you like to meet your sister tomorrow?" I ask while we wait.

She nods enthusiastically, "Yeah, I can't wait to meet her! Dad says she likes to play with dolls like me. It will be so much fun to play together!" Her excitement and innocence get to me, making my chest ache. I know in that moment everything will work out with Aubrey and her, everything will be fine.

I laugh lightly, proclaiming, "She'll like that a lot. That's the one thing she has trouble convincing me to play with her." She smiles and reaches for her ice cream. "I'll play other things with you two though and I'm sure if you twist my arm a little bit, I might even play dolls with you," I admit. We walk over to sit at a large table while everyone else places their orders and I let my dad pay for our desserts, so I

197

can spend the time getting to know a little more about my
new little sister.

Chapter 24

Blake

After ice cream, I drop Bree off and go back to my parents' house. I grab an old baseball out of the basket on the floor of my closet and collapse onto my bed. I stare up at the ceiling, tossing and catching the ball mindlessly. I can't stop thinking about how much alike Aubrey and Kari are. It's not just in their looks, but also in their likes and dislikes. I think about how Aubrey's interests haven't changed much, but Kari's will eventually change. My emotions are flying from love, to guilt to fear and I have no idea how to handle this. I want to do what's right for them, not for my dad, not for me, but for them. The worst part of it all is I don't have a clue if I even know what the right thing might be. Everything with my family keeps running through my head. I feel the need to talk to someone before I lose my mind. I pick up my phone and instinctively call Liz.

"Hi," she answers sounding surprised.

"Hey," I mumble closing my eyes as a feeling of relief washes over me with the first sound of her voice.

"I...I didn't know if you'd call. I didn't know if I should call," she stammers and I instantly realize she's afraid I'm still mad at her.

"I'm sorry Liz, I didn't mean to make you worry," I try to apologize.

"Why are you apologizing? I'm the one who should be saying I'm sorry. And I am sorry Blake, about everything. I should have come with you. I want you to know I trust you. I trust you more than I've ever trusted any guy," she proclaims and I believe her.

"Please don't apologize. You told me about your past and I should really be more understanding. I'm trying here. It's just I need your trust to be in this relationship and I want this relationship, Liz. I really like you," I admit to her.

"I really like you too, Blake," she confesses her voice cracking, "and I promise I'm trying to show you I trust you. Sometimes I just fail miserably," she jokes trying to lighten the mood. She succeeds in making me chuckle. I hear her breathe a sigh of relief before attempting to change the subject. "So, how's everything going with your family?"

"I don't know, I'm here and I'm trying." I take a deep breath and make an effort to let her inside my head. "I met Kari today, that's my new five-year-old sister." She gasps and I continue, "She's pretty amazing. She looks just like Aubrey did when she was five, except she has dark hair like her mom."

I sit on the phone with Liz for hours, telling her about Kari about Aubrey before and after the accident and how close my family used to be. "You know my dad used to be there for everything. He would play outside with Aub and I all the time. He never missed any of Aubrey's soccer games or a single one of my baseball games. Then, one day he's just gone," I attempt to explain. "But after everything that Aub has been through I feel so guilty for letting Kari in. I know this isn't her fault either, but it's always been just Aub and me," I groan in frustration. "I just want what's best for Aubrey and now for Kari, too," I add, guilt weighing on me.

"You have no reason to feel guilty Blake. None of this is your fault. You care so much for all of them. It's obvious you have so much love to give. You definitely have enough to share with both of your sisters." She pauses before adding, "I may not know your sister, but from what you've told me, I don't think she would ever want you to push Kari away. Like you said, she's innocent in all this too."

"She is and that's why I have to do what I can to protect her from our mess of a family. I know I was only a kid when the accident happened, but I always wonder if I could have done more." Liz's voice cracks through the phone like she's about to respond, but I interrupt to try to explain where I'm going with this. "Realistically I know I couldn't have, but that doesn't stop someone from questioning it. I would have done anything to protect her."

I close my eyes to try to squeeze out my visions of the accident. "I guess," my voice cracks with emotion, "that's why I always try so hard to protect the people I love, like my mom, both of my sisters now and even my close friends like Matt and Bree. I don't want there to ever be any doubt in my mind that I could have done more to help them or protect them and I don't want anything bad to ever happen to the people I love again," I emphasize. "I'm realistic, but I don't think I could take it!" I run my hand over my face and through my hair, dropping it above my head in exhaustion.

After a beat of silence, she murmurs quietly, "They are all really lucky to have you in their life, Blake."

"You have me, too, Liz. If you need me, you just have to tell me." The line becomes really quiet, "Liz?" I prod, questioning if she's still there.

"Yeah, I'm here," she barely chokes out and I can't help but hope her emotional response means she's getting it.

"You know I haven't done this in years," I state trying to lighten the mood after my spilling my guts to her.

"What?" she prompts sounding confused.

"Sit on the phone with a girl I like and talk for hours." I listen to the sweet sound of her giggling and smile to myself. "It almost feels like I'm in high school." She laughs again. "Except, I don't ever remember being this crazy about a girl in high school," I add and hear her breath catch through the phone. "Thank you."

"What are you thanking me for?" she prods sounding confused with a burst of laughter.

"For listening," I admit. "I feel like such a girl, but I fucking needed this," I tease.

"Hey," she snaps laughing harder. "I'm happy I'm the one you called," she concedes before I hear what I think is a muffled yawn.

"It sounds like it's time for me to let you go," I proclaim glancing at the clock reading 2:18 AM.

"I'm okay," she whispers sounding like she's fighting another yawn.

I laugh. "Why don't you get some sleep, Liz. I'll call you tomorrow after I go see my sister. Hopefully I'll make it back tomorrow night and come see you right after I drop Bree off."

"Ok," she agrees happily. "I'm looking forward to it."

"Good night, Liz," I murmur.

"Good night, Blake. And Blake? Everything is going to go great tomorrow; I know it will." I nod my head like she can see me and hang up my phone feeling as if a weight has been lifted off my shoulders. The only one who has ever helped me through my shit in the past has been Bree, but even with her here, Liz is the one I wanted to talk to tonight. I needed to hear her voice. I needed her to be the one to know me, which if I'm being honest with myself makes me a little crazy. With Liz's history and trust issues, I feel like I'm setting myself up for another failed relationship, but fuck me, I really want it to work.

Chapter 25

Blake

Just after dinner, Bree and I climb into my jeep about to head back to Maine. I sit behind the wheel for a minute and release a relieved sigh, dropping my head back to the headrest. "See, everything went fabulous Blake. I knew it would!" Bree exclaims.

"Yeah, it really did, Bree. Aubrey was fucking ecstatic! She absolutely adores Kari." I smile thinking of them playing happily together today. "Kari was so good to her too. She didn't treat her any different. I think she even looked at her with awe."

"She did. I think it's called the awe of meeting your sister for the first time," she claims. She smiles and I try to swallow down the emotion clogging my throat yet again.

"For the first time I can really admit I think it might all work out okay," I confess with a relieved breath.

She grins at me and jumps when her phone rings. She begins to dig around her bag, searching for it, but the ringing stops before she finds it, then immediately starts up again. She finally fishes it out of her bag. "It's Christian," she announces, then quickly answers. "Hi, Christian!" she states cheerfully.

I reach for my phone to check my messages seeing a bunch of missed calls from Liz. I look up to tell Bree I'm going to step out of the car to call Liz back, but when I look up Bree has gone completely pale and she's shaking. "Bree?" I ask with concern. She doesn't answer me and I'm starting to panic seeing her like this again. "Bree? Are you okay? What's wrong?" She just looks at me wide eyed and hands me the phone. "Christian? What the fuck did you do? Bree is freaking the fuck out!" I scream.

"Shut up, asshole! My sister was in an accident. She's at Boston Medical Center. I need you to take Bree and go there to find out if she's okay. They won't tell me anything on the phone. I'm on my way and my parents already left, but you guys are right there and can get there quick. Please," he begs. "Just get there and make sure she's okay."

"Okay," I nod in agreement as though he can see me. "We'll call you when we get there."

"And Blake?" he prods.

"Yeah?" I question.

"Take care of Bree for me until I get there?" he pleads his voice cracking.

"I will Christian. She'll be fine. They both will," I make a promise I pray I can keep trying to make all of us feel better. I haven't heard Christian like that since Bree was in the hospital. Honestly, I don't know how Bree will handle this if something happens to Christian's sister, Theresa. I toss her phone and mine in the cup holder and reach for Bree's hand, grasping it tightly. "We're going to head over to the hospital now and see what we can find out. Christian and his parents are on their way," I reiterate, struggling to reassure her. I give Bree's hand a squeeze and she looks up at me, still wide-eyed consumed with obvious fear. "It's going to be okay, Bree."

We arrive at Boston Medical Center and park in less than fifteen minutes. I practically drag Bree along by the hand up to the desk. "Theresa Emory?" I request.

"Are you family?" a woman with gray hair and pale blue scrubs inquires, never tearing her eyes away from the computer screen in front of her.

204

"She is," I lie pointing to Bree. "She's her sister-in-law." The woman looks up when I say that and looks critically from me to her to our clasped hands and rolls her eyes. I start blurting out an explanation, hoping she'll buy it, "I'm just a close friend of her and her husband. Her husband, Christian is Theresa's brother. He's on his way down from Maine, as well as Theresa's parents, but they won't be able to get here for a few hours. We are both from the area and we were here for our families. Her husband called when Theresa was in the accident. We said we'd call with an update when we got here."

She's still eyeing us skeptically, but turns to Bree and asks, "Do you have any ID?"

I try helping Bree scramble for her wallet and pull out her ID knowing I have to lie some more. "They were recently married, so she hasn't changed her name yet, but you can call the family to check with them if you need verification."

"I'll be back in a minute," the nurse informs us stepping away with Bree's ID in hand.

I quickly grab my phone and text Christian as fast as I can, "I told nurse Bree was your wife-only release info to family. Think calling to verify."

We stare at the spot where the nurse was, waiting for her to reappear. When she finally does, she looks at us with empathy, "The doctor is in with her now, he will be out to speak with you as soon as he can."

Bree nods numbly and I state, "Thank you," before putting my arm around Bree and guiding her to a couple pale blue plastic chairs in the waiting room. We sit down and I pull her into my arms trying to comfort her.

I send a quick text to Christian, "Waiting to hear from dr. Taking care of Bree, but she needs you. Drive safe."

About a half hour later, a doctor steps into the waiting room. "Family of Theresa Emory?" I jump up pulling an

205

almost catatonic Bree with me. "Theresa is stable for now, but she has a long way to go. She needs surgery," he begins and his voice trails off in my head as my focus turns back to Bree knowing Theresa is at least stable. I'm not even sure if she's hearing anything she's saying, her eyes look blank. I take a deep breath to calm my own anxiety so I can be strong for her.

When the doctor steps away, I guide Bree back to one of the uncomfortable plastic chairs. She sits and stares at the white walls in front of her as I text Christian, "She's stable. Drive safe." I stand to grab water for both Bree and me before sitting down with her. She takes a sip of water, then sets the cup on a nearby table. I heave a sigh and pull her into my side, rubbing her arm up and down for comfort.

We stay like that until Christian arrives. He makes it in record time, flying through the sliding doors. He frantically scans the room until his eyes land on Bree. He runs to her and immediately wraps his arms around her. He holds her like he's afraid she'll disappear if he lets go and barely loosens his hold until his parents arrive about thirty minutes behind him. Even with Christian and his family here, I can't leave Bree's side. I can't leave my family when they need me.

I glance down at my phone and notice the battery is finally dead. I have no way of charging the thing until I make it back home. I have no idea what I did with the charger. I sigh and put it away hoping there's no other emergency because I can't go anywhere until I know everything will be okay here.

The next twenty-four hours fly by in a complete blur. Theresa goes from surgery to the ICU (Intensive Care Unit). We sit in the waiting room doing just that, waiting for updates, barely eating or sleeping.

Finally, after forty-eight hours, Theresa is moved out of the ICU and on to a regular floor where I guess she will need a lot of physical therapy, but she will be okay.

"I'm going to go back to my parents' house and crash for a while before I drive back to Maine. Do you guys need anything before I take off?" I question.

Bree shakes her head and steps towards me, wrapping me tightly in her arms. "Thank you, Blake. I know how much you hate hospitals, but I don't know what I would have done if you weren't here," she whispers gratefully. "I kinda' freaked out," she adds with a strained smile.

I sigh and hug her back. "You don't have to thank me, Bree. You know I'll always be there for you, whether you're kinda' freaking out or completely freaking out," I proclaim trying to lighten up a shitty situation. "You're like a sister to me," I declare full of emotion and I really mean it this time.

Christian assesses me, giving me a small, grateful smile as Bree steps away. He wraps his arm around her before reaching his hand out towards me. "I know it's not even close to enough, but thank you again, Blake. It seems like I'm saying that to you quite a bit, but I appreciate it more than I can say," he emphasizes, his voice catching. He pulls me in and gives me an awkward one-armed hug with a firm pat on the back before stepping away.

I nod at both of them and give them a tight smile before walking out the door towards my jeep. I have to go see Aubrey. After the last two days, I need to see her and give her a hug. Then, I guess I'll have to get some sleep or I'll never make it back to Portland. But I really need to get back there. I feel such a strong pull to get back to Liz as soon as possible. If this week has reminded me of anything, I know I can't take Liz for granted.

Chapter 26

Elizabeth

Blake is coming home tonight and I can't wait to see him! I look through my closet trying to pick out something Sara would deem as cute to wear when my phone rings. I practically skip over to my desk hoping to see Blake's name, but I see my mom's name instead instantly bringing a frown to my face. I huff and regrettably hit answer before I flop on the corner of my bed. I uncertainly whisper, "Hello?"

"Elizabeth dear, why haven't you called?" my mom probes accusingly in her shrill voice.

"I'm sorry, Mom. I…I…I've been working a lot and I…" I stammer.

"No excuses," she snaps, interrupting me. "You know I hate your excuses. I expect better of you Elizabeth Stevens!" I gulp and stay quiet, waiting for her to continue berating me, but she changes the subject instead. "I want to go over your fall schedule with you. Are you registered for enough classes?"

"Yes, Mom. I have seventeen credits and I think you will approve of all my classes," I answer on an exhale, feeling resigned to getting this conversation over with. I stand up and start pacing, waiting anxiously for what she's going to say next.

"Well, thinking and knowing are two very different things. I still need to go over it with you," she demands trying to control my life again.

I try changing the subject to something she likes to talk about. "How's Scott doing?" I ask sweetly knowing the subject of my little brother always cheers her up.

"Oh, he's wonderful! He can't wait to start there in a couple weeks. He's moving into an apartment with some friends over Labor Day weekend. We'll definitely miss having him around here," she adds. I hold in my jealous sigh. "I'm sure he'll be home to see us all the time though since you are right in town," she states judgmentally.

"Mom," I begin wanting to defend myself, but pause because there's not really much, I can say. She's right. I do everything I can to avoid going to see her, even though she's only fifteen minutes away.

She quickly interjects anyway with her own news. "He's actually been seeing an older woman recently. I believe she was a friend of yours in high school, although she was involved in so much more than you ever were. She's such a wonderful girl," my mother gushes, at the same time, insulting me. I can't help but wonder whom on earth she could be talking about at the same time I'm disgusted with her tactics.

"That's great, Mom," I grit through my teeth with fake happiness. It's better than talking about me.

"You remember Tori Sheridan? Wasn't she captain of your cross-country team your senior year?" she prompts and my whole body instantly goes cold. I can't breathe and gasp trying to catch my breath. My stomach is turning so fast I think I'm going to throw up. This can't be real. "She took Scott to some banquet tonight her parents were putting on. He wore a tux and everything," she prattles cheerily, oblivious to my panic attack happening on the other end of the line, not that it would matter. "They looked so wonderful together," she continues to praise.

209

I completely zone out after that, not hearing the rest of the conversation about Tori and Scott, waiting desperately for her to hang up. "Elizabeth? Elizabeth, are you listening to me?" my mom practically screams into the phone sounding completely exasperated with me.

"Uh, yeah, Mom. I'm here," I stammer trying to shake myself out of my initial shock.

My mom huffs before declaring, "I'll expect you for dinner on Friday. Don't be late," she adds with disappointment dripping from her voice.

"Okay, Mom," I resign and hang up the phone trying to steady my hands.

I send a quick text to Blake showing my vulnerability, "I can't wait until you get home tonight. I REALLY need you..."

Sara walks in cheerily proclaiming, "Hey Lizzie!" She stops dead in her tracks when she catches the look on my face, her eyes wide. "What happened to you? Are you okay?"

"I'm...I'm...I'm okay..." I stutter.

She rolls her eyes and shakes her head at me before flopping down on the couch next to me. I didn't even realize I'd made it over to the couch. "Your eyes look like saucers, you're pale as a ghost, your knuckles are white from gripping your knees too hard...You want more? Cause there's a long list, or are you going to spill and tell me what's wrong?"

"Tori is dating my brother," I finally whisper my answer still in shock.

"What?!" she shrieks. "There's no way! Jax wouldn't date that bitch!" she snaps.

"No, no, not Jax...Scott," I correct robotically.

Sara's mouth drops open and closes like a fish before finally spitting out, "Scott?" completely flabbergasted. I just nod my head stiffly. "But, why?" I stare at her with my eyebrows raised waiting for her to clarify. "Not because Scott

210

isn't great and all, but he's obviously younger than her. Besides Kris who's basically the same age, she always dated older guys. I just..." she starts than her eyes suddenly go wide. "She's doing this to try to get to you I know it!"

Sara gets up, running to her room and comes back out with her laptop in her arms, already booting it up. "I haven't had a chance to look at the blog lately, but my guess is she has pictures up of her and Scott. Who told you this anyway?"

I sigh and close my eyes briefly while I answer bitterly, "My mom."

"Oh, boy, she must be thrilled considering what she thinks of the Sheridan family." I grimace in response. "Okay, here it is." She flips the screen towards me so we can both see it and the first thing I see is a picture of Tori and my brother all dressed up just arriving at her parents' banquet. Sara reads the caption out loud with disgust, "Just arriving at the big event with my new man."

She scrolls down and there are a couple more pictures of them with captions including, "Never thought I'd be dating a Stevens!" or "So happy to be dating the youngest and best of the Stevens siblings!"

"She writes the tackiest things in the world! No idea how anyone even reads her blog anymore. It's pretty much only about her. Yeah, she has her few make-up and fashion tips, but really, it's just a brag blog now. Or a blog meant to torture you. I just don't get it!" Sara exclaims. "She knew you would see these because your family would tell you about them and you would look. You can't let that bitch get to you!"

I shrug my shoulders and shake my head because there's nothing I can really say. Tori does get to me, every time. I feel tears form in the corners of my eyes and quickly try to blink them back. Sara looks at me and immediately pulls me into a hug. A few tears fall unwelcome and I quietly brush them away. "Don't let her get to you, Scott will be away from home and in college in a couple weeks and he'll realize there is so much more to this world than Tori fucking Sheridan!"

I nod my head and lean out of her embrace wiping more tears away. "Or she'll try to push their relationship in my face with both of them here," I suggest bitterly.

Sara shakes her head in denial. "Scott wouldn't let that happen. He may be dating her, but he was never there for anything that happened between you two. He doesn't know what she did to you. That's why she had to go after him, Jax would never, and Scott doesn't know better. If you tell him, he'll back off, you know he will."

"I know, but I don't know if I can tell him. I don't know if I can handle another person, even my little brother knowing something else so pathetic about me," I whine.

"It's not pathetic. She's the pathetic one in all of this. Don't you get that?" she asks exasperated. "She's the one trying to still act like she's queen of her own little world and tries to control everything when it comes to you."

"You know, it's not even completely about her. I guess I feel like Scott has already been the golden child in our family and with everything my parents expect of me…" I take a deep breath and try to calm my nerves. "My mom was already bragging about Tori saying how wonderful she is and putting me down at the same time. I just don't think I can handle it and now I have to go home for the weekend and…"

"Wait, why do you have to go home for the weekend? Your parents only live on the other side of town," Sara expresses looking confused. "Why can't you just show up for dinner or something and leave?"

"I could, but you know my mom, she wants to control me for the weekend," I retort sarcastically, but meaning every word.

She puckers her lips in distaste and asks, "Have you talked to Blake?" I shake my head in response. "Maybe he'll go with you," Sara suggests.

"I don't know if I can do that to him," I admit. I release another sigh, "He's supposed to be home tonight though, I'm just not sure when. He said he would stop over after he dropped Bree off."

"Why don't you grab a bottle of water and get some rest then before he gets back. Maybe it will help you feel a little better," she suggests.

I nod and wrap my arms around my best friend again. "Thank you, Sara."

"Anytime Liz, you know that." I drop my hands to my sides and offer her a small smile. "And besides, if a little rest doesn't help, amazing Blake can help when he gets here with a little sexual distraction," she jokes smirking at me.

I laugh quietly and blush. "Sara," I admonish.

She laughs. "Well, it would help, wouldn't it?"

I shake my head with a small smile and drag myself up off the couch trudging back to my room. "We haven't even...I mean...uhhh!" I scream. "Don't lock him out!" I shout over my shoulder and I hear her laughter in response.

I shut my door and leave it cracked slightly open, so Blake knows just to walk in. I curl up in a ball on my bed and check my phone, but I don't have any messages yet. I send Blake one more quick message, "I'm lying down for a bit. Just come over when you can. I really need to see you." I set my phone next to my head and close my eyes, hugging my knees tight to my chest.

I sigh with my futile attempts of getting Tori with my brother out of my head. "Blake, Blake, Blake..." I repeat trying to turn my dreams into happy ones about being wrapped in his arms instead of the disaster of the last couple days. I regret not trusting him, I regret not going with him

213

and I regret not being with him right now. I obviously can't change what's already done, but I can prove to him everything will be different now. I can't let my past affect me so much anymore and I can't let Tori trying to steal my brother away bother me.

Chapter 27

Elizabeth

Blake said he was coming home two days ago and I'm still waiting. I woke up the day after I expected him back in a panic. I had no messages from him, but I called his roommates and they said he's still in Boston. They would know if anything was wrong, wouldn't they? He hasn't called or texted me back even once and when I try to call him it goes straight to voicemail. I don't know if he's okay. I don't know if something is wrong. I just know he's with Bree and I'm the one who decided not to go with him. I keep telling myself it could be absolutely anything, but it's easier to say than to convince myself. I'm completely sick to my stomach.

I even tried calling Bree and Christian, but neither of them returned my call either. All I had was their phone numbers at their apartments, but still, I think someone would get the message and get in touch with me before I lose my mind. Then again, maybe she's not calling me back because something happened with the two of them and she feels guilty and Christian isn't calling me back because he's pissed. I know I promised I would try to trust him and not to think this way, but he's making it really hard when I can't get in touch with anyone! Besides the fact it's difficult not to think this way because the alternative means something is seriously wrong, but wouldn't someone know to call me if there was?

I have really needed him the last few days and he hasn't been there for me at all, but I keep praying there's a good reason. It makes no sense to me why I can't get in touch with him. Even before he left, he said he would be home at the latest by yesterday. I clutch my phone with increasing anxiety, my fingers turning white, not knowing what to do or what to think. I'm starting to feel like a crazy stalker. I'm trying to stay away from my phone without success. How am I supposed to trust him and depend on him when he not only doesn't show up, but he doesn't even call to tell me what's going on?

I'm sitting on the couch in our living room, concentrating on breathing in and out, about to lose my mind when Sara walks in with an audible sigh. I'm assuming she's trying to alert me of her presence and her annoyance with my behavior at the same time. "You have to get off this couch and get out of this apartment. You can't keep stressing about that stupid blog or your family or waiting to hear from Blake," she declares, her voice full of compassion as she drops on the couch next to me.

I slowly turn my head towards her. "I just…I just thought he was different," I sigh shakily in exasperation, trying to push back the tears. "And I'm the one who ruined everything by making up a stupid excuse to not go with him this week. He wanted me to meet his family and I ruined it. I ruin everything," I whine. She raises her eyebrows and looks at me with a question in her eyes. "I'm doing it again aren't I?"

Sara scrunches up her face in distaste. "I honestly don't know because we don't know why you haven't heard from him yet. But I do know you can't sit around like this, waiting to hear from him and wondering what you did wrong. All you're doing is torturing yourself," she insists compassionately. Reaching for my hand, she gives it a squeeze. "I know you think this is your fault, but I can tell you it's definitely not. If anything, he owes you a gigantic apology and an explanation. You already apologized about your freak out. In fact, you guys spent hours on the phone since then, so what happened after? Besides the fact that you really needed him the last couple days, where the fuck has he been?" she yells completely exasperated for my benefit.

"Yeah, but..." I begin.

"No buts, get your ass off this couch!" she interrupts me. Sara attempts to pull me off the couch and I reluctantly abide with a loud groan. "Go shower, then we'll go get some coffee," she proclaims. She pulls me into my room, throws some clothes at me and shoves me towards the bathroom.

At this point, I can't help but laugh at her forcefulness. "Okay, okay! I'm going," I finally relent.

Within twenty minutes I'm showered, dressed and Sara and I are in her blue Toyota Camry pulling up to the coffee shop near our apartment. We order our coffee and sit at a small table in the back corner, in hopes we won't run into anyone today. I'm really not in the mood. I'm positive I look like crap from crying and lack of sleep even after the shower Sara forced on me.

I close my eyes and take a few sips of my coffee, trying to calm my ever-present nerves, when the sound of my cell phone makes me jump. I set my coffee down on the table, thankful I didn't spill any on me. I reach for my phone and feel a rush of relief followed by nerves at the sight of Blake's name on the screen. My heart begins to pound like crazy out of my chest as I press answer. I take a deep breath before saying a shaky, "Hello?" My whole body begins trembling as I hold my breath, waiting to hear his voice.

"Liz...I...M..." Blake's voice echoes through the phone brokenly.

"Blake? I can't hear you. Are you okay?" I prompt still panicking like I have the last two days.

217

"Yeah…Bree…help…okay…home…" I hear every few words and my stomach clenches even more before the line goes dead. I feel lightheaded and stare at my coffee cup trying to regain my balance.

"Liz, is everything okay? You look pale. Is Blake, okay? What did he say?" I hear Sara inquire, but it sounds like she's far away.

I take a couple deep breaths and try to focus on the sound of her voice. Finally, I give my head a light shake and look up at Sara, "I…I don't know." I swallow down the lump in my throat and stare at her blankly. "I couldn't really hear what he was saying. The service was really bad, but it sounded like he was helping Bree with something the last few days and now he's coming back."

"And, he didn't have the decency to call you? They have service in Boston! What on earth could he have been helping her with that he didn't have one minute to call you to tell you what was going on?" she asks annoyed, voicing the same questions going through my own head.

I sigh, suddenly feeling defeated and alone. "My mom and dad want me to come home to stay with them for the rest of the weekend. I know it's just on the other side of town, but I can't deal with this and them at the same time anyway. I'm going to throw some stuff together after this and I'll be there for the next couple days."

"You sure you want to do that?" she prods skeptically.

"My mom expects me for dinner tonight anyway and I need to get it over with," I reply with only a hint of fear in my voice, to my surprise. I really don't want to deal with my family, but I can't stay here I think to myself. "And I don't think I can deal with Blake right now," I confess. "I'm too hurt. I've been trying so hard to trust him and look where that has gotten me," I croak out.

She nods at me with empathy and understanding. "Okay, let's get you ready to go home and remember it's only a fifteen-minute drive if you want to come back. I can always keep Blake at bay for you, so don't feel like you have to be there to stay away from him."

I stand up trudging towards the exit, sipping my coffee and looking down at my feet when I bump into someone. I feel a strong hand reach for my arm to steady me. I glance up quickly to apologize, lucky I didn't spill on either of us. I begin to stammer, "I'm so sorry, I…"

"Lizzie, I've been hoping I'd run into you, although not quite like this." I stare in shock with my mouth hanging open and my eyes wide. Kris is standing in front of me smiling down on me. "You look good. How have you been?" he prompts. I try to push any words out of my mouth but fail miserably.

"When did you get back?" I hear Sara ask.

"This morning," he answers her never taking his eyes off me. "I wanted to come by to see you and talk," he claims sounding more like a question, still holding my arm.

I shake my head like I'm shaking sense into myself and jerk my arm free before I run out the door without another word. I hear him call after me, but I ignore him and don't stop running until I reach Sara's car and quickly slip in the passenger side door. I put my coffee in the cup holder and wring my hands nervously in my lap until Sara drops into the driver's seat. She glances over at me before starting the car with a disappointed sigh as she quickly backs out of the parking space. She drives us back to our apartment without saying a word.

As soon as we get back to the apartment, I throw all my clothes and other necessary items into my purple duffle bag for the weekend at my parents. I keep a lot of clothes at home my mother will want me to wear anyway, so I don't need much. I pray it will go smoothly, even though I'm almost positive it won't. I could always come back here if I need to, I tell myself, trying to get the courage to walk out the door.

I reach for my keys and right before I pick up my bag, Sara places her hand on my arm to stop me. I look over at her and wait for what she has to say. "I know you're having trouble making sense of everything right now, but maybe we need to slow down and get the facts before we jump to conclusions." I keep staring at her, not responding, starting to feel numb thinking about everything from my family, to Tori, to Kris, to Blake and Bree, but feeling numb is better than feeling right now.

I finally nod at her figuring she's expecting some kind of response. She sighs and adds, "I also know that sucked for you seeing Kris just now, but I still think you really need to talk to him. I think it will help you with closure. Plus, he deserves to have to beg for forgiveness after what he did to you, even if you never talk to him after that and you deserve to hear it and you deserve to see him do it face to face."

I nod again and she sighs pursing her lips. Eventually she asks, "Are you sure you don't want to wait until Blake gets back so you can find out what really happened?" I just stare at her numbly without responding. She finally sighs in resignation and questions, "What do you want me to tell Blake when he stops by to see you? Because you have to know he will come by when you don't answer your phone."

I shrug my shoulders in response. "Whatever you want to tell him." She gives me a pointed look and I groan closing my eyes. I finally open them back up and look at her. "Tell him the truth. Tell him I'm not home. Tell him I really needed him the last few days and I was terrified when I couldn't get in touch with him. Tell him I don't want to see him right now."

She wraps her arms around me and concedes, "Okay. It's going to all work out Liz, I know it." She gives me one last squeeze before releasing me and waving. "Call me! I need to know you're okay. I love you, Liz!"

I nod as if in agreement, but don't open my mouth to say anything else. I turn as if in a trance to grab my duffel bag and purse before stumbling out the door.

Chapter 28

Elizabeth

As I walk into my parents' house, my mother rushes from the kitchen practically running and throws her arms around me like I live across the country and she hasn't seen me in years. Granted, I try to avoid coming home even though it is just across town, but this is still over the top for her, especially since I'm not her favorite person. I warily put my arm up and pat her on the back. "Hi, Mom."

"Elizabeth, dear, I'm so happy you made it home!" she exclaims. An all too familiar woman follows her down the hall smiling genuinely at the two of us. Now I know why my mother decided to show such theatrics to my welcome home.

"Elizabeth, have you ever met Mrs. Sheridan?" she prompts. "She came over for some tea," my mother informs me politely.

I can't help but raise my eyebrows in surprise since I didn't know they even talked to each other, let alone my mother doesn't drink tea. It only makes me wonder what my mother is up to. I smile tightly and nod my head in confirmation. "Yes, I remember Mrs. Sheridan," I state formerly.

My mother purses her lips at me, obviously unhappy about my reaction. "Yes, well, why don't you go get yourself cleaned up dear and put your things in your room. Mrs. Sheridan and I are going to finish our tea. Then you and I can chat afterwards in the study about your schedule," she informs me.

My eyes widen as I look at my mom like she's losing it since we don't have a study, but I keep my mouth pinched tightly shut knowing it will be so much worse if I argue with her. I'll assume she means my dad's office. I just nod again and plaster on my fake smile. I swallow and find the most polite voice I can muster, "Okay, Mother, I'll be down in a little while. It was wonderful to see you, Mrs. Sheridan."

I turn towards my room, hoping my mother didn't catch on to my sarcasm. I don't need to add any more layers to this already disastrous weekend, but how in the hell can she be serious about any of this?

As I'm walking away, I hear my mother talking to Mrs. Sheridan about me, her voice dripping with disappointment. "I don't know what's gotten into her lately, ever since her and Kris James broke up, we have to stay on top of her about everything. Her grades, her questionable friends," she huffs. "Someone needs to push her right back to that boy, maybe he'll knock some sense into her."

I swallow the tears and step quietly into my room. I know my mom always seemed to push me to be perfect, but I don't think I've ever heard her admit that she doesn't like my friends, or that she thinks more of Kris than of me. I close my door without a sound and slide down to the floor feeling defeated.

I glance at my phone and see some missed texts from Blake, but I don't bother reading them. Then I notice missed calls from him as well. I can't help but sigh heavily. He not only didn't bother showing up the other day, but he hasn't even bothered to try to return any of my messages until now. Why should I bother calling him back if he takes days to respond to me?

I try to swallow down the ache rising in my throat, as I wipe my tears away and push myself up off the floor. I take a deep breath and grab fresh clothes out of my closet, knowing those will be better suited for talking with my mother than what I brought in my duffel. I grab a pale green sundress with a white eyelet trim along with a white sweater and some fresh underwear before heading into my bathroom. I'm hoping if I dress the part for her, maybe she won't be so hard on me, even though I have this nagging feeling my efforts will be for nothing.

After I'm all fixed up, I grab my schedule and clutch it tightly in my hands as I slowly walk towards my dad's office. I try to pull myself together by telling myself there is no reason for me to be afraid of her, I'm an adult and this is my life. I sneak quietly into my dad's office and slink into one of the high back leather chairs on the other side of the desk, curling my legs underneath me and looking around at all the books, diplomas and family pictures. I don't think anything has changed since I was ten. At least that's something that makes me feel at home, even if it's a small comfort.

My dad is an attorney for a pharmaceutical company and he works a lot to say the least. I guess that's why my mom is always the one that tries to micromanage me. She tries to tell me what I need to do and who I need to be, then she tries to fill in all the little details, expecting me to be perfect. I'm just sick of working so hard to feel like I'm worthless when it comes to her.

I get so lost in my own thoughts I don't even hear her walk in. "Sit up straight, Elizabeth!" My feet drop to the floor and my back immediately straightens, although it's from stress, not from her order. "You should have been nicer to Mrs. Sheridan. I spent ten minutes apologizing on your behalf."

I grit my teeth and make every effort not to roll my eyes. "I apologize," I grumble stiffly. I mumble under my breath, "It's not like her daughter was ever nice to me."

I look up cautiously hoping I didn't speak too loud, but I have my doubts when I notice my mother's glare directed at me. "Elizabeth, you will be nice to that family if it kills you. Do you understand me?" she seethes. "I said, Do You Understand Me?" she pushes her voice raising an octave as she emphasizes each word. I nod my head trying to hold back the tears in my eyes. "Tori has grown up and gotten over the childish games you two played in high school. It's time you did the same."

I once tried to tell my mother how cruel Tori always treated me and that's exactly how she blew it off. She said I needed to stop playing such childish games and get over it. Then she said maybe it was me who was being cruel to Tori and she was just defending herself, but either way I better grow up and fix it. Who says that about their own daughter? After that, I never told my mom anything unless I knew I had to.

"Now, let me take a look at your schedule before dinner," she demands. I hand it over numbly and barely listen while she tries to insist, I take more political science and math. Sometimes I really believe she was meant to live in Washington D.C. and she's somebody else's mother, or maybe that's what I keep wishing for as I fight away the tears and do what I can to placate her.

Chapter 29

Blake

Glancing at my phone, the screen lights up. I breathe a sigh of relief, grateful it's finally charged, but my reprieve doesn't last long. I have a bunch of missed calls and messages from Liz. I press her number, letting it ring. My call goes unanswered, so I try again, but this time it goes straight to voicemail. "Fuck!" I yell as I slam my hand against the steering wheel.

I send a quick text, letting her know I'm driving back and pull out onto the highway, trying her number again, every chance I get on the drive home.

"Come on," I grumble, sitting at yet another light trying to get through Portland to her apartment. Her messages and texts all sound like something was wrong. It sounded like she needed me, but she couldn't get in touch with me because I'm a fucking idiot. What kind of asshole boyfriend does that make me? She sounds more and more upset with the last few messages and all of her texts. I should have left to go buy myself a fucking charger. She can't give up on us now!

I screech to a stop in front of her apartment complex and jump out of my Jeep. I run up to the front door and pound on it, calling, "Liz!" The panic in my gut surfaces more and more with every second that passes by without talking to her. "Liz!" I repeat, continuing to pound on the door hoping she'll answer.

The door finally flings open, but Sara is on the other side glaring at me, but no Liz in sight. "What the hell, Blake?" she demands.

"Where is she? Is she okay?" I ask frantically, pushing past her into their apartment.

"What the fuck do you care?" she accuses glaring at me.

I storm into Liz's room and my eyes fly around the rest of the apartment. When I don't see any sign of her, I look back at Sara desperately. "Where is she?" I ask, pleading.

"You ignore her for days when she needed you. Now you want to know where she is?" she prods still glaring at me.

I close my eyes and take a deep breath, trying to calm myself down. I know I'm not helping anyone right now, but after spending the last couple days in the hospital, then getting all of Liz's messages, I'd been holding it all in.

I eventually open my eyes and look her straight in the eye as I speak, "Sara, I've had a really shitty few days and I'm not in the mood." I take a deep breath and try to reign in my anger since it's not with her. "My phone died, and I didn't have access to a charger. I got her messages today on my way back and I've been trying to get in touch with her ever since, but she hasn't been answering. I'm worried. I came right here," I inform her with exhaustion apparent in my voice.

She's still glaring at me, probably trying to decide if I'm telling the truth or not. "It's the fucking truth," I spit out between my teeth before eventually sighing in defeat. "Can you at least tell me if she's okay?" I beg feeling as if I'm in pain, my chest aching.

She purses her lips, looking at me like she can find the answers with her eyes before finally answering, "Physically, yes."

227

My gut clenches in agony at the thought that I'm not there for her when something is obviously wrong. "Well, if you're not going to tell me where she is and she's not going to answer her phone, do you mind if I wait here for her?"

Her shoulders relax slightly. "She probably won't be back until Sunday night or Monday morning."

"What do you mean she won't be back until then? Where did she go?" I prompt feeling slightly more panicked.

"I'm not telling you anything unless she says she wants me to." She takes a deep breath and looks at me with pity, "Listen, I don't know what's been going on with you this week, but you can't ignore your girlfriend and think everything is going to be just fine when you get home. She needed you and not only were you not here, but she couldn't even find you to talk to you. She didn't know if you were okay or if there was something seriously wrong. After everything she went through with Kris, she deserves a boyfriend who respects her enough to find a way to call her when he doesn't show up like he said he was going to and that's only if it really was some kind of emergency," she proclaims. She glares at me again, showing her doubt.

"It was a fucking emergency!" I yell in exasperation. I take a deep breath, then look towards the ceiling and rub my hand down my face in both frustration and exhaustion. "Can you just tell her I'm back and I came by? I want to talk to her and see her and I...I just need a chance to explain and I need to make sure she's okay," I ramble feeling completely and utterly helpless, knowing she's not going to tell me anything right now.

She finally looks at me with just the slightest bit of sympathy and nods her head in agreement, "Yeah, I'll tell her when I talk to her, but I can't promise you anything."

I give her a tight smile and mutter, "Thanks." That's better than nothing. I turn and trudge towards the door before

I halt, quickly mumbling an apology, "Sorry to barge in like that." She doesn't say anything in response. Heaving a sigh, I keep moving, opening the front door and tugging it closed behind me.

I pull out my phone to scroll for anything I may have missed from Liz, but there's nothing. I send her yet another text, "Stopped at your place. Where are you? I'm worried about you."

I slide behind the wheel in my jeep and head to my apartment. I need to go for a run when I get home. Maybe it will help me focus and I can figure out where the hell I can find Liz so I can explain what the fuck happened the last few days. Then, I need to apologize and hope she understands and she's willing to forgive me. I don't want to lose her.

Chapter 30

Elizabeth

I walk into my apartment and drop my bag immediately on the floor feeling completely exhausted. "You're back early," Sara calls as she walks out of her room.

I sigh, "Yeah, one night in that place is all I could handle. My mom invited princess Tori over for dinner tonight and there was no way in hell I was going to endure seeing her or watching her with her paws all over my brother, so I…" I pause not really wanting to finish.

"You what Liz? Why do you look guilty? What did you do?" Sara asks accusingly.

I scrunch up my nose in distaste, "Well, I wouldn't say I did something wrong exactly, but I'm not really comfortable with this."

"What?" she prods eyes wide and completely exasperated.

"Well, I kinda' made a deal with the devil. My mom let me come back if I agreed to talk to Kris," I confess and instantly cringe at my admission.

"Well, that's not so bad. I think you should do that anyway. You need closure," she insists, nodding in agreement.

I sigh and close my eyes. I knew Sara would feel this way. "Yeah, but he's been calling my house too since I haven't been answering any of the messages here, so my mom got involved. He's coming here to talk to me. He's afraid I won't answer the phone." Sara's look tells me she thinks the same thing. I roll my eyes and continue, "My mom set it up as my get out of jail free card, but I don't want to see him. She told me I needed that boy to talk some sense into me like I'm some devil child," I grimace. Besides I have no idea what's going on with Blake," I groan.

"You didn't call him back yet?" she probes. I just shake my head sadly in response. "You're never going to know if you don't call him back," she reiterates.

"I know, but I don't want to let anyone hurt me anymore," I admit miserably. "I just can't do it Sara!"

Sara wraps her arms around me. "Lizzie, you can't live like that, you have to talk to him!"

"I know," I groan feeling sadness consume my whole body. "Maybe I'll call him tomorrow, after I deal with Kris."

"Lizzie," Sara starts, but we're interrupted by a knock at the door. I groan and drop my face into my hands. "Stay here, I'll get it."

I hear Kris's deep voice and try not to recoil, "Hey, Sara. Is Lizzie here?" I don't hear her answer, but seconds later Kris's voice is right next to me, "Lizzie?"

I look up feeling exhausted. "Hi, Kris," I croak out.

"Are you...I mean can we talk in private?" he questions cautiously.

I nod my head reluctantly and stand up figuring he'll follow me to my room. Sara yells, "I'll be in my room if you need anything." I wave my hand in her direction as a thank you and drop onto the floor in front of my bed, wrapping my arms tightly around my knees, hoping to protect myself.

Kris shuts the door and slides down the wall directly across from me with a sigh. His strong legs stretch out in front of him and he wiggles them back and forth, bumping my legs with his toes and I eventually look up at him from underneath my eyelashes.

"What do you want Kris?" I ask bitterly.

He sighs again and leans forward trying to squeeze my knee, but I flinch away. His hand drops and clenches into a fist before falling to his lap. "I just want to talk. I know I fucked up when it came to us. I should have supported you more when it came to Tori, but she's been through a lot, and I just thought it would be better if we left it alone."

I look at him like he's crazy. "Is this supposed to be an apology?"

He shakes his head. "This isn't coming out how I want it to. I wish nothing ever happened with Tori, I've never regretted anything so much in my life."

"A little late for that don't you think?" I snap.

"Well, I guess if you're still angry with me that means you still care," he suggests hopefully.

I shake my head already exasperated with this conversation. "Kris, you believed her over me. She kept screwing me over and you either ignored it or believed her instead of supporting me. Then she set it up, so I walked in on her fucking you and I'm the bitch. You made me feel like crap over and over again and then you cheated on me with her of all people. I can't..."

"Stop," he interrupts me. "Don't say you can't forgive me. I can't let you do that Lizzie. I told Tori off when I realized what really happened."

"You did?" I ask surprised.

He nods and swallows hard. "She manipulated me, and I didn't see it until it was too late, but I need you to know that I'm sorry. I never meant to hurt you. I loved you, Lizzie. I realize how good I had it when I had you and I'm so fucking sorry. I'm sorry for the way she treated you and that I didn't support you when she did horrendous things to you. I should have never tried to get you to push it to the side and I regret it more than I can explain. But I've never regretted anything more in my life than that night with her," he rambles desperately.

I finally look him in the eye and what I see completely floors me. He's downright vulnerable and everything about him seems to be radiating loss and regret. He looks utterly broken and I don't know how to respond, but I open my mouth to try, "Kris…"

"I'm begging you Lizzie, pleading with you to forgive me. I don't ever expect anything from you. I know how much I fucked up. I know I don't deserve it, but I'll keep trying to fight for your forgiveness. Please," he begs. "I'm so sorry," he repeats, his eyes glassy. He reaches up to wipe tears from my own face I didn't know had fallen. I gulp, swallow down the lump forming in my throat.

I know what I have to do for both of us to heal. I scoot a little closer to him and take a deep breath looking him in the eyes as I speak, "I forgive you, Kris." He stares at me questioningly and I repeat myself, choking back a sob, "I forgive you."

He pulls me towards him and wraps his arms around me and I let him, ironically finally feeling at peace with our past. I guess Sara was right and I needed this for closure. I place my head on his shoulder and he whispers in my ear, "Thank you." I feel him kiss my cheek gently and repeat, "Thank you, Lizzie."

I don't know how long we sit there holding each other, but I nearly jump out of my skin when my bedroom door flies open. I look up, shocked to see Blake standing in the doorway with his mouth hanging open. "You have gotta' be fucking kidding me!" he seethes right before he spins on his heel and stomps out the door.

Kris prompts, "Who was that?" shaking me out of my stupor.

I jump up and run out the door after Blake. "Blake," I scream just before he reaches the door to his jeep. He stops and turns around glaring at me.

"Blake, it's not what you think!" I exclaim.

"Who the fuck is that?" he questions bitterly.

"It…It…It's Kris, but it's not what you think," I stammer.

His fists clench at his sides and he stares up at the sky before settling his glare back on me. "And what the fuck do I think Liz? Do I think you cheated on me with your ex just like he did to you?" he spits making me flinch.

We stand quietly just staring at each other. He attempts to slow his breathing before continuing, "You want to know why I didn't call you those couple days?" He assumes my silence is his answer. "Christian's sister Theresa was in a really bad car accident." I gasp and he keeps talking, "Christian asked if I could drive Bree to the hospital in Boston where Theresa was and meet him and his family there. We were already in Boston so we were close to her and could find out what was going on, since they had to drive down from Maine and couldn't do a thing until they got there. I couldn't leave Bree until I knew everything was going to be okay. My phone died on the way there and I spent a couple days with all of them at the hospital."

When she was finally moved out of ICU and we knew she was going to be okay, I stopped to see my sister because anytime I'm in a hospital it's like reliving the fucking accident again and I had to see her. Then I went home to sleep for a couple hours so I didn't fall asleep at the wheel. While I slept for the first time in days, I was finally able to charge my phone. When I woke up, I got all your texts and messages and I've been trying to call you ever since, sick with worry. All I wanted to do was get home to you. Then I get here and you're gone and won't return my calls. Then

234

when you do finally come back," he pinches his lips tightly together. With tears in his eyes, he gestures his arms to my apartment behind us, insinuating what he walked in on.

"Blake, I'm so sorry," I start, but he puts his hand up to stop me, shaking his head.

He looks me in the eye. "I was so fucking worried about you, but you don't trust that I have a good enough reason not to call." I shake my head, but he keeps talking, "You don't trust me enough to tell me you're back from wherever the fuck you were and you're home in your bedroom talking with your ex. You seem to think there's something going on with Bree and I, no matter what the fuck I tell you," he declares sounding pained.

"Blake, I'm sorry, I do trust you," I grab onto his arm to try to get him to believe me, to understand, but he flinches away from me as though he's been burned, cracking my heart.

He nods his head at me. "Ok Liz, you say you trust me?" I nod at him with tears streaming down my face. "So, maybe it's time for the truth. You want to know the whole truth?" he challenges with vehemence but doesn't wait for an answer. "The truth is I was in love with her once. At least I thought I was. But my feelings for Bree are nothing compared to what I feel for you," he emphasizes. "And they could be so much more if you would actually consider trusting me. I would think by now I would have at least earned some of your trust, but..." he sighs in exasperation while the tears stream down my cheeks.

He shakes his head looking completely defeated. "Liz, I'm fucking crazy about you, in fact I thought I was falling in love with you, but I don't deserve this shit. I understand you have a past that makes it hard to trust, but I can't live my life with you always expecting the worst of me. I'm so sick of fighting so hard for you with all the ghosts of

235

our pasts and then feeling like I'm the only one making the effort. I need to have a relationship where the woman I'm with can trust me and love me knowing I'm not going anywhere. After everything my parents went through, that's one thing I know. If you can't trust me," he sighs again in resignation. I think I see a tear escape down his cheek through my own blurry vision as he takes a deep breath. "If you can't trust me," he starts again, "then I don't know what the fuck I'm still doing here. I'm sorry Liz, but I can't do this anymore, not when you don't even believe in me," he chokes out.

He shakes his head and starts to walk away from me with his shoulders slumped, looking completely defeated and resigned. Seeing him like this, I feel a deep ache inside my chest making me panic, "Blake, wait!" I run to him and grab his arm trying to stop him. "Please, wait!" He turns around and looks at me with devastation in his eyes. "I'm sorry. I'm so sorry, Blake. Please don't leave," I beg desperately clinging to his arm.

"What are you sorry for Liz? Hurting me? Lying to me?" he asks pausing to glance at my apartment in disgust where he saw me in Kris's arms. "Not trusting me? Or not believing in me when I have given you so many reasons to have faith in me…in us?" he challenges.

His words feel like a stab to my chest. "I…I'm sorry for everything," I reply timidly.

"Will it be any different next time?" he prompts. I stare at him blankly. I want to say something to try to make the words come out, but I can't. I don't know how to answer his question honestly yet. I close my mouth and watch as he visibly clenches his jaw and turns to get in his jeep. "Goodbye, Liz," he mutters with the hurt evident in his voice.

I let the tears stream down my face as I watch Blake leave through my blurry eyes. I know I can't stop him because I can't promise him it would be different next time. I may have closure now, but he just admitted he loved her. Can I ignore that? I stare numbly at the spot where his jeep was just parked.

My body begins to collapse when a warm arm wraps around me. I glance up reflexively as Sara urges, "Come on. Let's get you inside where it's warm."

As soon as I step through the doors of our apartment, my body starts to give out again and Kris steps up beside Sara and picks me up gently. He carries me to the couch and sets me down tenderly, his face full of concern. I ignore both of them and let my uncontrollable sobs take over until I pass out.

Chapter 31

Elizabeth

I wake up with a headache feeling like my whole face is swollen. I slowly crawl out of my bed stepping sluggishly into the kitchen. "Good morning, sunshine!" Sara yells all too cheerily.

I sit down next to her with a grunt at the kitchen table. She offers me a hot cup of coffee and I gratefully take it, "Thank you."

"You're welcome. How are you feeling this morning?" she asks hesitantly.

I shrug as I add cream and sugar to my cup before taking a sip. I curl my legs up underneath me and answer truthfully, "Awful. Sick. Stupid. What happened to Kris?"

"After you passed out, we waited until you were breathing normal, then he carried you to your room and tucked you in bed. He said he feels responsible for what happened with Blake," she concedes.

I look up warily. "Well, he kinda' is," I grumble guardedly. She laughs in response. Sighing, I continue, "But it's mostly my fault. I have to stop blaming Kris for my problems."

"Hmmm," she murmurs with a questioning gaze.

"What's that mean?" I prod skeptically.

"It means it sounds like you had your closure with Kris. Now maybe you can try to fix this mess you made with Blake," she suggests.

I huff and nearly cringe at the sound of my own whiny voice coming from my mouth, "But how am I supposed to do that?"

She laughs. "Lizzie, did you hear that man? He's crazy about you! He said he was falling in love with you! That doesn't just disappear because he's pissed at you. He'll calm down and talk to you. You just have to show him you trust him."

I drop my head to the kitchen table whining and bang it lightly three times. She just laughs even harder. "I messed up Sara. I should've just called him the first time he tried calling me back," I acknowledge.

She looks at me with sympathy. "There's nothing you can do about it now."

"Yeah," I admit regretfully. My cell phone rings suddenly. I rush to grab it hoping it's Blake, but an unknown number displays on the screen. I answer hesitantly, "Hello?"

"Liz?" a girl's voice asks for me.

"Yeah," I confirm waiting for more.

"It's Bree," she answers and the nerves in my stomach start to flutter. "Listen, Christian and I were on our way back to the lake last night from Boston when Blake called me, so we stopped here instead." I remain quiet not knowing what I'm supposed to say. "He's in the shower right now, but he's a mess. I'm wondering if I could come over and talk to you?" she prompts shakily.

"Um, I guess," I answer hesitantly. What could she have to say to me, let alone be nervous about?

"It will be fine Liz," she claims like she's comforting herself as well as me. "It's time for you to know some things. I'm going to leave now while he's in the shower so he can't stop me." I start to interrupt her when she insists, "It's okay. Christian is here to keep him sane." She starts laughing before she hangs up without even saying goodbye.

239

I set my phone down feeling completely confused. Sara probes, "Who was that?"

I look at her and attempt to swallow my nerves. "Bree," I answer. She raises her eyebrows in question. "I guess her and Christian stopped here last night to see Blake because of what happened. Now she's coming over here to talk to me. I…" I shake my head and swallow the lump in my throat. Sara gives me an encouraging pat on my arm. "I feel like I messed up so bad, I don't know if I can handle facing his best friend. I don't want her judging me, especially after he admitted he once loved her."

"Lizzie, you have to relax. Maybe this is a good thing." I look at her like she's crazy and she laughs at me again. "Think about it this way, his best friend is coming to talk to you because you guys had a fight last night. From what I can tell she's not the type of girl to call you so she can come over here and punch you, so I'm guessing she's trying to help fix things for him."

"You think so?" I feel the hopefulness in my question and try not to let it take over. She nods at me with a calming smile. I try to relax and sip my coffee while I wait anxiously for Bree to arrive, so I can hear what she has to say.

It feels like only seconds later when the doorbell rings. Sara lets Bree in before excusing herself back to her room, "I'll give you two some privacy. I have to shower anyway. It's nice to see you again, Bree."

"It's nice to see you again too, Sara." Bree smiles genuinely at her before Sara escapes quickly into her room.

Bree looks over at me and I can't help but think how pathetic I must look. I know my face is swollen and my hair is up in a messy bun. I'm wearing short light blue shorts with white paint splatters on them and an old ripped green Portland sweatshirt. "You're welcome to help yourself to some coffee," I offer pointing to the cabinet with extra mugs.

"Thank you," she proclaims, reaching for a mug and filling it before sitting down across from me. She adds cream and sugar as well, still staring at me, assessing me. Eventually, she announces with a small smile, "You look about as good as Blake."

My mouth drops open at her light-hearted teasing, but instead of responding I ask cautiously, "Is he okay?"

She sighs heavily, her eyes dropping to her coffee cup before she answers, "Not really." My heart twists with her response. "Liz, Blake has been my best friend for a few years now and I've never seen him like this when it comes to a girl. He's always dated, but never the same girl for long. I know he's crazy about you and he doesn't know how to handle it," she confesses.

I look at her uncertainly and ask, "What did you want to tell me? Why are you here Bree?" my voice cracking on her name.

"I think it's time you understand my relationship with Blake. I know how hard it must be to understand from someone else's point of view. I've even watched Christian struggle with it at times and he knows everything and fought with us through most of it."

"I don't understand what you're trying to tell me," I admit feeling even more lost.

She nods her head in understanding. "Do you mind if we go to the couch? Get more comfortable?"

"Sure," I concur, pulling myself up and grabbing my coffee to take with me. We set our mugs down on the coffee table and sit on opposite ends of the couch facing each other.

She looks me in the eye and mumbles, "Thank you." I see her swallow hard, her Adam's apple bobbing up and down. "Some of this is really hard for me to talk about," she admits.

241

"You don't have to tell me anything if you don't want to," I proclaim, even though my curiosity is beginning to get the best of me.

"No, I do. After everything Blake has done for me, this is the least I can do," she admits. I can't help but hug my knees, nervously waiting for what she wants to tell me.

"When Blake first moved to Massachusetts, we hung out a few times, but we didn't spend too much time together because it was nearly summertime. You see every summer I used to go stay with my grandma at the lake. That also happened to be the summer I met Christian. Christian was everything to me right from the start. I came home after spending the summer with him, knowing I had to make it through one year before I could join him at college here. We had plans to visit one another and everything. So, when I came home, Blake's friend Matt and Amy who was my only real friend were hanging out and so Blake and I spent even more time together."

I quickly cover my mouth to hide my shock at hearing her say Amy was her only friend then. That couldn't be possible, she seems so nice. I hold my breath trying not to react, while I wait for her to continue. "He helped me get my mind off Christian by making me laugh or keeping me busy. He knew when I needed to talk about him and when I didn't. He was always such a good friend."

She pauses and takes a deep breath. I could feel a different kind of tension in the air, anxious for what she was about to say. "I had some issues with my parents, but everything changed for me when I found out my mom was sick. She had leukemia," I gasp at her confession and scoot closer to her trying to give her support. "I told Blake, but I didn't want to ruin Christian's first year at college, so I kept making excuses why we had to push back our visits. I figured I just needed time until my mom got better, or until we knew what our plan would be to help her. Blake was honestly the only one I was able to talk to about any of it. Oddly enough, I think my problems helped him forget about his issues with his family."

She looks at me and I nod in agreement, "That sounds like him."

"You already know about his family, so I guess you could say we supported each other with all of the family stuff. Well, my mom decided she didn't want to go through any more treatments. She wasn't doing well and she didn't want the end of her life to be spent in the hospital enduring treatments she didn't believe would help. But she needed my dad and I to be there for her. I wasn't going to be able to leave for college in the fall like I had always planned," she pauses wiping her tears away.

"Bree, I'm so sorry," I murmur feeling helpless. I scoot closer to her again so I'm right next to her, but she puts her hand up to stop me.

"There's a lot more, I have to keep going or I'll never finish," she admits. I nod my head in understanding and wait for her to continue.

"I still hadn't told Christian about my mom and I knew he would be down every weekend to be there for me if I'd let him. I didn't want him to miss out on his college experience. So instead of telling him, I lied to him. I told him I started dating Blake and I broke up with him just before Christmas," her voice cracks and she clears her throat. She shakes her head, "I can't believe I was so stupid!"

She takes another deep breath before continuing, "Anyway, during that time, Blake was all I had. We really depended on each other. I cried to him about Christian, my mom and school. When summer came, everyone else started leaving for college or to start their new lives and it was just Blake and I left. A whole year had gone by and my mom kept getting worse. The holidays came and I was really depressed. I felt like I was losing control of my life and Blake was the only thing good thing left. But he was just a friend and I felt like I was putting too much pressure on him to help me. He had enough to worry about without worrying about me too. Right after New Year's my mom lost her battle with Leukemia. I tried to be there for my dad, but I was barely holding on."

"I'm so sorry, Bree. I didn't know," I brush a few tears that have fallen from my cheeks. I thought I didn't have any left after last night.

She shakes her head and gives me a small sad smile, "Thanks."

"So that's why Blake came second semester and you came here the next fall?" I ask trying to piece everything together.

"Not exactly," she begins shakily and takes another calming breath. "Blake said he stayed home for his sister, but I know part of it was for me. I became really depressed. He was really worried about me. I had some anti-anxiety pills and some sleeping pills the doctor had prescribed to help me. One night I just kept taking them until I passed out. So, when I didn't show up at the park later that night where I was supposed to meet Blake, he snuck into the back of my house and up to my room to look for me. He found me on the floor unconscious and called an ambulance. He saved my life that night. He was afraid to leave me alone after that. I had to force him to leave for school, promising I'd call him every day and even then, he left two weeks late."

"Anyway, when I finally came here, Christian and I found each other again. I never got over him, but we had a lot of things to work through. I'm not going to go into details because that's another whole story, but Blake was always there for me again. Then Christian and I were going through an exceptionally hard time, we were broken up and I lost my grandmother. My grandma was both my mom and my dad for me growing up. She was everything and I started slipping away again. This time I knew better, but I was such a mess about my grandma and Christian and I wasn't paying enough attention. I accidentally took too many pills trying to calm myself down so I could sleep. Amy found me, but just thought I was sick. Blake came in right after to check on me like always and saved my life again. Afterwards, Christian and I worked through our problems, and I went to therapy for my depression. I needed a lot of help."

Bree looks directly at me, wiping the last of her tears away. "I don't know if you've noticed yet, but Blake has a thing for doing everything he can to protect those he loves. I think it has to do with not being able to help his sister get better, or not being able to stop her from getting hurt in the first place. Blake and I may not be related, but he's my family and I'm his."

"I get it," I whisper still wiping tears away for what she endured. "I'm so sorry."

"Liz, Blake is like my brother. He has always done everything he can to protect me and I know he wants to do that for you too, but more in the way Christian and I do for each other. After everything Blake and I have been through together, and I've only told you a little, maybe you can understand our relationship more and know I'm not a threat. I need you to know, I'm completely in love with Christian, but Blake is my family too."

"I understand," I confirm nodding.

"I do have to ask though because just as Blake protects me like a sister, I'll protect him like a brother...last night with your ex?" she prods hesitantly.

I shake my head, "I promise, it was nothing but closure. He needed to apologize and I needed to give him

245

forgiveness to move on. I think if I couldn't do that, a part of me was still being held back with Blake and I want to try even though I'm terrified."

She nods her head. "I understand that and I'm sure Blake will too, but you need to tell him." I nod my head in agreement.

Throwing my arms around Bree, I mumble, "Thank you. Thank you so much for telling me all of this. My worries and jealousies seem pathetic after hearing your story. He kept telling me I needed to trust him and it wasn't his story to tell. Now I understand why," I concede looking at Bree guiltily. "I'm so sorry, I feel horrible."

"Don't be sorry, I get it. Christian was there and at times he had a hard time with my relationship with Blake. But don't let it ruin what you have with him. He deserves to have it all and with you I think he can. I've never seen him like this before," she claims and gives me an encouraging smile.

I groan, "I need to apologize to him again. I hope he'll listen. I'm so stupid!"

"Don't do that," she urges shaking her head. "Don't be so hard on yourself. There's no way you could have known. He's already calmed down since last night. I'm sure if you try to talk to him now, he'll listen," she confesses.

"Okay," I concede and lean back. "I'll try. I don't want to lose him," I admit.

"Then go get dressed and go get Blake back!" she encourages me. I stand up and smile at her. "I'll head back to his place and get Christian out of there before you come. Good luck!"

"Thank you, Bree. He's right about you, you are pretty wonderful," I declare. She smiles shyly at me in response. "Thank you for everything," I reiterate, giving her one last quick hug before running into my room to grab my things for a quick shower.

Chapter 32

Elizabeth

I'm standing outside Blake's apartment door in a complete panic. My heart is racing and I'm clenching and unclenching my fists over and over again trying to get my breathing to slow down. I have no idea what I'm going to say to him. I may understand his relationship with Bree more now since she told me her story, but I'm still the idiot who didn't trust him before.

What makes me think he'll forgive me and give me another chance? How am I going to prove to him I trust him?

I have to get myself under control before I knock. I bend over at the waist, putting my head down and placing my hands on my knees. I close my eyes and try to concentrate on my breathing when I hear the door open. I slowly open my eyes to see a pair of Nike running shoes in my line of sight and I stop breathing all together.

"Liz?" Blake asks hesitantly. I peek through my hair, still afraid to face him. "What are you doing?" he prods with a hint of laughter in his voice.

I quickly pull myself up, flipping my hair back and lose my balance from standing up too quickly. I start to fall backwards and Blake quickly reaches for my arm and pulls me upright. "Whoa, are you okay?"

I shake my head to get my mouth moving, "Um, yeah, I just…I just was wondering if I could talk to you. Are you leaving? I could come back," I ramble.

His hand drops to his side and I immediately feel chilled at the loss of his touch. He looks at me with indecision. He wipes both hands over his face and through his hair before clasping them behind his neck and looking up towards the sky like he'll find the answers he's looking for somewhere above. My mouth drops open at how tight and perfect his biceps and triceps look right now when he lets his arms fall and he eyes me quizzically. I feel myself blush a deep shade of red knowing he caught me ogling him at a completely inopportune time, but fortunately, he doesn't call me on it.

He finally breaks the tension when he answers, "I was going to go for a run, but I can do that later. Come on in," he urges.

He steps back and I brush past him into the apartment and wait for him to tell me where to go as my stomach turns full of nerves. "Let's sit down on the couch. My roommates are gone right now anyway." I nod my head, not ready to speak again and slowly walk over to their olive-green couch and squeeze into the far corner. Blake drops down next to me, leaving about a foot of space between us and places his elbows on his knees, clasping his hands together tightly in front of him.

I stare at the twitch of his strong jaw and the flexing of his biceps as he pushes his hands together with obvious tension. I open my mouth, but no words come out and I close it again. I turn my head to stare out the window, hoping to catch my breath and praying the right words will come to me.

I release a shaky breath and turn my head back towards him, but the only sound that comes is barely a whisper of his name, "Blake..."

He finally looks at me and speaks, his voice full of anger and hurt, "What do you want Liz?"

I squeeze my eyes closed to force my composure enough to speak. I hate that I didn't trust him. "I wanted to say I'm sorry. I'm sorry I didn't answer your calls or texts. I'm sorry I wasn't being fair to you. I'm sorry I didn't give you all of my trust when I should have." I open my eyes to look at him and he turns his head away from me causing my stomach to roil. I dare to scoot just a little closer to him and reach up to touch his arm. I can't help but feel a little relief when he doesn't flinch away from me. "I really like you, Blake. I want to trust you with everything."

"But you don't," he snaps. I flinch, pulling my arm away from him.

I close my eyes and take another deep breath before admitting, "Bree came to talk to me."

He drops his hands to his sides and slowly turns his head towards me. "When?" he gasps.

"Today," I squeak out under his burning gaze. I quickly continue, hoping he'll let me back in. "She told me her story and I'm sorry most of all for that. I'm sorry I doubted your relationship with her. I'm sorry I didn't trust you. I know I can't always use my past as an excuse, but that is exactly what I was doing. I was using it as my excuse not to get myself in too deep because I didn't want to get hurt again. But the problem with that is I already am in deep with you, Blake. I was afraid because I don't think I've ever had such strong feelings for anyone as I do for you. You could really hurt me Blake," I emphasize. "You could hurt me more than anyone ever has before." I pause to take another calming breath. "I've been trying to deny it, but this whole time, I've been falling in love with you, Blake," I admit quietly. I don't look at him as I continue, terrified if what I might or might not see, "But since I wouldn't let myself completely trust you, I hurt myself even more."

"That makes two of us," he concedes under his breath.

I flinch at his blatant insinuation. "I know it's not enough, but I'm sorry I hurt you more than anything," my voice cracks, pleading. I look away trying to blink back the tears pushing to overflow.

The air feels incredibly thick with tension before he finally releases a loud sigh. I glance back over to him hesitantly, waiting for him to speak. When he finally does, his words are not at all what I presume, although I don't know what I am expecting. "I understand what you're saying Liz and I forgive you. You don't have to put any more pressure on yourself about this. I'm over it. We can move on and be friends."

"Wha…What do you mean?" I prod in confusion.

His jaw twitches again before he declares, "I mean, I forgive you. We can be friends. No harm, no foul, right?"

"I don't understand," I spit out flustered as the tears start rolling down my cheeks.

He steps towards me with a look of regret and determination in his eyes and my hands start to shake. "Maybe you weren't ready, maybe I wasn't enough to help you through it, but you should have trusted me without knowing Bree's story. I forgive you, but I can't jump back into this right now. I just can't," he adds sounding desperate.

I nod my head, the tears flowing freely as I try to swallow down the stabbing pain in my chest. He steps into me wrapping his arms around me and holding me tight, but for the first time, his embrace gives me no comfort as the pain spreads throughout my body anyway. I don't understand how he can make me feel so safe and loved, yet so completely lost and alone at the same time. I hate the feeling of being helpless, but that's exactly what this is right now, complete and utter helplessness.

He finally releases me and the small bit of love and safety I felt in his arms, completely vanishes while the agony and numbness consume me. I stumble back to the door with him right behind me. Before I step outside, I turn around and look him in the eye. My whole body aches. I've never felt such loss as I choke out one more sincere apology, "I'm so sorry Blake." I turn and run to my car without looking back, trying to hold myself together.

I have no idea how I make it back to my apartment, but I do in record time. I numbly go immediately to my room. I shut the door and curl up into the fetal position on my bed so I can hug myself and attempt to hold myself together. Of course, I fuck up the one good guy that comes along in my life because of them. They ruin everything for me! I cry until my body can't take anymore and I finally fall asleep in complete exhaustion.

Chapter 33

Blake

I walk into my apartment, hot, sweaty and still completely on edge after a five-mile run. As soon as I watched Liz fly out of my parking lot, I took off running. My brain won't stop. How the fuck am I supposed to keep letting her in when she holds me at arms' length?! And now that she knows how fucked up my story with Bree is, I'm just supposed to say screw it? It's not supposed to matter she couldn't trust me without knowing everything? I can't do that. I can't set myself up just to lose again, like every other fucking time! Even though it about killed me when she was falling apart, I couldn't give in. I had to end it. It was the only way I could survive.

I go to my room and grab my phone off my dresser and see Bree's name. I open her text and read.

> *I talked to Liz. Did you talk*
> *to her yet?*

I quickly send a text back.

> *Thanks, but it doesn't matter.*

I get an immediate response.

> *What happened?*

But I ignore her and grab some clean clothes and head to the shower.

After cleaning myself up, I step back into my room hearing my phone ringing. I reluctantly answer with a groan, "What do you want Bree?"

"Don't you pull an attitude with me Blake Withers! What did you do?" she snaps.

I sigh in frustration. "Aren't you supposed to be watching a movie with your boyfriend or some shit like that instead of harassing me?"

"Blake," she warns sounding exasperated and I know it's time to drop my insolence. "Tell me what happened," she demands.

I groan again and run my hands through my damp hair before dropping down on the corner of my bed. "Liz came to apologize and I forgave her," I state attempting to leave it simple, even though I know Bree won't let me get away with it.

"And…" she urges me to continue.

"That's it. I told her we could be friends," I rush out, already cringing at the reaction I know is coming.

"What do you mean friends? She's perfect for you Blake! Weren't you the one who was so concerned about how to get her to trust you without her knowing the truth? You were so stressed about losing her because you didn't want to betray me. I told you I would talk to her for you because I could tell she was different for you!" she screeches at me. "What are you doing, Blake?" she challenges sounding infuriated.

"I'm not doing anything," I argue. "She couldn't even trust me until you told her about your history, our history," I reiterate exasperated.

"And, who wouldn't have trouble accepting our relationship, Blake? People who don't really know us think you and I are a couple sometimes and I know that drives Christian crazy. Can you really blame her for that? Especially when she didn't have the whole story, like Christian does?" she prompts. "I can see how she might have a hard time and so can you. She tried even before she knew," she reminds me. "Think about Christian and me. He had a really hard time with our relationship too and that's even after..." she trails off and I flinch at her harsh intake of breath. "You have to give her a chance. Don't make the same mistakes I did Blake because that's what you're doing, repeating my mistakes. She deserves a chance," she pleads.

I stay quiet with one hand fisted in my hair and the other clutching the phone trying to put everything together flying around my head. Bree finally breaks the silence, "This isn't just about her trusting you, is it?"

I sigh in consent. "Maybe." She knows me so well.

"This is about your sister and your family, isn't it?" I don't answer, but I know I don't have to. "Blake," she whispers with despair, "You can't keep yourself closed away in a box. Bad things happen to good people, things you can't control, but that doesn't mean you should shut yourself off from getting too close to someone."

"I don't. You and I are close. I'd do anything for you," I admit quietly.

"And I would do anything for you, but maybe that's why you..." she trails off.

"Why I what Bree?" I snap sounding agitated.

"Why you held on so tight to me. Why you never really dated anyone else. Why you go through girls like..." I wait for her to explain. "You're so afraid of getting hurt, of losing someone you care about that you don't let anyone get too close."

"I let Liz get close," I softly proclaim.

"Yeah, but you're pushing her away now that it's getting real," she reminds me and pauses, trying to let that soak in. "You protect those you love, but even you know you can't protect us from everything. Aubrey, your parents and I are all different examples of that. I think you're pushing Liz away to protect yourself," she declares gently.

I close my eyes and wipe my hands down my face feeling completely lost. Maybe she's right, I admit to myself. Maybe that's why I had trouble letting her go until Liz came along.

"Is that what I'm doing?" I whisper aloud, feeling my chest ache.

"Yeah, I think so," Bree answers even though I wasn't looking for a response. "You need to go talk to her. She's good for you Blake. I really like her."

"Yeah," I confess, "I like her, too."

"Then do something about it!" she encourages.

"I need to sleep on it, but I'll talk to her," I concede.

"Do you promise?" she probes.

"Yeah, I promise." I hear Christian calling her in the background, "And go talk to dickhead, I mean Christian," I tease laughing. "He sounds a little impatient."

"Go see her!" she repeats. She laughs into the phone then hangs up without saying goodbye.

I drop my phone onto the bed and then fall back with my hands above my head. I stare at the ceiling thinking about what Bree said. Maybe I have been holding her so close because I know we'll never be anything more than friends and I didn't want anyone to be more than friends. But then again, that's how we got so close. It's also how I kept all other girls away. I've slept with a few girls, but I've never had anyone I wanted for more until Liz. Am I just using her trust issues to push her away? Fuck, I have to get out of this room and clear my head.

I walk out into the living room and find all three of my roommates sitting in front of the TV with a couple pizzas and beer watching some action movie by the looks of it. Thad glances over at me, "Hey man. We haven't seen you in a while. Why don't you grab a beer? We have pizza."

I do as he suggests, walking to the kitchen and grabbing a bottle of bud light before dropping down on one of the brown faux leather recliners near the couch. I take a sip of my beer and reach for a slice. Without looking at me, Patrick informs me, "We're going to go down to Moe's later to play some pool or darts or something. You in?"

"Yeah, sure, I'm in," I agree, knowing I need time to think before I talk to Liz. I'm just not ready to deal with it yet.

Chapter 34

Elizabeth

It has been five days since I left Blake's house and I'm still a complete mess. I can't stop thinking about Blake and what I did. I know he said he forgave me, but I would give almost anything for a second chance. I just have no idea how I can get that chance. Bree texted me and told me not to give up, but I don't even know how to respond to that, so I never did. I've tried to text Blake, but his only response has been, "I'm really busy, we'll talk soon."

School starts this week, so a lot of students that go home for the summer are returning to campus. The café has been really busy with the end of summer tourists and returning college students, so I picked up some extra shifts to keep myself occupied. This past week has basically consisted of going to work and coming home. My tips have been horrible, but I have to admit I've been a horrendous waitress this week since my mind has been on Blake and not on what I'm doing. I actually feel bad for anyone who's been unfortunate enough to be in my section. Honestly, I've been so bad, I'm lucky I haven't been fired.

Today is my day off this week and I couldn't handle sitting in the apartment all day. Sara went on a date hiking at a park or something and I just couldn't deal with being alone for so long! So, I'm sitting at a small table in the back corner of the coffee shop, drinking a latte and watching all the strangers around me enjoying themselves while I wallow in self-pity.

"Want some company?" My head snaps up to see Kris smiling down on me hesitantly with a coffee cup in his hand. I purse my lips and gesture flippantly to the chair across from me. He chuckles lightly and mumbles sarcastically, "Well if that's not a warm welcome, I'm not sure what is." I scrunch my nose up in displeasure and he sighs heavily. "Lizzie, I'm sorry. I don't know how many times I have to say it to you, but I'm sorry. I never meant to hurt you and I would change things if I could."

I nod my head in agreement. "I know. Thank you."

"I thought we were friends?" he prods with a small, hopeful smile.

I sigh in resignation, "Sure, we are. I'm just...I just have a lot going on."

He bites the corner of his lip and looks at me thoughtfully. That look used to drive me insane, but not even the tiniest flutter erupts anymore. I look down into my coffee cup thinking of chocolate brown eyes I'd rather be staring at right now. Gulping, I fight back the tears threatening to burst free. "Some asshole hurt you again?" he questions threateningly.

"He's not an asshole," I instantly defend.

"Ah, so I'm still the only asshole, but he did hurt you," he states.

I grimace and shake my head in denial. "It was my fault."

"I doubt that," he claims, shaking his head with disbelief.

I look him directly in the eye and emphasize the first two words, "This time it was."

"Ouch!" he cringes. Sighing, he leans towards me, placing his elbows on the small table between us. "Lizzie, mistakes can be forgiven and I'm sure whatever mistake you made really isn't too bad." I look at him skeptically and he adds with a smirk, "You have always been pretty perfect you know.

I roll my eyes and grumble, "Kris, don't go there."

He laughs in response as he reaches for my hand across the table and I let him take it. He gives my hand a light squeeze looking me in the eyes. "Listen Lizzie, I always thought you were amazing. Even when I fucked up, I knew I was the one to blame. I never regretted anything so much in my life. You're human. You make mistakes just like everyone else. You deserve to be forgiven like everyone else too."

I give him a small smirk. "Are you trying to tell me you deserve to be completely forgiven?"

He grins with a sparkle in his eyes and mumbles, "Among other things." He leans in even closer, not yet letting go of my hand. "Lizzie, I think you're incredible and you shouldn't let anyone convince you otherwise." I shake my head in denial.

Behind him, someone clears their throat before I hear his deep voice, "Liz, can we talk?" I pull my hand away from Kris and into my lap, staring into Blake's round pools of chocolate in shock.

"Blake," I rasp out. He shifts back and forth on his legs looking incredibly uncomfortable as he stares at me waiting for my answer, to what I don't remember.

He raises his eyebrows at me in question. "I really need to talk to you, it's important."

I nod numbly and whisper, "Yeah."

Kris stands and turns towards Blake, sticking his hand out in greeting. "Hi, I'm Kris James."

Blake's head turns slowly towards Kris and when his eyes land on his face he pales immediately. I watch his Adam's apple bob up and down with a hard swallow as he appraises Kris, looks critically at his hand then back to his face. "

What did you say your name was?" he asks slowly in disbelief glaring at Kris.

Kris looks slightly taken aback by Blake's reaction before he answers hesitantly, "Um, Kris James."

Before anyone has a chance to react, Blake hauls his right arm back and punches Kris in the jaw. Kris's head and upper body flinch to the side with the unexpected hit, but his feet stay planted.

I scream, "Blake!" at the top of my lungs and jump in front of him before either of them has a chance to do anything else. "Stop," I shout and look in his wild eyes his chest heaving up and down in anger.

"What the fuck?" Kris yells from right behind me, but I put my hand up to stop him from saying or doing anything else. I glance at him to make sure he's okay. He's wiping his bloody mouth with the back of his hand and glaring at Blake. I know that look and Kris wants to fight back, but he doesn't want to do it with me here. I have to stay between them. He won't do anything with me in the middle. He would never put me in danger.

"How the fuck do you know him?" Blake bites out angrily.

"He's my ex," I explain shaking my head with confusion. "We just ran into each other. We were just talking."

Pain at this admission crosses every part of Blake's face and I'm at a complete loss as to what could possibly be going through his head because it doesn't seem like jealousy to me. "Stay the fuck away from her asshole! Hasn't your family already taken enough?" Blake accuses.

Kris stands wide-eyed looking completely stunned. "What the fuck do you know about my family?" Kris retorts.

261

"Does the name Withers mean anything to you?" Blake spits at Kris.

Kris shakes his head in confusion before his eyes light with shock and understanding.

He gasps, "My dad…" and begins to pale.

Blake's jaw twitches and he nods stiffly still glaring at Kris. My brain slowly catches up in comprehension. Kris's dad caused the accident that changed both their lives. "Oh, God," I whisper with dread, my stomach churning.

"Man, I'm so sorry. I…" Kris utters with pain, but Blake levels him with a deadly glare I've never seen from him before and silences Kris immediately.

"I have to get the fuck out of here," Blake grunts and turns striding quickly out of the coffee shop.

I then notice all the people staring at us but look at Kris with his mouth still hanging open. "I…" I start and Kris just points to the door in response.

I frantically run out of the coffee shop to find Blake. I look left then right and spot him feeling relief flood me at the sight of him, followed by anguish for his obvious grief. He's leaning against a red brick wall next to an office building and I stop in front of his feet. "Blake," I gasp, not knowing what to say.

He shakes his head. "Don't Liz. I don't think I can deal with listening to your shit right now," he grunts.

My breath gets caught in my throat and I try to remind myself of the kind of pain he's probably feeling right now. I force myself to breathe and stand with him, keeping my legs stiff so they don't collapse under me. I will wait until he wants to talk. He's going to need me I tell myself.

After what feels like an eternity, he finally opens his mouth, "His dad ruined Aubrey's life. He ruined my life, Liz. How am I supposed to feel about that?" I shake my head not understanding what he's trying to say to me, but afraid to ask

262

him. He shakes his head in disbelief. "I can't believe all this time...all this time the girl I was ready to give my heart to fucked the asshole that helped ruin me."

I cringe and tears immediately spring to my eyes, as my body starts to shake. "Blake," I grumble tearfully, "I'm sorry you're hurting but..."

"Why were you holding his fucking hand, Liz?" he accuses.

"I...I wasn't...I..." I stutter.

"I saw you! Don't fucking lie to me!" he screams. Reflexively, I cower away from him, but yet it's him I fear for right now. "We break up and you start fucking my enemy to get back at me? Well, you succeeded Liz, you fucking wrecked me!" he snaps before turning and storming away from me. I collapse against the brick wall he was just leaning against, my tears blinding me as I watch him walk away from me again, but this time it feels permanent.

A few minutes later, I feel a hand on my shoulder. I wipe my eyes and look up to see a concerned Kris. "Look, I know I'm probably the last person you want to see right now, but you left your purse and I thought I should help get you home." I nod my head and let him help me up.

He puts me in the passenger seat of my own car and then climbs into the driver's seat himself. "What about your truck?" I ask warily.

"I'll walk back here and pick it up. It's not far and I could use the walk," he informs me. I nod my head and close my eyes for the short drive back to my apartment.

When we get there, he gently guides me inside and walks me to the couch where I collapse and automatically curl up into the fetal position, trying to protect myself from the world. He walks over to the kitchen and when he comes back, he places a glass of water in front of me. He sits down on the opposite end of the couch, holding a bag of ice to his jaw. "Your boyfriend has a powerful punch."

The lump in my throat grows as I rasp, "He's not my boyfriend...anymore."

Kris sighs with regret. "I don't really know the whole story. I definitely had no idea who he was until tonight. I've always known there was a family by the name of Withers involved in the accident with my dad. Before the accident, my parents always fought and my dad was always drinking. My mom tried to get him to stop, but..." he drifts off, shaking his head in defeat. "I remember thinking maybe this stupid accident would make him change. Then the papers started reporting about the family. My mom tried to hide everything from us about them, but I saw it and I always felt like shit about it. My dad's suicide note was an apology letter to us. He finally got it, but it was too fucking late," he declares, his voice cracking.

I look over at him as a few tears fall down his cheeks. I don't have the strength to comfort him, so I just whisper as sincerely as I can muster, "I'm sorry Kris."

He nods his head in acknowledgement, "Me too. Thing is, I've always wanted to do something for the family, but didn't know how to find them."

"I don't know if they would want anything from you," I admit.

"What about his sister? I heard rumors she had it the worst, but I was always too afraid to try to find out," he confesses.

I nod slightly. "She's in an adult home in Boston."

His body tenses and he nods stiffly. "I gotta' go." He stands and steps towards me. "He's just hurt Liz, give him time."

I look at him warily. "What makes you the expert?"

"Any man in their right mind wouldn't want to lose you," he claims, giving me a weak smile. He leans down brushing my hair from my forehead and places a light kiss in the center. "Take care of yourself."

"Thank you," I whisper before he steps away from me and walks out the door. I close my eyes holding myself tight, praying for Blake to heal. I can't help but think I'd rather be in pain forever than see the amount of agony that consumed Blake today stay with him even a moment longer. It kind of puts the whole Tori thing in perspective. No matter what she does, she can't get to me anymore.

Chapter 35

Blake

I have an incredibly intense feeling that can only be described as feeling like a weight is sitting on top of my fucking chest. I don't know if I should go back there and beat the shit out of that asshole, go for a run or fucking self-destruct right now. My phone rings and I glance at the screen to see my dad's face. I hit the green answer button figuring anything is better than dealing with this shit right now.

"Yeah?" I snap into the phone.

My dad clears his throat. "Well, I guess it's better than you not answering." I sigh and wait for him to tell me why he called. "I was wondering if you could head back here this weekend. I have Kari this weekend and I want to bring her to go see Aubrey again. I thought maybe we could bring Aub to the park, a family trip," he suggests. "It's supposed to be good weather this weekend and…maybe you can bring your girlfriend too."

I flinch as thoughts of Liz with that asshole consume me. I take a deep breath and answer stiffly, "I'll be home tonight…alone."

"Are you alright, Blake?" my dad asks cautiously. I hang up without answering him, acting as if I didn't hear him. Unfortunately, I just don't want to answer because I haven't felt this helpless since…

I quickly pack a weekend duffle and tell my roommates I'm leaving for a few days before I jump in my jeep for the long drive back to Mass. I turn on the radio, but every song is fucking torture. They all seem to be about love or loss or family attempting to torture me and I quickly flip the speakers off.

Unfortunately, the silence isn't much better, it just gives me more time to stew and that's exactly what I do. My fist hits the steering wheel at the first red light and I relent to this being one of the longest fucking drives of my life.

I can't believe her ex is the son of the man who ruined my whole life. Realistically, I know it shouldn't matter, but I can't help but feel betrayed even thinking about it.

He has everything!

He can do whatever he wants and has the whole world in front of him with the means to do it. Let alone what he did to Liz makes me want to tear his body limb from fucking limb.

I shake my head, my heart beating hard inside my chest at the thought of her tears. This time her tears were caused by me and that fact breaks my heart even more. I can already hear Bree in my head telling me I'm making a mistake, telling me Liz is good for me. I spend the rest of the drive analyzing my feelings for Liz and trying to figure out where I go from here.

I walk into my parents' house and follow the sound of my mother's laughter to find them. I step into the living room and find both of my parents sitting on the rose floral couch. My mom is holding a glass of wine and my dad has a glass filled with what I can only assume is whiskey. I eye them skeptically. I haven't seen them like this since before the accident. "Hey, I'm here," I mumble.

Both my parents look over at me with gentle smiles. My mom happily shouts, "Blake! I'm so glad you're home!" I stroll over and give her a gentle hug with an overwhelming feeling of nostalgia causing a lump to form in my throat. She seems like the mom I used to know.

I lean back and look at my dad as he genuinely proclaims, "It's good to have you home." I can't help but look between the two of them and notice a sincere happiness in both of their eyes that has been missing for years. I don't know what's happening here, but I'm pretty sure my shitty mood might ruin it.

So instead of sticking around, I give them both a nod before announcing, "I've had a long week. I'm exhausted; I'm going to get some sleep."

"Okay, good night, Blake," they both call. I wave my hand and trudge up the stairs to my room. I drop onto my bed feeling at a loss as to the conflicting emotions fighting in my brain. I kick off my shoes and close my eyes, hoping to get my head on straight. Images of Liz completely take over my thoughts as I finally drift off to sleep.

The next morning, I wake to a pounding headache and my mouth feels like it's filled with cotton balls. If I didn't know any better, I'd think I went binge drinking last night, but thinking about it, it's probably the fact that I don't remember eating or drinking anything since yesterday morning. I drag myself out of bed and throw on some running clothes before heading downstairs for breakfast.

My mom is standing at the stove stirring scrambled eggs in one pan with sausage and bacon sizzling in the one right next to it. "Good morning, Blake," my mom greets me cheerfully. "Are you hungry? I'm just finishing making breakfast."

I nod my head and drop into a chair at the oak kitchen table. Pouring myself a glass of orange juice, I quickly gulp it down. My dad steps into the room and strides straight over to my mom patting her on the ass and kissing her cheek. "Good morning beautiful," he mumbles, and my mom actually giggles. I know I'm staring in shock when my dad turns, smirking at me. "Well, she is, isn't she?" I can't do anything but nod in agreement as I take the coffee cup my dad offers from him.

My mom brings breakfast over to the table along with some toast. She smiles and pats me on the head like I'm a kid again. At this point I can't help but shake my head and speak up, "What the hell is going on here?"

"Blake," my mom admonishes, but I don't react knowing what I wanted to say was so much worse.

My dad gets this smug look on his face and asks mischievously, "What are you talking about?" which makes my stomach turn at the insinuation.

I ignore my stomach and continue, "You're both different. Life has fu..." Clearing my throat, I start again, "Life has sucked since the accident. I don't remember you two acting like this since before..." I trail off knowing they understand me.

My mom sighs and looks up at me with determination. "Maybe it's time. I don't know if Kari is the one who has helped us see we can find happiness again, but we can Blake," she insists.

"What about Aub?" I prompt with pain clear in my voice. I have this overwhelming feeling that Kari is replacing Aubrey in their hearts and it fucking breaks mine.

"Aubrey is happy. She may not have the life we all wanted for her or the life she wanted for herself all those years ago, but she's happy. She loves where she lives. She loves her friends and the nurses who help care for her. She loves all of us," my mom pauses with tears in her eyes. "She would want all of us to be a family, Blake. Aubrey would want all of us to be happy too. She wouldn't want you to dwell in the past."

My jaw twitches with undesired tension. "I just want everything for her," I admit my voice cracking.

"I know, so do we," my mom acknowledges putting a comforting hand on my arm and squeezing gently.

"I met his son," I add quietly.

My dad's head snaps in my direction. "What…what do you mean?" he stammers.

I look directly in his eyes before confessing, "The man who hit us, I met his son yesterday." The room goes eerily quiet and I glance down at my bruised knuckles, "And I punched him," I admit.

I hear my mother's gasp and my father's grunt in reaction to my words. I reach for my fork not knowing quite what to say at this point. Eventually both of my parents start moving mechanically, eating their breakfast in silence along with me. When I finish, I rinse my dishes and place them in the dishwasher.

I grab another cup of coffee and turn to walk away from the tension. My mom stops me in my tracks with her choked words, "It wasn't his fault." I swallow hard and look at her through my now blurry eyes. She repeats, "It wasn't his fault. He had a father who was an alcoholic, caused an accident that changed all our lives and then took his life instead of facing his family." She looks me straight in the eye insisting, "They lost just like we did. They never forgot that night either, Blake," she gasps out painfully.

I look away not sure how to react and my dad adds, "Your mom is right. The only one we can blame is gone. It's not his son's fault." He pauses looking at me for my reaction, but I have no idea what they are seeing. "Aubrey would want us to be happy; you to be happy. She has always looked up to you."

I nod and try to swallow past the pain in my throat, not willing to admit I was wrong out loud. I look at both of

270

my parents, watching as my dad now stands behind my mom's chair with his hands resting on her shoulders rubbing soothing circles. I shake my head wondering how we ended up here.

Last time I was here I could barely get a few words of wisdom. Now all at once everything is coming out for us to deal with, but my parents seem to be better than ever. I set my coffee cup on the counter and place my hands on my hips trying to slow my breathing as if I just came from a run.

My dad looks at me regretfully. "I know I haven't been the best role model or father for that matter since then and I'm sorry."

I huff a humorless laugh. "Man, we're just getting it all out there today, aren't we?" I smirk unamused.

My dad swallows and continues, "Blake I couldn't ask for a better son. I'm sorry you had to deal with a shit for a father. I know I wasn't there when all of you needed me. Then, I show up and disrupt your life, but I was trying to do what was best for you." I can't help but feel bitterness rising in my chest with his words. "I'm not asking for your forgiveness, I'm just asking if we can try to be a family, you, me, your mom, Aubrey…and Kari?" All I can do at this point is stare at him thinking I've waited forever to hear some of the things that just came out of his mouth. My emotions overwhelm me. I feel a tear escape, but don't bother brushing it away.

"You deserve to be happy. We want you to be happy and I know your sister does too," he adds quietly.

I close my eyes and take a few deep breaths before I open my mouth to respond, "I'll try," I barely grumble out the words. I look at the floor and inform them, "I need to go for a run. I need some time alone to think about everything."

I see my dad nodding his head out of the corner of my eye and my mom adds almost desperately before I walk out

271

of the kitchen, "Maybe you can tell us about your girlfriend when you come back? You've barely told us about her. Her name is Liz, right?" I just nod my head because there is no way in hell, I can tell them how I fucked that one up at this point. I can only deal with so much at once and I'm way past my limit.

I raise my hand in a quick wave and run down the street at a sprint. I stop when I get to the park, placing my hands on my knees and panting for my breath that feels stifled from everything except the short run.

Chapter 36

Blake

I'm sitting at a small table in the corner of the coffee shop with Bree while she's waiting for Christian to show up. She stares at me with her arms crossed, eyeing me quizzically. "So, you're telling me you spent the whole weekend with your family?"

"Yup," I admit with a small smile, watching and waiting curiously for her response.

"And, everything went good?" she prods arching her eyebrows in surprise.

I chuckle with amusement at her reaction. "Mostly," I admit. "My parents are trying to act like parents again. To be perfectly honest, it's different for lack of a better word and I don't really know how to deal with it, but…I'm trying," I grimace. "We brought a picnic to the park on Saturday and I played with my sisters…" I pause realizing what I just said, "Wow, that feels strange."

"What?" she prompts inquisitively.

"Sisters," I repeat with complete awe. Bree smiles genuinely at me in response. "We really all had a lot of fun together. Kari is such an incredible little girl. Her and Aub like so many of the same things. Then, they thought it would be fun to try to pick on me together. Aubrey was smiling all day, Bree. She was so happy." I feel a smile pulling at my lips with the simple memories of my sisters playing together. "I don't remember the last time I saw her that happy at one of our family days. Then again…" I trail off not wanting to really talk about our past fucked up family days.

Bree gives me her own loving sisterly smile before inquiring, "What about Liz? Have you talked to her yet?"

I sigh and run my hand through my hair without answering when Christian steps up and scoots a chair right next to Bree and sits down. He places a cup in front of her and kisses her on her cheek before giving me a nod in greeting. "So, you're still being a pussy about getting your girl back?" he taunts with a smirk. Bree smacks him in the stomach and he lets out an exaggerated, "Oof," with a teasing grin. "I'm just saying he needs to suck it up and go to her, apologize. He fucked up big time and he needs to fix it. I should know," he adds for emphasis raising his eyebrows at Bree.

Bree rolls her eyes and shakes her head at him. "That's not going to get you Brownie points Christian," she mumbles.

"You love me," he murmurs, grinning, making her giggle. He kisses her on her cheek again and she gently pushes him away.

"As eloquent as my boyfriend here is," Christian chuckles at her comment, "he's right Blake. You need to figure out a way to apologize and apologize in a huge way!"

I groan loudly, knowing they're right. "I know, I know! But what I don't know is if she should even forgive me in the first place. The things I said to her the other day were so fucking cruel," I wince and sigh in disgust with myself. "I can't believe I did that; no one deserves to be treated that way. I made her fucking cry." I shake my head in defeat.

Bree's eyes begin to narrow as she's staring at me, more and more critically by the second. "So, what, you think if you don't apologize then she won't have a chance to

274

forgive you since you don't think you deserve it? That's what's holding you back?" she shrieks at me. I feel the eyes of many spectators as I shrug my shoulders as if it doesn't matter, but we all know it does. I stare out the window feeling empty and alone.

"Dude, you're a bigger fucking idiot than I ever was!" I don't even turn to look at Christian or give him a response, although I'm shocked to hear him speak up. "Think about what happened with me and Bree! Use your fucking head!" I remain quiet knowing even conceding that was difficult for him, let alone hard for me to hear.

After a few moments he continues, "I know we've never really been the best of friends, but Bree's right about you, you're a good guy and you know I hate admitting that." I grimace at his comment and let him carry on, "It's not just because of what you've done for Bree. Although I will owe you for the rest of my fucking life for that because I love her, and I wouldn't be here without her. From what Bree has told me and what's on that blog, Liz has a lot of shit going on right now and she really needs you. If that was Bree," he clenches his fists like he's holding in his anger and takes a deep breath to calm down. "Swallow your fucking pride and be what she needs you to be. Apologize, beg for her forgiveness and another chance and then be there for her."

I finally turn and glance at Christian trying to read him, but he's now staring at Bree like she holds the keys to the world. She has tears in her eyes making my heart stutter. She leans up and presses a kiss to his lips before glancing over at me. "I know you want to take all the blame, but this isn't all on you. You have both made mistakes and you both deserve another chance," she insists. "Be there for each other, Blake."

I nod in acknowledgement, but I can't help but think she deserves better than me when I hear someone clear their

275

throat behind me. I turn around to see Kris standing there with his hands stuffed in his pockets, shifting back and forth from one foot to the other, looking extremely nervous and uncomfortable. "Um, Blake, you think maybe I could talk to you for a few minutes?" he inquires.

I stare at him with my mouth hanging open in astonishment, not knowing how to respond. What could this asshole possibly want? Eventually, Bree stands and reaches her hand across the table and out in front of me to introduce herself, breaking the silence. "Hi, I'm Bree and this is my boyfriend, Christian. Are you a friend of Blake's?" she asks with a hesitant smile making me laugh humorlessly.

He quickly shakes both of their hands, apprehensively, my eyes never leaving his. "Kris James," he states in answer to her question glancing over for both her and Christian's reactions.

Both Christian and Bree's eyes register shock. "Oh!" Bree exclaims, quickly glancing back and forth between the two of us. Then she focuses on me and asks with her voice full of concern, "Do you want us to stay?"

I shake my head and mumble, "I'm good," feeling anything but.

She steps around the table and wraps me in her arms tightly. My arms reflexively wrap around her giving her a gentle squeeze before letting go. She eventually releases me too and I watch her step back around the table and tug gently on Christian's hand. He immediately stands, ready to follow. Before leaving he asks Kris, pointing to his own jaw, "So, is that from him?"

Kris nods stiffly, insisting, "Deserved."

Christian grins at me. "Yeah, he can pack those well-deserved punches." He chuckles and slaps me on the back in encouragement as Bree practically drags him out the door while he stares with what I would call morbid curiosity.

"Sorry about that," I say tightly, while I clench my fists and nod at his jaw. He slowly steps around to the other side of the table so he's in front of me.

"No, you're not," he retorts, smirking. I nod in confirmation and let it go.

"What do you want Kris?" I probe rigidly. I'm still struggling with seeing him even though everything my parents said to me this weekend keeps going through my head, knowing they were right. I continue to repeat the most important of those words over and over again attempting to keep me in my seat, "It's not his fault…It's not his fault…It's not his fault…"

He finally sits down opposite me with a heavy sigh. "Look, I get that you hate me and honestly you have every right to." I clench my jaw waiting for the rest, "But I want you to know I'm sorry."

I look at him like he just punched me in the gut. "I don't want your pity," I spit out venomously.

He nods his head in understanding. "I'm sure you don't and I'm not giving it. What I am giving is an apology for having an asshole as a father who didn't know how to get his head out of the fucking bottle enough to not ruin lives. I'm sorry we couldn't fix it before he fucked up more lives than my mom's, my sister's, and mine, let alone his own. I'm sorry we weren't enough to stop it. I'm sorry he didn't drive himself over a fucking cliff a helluva' lot sooner, not taking anyone with him. I know it does nothing to fix anything, but I'm sorry anyway. And I'm sorry for things that went beyond you and your family and had everything to do with my alcoholic father and his fuckups."

I stare at him for what feels like hours trying to gauge his pain, his honesty, his sincerity, but in reality, it was only a matter of minutes. I break the silence by nodding my head stiffly at him not ready to speak yet, but he takes that as the acceptance he should. I don't know what he's been through, but I can see the unwarranted guilt in his eyes for his fathers' crimes.

For the first time in my life, I can also imagine those weren't his father's only crimes as an alcoholic. I can see Kris has been through a life-altering kind of pain like me, yet completely and undeniably different. He may be apologizing for something that truly wasn't his fault, but maybe his apology and my acceptance will help us both move on somehow. I guess I can begin to understand that now.

I watch him as he visibly gulps before hesitantly adding, "I also know it's none of my business, but I really care about Liz and I can't keep my mouth shut." I immediately stiffen again with his mention of Liz. "I grew up with Liz and I've never seen her like this. She came close when I fucked up, but not like this. She's completely destroyed by what's going on with the two of you."

I glare at him. My protective instincts start to kick in. "You're right, it's none of your fucking business."

He nods stiffly and continues ignoring my warning, "She's a good girl. Treat her right. She deserves that. Her last boyfriend was a complete fuck-up," he states, offering a weak grin.

I let out an unwelcome chuckle with his admission. "Yeah, I heard he was a complete asshole."

He sniggers. Taking a deep breath, he proclaims, "Best of luck, man. I really mean it."

He stands up to walk away and I know I have to say something now while I still can or I will regret it. "Kris?"

"Yeah?" he asks, then turns to me waiting.

I gather my courage and strength and eventually look him in the eye. Taking a deep breath, I force out the words I know I need to say for all of us, "It's not your fault."

I can tell by the look on his face I completely floored him, but he quickly pulls himself together. He gives me a tight appreciative smile. He opens his mouth, his voice cracking as he responds, "Thanks." He gives me a stiff nod, his eyes glimmering before turning and walking out the door.

I drop back down in my chair feeling lighter about my past in a fucked-up way. I watch Kris walk away while I worry about Liz and how I'm supposed to fix the mess I made with her. I continue wondering if I even deserve for the mess I'm in to be fixed after how I treated her. Christian's words keep haunting me, telling me Liz needs me, telling me I need to apologize and be there for her. What I can't figure out is if those words are true or if I even warrant amnesty. I still think she deserves better than me.

Chapter 37

Elizabeth

We've only been back to classes for a week and I'm already letting Tori get to me again. Maybe it's because I don't have Blake anymore and I'm on edge anyway, but I can't seem to stop my emotions from getting the best of me.

I can't stop thinking about Blake either. I really am incredibly worried about him. I haven't heard from him or seen him at all since the day he punched Kris. Thinking about what happened all those years ago and knowing who they both are to me now is overwhelming. I can't imagine what he feels like. Rationally, I know it's not my fault, but I can't help but feel guilty for his feelings of betrayal.

Or maybe Tori is getting to me because my little brother Scott has started college here and suddenly him and Tori seem to be everywhere together. She always seems to be all over him and he's soaking up every second of it. I don't blame him, since he doesn't know anything about what happened between us, but it doesn't make it any easier. No matter what it is, I'm doing what I can to make myself more and more numb by the minute, attempting to shut out the outside world.

I feel a bump against my shoulder and try to catch my footing as I glance to the side to see what jarred me from my numbness. I look up to a smiling Sara and narrow my eyes at her. "Enough of your glowering! Let's do something fun tonight. Let's go out or something," she urges. I scowl at her some more and continue striding towards the library without responding. "Come on! We have to go out while it's still warm enough to walk around this town," she insists. She smirks begging me with her gaze. I maintain my silence and she sighs in defeat, finally redirecting her questioning, "Are we going to the library?"

"I am," I snap. "I have to pick up a book before my last class," I inform her.

She rolls her eyes and grumbles, "Fine. I'll go with you." I groan in response, but don't argue as I walk with her side by side. Eventually she probes, "So have you talked to Blake?"

I close my eyes and focus on my breathing, begging my tears to disappear before they begin. "No," I cry as a tear escapes, trailing down my cheek. I would think it would start to get easier to think about him, but it doesn't.

I quickly swipe my tears away as we make our way into the library. Standing up straight, falsely portraying my confidence, I easily find what I need. Grabbing it, I spin on my heel, striding towards the desk to checkout. An all too familiar voice suddenly stops me in my tracks, sounding like I've only heard it once before.

I freeze as I hear Blake snap, "I told you to leave me the fuck alone, Victoria!"

I dig my fingers into Sara's arm and slowly turn toward the sound of Blake's heated voice. He has his arms crossed in front of his chest, glowering at Tori who is trying to press up against him in the narrow hallway lined with books. "I'd be so worth it," she coos trying to reach for him causing my mouth to fall open and hang agape.

"Not a fucking chance," he spits out, gently pushing her aside. I drop my book and run as fast as I can, hopefully before either of them has a chance to notice me.

I crash into the front door with a grunt and shove it open desperately, needing to get away from them. I drop down in front of a tree just outside the doors of the library and lose control as my tears take over completely.

I soon feel a soft comforting arm around my shoulders, letting me know Sara found me and she's here supporting me, like usual. "I don't even know where to start with that!" I grumble, laughing spastically.

"I know, right?" she retorts, chuckling humorlessly. "What was that? We've always known she was jealous of you and that she's crazy but..." she shakes her head in disbelief. "It's disgusting and pathetic," she finishes.

I finally calm myself down enough to gasp between sobs, "I miss him, Sara. I miss him so much."

She gives me a sad smile, empathizing with me. "I know, sweetie, I know." She squeezes me tightly, hugging me for a few minutes before eventually reiterating, "I really think you should try calling him."

I shake my head in refusal. "I...I can't..."

She heaves a sigh and pushes, "You two need to talk."

I have to change the subject for a minute to get my thoughts and feelings under control, so instead I state, "Someone needs to tell Scott what we just saw, but it can't be me."

Sara groans in irritation. "Ah, I totally forgot about that! I still don't understand what he's doing dating her at all, but...okay," she relents. "I'll talk to your brother." She shakes her head in displeasure with another load groan, complaining, "What am I getting myself into?"

"Thanks, Sara," I mumble appreciatively. "I just know that's definitely something he can't hear from me." I shake my head in disgust.

"Now, back to Blake..." she prompts raising her eyebrows in question.

I heave another sigh and wipe the tears from my eyes as I rub my hands up and down my face. "I can't make him talk to me, Sara. He's the one who doesn't want to talk to me," I snap at her, the hurt evident in my voice.

She gives me a tight, sympathetic smile. Without pushing the subject further, she stands up. Holding out her hand, she requests, "Now hand the book over and I'll go check it out for you."

My eyes widen in shock, realizing my error. "I never checked it out!"

She smirks, taunting, "True, so you better hand it over before campus security shows up."

I hand her the book, watching her as she runs inside. My eyes close as the door closes behind her. Taking a deep breath in, I exhale slowly, focusing on my breathing while she's gone.

"You're good," Sara announces as she returns, startling me.

I open my eyes, mumbling, "Thanks."

She grins, nodding her head in acknowledgement. Reaching down she grasps my hands, leaning back with a tug, she helps pull me off the ground. "Come on," she urges. "It's time to get out of here."

"Okay," I mumble my agreement, strolling next to her back to our apartment.

Chapter 38

Elizabeth

Later that night Sara gets her wish to go out when her phone rings and my wasted brother asks for her to come get him at some house party. She had gone to see him earlier that day and told him about Tori, so he wanted to go out. I had convinced her to stay in and watch a movie with me since I wasn't in the mood to go out after seeing Tori hitting on Blake, even if he did turn her down flat. Now with my brother's call for help, even I had no choice but to go along.

We walk up to an old stone blue Victorian house with a white wraparound front porch overflowing with people. Scott had texted Sara the address and we can only hope it's the right one but judging from the flow in and out of the house, we're probably in the right place. "Is this a frat house?" I ask Sara as I spot three guys sitting on a couch on the lawn yelling obscenities at the people walking by.

Sara just shrugs her shoulders, shakes her head and answers, "No idea. Come on, let's go find Scottie."

"Scottie?" I smirk. She rolls her eyes and laughs in response.

We walk inside, finding the house flooded with sweaty people. Meghan Trainor is blasting through the speakers making it so I can't even hear Sara yelling to me with her mouth up to my ear. I scrunch up my nose at the smell of smoke and beer as I try to peer through the smoky haze looking for my brother.

I almost immediately get separated from Sara in the crowd. I scan the room little by little, desperately wanting to find Scott when a tall thin guy with longish black hair and blue eyes grabs me around the waist. He spills beer down the front of my shirt and mumbles, "Oops, I'm sorry, babe. Let me help you with that," he screams into my ear and reaches for me clumsily.

"Um, No," I screech immediately pushing him away and drying myself off the best I can. "I'm fine, thanks."

The guy tries to pull me towards him again giving me his drunk, sleazy smile. "I was just trying to pull you out of the way of all the assholes, I swear. I'm Dean and you're beautiful, what's your name?"

"Um, I'm just looking for my brother," I stammer. I try to step away from him again without answering his question.

"Not so fast, your name first and then I can help you find your brother," he offers.

I look around the room trying to find Sara, my brother or another familiar face feeling only slightly panicked. I really don't think this guy is something I can handle tonight, but I'm sure he's harmless in a room full of people.

"Well, well, well, if it isn't Elizabeth fucking Stevens practically screwing some guy in the hallway! What a surprise!" I hear the high-pitched screech making me freeze. I could handle this guy, I could handle about any guy right now, but I cannot handle Tori. I slowly turn my body towards her with dread, trying to keep myself from shaking. The guy that was just hitting on me is now looking at me with concern, which seems kind of strange to me, but who am I to judge? Maybe he's not a complete asshole.

Tori and I stand glaring at each other for what seems like hours before she finally opens her mouth again to speak, slurring her words, "So you get Scott to break up with me?" she accuses.

"I didn't do anything. I didn't even talk to my brother yet today," I whisper hoarsely.

She laughs bitterly, "Oh really?" She whispers so only I can hear her, "Then how did he know about Blake?" I don't answer and she shakes her head in response. Stepping closer to me, she whispers in my ear, "It doesn't matter. I'll get him to fuck me. I'll get Blake to fuck me too, just like I get all the men in your life to fuck me." She laughs manically as I gasp for breath. Tears run down my face, but I can't move. It's like I'm completely frozen and being forced to listen to every word she has to say.

She steps away and starts speaking louder, "Who here wants to play I Never?" There are loud cheers from around the room. She grins wickedly as she watches the tears stream down my face. "I have never fucked someone else's boyfriend." I block out everything around me, but I can't seem to block her out. Where is Sara? Where is Scott? I can't breathe. I need to get away from Tori, but I can't move. I start to shake just as she grins evilly with her next I never, "I have never fucked anyone on the Internet."

Before I know it, my legs give out, I feel arms around me murmuring comforting words in my ear and at the same time I hear so much yelling I can't decipher what's being said. My chest aches, my head's pounding and I attempt to get myself to focus.

By the time I'm able to wrap my head around what's happening, I'm buckled into the passenger side of Blake's Jeep with my brother lying across the back seat and Sara sitting next to him. Blake is yelling thank you out the window to Christian and Bree and a couple other people I don't know, including the guy who was hitting on me.

286

"I'm so sorry Liz. I wouldn't have left you even for a second if I knew she was there. I went out back to find Scott. I found him, but it took a while. I'm so sorry," Sara rambles shakily, attempting to apologize.

I shake my head, tears still streaming non-stop down my face. "It's okay, it's not your fault," I barely squeak out between sobs.

"Lizzie, I'm sorry she's such a bitch," my drunk brother mumbles and wraps his arm around Sara's waist. I'd laugh if I wasn't so depressed.

I glance over at Blake and his jaw is incredibly tense, anger completely radiating off him. "Thank you," I squeak out, the tears still flowing freely.

He shakes his head. "I'm so sorry Lizzie. She won't bother you again, with any of it. I'll make sure of it. It will all fucking go away Lizzie, I promise," he seethes.

"It's okay Blake. I appreciate your help, but it's not your problem," I whisper now that my breathing has calmed down a little bit. With my comment, I swear I watch his face go from anger to complete devastation and I can't quite figure out why. He's the one who wants to just be friends.

He swallows hard. "I want to do this for you, Liz. None of what happened tonight was okay. She can't be allowed to do shit like that. I'm not about to let her do something like that to you again. You told me she was harassing you, but I didn't know anything besides what you told me. This," he mutters angrily, "was fucked up and it can never happen again!" he declares, shaking his head in disgust.

I nod my head and turn to stare out the window letting the tears continue to fall. Blake pulls up to our apartment and he helps Sara and me get my brother inside. Assisting Scott to the couch, he lays him down as Scott flops over with a groan.

I walk Blake to the door feeling numb, not quite knowing what to say. He stuffs his hands in his pockets and looks at me, his eyes full of concern. He finally inquires, "Are you okay?"

I shrug my shoulders and mumble, "I will be I guess." Then, I look at him curiously and prod, "How did you know I was there? And what was going on?"

"Christian texted me," he answers simply. I must have looked confused because he explains further, "That was Christian's house. He saw you walk in, then you were talking to his roommate," he adds the last part looking slightly hurt, but I don't have the energy to comment. "I didn't really know what was going on with Victoria until I got there. Christian saw you with Dean and he doesn't trust him, so he texted me." He shakes his head in disbelief. "I'm really fucking glad he did!"

I just nod in understanding. "Thank you," I whisper again.

He nods his head in acknowledgement. "Good night, Lizzie." He turns and walks out the door. I'm left with Sara and my brother feeling completely alone and devastated again.

Chapter 39

Blake

It has been two weeks since I saw Liz at the party and as Christian put it, I', still being a fucking pussy when it comes to apologizing to Liz. I am at a point where I know I need to do it though, whether she forgives me or not. She deserves a real apology even if I don't deserve forgiveness, so I've decided today is the day I'm going to make it happen. If she never forgives me, I'll have to deal with the consequences. It would be a well-deserved punishment for being such an asshole.

I have been able to use the last two weeks to get Tori completely away from Elizabeth, hopefully for good. She was terrified of the lawsuit I threatened her with and actually completely cooperated with me. Ironically, I teamed up with Kris James and with his support, she had no choice but to do everything we asked. She pulled everything off her blog and gave us all her files on Liz. It's sick what she did to her.

Hopefully what we did to protect her was enough because I know Liz doesn't want to go through any kind of lawsuit or she already would've done it. As for Kris, I have no idea what made him support her now, maybe it's his guilt, but I honestly don't care, I'm just glad he did it because she really fucking needed this.

I've been sitting in the parking lot of her apartment complex for the past hour trying to figure out what I'm going to say to her. I hope she's actually home when I get the nerve to get off my ass and knock on her door because I don't know if I can do this part again. I drove by the café first and her friend Katie said she's not working today, so at least I have that going for me. I finally take a deep breath stepping out of my jeep, knowing it's time to man-up.

I trudge up to her door and raise my hand to knock when it opens and my eyes collide with Liz's sparkling green ones, taking my breath away. My chest feels like it takes on the weight of a mac truck seeing her again and I have trouble speaking. She bites her bottom lip when she sees me and fidgets with her purple backpack strap, slung over her right shoulder.

"Um, Hi," she stutters uncertainly with the surprise of seeing me. "What are you doing here?" she asks looking at me nervously, still biting her lower lip. I have to hold myself back from reaching out to pull her lip free with my fingers or even with my teeth for that matter and quickly run my raised hand through my hair.

I shake my head to get my thoughts back on track and raise my eyebrows at her instead gesturing inside. "May I come in?" I ask tentatively. She looks terrified of my question and a huge wave of guilt washes over me. "I just need to talk to you, it's important. Please," I quietly beg, my heart pounding outside my chest.

She nods her head slowly and backs up to allow me to pass by her to come inside. She closes the door behind me and drops her backpack down on the floor by the door before turning to face me, watching me hesitantly. Finally, I realize I'm still holding the bouquet of partially strangled yellow, purple and white lilies and daisies I'd brought for her. "These are for you," I offer lamely.

"Thanks," she mumbles timidly. Reaching out, she takes them from me with a tight smile. I watch as she grabs a large glass and fills it with water like I did the first time I brought her flowers and places them in it without saying a word. When she's done, she wanders quietly towards the couch but doesn't sit down.

"Is Sara here?" I ask nervously, needing to know if we might have an audience or if she would have support if she didn't want mine. My heart clenches at that thought. She shakes her head stiffly in answer. "What's with the backpack?" I question, still needing a minute to gather my thoughts and courage.

"I was just headed to the library to study," she responds quietly, looking anywhere but at me. I nod my head in acknowledgement, struggling, having no idea how to even begin this conversation. She eventually does it for me asking cautiously, "So…how are you?"

"Shitty," I answer honestly. I love the way her mouth rounds in surprise. I release an emphatic sigh and drop down on her couch placing my elbows on my knees and look directly at her. "Look Liz, I know this isn't even close to enough, but I need to start by saying I'm sorry. I'm so fucking sorry for the way I spoke to you and for hurting you. I know I don't deserve your forgiveness, but I need you to know how much I regret what I said to you when I saw you with Kris. I didn't mean a single word of it."

I pause but hold my hand up when she looks like she's about to say something, trying to let her know I'm not done. I take a deep breath and look directly into her beautiful green eyes as I continue, emotion overtaking my voice, "I know it's no excuse, but I've gone over this in my head constantly since it happened and the only way I know how to explain myself right now…seeing him, hearing his name brought up so many painful memories I don't even know where to begin. It was especially too much having him show up in my life right now with all the changes going on with my family," I emphasize. "I'm trying to adjust to those and make sure we're all going to be okay. But seeing him of all

291

fucking people grab your hand," I grit through my teeth, cringing slightly and shaking my head with disbelief, as I allow my expressions to finish the statement. "Then when you didn't pull away like I expected, it didn't only put me over the edge, but put me directly into the seriously deranged category. I couldn't see straight. It fucking wrecked me," I claim, my voice cracking.

She tries to hide her laugh at my comment and accidentally snorts instead. She instantly turns bright red, making her look even more gorgeous, if that's even possible. "Nothing happened," she starts to enlighten me.

I again interrupt her, "It doesn't matter, Liz. I had no right," I insist, shaking my head. I notice her face immediately cloud over. Realization hits at what she thinks with my comment. "Wait, that's not what I meant. I just meant I had no right to treat you that way under any circumstances. I should have talked to you instead of jumping to conclusions. I can't even express to you how sorry I am Lizzie. I know I don't deserve it, but I'm going to ask for your forgiveness anyway."

She looks at me uncertainly and I don't blame her. "So, what, you want to be friends?"

I shake my head and laugh humorlessly. "I don't think we were ever really friends, do you?" She shakes her head and looks away from me with tears in her eyes. My heart breaks because right now I feel like as much of an asshole as the guy who cheated on her, if not more.

"I'm actually hoping you'll give me a chance to show you that I'm fucking crazy about you," I declare, my voice catching. "I'm hoping you'll give me a chance to show you how good I can actually be to you. I'm hoping you'll give me a chance to be there for you when you need me like I should have always been and I'll try to let you do the same for me," I smirk slightly as I watch her brush away another tear.

"Lizzie these last few weeks I have fought with myself so much about whether or not I even deserve you," I tell her honestly. "That's one of the reasons it has taken me so long to get here to apologize to you. I was so fucking cruel; how could I even ask you for forgiveness?" I shake my head, disgusted with myself. Then, I stare at Liz in awe, "You are incredible and deserve the best. I don't know if I can give that to you, but I sure as hell want to try," I plead.

"Blake," she steps towards me hesitantly and sits down beside me on the couch. Her tears are now flowing freely down her cheeks. I want so badly to wipe them away for her, but I hold back waiting for her response. I need to give her space. "What are your other reasons?" she probes quietly.

"What?" I question, struggling to keep my voice steady as I look at her with slight confusion albeit a little bit of reluctance, since I'm pretty sure I know what she's asking.

"For staying away so long?" she prompts with such curiosity and hope I pray she's okay with my answer.

I close my eyes to gather my thoughts then open them again staring straight ahead when I start to speak. I can't look at her if I'm going to see her disappointment in me in her eyes. "I didn't like how things went down at the party," I confess. "I did some research and found out Victoria and Tori are one in the same. I figured as much after the other night, but I wanted to be sure and I just couldn't ask you. You're always so upset anytime her name is even mentioned. You already told me what happened with the two of you, although I had no idea it was still happening." I shake my head in abhorrence.

I steal a glance at Liz out of the corner of my eye and notice she has completely tensed up. I need to talk quickly if I'm going to get this all out. "I found her blog and went through her history that wasn't already removed when she got in trouble the first time back in high school," I don't know what to do besides shake my head as my body starts trembling with my anger. "You told me but seeing it…seeing it makes me understand why you had such a hard time trusting me."

"Blake…" she whispers hoarsely.

"I know you didn't want to do anything, but I couldn't just sit back and let someone hurt you like that," I spit out.

"What did you do, Blake?" she prods shakily. I slowly turn towards her and see more tears on her cheeks. I reach my hand up to wipe them away, but she flinches away from me. I nod, but my heart breaks with her reaction. I need to tell her the whole story and then she can decide.

I take a deep calming breath before I continue, "I went to Kris and asked for his help. I figured between the two of us we could effectively threaten her without you having to get involved."

"And he agreed?" she prods completely shocked.

I nod stiffly. "We went to Tori and threatened her with a lawsuit. She took down her blog, gave us all the pictures and videos she had of you and Kris," my voice cracks unintentionally on the thought of what's on the videos and pictures. I swallow hard and force myself to continue, "She gave us her word, which I know doesn't necessarily mean too much, but with Kris's help..." I trail off knowing she understands. "She also promised to leave you, your family and friends alone whomever that may include. Like I said, I don't know how good her word is, but I know you didn't want to go to court or you would have already done it. I also know she doesn't want that either. She was pushing it as far and as long as she could. She finally hit the bottom when Kris and I came at her." I stop talking still not able to look at her for fear that she hates me for what I did.

"Th…Thank you," she stutters, which gives me the courage to snap my head up and look at her beautiful face again. She's still wiping tears away and I swallow hard at the sight, trying to get rid of the ache in my chest. I would give anything to mend her broken heart. It fucking breaks me to see her like this.

"I wish I could do more Liz. I would do anything I could to protect you," I admit.

"You've done more than enough Blake. Thank you," she mumbles sincerely and this time she lets me wipe her tears away with my thumbs. The smallest of things makes me feel incredibly grateful and hopeful at the same time.

"I need you to know, Liz, I want you back. I want us to work. I'm so sorry for how I've treated you the last few weeks. I need you to know I will always do everything I can to protect you, but I want you with me so I can do that. So, I don't have to worry about my phone dying and not being able to get in touch with you," she laughs humorlessly. "I hope you forgive me for what I did with Tori," she grimaces and nods at me, tears still streaming down her face.

"As you know, my family takes up a lot of my time and they are one of the reasons I haven't really done relationships in the past. Of course, I have other reasons, like not knowing the right girl until now, but…" I pause and smirk at her. "I don't know if you've noticed, but with you, I want to go all in," I cradle her face in my hands continuing to wipe her tears away with my thumbs. "What I mean is, I can't stop thinking about you. I want to be with you, have fun with you, and share who we are and who we were with each other. I want to fight with you, make up with you and protect you. I want to kiss you, touch you and hold your hand. But most of all Lizzie I'm hoping you'll give me a chance to show you how much I'm falling in love with you because that is what's happening here for me. I am falling in love with you. And let me tell you, being without you like I have been the last few weeks, would be the death of me. I can't fucking take it anymore! You're constantly in my head and my heart and I can't let you go. I don't want to let you go," I plead.

Liz bursts into uncontrollable sobs and collapses in my arms. I wrap my arms around her and rub her back, savoring the feeling of having her in my embrace again. Her sobs eventually begin to even out and I feel my body start to relax right along with hers. When I think she's calm enough to talk, I kiss the top of her head and ask hesitantly into her hair, "Does this mean you forgive me?"

She bursts out laughing and I smile at the beautiful sound. She pulls back to look at me, her face beautiful even when streaked with her tears. She smiles so bright, her whole face lights up, stopping my heart. "I forgive you, Blake," she whispers. I feel a lump catch in my throat. "How can I not when I'm assuming with everything you said that you forgive me for how I acted with you and Bree?" she prompts.

Instead of answering her with words, I know I can't wait another second to kiss her. I lean in and gently press my lips to hers, tasting forgiveness in the form of the salt of her tears. I move my lips with hers trying to show her not only my forgiveness, but also my love for her. I'm finally right where I need to be.

Chapter 40

Elizabeth

Blake and I have been inseparable over the last three weeks, besides going to classes. I must admit I feel incredible about our relationship. Realistically, for the first time I have no doubts about us anymore. He'll bring me coffee in the mornings and we'll walk to campus together, or we'll leave early and buy our coffee down the street, so we can sit and talk before we go to class.

Sometimes Sara joins us, as well as Bree and Christian, whom I'm really beginning to love being around. When we're not in class, we're trying to enjoy every bit of the good weather while we still can, but more than anything we enjoy each other. We still spend a lot of time walking, talking and laughing down at the harbor, one of the places we consider our own.

This weekend Blake brought me to meet his family. In all honesty, I was completely terrified, but so far it has gone pretty well, all things considered. A thickness remained in the air while we were at his parents' house. I think it stems from Blake having a long way to go before he's comfortable with his parents' relationship with him and with their relationship with each other.

Also, with everything they've endured in the past and now with their new family and where it will lead them, even though he accepts it the best he can. His strength in dealing with it all is indescribable and so unbelievably sexy. I wanted to do everything I possibly could for him. Mostly, I stood by him trying to support him in every way I knew how. Blake held tight to me while we were at his parents and it meant the world to me that he was looking to me for support.

As soon as we walked out the front door of his house, his whole body visibly relaxed. He took me around the town he lived in for only two years, but I know it felt more like ten years to him with everything that occurred in that short time. He showed me the park where he used to meet Bree, Matt's house where he spent a lot of his time, the high school where he graduated and finally Bree's house where we're sitting now.

I look up at the white colonial house in front of us that reminds me so much of Blake's but hasn't had the love of a family within its walls for a while. I choke down the emotion I feel, imagining what it would have been like for him to find his best friend unconscious on the floor, a girl he loved on some level, terrified wondering if she would live. He had so much of his own family issues to deal with. I almost hate myself for ever fearing their relationship because of the trauma of it all.

I know he loved her once and still does on some level. I guess that's what scares the hell out of me, but neither of them deserves my doubts with what they've endured. Then of course there's the fact that Bree is obviously completely in love with Christian and I don't need to worry about her falling for Blake. I want to have the kind of love with Blake that Bree and Christian have more than anything. I think we're finally headed in that direction.

Jealousy and guilt for having those feelings again attempt to consume me while we sit quietly in front of her house. Blake must see my anxiety and immediately tries to reassure and comfort me. He cups my face gently in his hands looking deep into my eyes, "I'm so happy you kissed me at the concert. I don't think that is a night I'll ever forget, not only because you surprised me with your kiss, but mostly because it's the night I found you. You make me so happy Lizzie. Thank you for being here for me. Thank you for coming back to me. Thank you for forgiving me, even though I'm not always sure I deserve it," he proclaims his voice full of emotion. "I'm not falling anymore Lizzie, I love you," he whispers his declaration against my lips. Then, he kisses me gently and lets our lips fall apart.

A tear escapes out of the corner of my eye as a small smile covers my lips. "I love you too, Blake," I whisper back feeling the joyful truth of it all wanting to pour out of me. He closes the distance between us pressing his lips to mine and it feels like he's shocked my heart sending tingles everywhere. He moves his mouth deliberately over mine. His kiss starts slow and sensual, but quickly grows hungry when his tongue pushes inside, tangling with mine, tasting every corner. I want more of him. I press my body into his as much as I can in his jeep and let my hands travel down his muscled arms with a whimper.

Blake groans into my mouth in response and pulls back, giving me a chaste kiss before pulling completely away with another groan. I don't want to let go so I fist his shirt in my hands, with my futile attempt to pull him closer. He laughs and shakes his head like he's trying to get rid of the sexual tension enveloping us.

"What?" I prod innocently, attempting to keep a straight face.

He gives me a disbelieving grin and shakes his head again. "Now you're ready? When we still have to go to Boston to spend the day with my sister and then drive back to Portland? We aren't going to be able to be alone today unless we're on the road for what will feel like forever!" he exclaims, joking and exasperated at the same time.

I know he's teasing me, but I shrug and can't help but giggle at his reaction. I feel a blush creep over my whole body when understanding sets in and I know how well he truly reads me. He groans again, reaching for me. "Come here." He gently kisses me again, keeping it light. "You know I didn't tell you I love you so you would have sex with me," he states, watching my reaction.

I smile timidly. "I know, Blake, but I don't have any other reasons for waiting to be with you, but I do have a million reasons for wanting to give you all of me," I admit sheepishly.

His chocolate eyes glow with happiness. "Only a million?" he challenges giving me another chaste kiss and chuckling softly. I don't say anything in response, but I look at him with adoration and he gazes back at me like he's memorizing every one of my features making my heart beat even faster if that's possible. He finally opens his mouth again and suggests, "Who knows, maybe we'll be exhausted and have to find a place to stop to sleep on the way back." He smirks.

I don't know if he's serious, but I like the idea of us being completely alone without worrying about either of our roommates or any other distractions for our first time together. He's been so incredibly patient with me and I'm more than ready for that time to be now. I scoot back and buckle my seatbelt before answering, "You know I think that's a really good idea, Blake."

I watch as looks of mild surprise, excitement, lust and love pass through his features before he settles back into the driver's seat and buckles his seat belt. He starts his jeep and reaches across the seat to clasp my hand with his. He pulls it to his lips, placing a light kiss on the back of my hand before resting our hands together on his thigh. "Let's go to Boston then," he states as he pulls away from the curb. I smile back at him and enjoy the quiet of the short ride into Boston.

The moment we walk into the adult home in Boston, I see a real difference in Blake when it comes to how he is with his family. I know he's nervous about me meeting his sister, even though I know he wants me here, but it's different. I see the sincerity of his love for Aubrey every time he talks about her, but seeing it play out in front of me is amazing to say the least. We walk into the main room used for activities, parties and meals holding hands and Aubrey spots us immediately.

Blake's whole face lights up when he sees her. She runs directly to Blake and throws her arms around his waist. He instantly drops my hand and wraps his sister up in his arms and swings her around causing her to squeal with glee. I don't think I've ever seen anything so beautiful, watching their mutual love and admiration.

When she lets go of her brother, she looks right at me smiling shyly. "Are you Lizzie?" she questions hesitantly.

"I am," I answer nodding back at her with a wide smile. "It's so wonderful to finally meet you, Aubrey. Blake has told me so much about you," I declare. I'm trying not to let my nerves get the best of me, but it's hard not to; I really want her to like me.

She rolls her eyes and mumbles in an exaggerated groan, "Blake talks about you all the time, so I've heard a lot about you too."

"Aubrey," Blake laughs.

She shrugs her shoulders innocently and exclaims with a smile, "Well it's true!" The heartbreak of that small gesture almost overwhelms me because it truly is innocent. This gorgeous eighteen-year-old girl has the purity and heart of a child because of a horrific accident, an accident caused by Kris's dad. It's a shock to see more of the effects on Blake's family.

The moment Blake notices the emotion on my face, he leans close and whispers in my ear, "She's happy. So, we need to be too."

I swallow hard and nod my head in understanding and agreement. "So do you want to go to the zoo with us today, Aubrey?" I propose pasting a smile on my face to the best of my ability.

"The zoo?" she repeats with eagerness. I nod and she hugs me in pure delight. "I love the zoo!" I hug her back with a quiet laugh.

We spend the rest of the afternoon at the zoo with Aubrey. With every minute that passes I think I fall more in love with Blake. He's so caring and protective of his sister. Although I've seen this loving and protective side of him with Bree and now, I'm starting to see it with me, which makes my heart warm.

Watching Aubrey and Blake together is so simple and beautiful. They imitate the monkeys together bouncing around outside the cage laughing. He has contests with her on who can sound more like the animal we're observing. Everything he does makes me smile from the inside out. He's an incredible man and I couldn't be happier with the way things are turning around for us.

After we eat dinner at a Mexican restaurant, we bring Aubrey back to her home. She throws her arms around me to say goodbye, bringing tears to my eyes. "Thank you, Lizzie. I had so much fun with you and my brother today! I'm so happy to meet you and I hope you come back with him next time too."

I give her the biggest smile I can as we step out of our hug. "I had a wonderful day too, Aubrey. Thank you for inviting me to spend it with you and Blake. I'll see you soon. I promise."

She grins at me before throwing her arms around Blake. "I love you, Blake."

"I love you too, Aub." He smiles and kisses her forehead. "We'll see you soon, okay?" She nods her head in agreement and walks back into her room.

Blake tugs me with him to the nurse's station. "Hi, Maria."

A beautiful woman looks up in response. She's probably in her thirties, with short dark hair and brown eyes and wearing bugs bunny scrubs. She smiles genuinely at us. "Hi, Blake. How was she today?"

"She had a great day. She was talking a lot and barely needed to use sign language at all. There were no problems and she was so strong and full of energy today. We had trouble keeping up with her," he jokes.

"Dinner went well, too?" she probes.

"Yeah, she had a soft taco and a lemonade. She didn't want to cut it up, but I kept a close eye on her and she ate with small bites and had no problems at all. I also gave her the two pills with her dinner and she swallowed them like a champ." I listen to Blake give the nurse a recap of everything else she ate during the day, along with the number of times she went to the bathroom. As they continue to talk about Aubrey's day and her care, I'm overwhelmed with the thought of how no one could be more caring than the man next to me. I truly have no idea how I ever had any doubts.

He says goodbye and reaches down, entwining our fingers together when the nurse stops us, "Wait, there's something I almost forgot to tell you." Blake and I both look back at her, curious as she gives us a kind smile. "We received a substantial grant this week from an undisclosed benefactor. The money will help pay for the medical care for young residents like Aubrey who may spend much of their life here, as well as additional activities and programs. I already talked to your parents about it, but I thought you should know. It will really help your sister and hopefully all of you."

I search Blake's features, trying to read how he feels about this news. This should be a good thing, right? Why does he seem tense? He forces a smile and speaks up almost rambling, "Thank you, Maria. That's great. We'll see you soon. Have a good night." He tugs on my hand and hurries out the front doors and over to his jeep. He mindlessly releases my hand and climbs in without saying a word.

"What's wrong?" I rasp, trying to break the unexpected tension after such a fabulous day.

He finally turns to look at me with his eyes full of pain and right when I think he's about to speak, he sighs collapsing into me and enveloping me in a hug so tight. I'm almost afraid to ask again, for fear I won't like the answer, but for him I do, "Blake, what's wrong? I don't understand, isn't the grant a good thing?"

He gradually loosens his hold on me and I breathe a little easier, but still fear for him, watching him struggle to speak his thoughts. Eventually his voice cracks, "Lizzie," he says my name and holds onto me like he's using me as his strength. "I'll be okay."

I let my hands run down his arms until I meet his hands and grip them tightly. I lean back slightly so I can see him better, but yet I'm still able to hold him and show him I support him.

He sighs and releases one of my hands to run it through his hair before resting it on my knee. He nods his head. "It is a good thing," he concedes with a grimace. "Aubrey deserves this, hell, even my parents deserve this.

304

I'm just pretty sure I know where the money came from and it makes everything come flooding back to me."

Realization finally hits me and my body begins to relax. "Kris," I whisper. "He asked me where your sister was. He had heard rumors. I never really told him anything, I just said she was in a home near Boston," I admit nervously.

Blake nods in agreement. "Yeah." He takes a deep breath, "Ironic, but it seems Kris and I are more alike than I ever thought. I don't like to admit that," he mumbles glancing quickly up at me through his eyelashes, "for more than one reason."

I can't help but chuckle lightly at his insinuation. "It might not be from him," I suggest, but not really believing that to be true.

He sighs, again. "Yeah, but it's okay if it is." He closes his eyes slowly and then finally opens them to focus on me. "I'm okay. It was just a shock. I know it's not his fault anymore. I've just hated him for so long." He pauses, "If he feels even a little of the guilt like I have since the accident," he shakes his head like he's trying to shake away the pain, "then maybe doing this for Aubrey, for our family will help him heal and I can't deny him that."

With my heart pounding in my ears, I lean towards him and gently press a kiss to his lips. "I love you, Blake. You're the most incredible man I know."

He looks into my eyes as a smile touches his lips. "I love you too, Lizzie."

Chapter 41

Elizabeth

After sitting in Blake's jeep for half an hour just holding each other and talking, I suggest, "Let's find a hotel. I'm exhausted physically and emotionally from today."

"Are you sure?" Blake prompts.

Nodding, I add, "We still have an overnight bag since we stayed at your parents' house last night. We'll just have to dress in the same clothes tomorrow morning for the short drive home, but that's okay.

"Well, I guess it's either the hotel or Matt's house," he states, offering me another option, probably to make me comfortable. I just shake my head and point to the hotel in front of us.

After we check in, Blake grabs a bunch of candy bars and drinks from a small area in the lobby near the desk and pays for them. "We might want some dessert later," he smirks at me, and I can't help but laugh. I shake my head at his idea of dessert and how adorable he looks right now.

As we make our way up to our room on the second floor, my whole body practically fights me with each step I take, feeling like dead weight from complete exhaustion. I barely register nerves about sleeping with Blake, which we haven't done since we stayed at Bree's house on the lake. One of us would always leave before anything could stray too far, although it definitely has not been easy. Let alone, I haven't been able to think about the fact we talked earlier today about finally having sex tonight.

Blake puts the key card in the lock and pushes the door open, propping it wide for me. I step through the door and immediately drop my duffel before collapsing face first onto the king-sized bed.

Blake laughs and I soon feel the bed bouncing me up and down with his weight. "I already wore you out, huh?" he taunts lightheartedly.

I roll over and smile up at him from underneath my lashes, even though I know my face is turning pink. "I had a big twenty-four hours. I met your parents, you showed me around your town, I met your sister and we spent the day at the zoo. We found out about a huge grant that will help her and I found out you love me," I add the last part letting my smile widen. "I think that covers most of it and it definitely qualifies as big enough to tire me out," I add playfully.

His smile softens as he reaches his hand towards me. I close my eyes as he runs two fingers tenderly down the side of my face and drops them softly to the bed when he reaches my chin. "Well, my parents loved you and they were relatively normal today, so that's a bonus." He smirks.

"My sister absolutely adored you and she had a fantastic day. You still have to meet Kari, but you will, maybe next time. Hopefully the fact that you're so well loved makes you feel just a little bit better. Although it's not really a surprise since you are so amazing." He pauses, his eyes turning playful, "But then again, it takes someone pretty special to get a catch like me."

I lightly smack him in the chest and he laughs. "I love that sound," I whisper inaudibly. Blake raises his eyebrows in question, but I just shake my head. "You're incredible Blake Withers," I proclaim with a content sigh.

Blake's smile lights up his whole face as he leans towards me. "You're pretty incredible yourself. And so

307

beautiful," he whispers looking at me in awe as his thumb trails across my bottom lip.

Blake's warm, soft lips meet mine. His hand curves around the back of my head, holding me in place while he kisses me. The slow, sure movements of his mouth over mine, the sweet minty taste of his tongue, and the strong comforting feel of his hand in my hair, instantly heat my whole body. I instinctually let out a soft whimper and roll into him.

"Lizzie," Blake groans. "I know you said you were ready, but we don't have to do anything more than this." He kisses me deeper, exploring every part of my mouth and I push back wanting to explore every part of him.

He pulls away just slightly, panting for breath and I look down at him with a playful smile. "I'm not tired anymore," I confess. I press my lips lightly to his neck with a giggle.

"Lizzie," he groans holding me tight. "That's not telling me anything!" he exclaims. I laugh outright, my lips tickling his ear.

He quickly rolls me over, pressing my hands above my head and his body pressing the length of mine, sending chills down my spine. "You think you're pretty funny, don't you?" he teases. He smirks at me as goosebumps slowly appear covering nearly my whole body.

"I think I'm hilarious," I claim, grinning back at him.

His smirk slowly turns into a loving smile. "Lizzie, Lizzie, Lizzie," he mumbles shaking his head. "What am I going to do with you?"

"I don't know, but I think it's time to find out," I throw out friskily and his smile turns from mischievous to full of want for me. I need him to know I truly am ready. "I love you, Blake. I want you to make love to me."

I see the love shining through his gorgeous chocolate browns. "I love you too, Lizzie." He leans down just enough to softly press his lips to mine. Then he barely pulls away, so I can still breathe him in, but our lips are no longer connected. "I want to cherish every inch of you," he murmurs. He kisses me again, our breaths picking up speed, just like our kiss before he pulls away yet again. "But I want you so much right now," this time his kiss devours me and I whimper trying to pull my hands from his grasp, needing to touch him as he presses his body into mine, our hearts racing.

He releases my hands and runs his hand gently over my jaw and down my neck. He pulls back from me and I ask almost desperately, tugging at his shirt, "Please take this off?" He smiles; obliging me he reaches behind his head and with one hand, swiftly pulls his t-shirt over his head. My mouth nearly goes dry at the sight of his lean, tight abs and chest. I love looking at him. I lightly drag my fingers down his chest.

He clears his throat and I regretfully drag my eyes from his chest with my eyebrows raised, meeting his intense gaze, his eyes turned into pools of dark chocolate. "Need help with yours? Or are you still ogling me?" he prods cockily.

I feel so confident and playful around him, especially right now and can't resist my response, "I'm definitely not done, but you can absolutely help me too."

He laughs lightly before leaning down and gently pushing my shirt up, trailing kisses up my stomach as he goes, leaving me nearly breathless. "You're going to be the death of me, Liz," he groans into my skin.

When he reaches my chest, he stops his kisses and leans up to assist me with my shirt. Then his kisses continue again down my shoulder as he gently pushes the strap of my bra to the side. "Take it off," I cry desperately as I plant kisses on his chest tasting a little bit of salt on his smooth skin.

He chuckles, slowly sliding his hands around my back. "My we are demanding tonight." He easily unhooks my bra and slides it down my arms dropping it to the floor.

Pressing his lips to mine, he kisses my lips like he can't get enough of me as his hand trails lightly across my breast and my nipple, causing me to inhale sharply. He drags his fingers slowly to my other side and does the same, teasing me and eliciting the same reaction. Pulling away from our kiss, he resumes a trail down my neck and chest with his tongue flicking out, tasting my skin. He presses his lips to the side of my breast before making his way to my nipple, teasing it with his tongue and then taking the whole thing in his mouth, while he plays with the other with his fingers and thumb making me cry out.

I can barely comprehend anything but being in the moment with Blake. His touch is making me lightheaded, causing my head to drop back from his chest as I moan for more.

He releases me and quickly moves back to my mouth, devouring me. I reach for his jeans and unbutton the top, followed by his zipper and pull back enough to pant, "Let's both get rid of these," I request.

He nods in agreement. Standing, he swiftly removes his, staring at me remaining only in his boxer-briefs. I sigh with contentment and lust for this sexy man before me.

He tosses something on the nightstand next to the bed, then reaches up to help me remove my jeans and I do nothing but lift my butt and smile as he tugs them down to find my jade green lace trim underwear. I love the groan that comes out of his mouth causing my stomach to twist. "You are so damn sexy," he practically growls at me. I smile lovingly at him, believing what he says because he makes me feel that way with a simple look.

He crawls back on the bed and slowly up my body, placing kisses with every move he makes. His hand curves over my hip and around to the inside of my thigh. I inhale sharply the second his fingers rub over my clit. In the very next moment, we are both lying naked in each other's arms and his fingers rub over me again eliciting another uncontrollable gasp. I grab his arm to stop him and he immediately pulls back, breathily asking me, "Are you okay, Lizzie?"

I nod out of breath as he looks into my eyes with such concern and love I have trouble finding my voice. I'm finally able to croak out, "I want you now. I don't want to wait another minute. I want to be completely yours. We can save the rest for next time."

"Are you sure?" he prompts, his eyebrows drawing down as he looks me over, assessing me for the truth.

Nodding, I smile in affirmation. "Yes."

He then reaches for the nightstand and grabs what he tossed there earlier, ripping open a silver condom package with his teeth before quickly rolling it on. "I'm going to go slow, tell me if it hurts or if you need me to stop. Okay?" he pleads needing me to answer. I nod caressing his arms in anticipation.

Blake leans down and kisses me hard. I swear I can feel all his emotions in his kiss and I do everything I can to show him all of mine right back. He slowly eases into me, never pulling away from my lips and I can feel myself attempt to adjust to him. He pushes all the way in and stops as we both gasp breaking our kiss.

"You okay, Lizzie?" he prods looking me directly in the eyes with so much love I feel like my heart will burst.

I can't speak, so instead I nod my head and push my hips into his to let him know I am good. He doesn't tear his eyes away from me but continues to devour me with kisses as we slowly move together. I wrap my arms tightly around him, feeling like I'm exactly where I'm supposed to be, getting lost in this wonderful man.

We pick up the pace making it so I can no longer kiss him and keep breathing. I tear my lips away from his with a groan, trying to catch my breath. Sliding my hands up and down his back as we move, I feel his rigid muscles ripple underneath my touch.

Lifting my head, I stare into his eyes as we move together, faster, harder, deeper. Panting desperately, I cling to him as he pushes me all the way to the top, making me feel like I can't take anymore and shoving me right over the edge. I feel my body releasing, clenching around him.

He soon follows right behind me, his eyes never wavering from mine causing my heart to skip a beat. I have a moment to treasure the look on his face as he's falling, just before we collapse together in a sweaty mess of limbs.

After we catch our breath, Blake kisses me lovingly and pulls away from me. I immediately feel the loss and take a deep breath. "I'll be right back," he murmurs giving me a chaste kiss before jumping off the bed. I grin happily as I watch his firm ass striding to the bathroom. He's back quickly with a cloth to help me clean up. Then he tosses the cloth on the floor and settles back on the bed wrapping me in his arms. "What are you smiling at?" he questions.

"You," I concede simply.

"You know you didn't have to jump me as soon as we walked in the room," he jokes and I immediately elbow him in the gut. He chuckles and reiterates, "I love you, Liz. I wish there was a way to say more, but I love you and I'm not letting you go."

"So, I'm stuck with you then?" I prod. He laughs again. I grin and admit, "I'm not going anywhere. Thank you for being so patient with me."

"You're worth it," he declares kissing me lightly on the lips and giving me a tight squeeze. "Honestly, I'm incredibly grateful every day for your forgiveness," he confesses and my heart pounds erratically with his words.

I shake my head, overwhelmed. "I'm the one who needs to be grateful Blake. You're so good and incredibly patient with me. All you asked me for is your trust and it took me so long to get there. I look at Bree," I huff and look away from him disgusted with myself. "I ask myself why nearly every day," I grimace at my admission.

He turns me towards him and tilts my chin up so he's looking in my eyes as he pleads, "Don't do that. God, Liz, sometimes I wish I were better with words so I could let you know what you do to me. When I need someone to talk to, you're the one I want to call. When something good happens, you're the first person I want to share it with if you're not with me already. I've wanted to kiss you, touch you and who knows what else since the day you kissed me at the concert."

I gasp, my heart and body warming with his words. Licking my lips, I open my mouth to respond but his thumb gently brushes over my lips, halting my actions.

"I've struggled to hold back because you are so good, probably too good for me. You make me happy just by being there, by listening, by laughing, or just by looking at me like that," he chuckles softly, tapping my nose for emphasis. "I hope I do the same for you because I'm going to try to do that for you every fucking day. I've never had this feeling before Liz, and it is all because of you. Don't question it, just let us be," he begs.

Blake kisses me again, electrifying every part of me. Overwhelmed with emotion, a tear escapes down my cheek without my consent. I can't squeak out anything more than, "I love you so much, Blake," and hope for now I've said enough to this man who has stolen my heart and soul.

I curl into him as tightly as I can. Pulling me in closer, he places another soft kiss on my lips, taking my breath away. He molds his body into mine, chest to chest and tangling our legs together.

Blake has a way of making me feel incredibly loved and protected like no one ever before. Within minutes we both fall sound asleep wrapped in each other's arms. Sighing with contentment, I know I'm right where I belong.

Chapter 42

Elizabeth

Blake and I are headed to my parents today for a family dinner and I honestly don't know if I can handle it. They're meeting him for the first time as my boyfriend. I'm terrified my mother will make some embarrassing comment or do something I don't want her to do, but I'm ready. I've been trying to prepare myself for her, knowing this time, I won't let her get away with it because if I don't say something Blake will, and I can't do that to him the first time he meets my family. Let alone, around him I feel stronger and confident with myself again.

I tried on so many different outfits, while Blake just sat and patiently waited, telling me I look beautiful every time. Then when I wanted to try on another outfit, he offered to help me change making me laugh and blush. I couldn't help but roll my eyes at him after a while because he knows he's really no help at all with this.

When he asked what I wanted him to wear, I told him anything he's comfortable with because I know he'll look good in anything. Besides, I don't want him walking in there trying to fit my mom's mold; he's too good for that. Let alone I've done enough of trying to please her in my life and it's time for it to end.

I fall more in love with Blake every day for so many reasons. I don't care what my mom thinks about him, although even I can admit life will be easier if things go well today. Blake is more than incredible I think to myself, glancing over at him with a small smile as he pulls into my parents' driveway. They would be crazy not to agree.

315

I let out an audible sigh as he puts the car in park and turns to look at me with a smile curving up at the corners of his lips. "None of that," he urges. He smirks and kisses me chastely. "Not with me. Today is going to be a good day."

His smile lights up his chocolate brown eyes as he places his hand along my jaw, pulling me to him for a gentle kiss and making my lips tingle. When he pulls back, I breathe a sigh of pleasure and contentment. "Much better," his smile broadens, briefly tasting me again before slowly pulling back so our faces slide leisurely apart as his hand gradually follows. "You ready?" he prompts, raising his eyebrows in question.

"As much as I'll ever be," I admit offering him a timid smile. He gives me another chaste kiss before jumping out of his jeep and quickly jogging around to the other side to help me out. My feet are already on the ground when he's by my side. He reaches for my hand, entwining our fingers together. I step out of the way of the door for him to close and smile up at him as we walk up to my childhood home.

We walk in the front door and my mom immediately greets us. "Elizabeth? Is that you dear?" she calls from down the hall.

"Yes, Mom. We're here," I answer stiffly.

"Come on into the kitchen, I'm finishing up dinner," she calls back.

I walk towards the kitchen gripping Blake's hand as tightly as I can as my lifeline, hoping I'm not cutting off his circulation. He gives my hand a squeeze and reaches over with the other to rub the back sandwiching my hand in. I take one more deep breath before stepping into the kitchen. "Hi Mom." I step over to her and give her a gentle one-armed hug and kiss on the cheek before Blake steps up beside me.

Turning towards him, I grin, his presence giving me the strength I'm searching for. "This is my boyfriend, Blake,

I told you about," I introduce him, reluctantly letting go of his hand so he can shake my mother's hand.

"Hi, Mrs. Stevens. It's wonderful to finally meet you. I've heard so much about you," he gushes with his radiant smile.

"Hmm, welcome," she murmurs eyeing him. I already feel the nerves churning in my stomach with her cold greeting. I think I might throw up. "Where are you from, again?" she asks curiously.

"I'm actually originally from Portland area, but we lived on the other side of town. My family lives in Massachusetts now though, in the Boston area," he answers with confidence, ignoring her critical look.

"Why'd you move there?" she probes with distaste. She's not one to worry about getting too personal, especially when it comes to embarrassing me.

"Mom," I warn.

Blake puts his hand on my arm and answers bluntly. "My family was hit by a drunk driver when I was younger and my sister sustained life changing injuries from the accident. We moved to the Boston area when my dad found a really great adult home, we believed would be able to help her."

My mother stands wide-eyed, completely stunned, not knowing quite how to respond to his honesty. The pride I feel for Blake must be shining through the smile I'm giving him. I've never heard him talk about the accident so easily before. I could hear in his voice he was finally letting go of the hate he's held for so long, although I know it will never completely disappear.

How could it?

Then again, I have a feeling some of the reason he told my mother all of that might be the shock factor, to put her in her place. It's the first time he's meeting her and yet he already knows her so well I can't help but think. I glance at the ground trying to hide my amusement. After a moment, I'm finally able to look up at him and give him an encouraging smile.

My mother eventually finds her words and clears her throat to respond. "I'm so sorry."

"Thank you." Blake offers an appreciative smile to my mother needing a subject change. "Can we help with anything?" he offers.

"No, you're our guest and Elizabeth needs to introduce you to her father. Elizabeth why don't you go on upstairs and change for dinner and then I should be about ready when you come down," my mother suggests. My whole body stiffens with her blatant scrutiny.

"I'm fine mother. I dressed for dinner before I left my apartment," I grit out pasting a tight smile on my face.

"Don't you think," she starts as Blake steps back up next to me, placing his hand on the small of my back for support.

I take a deep breath and interrupt her immediately, "Mother, while I completely respect your opinion and your taste, I know we don't always agree." Briefly pinching my lips together, I look at my mother, trying to let her know I won't waver this time. "I like this dress. Blake likes this dress on me," I add nodding towards him. He grins with a sparkle of pride in his eyes.

Taking a deep breath, I continue with confidence, "And at one time you liked this dress. Even if you don't like it for today, it is what I'm wearing for dinner. It's time I make my own decisions when it comes to my choice in clothes, don't you think?" Arching my eyebrows, I stare at her with unwavering confidence; yet knowing if Blake wasn't behind me, supporting me, my legs likely would give out.

With a shake of her head, she finally breaks our stare. "Yes, yes, go introduce Blake to your father," she mumbles waving us both away from the kitchen like she's shooing a fly.

As soon as we step back into the foyer, I try to stifle a giggle. Blake steps into me from behind and gives me a quick squeeze around my middle whispering in my ear, "I'm so proud of you, Lizzie." His breath sends chills down my spine as he leans in placing a kiss to my cheek.

"Oh, it was nothing, it was just about my clothes," I claim blushing; attempting to act as if it was no big deal when we both know it was a monstrous feat for me.

"Don't downplay it," he insists. Turning me towards him, he reaches for both of my hands. "We both know how much you have been stressing about your mom and standing up to her. You are incredible," he declares with awe evident in his voice and eyes.

"Yes, she is, isn't she?" my dad reiterates from behind me making me squeal and nearly jump out of my own skin. My dad chuckles at my reaction. Blake covers his mouth to hide his own laughter when I glance over at him and I feel myself quickly turning red.

"Dad, you scared me!" I shake my head and both of their smiles widen. I sigh and grin back at them. "Dad, this is my boyfriend, Blake."

"It's good to meet you Mr. Stevens," Blake proclaims, reaching out his hand to shake my father's.

My dad reaches his hand out with a smile, "It's great meeting you too, especially since I now know you think so highly of my daughter." My dad and Blake chuckle again and I respond by turning an even darker shade of red.

My mom calls me to help bring everything to the table for dinner and I quickly and quietly oblige. We sit at the dining room table passing around the marinated chicken, mashed potatoes, broccoli, rolls and salad. My mother recites our dinner prayers, picks up her fork and promptly starts in on me. "Elizabeth, I ran into Mrs. Sheridan yesterday at the grocery store."

I flinch slightly and watch Blake's fork freeze halfway to his mouth. His eyes immediately lock on mine. I take a deep calming breath and tell myself I can do this one way or another. "Oh?" I question still observing Blake as he gently sets his fork back down on his plate watching me cautiously.

My mother continues with her eyes burning into the side of my head, "Yes, I haven't seen much of them since Tori and Scottie broke up." She pauses and I keep doing everything I can to just keep my hands from shaking. "She seemed very upset about their break-up. She said Tori was bullied into it and she thought I might have some insight into it. But she says Tori won't really talk about it." She pauses again before prompting, "Well?"

I swallow the lump in my throat and fight to keep my voice steady, "What do you want me to say, Mom? Tori and I aren't friends, we never were. As for Scott, he never tells me anything about who he's dating."

Her eyes narrow reproachfully. "So, this has nothing to do with you? You were always so jealous of her. I remember you used to make wild accusations against that poor girl!" she declares with distaste.

I fight the tears forming in my eyes and Blake turns to my mother, "Mrs. Stevens," he begins with controlled anger, but I can't let him say a word. This isn't his fight.

I jump up, interrupting him, "Mom, your accusations as you call them, were facts. I could prove it to you, but I never wanted you to hear or see all the bad things she did to me. I thought it would make you think even less of me. You always found some way to think poorly of me on your own. I

320

didn't want to give you any more ammunition. Tori bullied me and tortured me for years. Even Kris James would tell you she bullied me. You should be thankful she's not dating your precious Scottie anymore because he is way too good for her!" I glare at her seething.

"Don't talk to me that way young lady," my mother reprimands, her face turning red with embarrassment and anger.

"Judy," my father commands forcefully. "That's enough!"

All our heads swing to look at my father. My mouth hangs open, stunned from his simple actions. He doesn't let the silence hang in the air long. "I know I was always working while the kids were still living here, but if my daughter says she was being bullied by Tori Sheridan, then we as her parents should believe her. She has never given us any reasons to doubt her. I don't care who Tori's parents are. She's not our daughter. Our daughter is sitting right here, and I want her to come back. If we treat her like she's the problem, you won't have a daughter anymore."

Stunned, I slowly drop down into my chair staring at my father. I just always thought he was on her side. Silence looms around the table as my father picks his fork back up and resumes eating his dinner. After taking a bite, he glances up at me and winks.

Exhaling with relief, my chest tightens. I smile at him and wipe the lone tear that spilled over onto my cheek without notice.

After what seems like hours, but in reality, is only a matter of minutes, my dad looks at Blake and asks like nothing out of the ordinary just happened, "So, what are you majoring in, Blake?"

Blake gently shakes his head and clears his throat before answering. The rest of dinner continues with my dad making every effort to get to know Blake. My mom remains silent, only nodding her head as if she's listening, although I wonder if she's paying attention at all. I know she's fuming from what happened and probably blaming me for all of it.

When we walk out the door that night, my mother goes up to bed, claiming a headache with a quick wave of her hand to say goodbye. My dad walks us to the door and shakes Blake's hand. "Thank you for putting up with us tonight," he proclaims, grinning.

Blake responds simply, "Thank you for having me, Mr. Stevens."

My dad nods his head and pulls me into his arms. "I love you, Elizabeth and I'm very proud of you."

I attempt to hold back the tears about to spill over as I choke out, "I love you too, Dad." I hug him tighter than I have since I was a little girl. I finally let my arms fall and smile up at him.

"Take care of my little girl, Blake. Elizabeth, let me know if you need anything," my dad emphasizes looking me in the eye, waiting for my acknowledgement. I nod my head and we turn, walking out the door.

We quickly climb in Blake's jeep and he turns to look at me immediately. "Are you okay?" he prods with concern lacing his voice. I nod my head, a few more tears escaping. He pulls me into his arms, comforting me. "I'm so proud of you," he repeats. He pulls back and delicately cradles my face in his hands. He looks deeply into my eyes and proclaims, "I love you, Lizzie."

"I love you too, Blake," I whisper feeling loved and cherished. I don't think I ever thought that would happen. He pulls me tightly to him placing a gentle kiss on my lips.

Epilogue

Blake

I stare out at the road in front of me as I drive over to Liz's apartment to pick her up for our date. My thoughts drift to Thanksgiving this past weekend since we just got back to town this morning.

We spent Thanksgiving at her house with her parents, her two brothers and a couple aunts, uncles, and cousins. I got along great with her brothers and her dad continued making me feel welcome. He made sure to constantly praise Liz for everything, attempting to reassure her of his feelings for her. For Liz's sake, I'm grateful to see this change.

Her mother, on the other hand, was at best cordial, but I noticed she seemed to be that way with Liz's brother Jax as well. Liz's brother Scott really does seem to be the golden child in her eyes. It's sad, but Liz amazes me with how she deals with it all.

Then, on Black Friday we had a second Thanksgiving with my family. My parents decided that was the best way to celebrate the holiday this year, so Kari could spend Thanksgiving with her mom and her family and still have Thanksgiving with us. My mom and dad spent Thanksgiving Day with Aubrey at the home. Then Friday morning, Liz and I were able to pick Aub up and bring her back to my parents for our celebration.

The whole day felt perfect. Liz played with my sisters like she was still a little girl herself making me love her even more for it. It was so much fun to watch her with them, making my heart full.

My dad and I are still more civil than anything, but I don't know if it will ever be different between us. I'm just thankful he puts forth an extra effort to make Liz comfortable and feel welcome because she's exactly where she needs to be, right here with me.

Tonight, Liz and I plan on meeting up with Bree and Christian for dinner at a quiet local pub for burgers and beers so we can actually hear each other talk. We're hoping to catch up before we start classes again tomorrow since we haven't seen them in a while.

I walk up to Liz's door and knock, impatiently waiting for her beautiful smile. She pulls the door open and stands in front of me in dark blue skinny jeans and a white t-shirt with a green and white flannel shirt layered over top and tied at her waist. I love that looking at her in clothes so simple completely takes my breath away.

"Hi, Lizzie." I grin and lean in pressing my mouth to hers because I can't wait another second to taste my girl.

"Hi, Blake," she murmurs as I pull back, smiling brightly. "I'm ready to go," she declares as she tugs a small brown leather purse over her shoulder.

"You look beautiful," I proclaim as I help her into my jeep. I gently grab her chin, giving her another soft kiss before I pull away and shut the door.

I run around to the driver's side, climbing in to hear her mumble a quick, "Thank you." I smile genuinely in return and pull out of the parking lot quickly before I don't want to leave at all.

I reach across the seat and entwine my fingers with hers, needing to touch her on the short drive to the pub. I never want to be very far away from her though, so that's really no surprise. I have no idea how I got so lucky, but like I said to Liz, I'm not about to question my good fortune. I'm just going to enjoy everything with her and soak up every fucking second.

We walk into the pub hand in hand and I quickly spot Bree and Christian snuggled into one side of a large wooden booth. I tug Liz with me as weave our way through the tables over to them. Bree jumps up, throwing her arms around me. "Happy Thanksgiving!" she practically squeals in my ear.

I chuckle, giving her a quick hug in return before releasing her. "Happy Thanksgiving, Bree." She lets go of me, throwing her arms around Liz and doing the same. I smile with warmth filling me at the sight. The happiness emanating from both my best friend and my girl is overwhelming with all we've been through. I shake my head and tap Liz lightly to slide in the booth before me.

"Hey, Christian," I greet him with a nod. He smirks at me knowingly, causing me to raise my eyebrows in question, but he just shakes his head and chuckles lightly in response.

"We just ordered beers for everyone. Hope that's ok," Christian informs us. Both Liz and I nod in agreement.

"So how was your Thanksgiving?" Bree prompts when we're all settled into the booth.

I grin. "We survived. How was yours? Did your dad make it to Maine in time?" I question knowing that's what would make Bree's Thanksgiving.

Bree nods in confirmation. "Yeah, he made it to Christian's. He had a few of his aunts, uncles and cousins there too, so it was a full house," she adds nodding towards Christian. "We had a really great time," she claims. She smiles then a melancholy look passes over her face.

Christian immediately wraps his arm around her and slides her a little closer in support. I assume she's thinking about her mom and grandma who were not with them, at least not physically, causing my chest to ache at the thought.

Liz inhales sharply and smacks her hand on the thick wooden table. I startle slightly and turn to her in confusion, surprised by her outburst. "Is that what I think it is?" she shrieks at Bree.

Bree blushes and Christian grins with a slight nod. Liz squeals and reaches for Bree's left hand, admiring an oval diamond solitaire on her hand. I feel a slight twinge in my gut before relaxing into the booth. I watch Bree carefully as Liz proclaims, "Congratulations!"

She smiles genuinely and mumbles, "Thank you." Then she glances at Christian with so much love and commitment. I know I could never want anything more for her than the happiness I see on her face right at this moment. It doesn't get better than that.

A proud grin slowly creeps over my face. I look over at Christian. "Congratulations, man. I'm glad you finally found the right time to ask her."

Bree turns to me with a look of surprise, eyes wide. "Wait, you knew?"

I just nod in confirmation and stand up with my arms wide as I wait for her. She jumps up and throws her arms around me, hugging me tight. "Christian talked to me quite a while ago," I concede without apology. "Congratulations, Bree. I really am so happy for you guys. If anyone deserves to be happy, it's you." Giving her one more squeeze, I kiss her on the top of her head before releasing her and stepping away. I sit back down next to Liz and instinctively reach for her hand.

"Besides, it kills me to admit this, but I think Christian was right." All three of them eye me with extreme curiosity. Laughing, I nonchalantly shrug my shoulders. "I don't think I've ever seen you so happy. Congratulations, guys," I repeat tipping up one of the beers as the waitress sets them down at our table.

"Thanks, Blake," Christian states. Reaching across the table, he grasps my hand and shakes it before reaching for his own beer and toasting me. We order our burgers and enjoy the rest of the night catching up and celebrating.

At the end of the night, I escort Liz into her apartment, not ready to leave her yet. "Are you okay?" she questions while she looks for something for us to watch on TV.

"I'm fantastic," I confess tucking a lock of hair behind her ear with a smile.

"So," she begins fidgeting and staring at her lap uncomfortably, "how do you feel about Bree and Christian getting engaged?"

Heaving a sigh, I wrap my arms around her middle pulling her close to me before dropping us both back on the couch. In this moment, I need her as close to me as possible. I keep maneuvering us until the length of her body is pressed to mine. I glide my hands gently over her back and let one slide back down, while I bring the other one around to cup her cheek.

"I seriously think it's phenomenal. I meant it when I said I've never seen her so happy. That's all I ever wanted for her and it's obvious Christian is it for her. My fear was what would happen to her if she lost him again, but I finally realized he's not going anywhere. He'd be just as lost without her. That's all I have ever wanted for her."

She nods, still not looking me in the eye. I don't like where her mind is straying and I'm desperate to rein it in quickly. I bring my other hand up to the other side of her face so I can gently tilt her head further, urging her to look at me.

"As for me, I've never been happier than I am when I'm with you, Lizzie. The things you do to me by just being you," I shake my head in admiration. "You have to know I will treasure every minute you ever give me for the rest of my life," I admit, hoping she sees the truth in my eyes.

"My life without you is unimaginable. For the first time in over ten years, I feel like I'm home again, but that's all because of you. I love you," I whisper into her mouth. Then I gently tug her in the rest of the distance, desperate to taste her. I move my mouth over hers, needing her to feel how much I want her, how much I love her. I put everything I have in me into my kiss.

Soon she breaks away from my lips to catch her breath. She whimpers, "I love you too, Blake." She leans back into me and kisses me back with complete abandon. Suddenly I can't get her close enough to me. My hands start to wander down her sides and I lightly graze her nipple on my way down, appreciating every sound emanating from her gorgeous mouth.

My hands go down to her ass and I give her a gentle squeeze. "Wrap your legs around me," I gasp breathlessly. She does as I request and I sit up, putting my feet on the floor and stand with her wrapped tightly in my arms. I feel her heat for me at her center trying to pull her tighter, get her closer. I carry us to her room without breaking our kiss. "Don't want Sara to walk in on us," I admit over her lips making her laugh.

"What about the movie?" she pulls away asking innocently.

"What movie? I thought you were trying to watch something on TV?" She shrugs making me laugh. I shut the door to her room and devour her mouth again as I lay her down on her bed. I pull away and glance at my girl, my love and struggle to catch my breath. "I need you now," I whisper desperately.

"I'm all yours," she admits with a sexy smile, "always." I know I will do everything in my power to show Liz just how much I want to keep it that way forever.

Acknowledgements

Although this is a 2nd edition, the acknowledgements will remain mostly the same. For those of you that know me, you know I've had a tough year. I planned on having this book out sooner, but the sudden loss of my dad drastically slowed me down, although he's also one of the reasons I continue to write. My dad and I both have always loved to read and we would share books we'd love. Both him and my mom constantly encouraged me to do the things I love like writing and although it took a little longer this time, I knew I couldn't stop. I miss you dearly dad, but you are still an inspiration to me every single day.

I want to thank my family for all their support. It's a wonderful feeling to overhear your kids tell other people their mom is a writer with their voice full of pride. I'm so proud of both of you too for all that you do! My husband, Michael surprises me every day. Thank you for reading my books and giving me your feedback as well as your continuous love and support. I know I don't say it enough, but I appreciate you and all you do.

Thank you, Kelley for your constant encouragement, as well as reading my book and sharing your thoughts. It means the world to me, just like you do. Kelley, my girl, the most basic way to say it is you rock!

Thank you to all of my Beta readers, my ARC readers and my fans who have read, shared, or reviewed my books. I greatly appreciate every single one of you! Keep reading and sharing! Enjoy!

Thank you to my incredible cover designer, Jessica Scott of Uniquely Tailored, who gave The Unforgettable Series a fresh new look. I'm in love with every single one of these new covers! Thank you so much!

What's Next?

It's time to find out more about the eldest Emory sibling, Jason in Unforgettable Dreams, book 3 in The Unforgettable Series. Each book in The Unforgettable Series is a standalone novel, but better read in order. The series in order includes:

The Unforgettable Summer (Bree Summers & Christian Emory)
Unforgettable Nights (Elizabeth Stevens & Blake Withers)
Unforgettable Dreams (Sara Miller & Jason Emory)
Unforgettable Memories (Theresa Emory & Jax Stevens)
The Unforgettable One (Matt Emory & Sadie Rossi)
Unforgettable Mistakes (Matt Young & Amy Stone)

A spin-off from The Unforgettable Series Coming Soon:
Breaking Cycles (Grant Young & Gabriella Howard)

Nikki is also the author of The Home Duet. The Home Duet must be read in the following order:
Dreams Lost and Found (Samantha Voss & Brady Williams)
Finding Home (Samantha Voss & Brady Williams)

Connect with the Author

For more Adult Contemporary Romance, read more by
Nikki A. Lamers. Connect with her here:

Official Author Website
www.nikkialamersauthor.com

Linktree for All Author Links
https://linktr.ee/NikkiALamersauthor

For Clean Contemporary Romance
Read books by Nicole Mullaney. Connect with her here:

Official Author Website
www.nicolemullaneyauthor.com

Follow Me on Instagram
https://www.instagram.com/nicolemullaney/

Author Facebook Page
www.facebook.com/Nicole-Mullaney-Author-
103006415283835/

BookBub
@NicoleMullaneyAuthor

About the Author

Nikki A Lamers has always had a passion for reading and writing, especially romance. She grew up in Wisconsin with her sister, mom and dad. She always loved reading romance books and watching romance movies with her dad, something they both enjoyed. After college she lived in Florida for a few years working for the "Happiest Place on Earth," where she met her husband. She now lives on Long Island in New York with her husband and two kids. She spends her free time reading or hanging out with friends and family. She would love to spend more time traveling, visiting new places and meeting new people as well as continue creating stories, each of her characters becoming part of her family.

www.ingramcontent.com/pod-product-compliance
Lightning Source LLC
Chambersburg PA
CBHW070844260626
47170CB00007B/2498